D0261449

YE 17.50
5.95

■In the poetry of our youth, myths speak through us. When old we speak in myths; women shall remain silent no more, nor shall they 'come and go talking of Michelangelo.' And the scholarly literature on T.S. Eliot shall grow.

The contradictions and paradoxes continue. New schools of thought emerge, new definitions and formulas are advanced to seduce History to yield her enigmatic secret; and yet 'History never confesses, not even her lost illusions, but neither does she dream of them again.' And Merleau-Ponty is gone, and Oedipus blinded himself, for he looked Truth in the face.

And if Truth is a woman, philosophers must become lovers. But Nietzsche was mad and Oedipus married his mother; we are sane and utterly proper. We love books.

■These are hard times, we are told. For the poor, life has always been hard. But they are tough. The rich are sensitive, delicate, special.

The quiet hour, when night is about to devour day, the poor are exhausted and forget to curse or thank god; the wealthy are preparing for their night life after the toil of a lifeless day. Ritualistic cocktail parties are organized gravitating towards opulent, unhappy bedrooms. The bedrooms of the poor are dull. Inhabiting the margin of survival kills passion and imagination.

The rich inherit the earth; the poor inherit the whispers of the sea. We are the children of god.

We must sail to the 'heart of darkness' to pay homage to the last sailor. But sailors shun dangerous voyages, don't know Conrad, and long for security: a steady income, a home erected on stable land.

We are created in god's image. Come, let us visit asylums, hospitals, prisons, brothels; let us see god's face in the empty eyes of the anguished, angry, abandoned, forgotten souls of humanity. But always remember the innocence of children. And Freud was pensive and melancholy; Hitler once was a child.

Our age is 'barbaric, mystical, bored' Günter Grass tells us. The bored are tearless.

Hitler shed tears over the death of his canary. Hitler did bring tears to the world. Six million times over. 'And the Greek sea's curly head/Keep its calms like tears unshed' Lawrence Durrell.

'Commanding is breathing... And even the most destitute manage to breathe. The lowest man in the social scale still has his wife or his child. If he's unmarried, a dog' Camus. I know married couples with children and dogs. But times are changing.

Cruelty to animals is strictly forbidden; cruelty to human beings goes by other names.

Of dogs, human beings, and their destinies, André Schwarz-Bart knows best. His exquisitely graceful song-tale begins thus: 'Our eyes register the light of dead stars.' But those were the Dog Years. Grass again.

'To-day, people are more persuaded than ever that they have perfect freedom, yet they have brought their freedom to us and laid it humbly at our feet' Dostoevsky. When this occurs a new disease arises on the horizon distinct and more dangerous than what Marx spoke of as the phantoms of the mind.

■The silent sovereignty of death shall reclaim every single individual. The ruins of time like oceanic waves shall engulf everything. From nothing to nothing, the boundaries of the agony of 'the educated imagination' Northrop Frye – the trajectory of the chances of freedom.

No litanies, no threnodies. Neither paeans. A pause.

'To the future or to the past, to a time when thought is free...greetings' Orwell.

Essays Edited by Alkis Kontos
for the University League for Social Reform

DOMINATION

UNIVERSITY OF TORONTO PRESS

Toronto and Buffalo

© University of Toronto Press 1975
Toronto and Buffalo
Printed in Canada

ISBN 0-8020-2219-7 (cloth)
ISBN 0-8020-6254-7 (paper)
LC 75-37172

Contents

Preface ix

Dominance in children 3
O. WEININGER

Towards a happier history: women and domination 17
ELIZABETH BRADY

Dominion of capital: Canada and international investment 33
R.T. NAYLOR

The Third World: powerful or powerless? 69
R.O. MATTHEWS

Liberalism and the political theory of property 89
C.B. MACPHERSON

Merleau-Ponty: the ontological limitations of politics 101
MONIKA LANGER

Domination and history: notes on Jean-Paul Sartre's 115
Critique de la Raison Dialectique
KEITH MCCALLUM

Form and metaphor in Fanon's critique of racial and colonial
domination 133
ATO SEKYI-OTU

Magic and domination 163
CHRISTIAN LENHARDT

On science as domination 185
BEN AGGER

Albert Camus' *Caligula*: the metaphysics of an emperor 201
DAVID COOK

Domination: metaphor and political reality 211
ALKIS KONTOS

Contributors 229

Preface

The present volume is the result of a project conceived under the auspices of the University League for Social Reform and carried out under my editorship. The origins and subsequent development of the ideas that structured the orientation of the project stem directly from our growing common concern with the dimensions and modalities of human bondage and, inevitably, the chances of freedom.

The volume is an exploratory exercise, drawing from various perspectives, in an effort aiming simultaneously at a better understanding of the nature of domination and a greater awareness of its complexity. Our task was meant to be theoretical in nature and speculative-diagnostic rather than therapeutic in aspiration.

We did not work with a given definition of domination. Each essay stands as an individual voice, a perspective, deriving its full strength and scope from the orchestrated theme of the volume as a whole, for which I carry sole responsibility.

I am grateful to Ms Pamela McCallum now of Girton College, Cambridge, England, who served as my editorial assistant with intelligence and diligence. Her services were indispensable. The two individuals to whom I am most deeply indebted are Ms Patricia Lagacé and Mr R.I.K. Davidson of University of Toronto Press. Ms Lagacé's calm, elegant intelligence is skilfully employed for, not against, the author. Mr Davidson's creativity and natural sense of excellence inspire and guide.

Publication of this work has been assisted by the block grant program of the Ontario Arts Council.

AK

Domination

O. Weininger

Dominance in children

Most people who have worked with disturbed children, especially those who work in family therapy, recognize that in the complicated dynamics of the troubled family the question of dominance – who has it, why, and how it is used, to what degree, and for what purposes – is a central question which must be carefully unravelled if the family is to readjust and develop better human relations. Yet there is very little in recent psychological research or literature that attempts to delve into this complex area. In the 1930s, some work was done in social psychology on dominance, but the focus was on adult social relations, and since then the only work done has been on dominance in families with schizophrenic members. At no time has the question of dominance in children, in their relations with their families and their peers, or in their adjustment to and progress within the educational system, been thoroughly investigated.

This article is concerned with the concept of dominance as it relates to children. It is very much a questioning, investigative paper and does not purport to have answers. In fact, one of my major purposes is to define dominance as I have seen it at work in families and begin to find a way to probe it in depth. I shall look briefly at some of the work which has been done in the etiology of dominance, with particular emphasis on the power motive; I shall also be looking at the involvement of the family in the development of feelings of dominance, at the survival value of dominance or submission, at dominance as it affects learning, and at the politics of dominance. In many cases, I am operating on insights gathered in work with children, adolescents, and their families. I hope to be able to pose some questions and draw some guidelines for further thought and research, both for myself and for others concerned with the dynamics of families.

The first stumbling block to a thorough study of dominance is the difficulty of reaching a satisfactory working definition of the concept. Dominance has been defined as 'the need to direct or control the actions of other people, including members of the family and friends. To have every action taken be that which he suggests.'[1] In the 1930s, A.H. Maslow suggested that there was an intrinsic difference between dominance status (which is ascribed to one by others in social interaction for many cultural and ethnological reasons), dominance behaviour (which is behaviour attempting to control or influence others), and dominance feelings (which are difficult to define succinctly). He listed thirteen near-synonyms which together give a picture of a dominant individual: self-confidence, self-esteem, high self-respect, consciousness of feeling superior, forcefulness, strength of character, sureness, a feeling of being able to handle others, masterfulness, feeling that others do and ought to admire and respect one, capability, absence of shyness or timidity or self-consciousness, and pride.[2]

Yet none of these definitions states exactly how dominance functions for those who work with children. Three factors stand out as central to the concept. First, dominance in children is often, but not always, unconscious. Children are not consciously trying to control others or to have 'every action taken be that which they suggest.' Rather there is an air of survival necessity in the young child's often frantic attempt to order a chaotic world, to make the behaviour of siblings and adults predictable, consistent, and safe for himself. Rather than being self-confident and calmly assured, as dominant adults may well be, the child seems to have a desperate need to structure coherently and tightly his own world. The children I have worked with who had the highest need to dominate were those most frightened, most insecure, most afraid of being abandoned or passed by in an inexplicable adult world. In adolescence this strong need to dominate and manipulate seems even more obviously connected with a basic insecurity and fear of rejection or failure.

Second, dominance in young children seems to be a fairly logical outgrowth of the kind of egocentric thought typical of the young – an unquestioning assumption that what they want and need should be the key consideration for everyone else. Most young children, before they are suitably socialized, feel that adults exist only to serve their needs.

Third, and related to the second point, is the thought that dominance is basically an ethnological concept; for example, what might be considered unsuitably dominant behaviour for a female in a patriarchal society could be quite appropriate in a matriarchal society. North American society has been accused for many years of catering unnecessarily to its young; perhaps the strangely contorted families where young children are pulling all the strings are extreme results of a twenty-year tendency to put children's needs far above adults' needs, especially in areas of privacy, time for oneself, and material possessions. Perhaps in more adult-centred cultures strangely skewed families do not exist with the same frequency or intensity.

Most research dealing with etiology of dominance is vague. A. Thomas, S. Chess, and H. Birch found that children who developed behaviour disorders had certain features of temperament which, together with organization and patterning, played significant roles in the evolution of their disorders.[3] This is hardly an unexpected finding, nor is it particularly enlightening. They went on to suggest that development was the 'rest of interaction between the child with given characteristics of temperament and significant features of his intrafamilial and extrafamilial environment. Temperament ... also interacted with abilities and motives ... as well as with the environment in determining the specific behavior patterns that evolved in the course of development.'[4] This does not really tell us anything about why dominance develops to a greater degree in some children than others, or at what stage it begins to be pathological in range and depth. A. Bandura provides slightly more of a clue for the maintenance of already established dominance: 'By aggressive behavior, or dominance through physical and verbal force, individuals can obtain material resources, change rules to fit their own wishes, gain control over and extract subservience from others, terminate provocation and remove physical barriers which block or delay attainment of desired outcomes.'[5] In other words, aggressive or dominant behaviour is strengthened and maintained to some extent by its positive social consequences. Again, although this sounds plausible for adult behaviour, or for perhaps a ten-year-old child, dominance as personality trait must become part of the range of behaviour much earlier, and it is difficult to credit a two year old with these complicated motives or actions.

Blau perhaps comes closer when he states that power is based on a resource – for adults, training, knowledge, experience, or size, and for a child, 'such qualities as a reserve of emotional responsiveness that may be freely given or withheld.'[6] A one- or two-year-old child easily and quickly learns that some behaviour gets more attention than others. It is a quick step from that learning to deliberately 'performing' to get attention or just as deliberately not performing to unsettle adults; for example, a two year old who is toilet-trained but 'forgets' always at the moments most inconvenient or embarrassing for his parents, thus forcing them back to the level of having to cater to his bodily needs before their own activities could be carried out. A child who has mastered anal actions has acquired 'social power' over his parents and can now effectively express his feelings of opposition, displeasure, and anger to them – he has, perhaps, a feeling of omnipotent dominance through his magical control over his own bowel movements and his parents' total lack of such control over him.

I suggest that dominance develops in a child through his early relations with his parents, through their reactions to his needs both physical and emotional. An infant is helpless, dependent on the good will of ministering adults, and aware so early of his smallness and powerlessness. It seems obvious that one of the major reasons a two year old gets such enjoyment out of overusing the word 'no' is that speech gives him the power to say what he wants even if he knows that, in the end, the adults decide – after doing, eating, wearing, going, and sleeping on someone else's schedule, at someone else's desire, it must feel great to scream no loudly, to register one's existence as an individual. I suggest that, at this point, patterns of interaction are established: if the parents always give in, the child learns to dominate very quickly; if there are rules that never change, things that are never allowed, but also some choices available, he learns that, by and large, although adults run things some situations are open to his dominance. A child who is never allowed to decide anything becomes enormously frustrated and probably very submissive until the day finally arrives, when he is thirteen or fourteen, when 'they' cannot *make* him do anything any more and all hell breaks loose.

Many examples of a young child's attempt to define himself, his position, his status in the world, could be given. I shall give one example and then explain the ramifications of such a dialogue as the child grows older and uses dominance successfully or pathologically.

CHILD: 'You're so big.'
ADULT OBSERVER: 'You'll be as big as me when you are older.'
CHILD: 'I'm big when I stand up, I'm small when I sit down. You might not see me, I'm so small when I sit down.'
ADULT OBSERVER: 'I see you when you sit or when you stand.'
The child places himself in an inferior submissive position, and experiences his own inferiority in relation to adults.
CHILD: 'I will be big as you when I stand up on the chair.'
ADULT OBSERVER: 'You'll be as big as me.'

The child attempts to gain identification with the adult, to regain the loss of self-esteem by being small. He identifies with the adult to gain power and dominance.

CHILD: 'I squashed a bug. I squashed a big bug, and yesterday I killed a tiger. I'm going to kill the biggest bear and eat it all.'

The child imagines power and control over objects in his fantasy. He sees himself as powerful in a little way (bug-killing), but then, becoming eloquent, claims he has killed a tiger and will kill the biggest bear and eat it, an act of incorporating the powerful object and thus gaining its power and control, thereby making himself more powerful and potentially a more dominant individual.

CHILD: 'I think I'll give you a piece of the biggest bear. It's good food.'

The child, fearing retaliation from the adult, tries to appease the adult by offering food to him. This, in effect, helps him to maintain his incorporated strengths, yet does not alienate the adult whom the child feels or fantasizes might become angry at too powerful a child and try to take away his power totally. The child shares power with the adult (through identification with the adult who supplies the needed food, warmth, and love), in an effort not to lose the adult omnipotence which the child must have in order to feel like a 'good' child (self-esteem is gained only by the adult giving supplies to the child, such as food, love, etc.). The child is actually afraid that his own power, wishes, and fantasies could destroy the adult and that he would thereby lose the adult as a potential source of supplies. He consciously sees the adult as being threatened by his power, the reverse of his actual feeling, saving the child from the anxiety of loss of control over primitive wishes. No doubt the ego of the child is not sufficiently developed to cope with 'pure dominance,' and so it must be tempered with identification, which we call prudence, or by ego control. This prudence might be compared with diplomacy, which permits the child to acquire the feeling of dominance over adults without risking the loss of gift supplies.

Now the child really has dominance over his environment, both in his fantasies and in reality, and he can go on to explore the extent of his dominance. Periodically, he will have feelings of inadequacy, either when his fantasy gets out of control, or when the adults offer greater resistance to his attempts to dominate. In such situations, the child will either fight or withdraw to an earlier phase when he felt more in charge of the situation. To fight is to feel powerful, to have sufficient self-esteem to think that he will win or have a good chance of winning. The child now has incorporated the powerful objects, the adults, and is able to test his use of them. He will go on to achieve even greater control of his environment, both at home and at school; he will achieve academically, socially, and emotionally. His feelings of dominance are sufficient to permit him to cope with his environment and to suffer the dangers and anxieties of possible tragedy because he has incorporated the strong dominant elements of his parents. These dominant elements act with his own aggressive forces and thereby acquire even greater emotional energy, which is necessary for the satisfaction of his needs. The child is now able to explore new situations and relations because he has emotional resources to call upon. Leaving his parents for the first time to go to school is still a danger but one he can handle because his past experiences have allowed him to gather sufficient resources. He need not withdraw or become excessively anxious. He can go on and fight if necessary, or, as some teachers have seen it, become too active or too questioning in an effort to understand and master the new environment – to dominate it. The dominance is a necessary condition for learning and achieving within the academic situation.

If the child has to withdraw to an earlier phase, he must do so in fantasy. If the fantasy becomes so strong that it blocks out reality, then dominance is acquired in imagination, although it is felt by the child to be real. Dominance acquired by fantasized aggression, while powerful, is also dangerous. The child uses fantasy in an attempt to shore up his dissolving feelings of dominance; he then has little energy to involve himself with such realities as school, family, peers, or even his developing self. He almost maintains a kind of status quo in order to prevent himself from collapsing, but he is actually regressing because he continually has to block out reality.

Thus dominance seems to be a necessary component of personality development and interaction patterns in childhood, a way of placing oneself in the spectrum of the family and the school which may be more or less successful depending on the reactions and responses of the environment to the infant's first attempts to have some control over his environment. A child exhibits dominance as a natural part of the range of human behavioural development, and I think that the dominance *feelings* of adulthood come after the dominance *behaviour* exhibited by all young infants and children.

The aggressive, noisy, bossy, possessive, and obnoxious child (whom everyone knows but no one seems to have) would seem to be the child whose family's reactions to his first attempts at control have been to 'give-in' to his every demand. These are the frightened children, the ones who sense no safety in the adults around them, who keep pushing in hopes of finding limits. The shrill voice of a three year old ordering his parents around is not that of a child who truly seeks dominance, I think, but that of a child who looks wildly for someone to be dependent on or submissive to, someone who will say no and mean it. In families where the ten year olds are running the show, where the adults' feelings and moods depend on the child, where his wants determine family spending and scheduling, or where teenagers are making all the decisions, the parents have abdicated their roles as adults and forced the child to become the 'ruler.' Thus the child's initial attempt to identify with the all-powerful adult in order to feel dominant has been negated because the power is quickly given over to him, thereby arresting his attempt to form the satisfactory identification necessary for maturing.

Dominance in children is not simply behaviour by which the child 'satisfies its needs before or at the expense of others, or when, in face-to-face situations, it induces submissive behavior in others.'[7] Dominance is an experiential relation of the child with powerful, giving adults. It is the kind of relation where the child acquires dominance by identification with the strong adult in his home; yet, the child does not simply take over the powerful role – he does not have the resources to do so – but, if forced by inadequate adults, he does take over by hyperactive, hyperdemanding, continuously irritable, whining, belligerent behaviour. This is his way of handling a difficult situation where he has to play a role for which he is unprepared. He uses only those devices which are available to him – primitive, generalized hostilities. Dominance then may be the result of 'activation within the organism of two antagonistic disturbances or drives – pugnacity and fear.'[8] If dominance is established too early, it is seen as an attempt upon the part of the child to cope with his fear of not gaining satisfaction from inadequate parents. Pugnacity or aggression takes over and the child becomes the overly dominant member of the family. Adequate ego development is then thwarted.

Obviously the role of the family cannot be underestimated in the development of dominance and in the emergence of raw power in the older child and adolescent. In *The Politics of the Family*, R.D. Laing speaks of attribution as a basic method of setting personality traits in young children.[9] It is not a question, he says, of telling them they must *be* good, but of constantly asserting that they *are* good, and thus setting expectations for them. A family that constantly repeats, 'John is a very stubborn little boy who likes his own way' to the child, siblings, relatives, and teachers is programming that child to become aggressively dominant. Research suggests that parents seldom perceive girls as being dominant; this reveals a very clear sociological expectation based on sex, a patterning which suggests strongly to boys that dominance and aggression are good and reinforces this suggestion during childhood and into adolescence, especially in terms of physical and sexual aggression, and which suggests to girls that 'softer and more feminine' qualities are desirable. W.D. Pienaar found that boys were perceived as more powerful than girls in families with high and low adjustment ratings, and by all family members.[10] M. Rothbart and his colleagues even assume bluntly that 'a valid measure of dominance should at least show females exhibiting less dominance with males than with other females ... '[11] Although children of both sexes may develop dominance in the same way in infancy, the reinforcements and attributions of their families quickly alter and channel their dominance behaviours in ways that irrevocably affect their later dominance feelings and status as adults. After its initial appearance dominance, to a great extent, is a sociological aspect of development and no longer a purely psychological development.

An interesting perception of the role of the family in determining pathology is found in George Frank's theory that the experiences to which the individual is exposed over a period of time do not necessarily lead to the development of learned patterns of behaviour. He suggests that it is not the reality of the family that is the important dimension in determining the child's reactions, 'rather, it might be the perception of the family members, and this might often have little or no relation to the people as they really are. This would mean then that in many instances the important variables in the development of psychopathology might be the factors which the child brings to the family ... Indeed we are left to wonder ... whether the proclivity towards fantasy distortion of reality might not be *the* factor in the development of psychopathology, and this proclivity might not always be determined by the child's experiences per se.'[12]

One wonders, however, what forms the child's original perceptions of his family members. I cannot see that it can be anything but the responses to what he sees, hears, feels, and senses around him. Granted that every human being will assimilate and accommodate in his own unique fashion, that perception is perhaps the infinite individual act, identical for no two people however similar their experiences, and that reality is not external but rather internal, a combination of perception with previous experiences and knowledge blended instantaneously and mysteriously by the mind, it still must have *some* raw material to assimilate to begin with.

The newborn infant is biologically totally dependent upon adults, particularly the adult responsible for his care – usually his mother. If she does not care for the child, his existence will be threatened by lack of warmth, lack of touch, and lack of food. If she cares for him well, his physical needs and emotional drives will be attended to and he will thrive. Because of his dependence in these primary experiences the child develops a sense of unity with the adult. During this early period of his life, she is little more than an object that satisfies his needs and wants; she tends to become a personalized individual only through the caring experiences she gives him. This sense of unity with the adult must provide the infant with important and powerful fantasy experiences. This unity subsequently provides the basis for the powerful, controlling, dominant feelings the infant has, and his wish demands are activated by the full pleasure principle which determines his existence at this time in his life.

The young child invests the adult caring for him with feelings even though he is not fully aware of her as a person as yet. If she satisfies his needs, she is the 'good mother'; if she frustrates his needs, as is inevitable at times, she is the 'bad mother.' Since the young child's needs are at times satisfied and at times frustrated, this non-complete satisfaction forces the young child to begin to cope with the impinging reality. He must now begin to distinguish not only between the good and bad mother, but also to see her as having an existence separate from his own. As the emotional investment that the mother makes in her child increases, and as he develops, he begins to perceive her as a separate person. I think that it is this separation of himself from his mother that forms the basis of ego development. The child will be able to maintain the mother's original emotional investment in himself if he gives up direct satisfaction of his pleasure needs. He begins to depend upon her and to regard her as a separate person capable of satisfying his needs. But the satisfaction of these needs and the timing of these satisfactions will be dependent upon the cues which he gives her or which she picks up from him. The most prominent cue is crying. If she responds quickly, then the child receives satisfaction and the feeling of control and fantasized dominance are present. This dominance is a desirable emotional feeling if the child is to cope with his feelings of frustration. His capacity to make emotional investments in himself and other significant people in his life seems to depend upon the ways in which these early needs are satisfied. When frustration is not excessive and his needs are quickly satisfied, he sees himself as having some control and dominance over his environment and is able to tolerate longer and longer delays as his ego capacity for delay increases. This latter aspect, ego capacity for delay, increases as the old dependency situations change to new dependency situations. The expansion and discovery of new feelings, new demands, and new dependency situations rests upon the child's capacity to have internalized his mother's characteristics and to have established his own psychic reality. The child is no longer dominated by the need for immediate satisfaction, for he is now capable of maintaining an image of his good, satisfying, caring-for mother, and so can overcome some anxieties because of his incorporation of her characteristics. This basic dependency relation with his mother alters and grows to become the origin of feelings about himself and others in his family. He cares for himself because his mother cared for him, but he can extend himself and carry on in the face of anxiety because she has made an emotional investment in him and he has been able to carry around in his psychic reality an image of the caring mother.

The young child learns that he cannot get everything he wants right away, and that he is essentially a different being from his mother. The child forms an identification bond with the mother and thereby incorporates her power to satisfy his needs and drives; because she is powerful, the child identifies with her to assume her power and thereby her control on fantasized dominance. The child's feelings of dominance stem from this identification with the powerful adult and exist as a source for satisfaction of needs – perhaps for biological survival. The identifying process that each member of the family goes through exists in accordance with the common bond which unites the family; that is, all members of the family are in fact united to a mother who is felt, in fantasy at least, to be the unusual provider.[13] Laing, then, may in fact be saying that parents must tell their children they are good in order to ensure that the mother be the provider and not the punitive, limiting, or bad mother. If she sees her children as good or perhaps potentially good, then she will provide and care for them. If she is able to accept their identification with her and not feel devoured by their dominance, then she will in fact provide the basis for allowing her children not only to see themselves as good, but also to see her as a good mother. Politically, when parents have unconscious motives which create opposition to the expression of care and to interaction with their children, then the above cannot happen; when society insists that children have no rights, the basis for inadequate parenting is laid because the parents are not living within a social milieu which reinforces the needed primary relations.

An extension of this theory is the idea that there is survival value (which a normal child will quickly learn to gauge accurately) implicit in being dominant or aggressive, passive or submissive, as the situation requires. Certainly an ability to be dominant or submissive on demand is necessary for survival in the school system. If a child is to make an impact on his learning environment, he must in a sense attack it through aggression and ambition. Every teacher knows that the child whose needs are most easily left unmet is the quiet one in the corner of the classroom whose name one never can quite remember. The child who knows when to act up, and how most effectively to draw attention to his needs, will get attention, although sometimes not of the kind he is seeking. An intelligent and ambitious child knows how to make the teacher teach him, to make the teacher feel that he is important and that his vocation is important and useful, and thus to reap the rewards of the teacher's own satisfaction with a responsive student. Again, a child who is perhaps used to always having his 'own way' at home, who has become overly dominant in interactions with peers and adults, is apt to have a difficult time in school unless he learns to control his aggression enough to make the teacher feel useful and not irritated. A child who has not learned successfully how to be dominant or submissive within a situational context, or one who has not been able to exercise any dominance at all because he has been taught that aggression is always wrong, will find success difficult or impossible to achieve.

Four factors seem to be involved when a child has had his aggressive and dominance feelings thoroughly closed off: 1/ he may feel guilt over feeling aggression, due to familial responses to his aggression in the past; 2/ he may have a fear of outdoing his parents, of being so aggressive that they will simply collapse under the pressure, a variation of the fear that one's anger is strong enough to damage or destroy others permanently because one has never had a chance to try it out and find out that it is not, in fact, fatal; 3/ he may fear that he will have to take over the family role as provider or leader, sensing that his parents are not strong, and feeling his own aggression as relatively much stronger, particularly if his parents are quiet, never displaying much aggression themselves; 4/ he may fear growing up, as most adolescents do at some time, and avoid dominance or aggression because he so thoroughly identifies it as an adult trait, or a prerequisite of adulthood, a part of decision-making he is afraid to grow into; in other words, he hangs onto a much earlier pattern of distribution of power, perhaps feeling he is not strong or wise or resourceful enough to attempt a different way.

It is clear that these questions and areas are all almost inextricably interwoven. The etiology of dominance has to do with family interaction, - what the parents expect, and how they respond to a child's first attempts at control and independence - in turn this interaction becomes a very political question as children grow older and are more easily drawn into alliances, (which reflect the various desires for, or fears of, power and aggression), with one or the other parent or with siblings. At the same time, a child's usual patterns of dominance and submission within the family are carried over into his peer relations and into his attempt to carve out a niche in the school system. Whether a child's needs or feelings of dominance lead to dominance behaviour which is acceptable to his particular culture and society, and whether a child's initial dominance strivings lead to dominance status within the adult world, all seem to depend on the patterns of interaction which are part of his familial environment and which may be pretty well set by his parent's personalities, temperament, philosophies, and experiences by the time he arrives.

A young child may come to sense that he has the power to control the behaviour, actions, and even feelings of other people, especially those people who are members of his family. He can gradually acquire the position of holding authority influence over them, and his demand for control and his observations of his influence may thus lead him from dominance to domination. In other situations, the dominance in the young child can be demonstrated, not by direct command, but rather by exerting an emotional pressure on another person, usually the mother, to act for him. The child is then able to maintain a 'back-seat driving' position. A change in domination would not occur by change in the mother, for the child could make use of another person, within the family or without. A change away from domination could occur only through changes in the personality structure of the child.

Perhaps it is impossible to causally distinguish whether the child's behaviour is learned by the responses of his family, or whether the responses of his family are learned by his behaviour. Obviously the two are related, and obviously a change in one will affect the other, and perhaps the changes and the realignments are so minute, so sensitive, so dependent on the context of the family patterns being unbroken or unchanged by any observer, that it will be impossible to ever really know exactly how or why any one family functions. Psychology has not had remarkable success in figuring out all the hows or whys of the functioning of individuals, much less the infinitely more complex group, the family, with all the historical, social, economic, political, cultural, and generational pressures operating on it.

Perhaps I am not arriving at a very distant spot from that at which I began: my thinking is that dominance in families is a central determinant of family adjustment and of the satisfactory development of individual children within that family; this is largely based on seeing a good many children whose dominance needs had been pulled or warped by their interaction with their families and with the schools. The study of the etiology of dominance, and of the ramifications of dominance, will indicate the importance of dominance in the development of the human personality in childhood and in the stability of the human personality in adulthood.

NOTES

1 B. Rotter, J.E. Chance, and E.J. Phares, *Social Learning Theory of Personality* (New York 1972), 32
2 'Dominance, Feelings, Behavior, and Status,' *Psychological Review* (1937), 44, 404-29
3 *Temperament and Behavior Disorders in Children* (New York 1968)
4 Ibid., 182
5 *Principles of Behavior Modification* (New York 1969), 380
6 Quoted in E.G. Mishler and N.E. Waxler, *Interaction in Families* (New York 1968), 119
7 N.L. Munn, *Handbook of Psychological Research on the Rat* (New York 1950), 468
8 J.P. Seward. 'Aggressive Behavior in the Rat: 1. General Characteristics: Age and Sex Differences.' *Journal of Comparative Psychology* (1945), 38, 175-98, 191
9 (Toronto 1969)
10 'Dominance in Families,' *Dissertation Abstracts Int.* 30 (6-B), (1969), 2914-15
11 'Sibling Configuration and Interpersonal Dominance,' *Proceedings of the Annual Convention of the American Psychological Association* (1970) 5 (part 1), 367-8
12 G.H. Frank, 'The Role of the Family in the Development of Psychopathology,' *Abnormal Psychology*, ed. E.A. Southwell and H. Feldman (California 1969), 300
13 W.R. Bion, *Experiences in Groups* (London 1961)

Elizabeth Brady

Towards a happier history: women and domination

SOME PROBLEMS WITH LANGUAGE

' ... the happiest women, like the happiest nations, have no history.'[1] Woman's growing knowledge of the history of her sex may preclude idiot joy, but it also marks the beginning of freedom through self-consciousness, of informed choice governed by a new awareness of real options and illuminated by the conviction that the present is Now and subject to her will. Learning how and why chains were forged tells something about how they can be smashed.

In the past Canadian historians have ignored the impact – or failed to explain the want of it – of women, individually and collectively, on society.[2] Yet the most significant aspect of contemporary woman's consciousness is her sense of the historical context from which her sex has emerged. What are the realities, historical and existential, on which abstractions like 'domination' and 'women' have been grounded? How have Canadian women conceived of themselves and of their role in this society from settlement to the present day?

In view of the paucity of historical documentation in these areas, I shall draw on the imaginative record women have created, using three novels by Canadian women, written over a period of two hundred years, falling almost exactly a century apart. In them one can perceive the meaning of domination in the lives of Canadian women and trace the gradual evolution of a distinctly feminist consciousness alongside the parallel and necessary growth of political awareness. Like the minds of Plato's cave dwellers, the female psyche, as it matures through the course of these three novels, moves progressively from relative ignorance to informed lucidity. In charting this evolution, this essay becomes an exercise in naming, an attempt to locate and describe where we have been. It does not offer a new alphabet: any program for social change aimed at levelling inequality must be developed collectively.

I would first like to look briefly at two conflicting concepts of the male/female relationship – the hermaphroditic and the symbiotic – with a view to illustrating the role played by language in our conceptualizing of the terms 'domination' and 'women.'

In the botanical world, the hermaphrodite has its stamens and pistil in the same flower, with the peculiar result that any struggle for sexual domination is confined to a local habitation. When in his *Symposium* Plato narrates the myth of Eros, he seems to have had in mind some such androgynous ideal. Zeus conceived a plan of cutting into two parts each of the three sexes (man, woman, and the androgyne or union of the two). 'After the division,' so the legend goes, 'the two parts of man, each desiring his other half, came together, and throwing their arms about one another, entwined in mutual embraces ... human nature was originally one and we were a whole, and the desire and pursuit of the whole is called love.'[3] However removed from experience the myth may be, its interest largely resides in its *political* significance: Zeus saw his plan as an effective means of maintaining the domination of the gods over man and of obtaining his sacrifices and worship.

Yet the androgynous ideal has persisted over the centuries. In her first feminist tract, *A Room of One's Own* (1929), Virginia Woolf concluded her case for sexual equality by sketching future guidelines: writers of both sexes must put aside any insistence on preserving sex differences and recognize instead the androgynous or bisexual nature of the creative mind. She suggests that 'there are two sexes in the mind corresponding to the two sexes in the body' which 'require to be united' through spiritual cooperation.[4] Because this 'man-womanly mind' will be free from the didactic impulse to proselytize on sexist grounds, the new person can then develop a lifestyle more completely expressive of his/her total being.

In spite of its appeal, androgyny remains merely an ideal, perhaps because it provides such an unconvincing blueprint for reality. In his article 'Goddesses of the Twenty-First Century,' Buckminster Fuller offers a diametrically conceived notion of male/female relations. Male and female are fundamental complementaries, and as such they mirror a dialectically structured universe: 'Only in the mid-twentieth century did it become scientifically clear that unity is plural – and, at a minimum, two; that all experimentally detectable phenomena have their unique opposites, and that the complementary opposite behaviors [for example, male/female] are never mirror images of one another. Science is remiss and unnecessarily prejudicial in calling one of a pair of complementary behaviors "negative." There are always much better descriptive terms.'[5]

Certainly Fuller's dialectical conceptual framework serves as an accurate description of how language has evolved, and his plea for 'better descriptive terms' can function as a useful guideline in this essay. For if there is a general agreement on what the key terms of reference, 'domination' and 'women,' *really* mean, much preliminary discussion about ordinary language and contemporary usage can be dispensed with. At the same time it will be discovered that the concepts domination (from which 'liberation' by apposition derives its meaning) and women (which by apposition to 'men' derives its meaning) remain unanalysed – and any clarification of their respective meanings falls a victim, in so many feminist and anti-feminist arguments, to an immediate emotive onslaught.

This insistence on a clarification of the meaning of two such frequently used words may make the reader impatient, but such clarification is needed – as recently as 1928 the Supreme Court of Canada ruled that women were not 'persons' in the terms of the BNA Act. In this attempt to elucidate meanings I shall be examining not merely two words in ordinary language but the *realities* we use these words to describe. Words do not float, clear and pristine, above their contexts, but trail after them a bewildering complexity of ambiguities, concealed intentions, emotional responses, traditional associations, and personal connotations. This is particularly the case with words like domination and women which, whatever their ostensible meanings, are generally used *politically* – that is, both to describe a specific condition and to prescribe the means of its modification.

Objectively 'domination' is simply a word used to describe a context within which certain conditions prevail. In that particular context, individuals may or may not be content; to suggest otherwise at this juncture would move us from factual statement into value judgment. That 'domination' has acquired a negative connotation in ordinary language is confirmed by the manner in which politicians so warp its meaning that the word becomes synonymous with its opposite. For example, when the Americans used political force in southeast Asia to enforce ideological and economic domination without the consent of the populace, they claimed to be 'keeping the world free for democracy.' In this process of translating fascist brutalities into palatable rhetoric, dictators fight wars of 'liberation.'

Now what is most offensive to common sense and to the historical record in this abuse of language is its total disregard for the central meaning of 'liberation.' In a state of political domination, free choice is a dispensable commodity. And it is only within this context of *will* that the term 'liberation' derives its meaning. 'Liberated' or 'free' means only that we act *not* under domination: it rules out the suggestion of its generally accepted antitheses.

The relation between the terms domination and women is not always clear; undoubtedly this is why the mere phrase 'women's liberation' provokes such conflicting responses. And I'm not being facetious when I suggest that these conflicting responses are, in turn, partly attributable to a general confusion about the meaning of 'women.' It might be unusual to find any full-blooded North American male confessing to this kind of confusion. But it would be equally exceptional to discover a woman who isn't at this moment experiencing a great deal of personal conflict over the subject. People's lives are governed, not in terms of dictionary definitions, but in relation to a whole nexus of traditional roles, conditioned behaviour, and social expectations. Even a cursory examination of woman's contemporary role in society, whatever that society, suggests that this role has undergone radical and irreversible transformations in the past decade. That transformation has been accompanied by a corresponding change in the usage of the word 'women.'

I remarked earlier that words are never 'clean.' Most of the meanings traditionally associated with 'woman' are derogatory – qualities generally (although entirely arbitrarily) attributed to the female sex are capriciousness, proneness to tears, gentleness, devotion, fearfulness, passivity, etc. The list is limited only by the volume of male hang-ups being exorcised through the word. Freud's disciples could not conceive of a woman but as a castrated male – hence Germaine Greer's 'female eunuch.' The post-Freudian definition, then, was negative. As Buckminster Fuller said, we can do a lot better than that.

We want *open* words. The term 'woman' must be granted as much flexibility as 'domination.' Only in this way can we continue to enlarge the parameters of women's experience and potential. So (1) while we can refer the definition of 'female' to experience and agree that the female sex is biologically defined by its capacity for maternity, any woman who remains childless for whatever reason does not thereby forfeit her membership in the sex; (2) nor does a woman define herself *as a woman* by what she does with those specialized genitalia for purely sexual, as opposed to reproductive, purposes. We are left without a definition, free to watch women grow and in the process invalidate every attempt to categorize them.

When the author of *Das Kapital* attacked Hegelian idealism, he was in effect attacking an entire political philosophy. Philosophical idealism, he so profoundly observed, is an apology for the status quo. And in noting this seminal connection between a philosophical system and its political application, Marx attempted to bring theory and practice back into a working relationship. Only by grounding abstractions in fact, by putting them to the test of experience and history, can we begin to establish moral priorities.

The three novels before me verify the value of this kind of procedure: by allowing the concepts 'domination' and 'woman' free play at the outset we ensure that they gather their related meanings directly from and within their original source of integrity in women's lives. This method of proceeding also underscores how 'closed' definitions of the role/function of women serve to circumscribe their full human potentiality.

The first novel, *The History of Emily Montague* by Frances Brooke, was published in 1769 (this date establishes it as the first North American novel). The second is Rosanna Leprohon's *Antoinette de Mirecourt*, first published in 1864. The final novel is Margaret Atwood's *The Edible Woman*, which appeared in 1969. I'm going to interpret the two early novels as raw material, that is as *descriptions* of the predicament of Canadian women, and *The Edible Woman* as an analysis of the over-all domination structure.

One important qualifying point. Until quite recently it was very unusual for a woman in this country to write a book at all. If she did so it is relatively safe to assume that she occupied a position of economic privilege in relation to the rest of her sex. In *A Room of One's Own* Virginia Woolf convincingly argued her thesis that 'a woman must have money and a room of her own if she is to write fiction' by demonstrating the combined negative effects of poverty and deference to male authority on English women novelists in the past. Only by gaining financial autonomy can a woman begin to enjoy the intellectual freedom out of which literature grows. We can expand the relevance and general application of this notion by reasoning that only by achieving economic independence can *any* woman realize her creative potential as a total person.

THE EIGHTEENTH CENTURY: 'PROPER IDEAS OF PETTICOAT POLITICS'

'They are squabbling at Quebec, I hear, about I cannot tell what, therefore shall not attempt to explain: some dregs of old disputes, it seems, which have had not time to settle ... For my part, I think no politics worth attending to but those of the little commonwealth of woman: if I can maintain my empire over hearts, I leave the men to quarrel for every thing else.'[6] This quotation contains in essence the two central themes of *The History of Emily Montague.* The 'squabbling at Quebec' refers to the political context of the novel. Most of the action takes place in Quebec City in the mid-1760s, shortly after the cession of Quebec to Great Britain at the end of the Seven Years' War, when the colony became the centre of a clash of rival imperialisms – the French seigniorial and the British colonial systems.

This historical setting has for its social counterpart the garrison society of Quebec, where Frances Brooke resided from 1763 to 1768, during her husband's period of tenure as chaplain to the garrison and deputy to the auditor general. In fact, as a focal point, the historical context soon gives way almost entirely to the social milieu, 'the little commonwealth of woman.' But for the modern reader, this lapse into the stock-in-trade of the eighteenth-century sentimental novel is not accomplished before the book's real significance has been imparted – the line of relation (almost of causality) it traces between political philosophy and the status of women. Imperialism, the prevailing political mode, provides the only sexual modality permitted in male/female relationships. As the colony is subject to the domination of the patriarchal state, so women are oppressed in the economic, political, and legal spheres by the agents of imperialism. Whether or not one consents to Engels' theory (in *The Origin of the Family, Private Property, and the State*) that we can trace the origin of this governing hierarchy of wealth and class back to sexual domination, the fact remains that women can not be free agents within a system that denies them economic independence.

The novel has a simple plot: three pairs of lovers, through an interminable exchange of lengthy letters, triumph over a series of patently phony obstacles in their paths to true romance. What is interesting is the narrative perspective. Everything is purveyed to the reader from an upper-middle-class British point of view. *Emily Montague* is dedicated to 'His Excellency Guy Carleton, Esq. Governor and Commander in Chief of His Majesty's Province of Quebec,' and the spirit of sycophancy written into the prefatory letter of dedication informs the entire novel. Underlying the British imperialist mentality of the main characters is an exploitative belief in the value of colonies in so far as they embellish the prestige and fill the coffers of the mother country. The flow of profit derived from securing foreign markets and raw materials is one way. The relationship between mother country and colonies is based on the model of parent/child relationships: 'Every advantage you give the North Americans in trade centers at last in the mother country, they are the bees, who roam abroad for that honey which enriches the paternal hive ... Yet too much care cannot be taken to suppose the majesty of government, and assert the dominion of the parent country.'

British imperialism repeatedly expresses itself in terms of an uncritical master-race theory of colonial domination. The settlers take with them to the colonies an arrogant assumption of their innate superiority in governmental, religious, social, and cultural spheres. They are fired by a messianic conviction that the French and the Indians will happily cooperate in their own cultural and ideological assimilation. These attitudes are imported intact from the Old World into the New, where they are perpetuated with relatively little modification by the *Canadian* experience.

Emily Montague is, however, occasionally illuminated by passages of insight into the unsatisfactory nature of the role, education, and political status of women. The same kind of paternalism that characterizes Britain's treatment of the American colonies also characterizes the state's treatment of women. Britain, it is suggested, might do well to study the political equality of Indian women: 'The sex we have so unjustly excluded from power in Europe have a great share in the Huron government; the chief is chose by the matrons from amongst the nearest male relations, by the female line, of him he is to succeed ... In the true sense of the word, *we* are the savages, who so impolitely deprive you of the common rights of citizenship ... By the way, I don't think you are obliged in conscience to obey laws you have had no share in making; your plea would certainly be at least as good as that of the Americans, about which we every day hear so much.'

This political analogy the novel draws extends both to the American colonies and to male-dominated women a mandate for civil disobedience, if not for revolution. The struggle of women against male domination is comparable to that of the oppressed Americans who were rebelling against colonialism. Although this concept of solidarity among oppressed groups is merely adumbrated here, the fact that it pre-dates by almost a century and a half the first great feminist movement is noteworthy. The rationale echoes the informing spirit behind the colonists' rejection of the Stamp Act (no taxation without representation in Parliament) and the Declaration of Independence: governments derive 'their just powers from the consent of the governed' and it is the right of the people to revolt when those powers are abused. These democratic principles later became the platform of the Woman's Suffrage movement.

Unhappily the egalitarian standards expressed above are never translated into action in the novel. Frances Brooke's main concern is to depict the stylized ritual of courtship among the British gentry in Quebec, a ritual governed entirely by the conventions of romantic love. The woman assumes in the eyes of her beloved a glorified and idealized role which serves as a pretext for her continued domination by him. She is described in terms which emphasize her passivity and dependency. Emily Montague's three characteristic attributes are 'that bewitching languor, that seducing softness, that melting sensibility.' Such an ethereal personage is obviously unsuited to any serious involvement with the real world and the lifespan of male domination is thereby extended.

Although Emily eventually receives a large inheritance, which might have conferred on her some measure of independence, she remains a clinging vine because of the deep-rooted effects of her upbringing. At the conclusion of the novel, the respective roles of the sexes are rigidly and patriarchically defined: 'In one word, they [men] would have been studying the useful, to support us; we the agreeable, to please and amuse them; which I take to be assigning to the two sexes the employments for which nature intended them, notwithstanding the vile example of the savages to the contrary.' Here is a powerful expression of the vicious circularity of sexual dominance: men convert women into decorative objects; women in turn must collaborate in their own oppression because of the *economic* character of bourgeois marriage (essentially a system of barter or institutionalized prostitution in which the wife receives lodging and commodities in exchange for domestic and sexual services rendered).

What we have in *Emily Montague* is an imperialist viewpoint (reflected in both political and sexual matters) which is only marginally responsive to the very divergent demands and circumstances of the new country. There is little sense of the pioneering spirit which was eventually to transform the transplanted culture into a more recognizably home-grown product. This was partly due to the resilience of the British to the aboriginal and French-Canadian cultures they encountered. Their conservatism is, to some extent, also the natural defensiveness of the newcomer. But it seems to stem principally from the fact that these characters are visitors: they emigrated to Canada only as temporary residents (like Frances Brooke) and resumed their upper-middle-class life in England when their fortunes were re-instated. As a result their commitment to Canada is imperfect and their point of view usually that of the intelligent observer, seldom the participant.

Also of interest here is the politics of novel-writing in the late eighteenth century, a subject centrally related to sexual politics. At this stage the form of the novel was in its infancy. Samuel Richardson's *Pamela*, which is generally regarded as the first English novel and which served Frances Brooke as a model for *Emily Montague*, was published only twenty-nine years earlier. The major novelists were men, and their work was directed at a readership of middle-class ladies, as much for their moral edification as enjoyment. Many novels of the period were no more than extended and prolix sexist sermons. It would be less than realistic to demand radical feminist tracts in 1769: the first book on the subject did not appear until 1792 with the publication of Mary Wollstone-craft's *A Vindication of the Rights of Woman*. In this context the tentative, somewhat self-conscious feminist insights of a Frances Brooke are much to be admired as precursors of a later and braver assertion of woman's rights.

One does note in *Emily Montague* the beginning of the long dependency of much early Canadian literature, for both its forms and themes, upon the richer cultural models of Britain. This extended reliance resulted in, among other things, the 'genteel tradition' of Canadian letters, and so many second-rate derivative works, pot-boilers written by authors trapped in a situation in which they could rely on virtually no market at home, were discriminated against and exploited by foreign copyright laws, and consequently were compelled to write with a wary economic eye on Britain and the United States.

As we move into the nineteenth century we can begin to chart as well the more positive side of the story – the growing recognition on the part of our early writers of the basic recalcitrance of Canadian experience in the face of the transplanted heritage, and the development of this recognition into forms of defiance from which emerged a more truly native culture – and with it a new female consciousness.

THE NINETEENTH CENTURY: 'A PRUDENT HORROR OF SECRET MARRIAGES'

In *Antoinette de Mirecourt: or, Secret Marrying and Secret Sorrowing*, Rosanna Leprohon chose for her novel the same historical setting as Frances Brooke's, post-Conquest Montreal. But when she examined that unsettled period Mrs Leprohon had the advantages of a century's hindsight and a bicultural heritage. Born and educated in Montreal, the daughter of a wealthy Irish immigrant family, and married to a French-Canadian physician, she moved comfortably within two cultures. As a result, a much more independent and objective poli-tical sense informs this novel.

The dedication to *Antoinette* opens on the intensely nationalistic note that infused so much post-Confederation literature: 'Although the literary treasures of "the old world" are ever open to us, and our American neighbours should continue to inundate the country with reading-matter ... yet Canadians should not be discouraged from endeavoring to form and foster a literature of their own.'[7] The controlling viewpoint in this novel, as in *Emily Montague*, is upper class (wealth and family influence remain the status quo), but with a significant difference: the events following the 'capitulation of Montreal to the combined forces of Murray, Amherst, and Haviland' in 1760 are narrated from the French-Canadian perspective. In this light the British victory is seen as 'that darkest episode in the history of my country.' This perspective provides a strong qualifying commentary on Frances Brooke's ardent and uncritical imperialism.

British imperialism is examined in reverse focus as an economic and ideological system founded upon conquest and perpetuated by the subjection of the conquered people to military force. But the true target of attack here is *not* the fact of oppression under imperialism, it is that the exploitation is British rather than French.

The superficial social world in which Frances Brooke's characters found themselves at ease is also held up to moral scrutiny. *Antoinette* is a cautionary tale, significantly sub-titled 'Secret Marrying and Secret Sorrowing.' Its specific didactic concern is the problem of clandestine marriage 'unhallowed by a father's blessing, and that religious benediction, which she [Antoinette] had been taught from childhood to regard as so solemn and necessary a part of the marriage service.'

The female protagonist (not surprisingly a beautiful and wealthy heiress) is at the beginning of the novel a naive and unworldly child of seventeen. Among the opportunistic adventurers within the ranks of the English officers is Major Audley Sternfield, a 'super-refined dandy' who typifies to perfection everything in the fashionable life of Montreal the novelist condemns. Antoinette's cloistered, country innocence is soon corrupted by the fortune-seeking Sternfield. She is emotionally blackmailed into a secret marriage to this man she doesn't love by social and family pressures beyond her control and understanding. Dominated by a loving but despotic father who attempts to force upon her the suitor of his choice, she is unwittingly persuaded into contracting a tragically unsuitable marriage of her own 'choice.'

The morality of the novel is unflinchingly doctrinaire, often to the point of insensitivity. A virtual child is callously manipulated by a male-dominated family, Church, and society, but her victimization by these patriarchal forces never becomes a target for their condemnation or a plea for their revision. To plead for any significant revaluation of woman's monolithic and exclusive status as wife and mother in this context would entail a major critique of the patriarchal system. *Antoinette de Mirecourt* is not a novel of social protest:

Rosanna Leprohon writes from the rigid confines of a brutalizing Roman Catholicism which, rather than accommodating its laws to human (specifically female) needs, stolidly and consistently condemns the innocent transgressor for falling short in faithful and rigorous observation of those laws. Indeed, at times the vindictive tone which surrounds the various descriptions of Antoinette's misconduct approaches misogyny.

Although her misfortunes are reversed at the end through a second marriage, this time to the honourable Col Evelyn and with her father's consent, her escape from the 'system of persecution and intimidation' enforced on her by the tyrant Sternfield is achieved only by the novelist's moral evasiveness. Divorce is ruled out on religious grounds as an alternative to a lifetime of 'wifely submission' to male tyranny – so Mrs Leprohon has Major Sternfield conveniently disposed of in a duel, thus leaving Antoinette free to enter the kind of union endorsed by Church and father. Without the introduction of her first husband's fortuitous death Antoinette's story could have ended only in suffering. This brutal fact the novelist studiously avoids, for to acknowledge it would force upon her a critical examination of her Roman Catholic morality, with its extreme prejudice against women who, like the American colonies, were obliged to obey unjust laws they had no share in framing. Instead, she opts for a little therapeutic male violence.

In *Emily Montague* patriarchal domination reflected itself politically in the form of British imperialism and sexually in the institution of marriage. The domination of women in *Antoinette de Mirecourt* is enacted on a religious level, by the Church (which is shown in the novel to function for the French-Canadian community as a surrogate government and law court), and within the family by the father whose paternal authority is absolute. Filial obedience, however misguided, is as sacred a female duty as submission to the Church. And again, the woman's motive for submission to parental (as to marital) tyranny is economic.

As the French-Canadian viewpoint of *Antoinette* qualifies the British imperialist viewpoint of *Emily Montague*, so the non-fiction literature of pioneer women which emerged during the nineteenth century qualifies the essentially upper-class view of both these novels. Any student of the period should contrast the refined and sophisticated ethos of the latter to the painful realities of the settlers' coming to terms with the harsh backwoods of the new world without the softening luxury of a fixed income and inherited wealth.[8]

THE TWENTIETH CENTURY: 'OH, SCREW MY FEMININITY'

The Edible Woman is an interesting measure of the distance travelled by women during the hundred years since the publication of *Antoinette de Mirecourt*. Margaret Atwood has assimilated many of the feminist ideas and values current during the second phase of the woman's movement in the late 1960s. She develops a female protagonist (who has a job) sufficiently enlightened to relate her analysis of woman's predicament to the larger sociopolitical system which victimizes her. The novel offers a probing criticism of consumerism in capitalist society,[9] the specific targets of her attack being market research and advertising, those businesses which create and sustain the media myth of middle-class Domestic Woman.

At the beginning of *The Edible Woman* Marian McAlpin is employed by Seymour Surveys, a market research firm which exploits women, whether in the guise of its own employees or as consumer housewives: 'As market research is a sort of cottage industry, like a hand-knit sock company, these [the interviewers] are all housewives working in their spare time and paid by the piece. They don't make much, but they like to get out of the house. Those who answer the questions don't get paid at all; I often wonder why they do it.'[10] Although Marian senses the unreality and manipulative nature of her work (ironically, she has become an instrument of consumer capitalism), her employment options after university graduation were so limited as to preclude any less exploitative work. In any case, the prevailing system of university education itself has become part of the larger throw-away nexus: 'Production-consumption. You begin to wonder whether it isn't just a question of making one kind of garbage into another kind. The human mind was the last thing to be commercialized but they're doing a good job of it now; what *is* the difference between the library stacks and one of those used-car graveyards?'

As the novel proceeds, Marian's growing revulsion against the 'production-consumption' syndrome is reinforced by her recognition that the image of woman created by the ad men is no less synthetic than the thousands of non-products marketed to enhance her 'femininity.' The women who identify with the plastic humanoids in the ads are themselves in danger of becoming those depersonalized objects – the 'purchasers' are ultimately transformed into the 'package' which is promoted to maintain consumerism. Women who defer to such warped male standards of what is 'feminine' and desirable, standards which exist only to support the whole consumer ethic, become frightening parodies of real persons. And their inferior status as commercialized dolls provides a strong pretext for their future domination.

Yielding on one occasion to the pressure of male opinion (in the person of her fiancé, Peter, who is a conservative law student), Marian allows herself to be metamorphosed into a self-mocking caricature of herself. Encased in a 'short, red, and sequined' dress, adorned with 'nailpolish and makeup and elaborate arrangements of hair,' she becomes detached from the soul-less doll's body she inhabits, unable to 'grasp the total effect.' The process of alienation which has taken effect here, one which is certainly not unfamiliar to women

who grew up during the 50s, is a serious mind/body schism in which the 'real'
woman can no longer relate to her own physical being.

So pervasive is the influence of the ad world that the entire range of Marian's
experience begins to conform to its terms of reference. Even her boyfriend is
'nicely packaged,' 'ordinariness raised to perfection, like the youngish well-
groomed faces of cigarette ads.' Peter is quickly becoming a good middle-class
member of the martini set. Unable to respond to Marian as anything but an
embellishment to his own self-image, he treats her 'as a stage-prop; silent but
solid, a two-dimensional outline.' His ideal of marriage is not unlike the form
of marriage among the upper classes criticized almost one hundred years earlier
by Engels, a marriage of convenience in the process of becoming 'crassest
prostitution.' The explanation of Peter's initially powerful domination over
Marian lies in the fact that he represents a strong social norm which is but-
tressed by the group. Thus her decision to marry him gives her a temporary
feeling of stability and normality, if only because her sexist conditioning has
led her to regard marriage as the inevitable, perhaps exclusive, outcome of a
young woman's training. Within the crippling bounds of these social mores, an
unmarried woman is regarded as (at best) a misfit and (at worst) a pervert.

Marian's eventual ability to reject the sexist role imposed on her is developed through her awareness of her identity with the various things *consumed*:
she is being eaten! She mentally strips from an activity as habitual and basic
as meat-consumption its veneer of 'civilized' refinement. Like the once real
cow that now lies encased in pre-packaged cellophane, she sees herself as the
hunted-down victim of another male predator, her fiancé: 'That dark intent
marksman with his aiming eye had been there all the time, hidden by the
other layers, waiting for her at the dead centre.'

Marian's predicament is not neatly resolved; unlike those of Emily Montague
and Antoinette de Mirecourt her dilemma is real and multifaceted, and cannot
be effaced in a contrived, happy marriage. Her anxiety, which manifests itself
in a variety of ostensibly irrational actions, stems from the very act of self-
liberation she is undertaking. In freeing herself from all imposed, fixed definitions of woman's role she places herself in a state of *becoming* – and without
clear guidelines the process is frightening. Having rejected the particular conventions which hemmed her in as tightly as her party girdle, she finds the alternative female 'masks' equally inappropriate and oppressive.

There is her roommate Ainsley who, having decided that maternity 'fulfills
your deepest femininity,' embarks as a 'scheming superfemale' on a quest for
a suitable stud with good genes. There is a married friend Clara who is mother-
earth, pregnant for the third time. And at the office Christmas party, Marian
develops a near-misogynist revulsion against her fellow workers when she is
almost suffocated by 'this thick sargasso-sea of femininity.'

This false notion of femininity which is dominating her own identity Marian symbolically rejects at the end of the novel. With sponge cake, coloured icings and 'globular silver decorations' she creates an edible synthetic woman which she ritualistically offers up to her fiancé: 'You've been trying to destroy me, haven't you,' she said. 'You've been trying to assimilate me. But I've made you a substitute, something you'll like much better. This is what you really wanted all along isn't it? I'll get you a fork.' So dies one unnatural definition of woman.

Atwood's analysis of woman's predicament has been executed on several levels: each of the different female roles is examined – woman as underpaid worker divorced from production; as lover/mistress alienated from her emotions; and as mother/wife whose capacity for maternity subverts everything that falls outside of her reproductive function – and each of these roles is systematically rejected. The novelist's real achievement is to have examined the inter-relationships between the various forms which male domination assumes in a woman's life, and then to have related these forms to the larger domination structure of consumer capitalism. Thus the woman proceeds from a consciousness of her personal dilemma to an awareness of it as a socio-political problem.

The tentative, deliberately undogmatic note on which this novel concludes is a realistic one. By refusing to conform to the zeal for role-definition and stereotyping which characterized earlier periods, it takes an important first step towards depriving concepts like 'domination' of their referential grounding in contemporary woman's experience.

If we have learned anything from the past, it is that the status of women can not be studied apart from political systems. It is significant that Rosanna Leprohon's clarion call for nationalism is echoed a century later by Margaret Atwood. Both women recognize the relevance of domination within the economy to women's status in society.[11] This is not to claim that any one political system in itself provides a guarantee of egalitarian treatment or an instant blueprint for more humane modes of relation between men and women.[12] It does indicate that the political focus of the struggle against male domination must now be enlarged to include attacks on specifically sexist abuses *within* an overall struggle against domination, in whatever guise it manifests itself.

We are faced not simply with a question of enlarging woman's role within the socioeconomic system as it now functions, but of so modifying her role that the system itself is concurrently modified beyond our present recognition of it.

NOTES

1 George Eliot, *The Mill on the Floss* (London 1951), 374

2 See Sandra Gwyn, 'Women,' *Read Canadian*, ed. Robert Fulford, David Godfrey, and Abraham Rotstein (Toronto 1972), 144. However, three recent publications that contribute to our knowledge of this subject should be noted: *Women at Work: Ontario 1850-1930*, ed. Janice Acton, Penny Goldsmith, and Bonnie Shepard (Toronto 1975); *Never Done: Three Centuries of Women's Work in Canada*, the Corrective Collective (Toronto 1974); and Catherine L. Cleverdon, *The Woman Suffrage Movement in Canada* (Toronto, 2nd. ed. 1974).

3 *Plato's Symposium*, trans. Benjamin Jowett (2nd ed. rev., Indianapolis and New York 1956), 32-3

4 (London 1967), 147

5 *Saturday Review* (2 March 1968), 14

6 Frances Brooke, *The History of Emily Montague*, New Canadian Library edition (Toronto 1961), 86

7 New Canadian Library edition (Toronto 1973), 17

8 Such realities are documented in Anna Brownell Jameson, *Winter Studies and Summer Rambles in Canada* [1838], New Canadian Library abridged edition (Toronto 1965); Susanna Moodie, *Roughing It in the Bush* [1852], New Canadian Library edition (Toronto 1970); Catharine Parr Traill, *The Backwoods of Canada* [1836], New Canadian Library selected edition (Toronto 1971), and *The Canadian Settler's Guide* [1855], New Canadian Library edition (Toronto 1969). See also Eve Zaremba (ed.), *Privilege of Sex* (Toronto 1974); and Anna Leveridge, *Your Loving Anna: Letters from the Ontario Frontier*, ed. Louis Tivy (Toronto 1974).

9 At a later stage in Atwood's intellectual development, her critique of capitalism extends to a broader criticism of the economic umbrella under which Canadian capitalism is subsumed – American imperialism.

10 Margaret Atwood, *The Edible Woman*, New Canadian Library edition (Toronto 1973), 19-20

11 For a good Marxist analysis of the relation between class struggle and the struggle of women as the most oppressed people, see Juliet Mitchell, *Woman's Estate* (Harmondsworth 1973).

12 See Kate Millett, 'Reactionary Policy: The Models of Nazi Germany and the Soviet Union,' *Sexual Politics* (New York 1970).

R.T. Naylor

Dominion of capital: Canada and international investment

Over the past decade the world economy has witnessed a multilateral movement of capital on a scale unprecedented since the great era of international
investment prior to the First World War. Britain was then the chief metropolis
from which finance capital spread to the far reaches of an ever-expanding empire, formal and informal, while lesser powers struggled in emulation. Since
the Second World War, American international economic power based on the
global operations of the multinational corporation has dominated the Western
economy, although over the past ten years other, less potent, industrial states
have striven with increasing success to challenge American hegemony by their
own corporate expansion. In both eras the international flow of capital has
been the instrument of economic and political domination par excellence. And
in both periods Canada has been the leading example of a 'borrowing' country, a recipient on the greatest scale of the flows of economic power crossing
national borders in the form of international investment. The contours of
Canadian economic evolution under the aegis of capital invested from abroad
provide an illuminating view of the structure of dependence inherent in the
international capitalist order, past and present. They show well the patterns of
dynamic development and underdevelopment experienced by a hinterland
economy, given that a substantial degree of critically important economic
decision-making originates from outside its borders.

Economic domination by itself clearly does not preclude economic development in the sense of the growth of national income, population, and even per-
capita income. It need not even exclude the possibility of innovation and
changes in technology and industrial structure. But what domination does imply is that the direction of economic development – that is, which sectors of
the economy flourish and which stagnate – is dictated by the needs of the
metropolitan economy. Economic domination minimizes autonomous growth
and change. Furthermore, it necessarily implies a net outflow of surplus from
the hinterland to the metropolitan economy either through repatriated earnings from investment or through adverse terms of trade – a surplus which
otherwise could have been captured by the economy to generate local capital
formation.

The crux of the problem of domination inheres in the relation between
metropolitan capital and local capital in the hinterland. Acrimonious debate
has turned upon the question as to which of two antagonistic positions best
describes the hinterland-metropolitan capitalist linkage. Does domination
from abroad by virtue of the greater economic power of the metropolis admit
of or lead to the creation of a national capitalist class whose long-term interests are inherently at variance with those of the metropole? Does it on the
contrary produce only a local capitalist class that is either totally subordinate
to or completely integrated with that of the metropole, whose raison d'être is

at one with that of the metropole, and who can never be expected to challenge its relative position? In brief, does capital have an address and a nationality, or is it truer to say that it has no country, that any complication produced by the coexistence of big and small is simply a sideshow in its universal game of despoiling the globe's resources? The Canadian experience sheds a great deal of light on these questions. But to understand the Canadian experience, one must first make explicit reference to the metropolitan economies out of whose process of economic expansion the Canadian economy and society sprang into being.

THE EXPANSION OF THE METROPOLES

The evolution of the contemporary international capitalist order proceeded in discernible stages from its birth in sixteenth-century Europe, where the old feudal order had decayed, the population was growing again after the ravages of wars and plagues, and the pace of commerce had accelerated. Prices rose with the economic expansion of the late fifteenth and early sixteenth centuries, and the resulting quest for gold and silver assumed an awesomely destructive dimension as entire civilizations were sacrificed in the scramble. Gold and silver took on a new significance in this era because the expansion of trade and rising prices necessitated a greater quantity of circulating medium. The rise of the nation-state in the wake of economic resurgence led to the assertion of national political power and to demands for currency unification and national capital markets for government finance, as well as to the breakup of the old cosmopolitan medieval credit system on the shoals of antagonistic sovereignties. The spread of commerce beyond the old European trading system to new and distant peripheries demanded a greater supply of cash, and the growth of multilateral trade also made cash payments necessary. Finally the change in the foundation of social power from the ownership of land, whose more or less fixed rent yields at a time of rising prices threatened and often destroyed feudal nobles, to new, more portable forms of wealth was predicated on an expanded supply of bullion.

The first stage of European capitalist expansion was that of overt theft, of the plunder and enslavement of Amerindians for work in the mines. It was the great era of publicly sponsored piracy as other nations who lacked Iberia's direct access to New World gold and silver sought their share of the spoils in other ways. The cod fisheries and the exchange of fish for Spanish gold became an early source of imperialist rivalries in the North Atlantic. Actual European settlement, apart from that strictly required for looting or supervising the mining of gold or the drying of fish on a seasonal basis, was minimal in the early years.

In stage two, piracy or overt theft gradually evolved into trade or covert theft. For example, Queen Elizabeth's share of the booty brought back by Sir Francis Drake in the Golden Hind sufficed not only to pay off her entire foreign debt but left enough to establish the Levant Company with a monopoly of the Mediterranean trade. The profits of the Levant Company in turn spawned the East India Company. The age of the great chartered companies, state sanctioned monopolies charged with military and governmental powers as well as economic privilege, had begun. And although these companies were the instrument of mercantile expansion of all Western powers, the English in particular perfected their use. These conglomerations of capital, the first historical instances of economic organizations with bona fide modern corporate characteristics, signaled a change in European attitudes to the colonies. Companies with commitments to colonize and governmental powers replaced the casual gift of New World territory as fiefdoms to court favourites. Agricultural settlement and the more intensive exploitation of the colonies for their staple products proceeded, and the demand for manpower increased. Chartered companies, such as England's Royal African Company, flourished when slaves replaced gold as the most lucrative traffic of the Atlantic adventures. In the British West Indies early tobacco farms based on small holdings and indentured labour were eclipsed by the rise of the sugar plantation based on Black slavery. In the Spanish islands where sugar was a lucrative crop, the Indian population was nearly extinct within fifty years of the Spanish arrival and was replaced by Black slaves. Black slaves also spread across the mainland of the Americas, south, central and north, wherever the plantation mode of staple production became feasible. New products, foodstuffs, and basic raw materials for mass consumption or industrial use now flowed in trade from the colonies to the metropolis – in contrast to the spices, jewels, and specie for luxury consumption that had been the backbone of pre-capitalist trade between Europe and the East.

Stage three saw the Industrial Revolution begin in late eighteenth-century Britain and spread throughout western Europe. Until the 1870s British industrial hegemony, based first on cotton and later on iron and steel, saw few serious challenges. It was a period when the character of British investments abroad underwent substantial change. Until the end of the Napoleonic wars, British capital flowed abroad chiefly in the form of mercantile credit in conjunction with international commodity flows, or the operating of chartered companies, or in the form of British government loans and subsidies to allied states for military and related purposes. Thereafter the earnings of British shipping, insurance, and other services abroad more than offset a fairly steady balance of trade deficit and provided the funds for a sizeable expansion in the flow of private long-term capital abroad. Capital flowed through the 'mer-

chant banks' like the Baring Brothers or Glyn, Mills and Company to government finance, canal, railway, and other infrastructural investment guaranteed
by or closely linked to government, and only to a much lesser degree industrial or mining funds, which remained overwhelmingly the product of private
subscription, rather than the work of the British capital market. Capital, of
course, continued to move abroad on a private basis to the British planters and
entrepreneurs who controlled and directed staple extraction abroad. But the
great mercantile monopolies, apart from the Hudson's Bay Company which
still had a lease on life, were defunct institutions in terms of aiding and abetting
British overseas expansion.

Stage four began with a crash – that of 1873 and the ensuing Great Depression. The era of a free flow of commodities typical of the age of the Industrial
Revolution ended in a wave of tariff building by the industrializing nations
in an attempt to prevent the worldwide deflation from undermining their
industrial hopes. Britain, with its enormous stake in international commodity
flows, was the major abstainer.

As the free flow of finished commodities was increasingly inhibited by
tariff and other barriers to trade, the international economy underwent some
major structural changes. Countries began to seek their own spheres of market
influence for the export of finished goods and their own assured supplies of
raw materials. At the same time international capital flows in the form of
financial capital accelerated as did the international migration of labour to
populate the white settler states of the peripheral areas.

Britain was the world leader in these transformations. By as early as 1893
some 15 per cent of her natural wealth was invested abroad. And her domestic
savings available for foreign investments were supplemented from abroad by
the workings of the key currency system built around the pound. Since the
tenure of Sir Isaac Newton as Master of the Mint, the gold standards he had
created ensured that the world of commerce and finance would revolve about
the City of London. Instead of sterile gold, countries began holding their foreign exchange reserves in the form of short-term, interest-yielding balances in
London, which could be channelled off by British financial institutions along
with Britain's own savings into long-term investments overseas.

The need for markets, the search for raw materials, the defence of invested
capital, all dictated a scramble for colonies not only by Britain but, especially
after 1896 when world prices began to rise again, by other Western powers.
Between the partial economic recovery of 1878 and the end of the war for the
seizure of the Boer republic's gold resources, Britain alone added 5 million
square miles and 88 million people to an already vast empire. Especially desirable were the white settlers' states whose output of cheap raw materials led to
a secular improvement in the British terms of trade and, of course, a deterior-

ation in their own. Australia provided wheat and wool, New Zealand dairy and meat products, South Africa gold, diamonds, and a wide range of agricultural produce. Grains and livestock from the Argentine and Canada supplemented the traditional staples of the old Empire. These white settlers' states functioned not only as raw material hinterlands but also as important markets for British industrial products.

But major transformations in the world order were already taking shape, changes of such a radical nature that the old metropolis would be swept aside in a maelstrom of wars and depressions. The world expansion after 1896 saw the birth of the age of electricity, the internal combustion engine, and a vast increase in the chemical industries. The centre of industrial activity shifted irrevocably from the old metropolis to the new. From 1914 to 1939 came twenty-five years of cataclysmic change, the death of the British empire, and the end of the world hegemony of finance capital.

Finance-capital represented the portfolio investments of financial institutions or rich individuals. Such capital moved easily into government finance in the colonies, into mortgages, into railroad finance, into public utility finance, and sometimes – but much less so – into mining. British loans went abroad seeking an assured rate of return in investment outlets with safe collateral, with the implicit or explicit guarantee of governments, or into utility and similar investments that generally had an assured monopoly to guarantee a return. British direct investments abroad were much rarer, and industrial investments were particularly scarce. The new age of automobiles, electricity, and chemicals was outside the purview of the British investors. It was quite otherwise for the new behemoth.

Stage five had its origins well back into the nineteenth-century development patterns of the United States, and in particular of the American firm. American industrial growth began effectively in the great era of individual enterprise following the War of 1812, when the old colonial commercial oligarchy was displaced from the seat of economic power by the nascent industrial and agribusiness class. With the expansion of the 1850s and the Civil War, the railroads spanned the continent, creating a national market and with it a national firm reaching to integrate horizontally across the country. As the Civil War expansion gave way to the depression of the 1870s and 1880s, the new corporate giants began in earnest the process of integrating vertically to control their raw material resources. And as the world economic revival of the 1890s dawned, the American firm began its international expansion in the form of the multidivisional corporation, integrated vertically and horizontally over a multitude of product lines and challenging the old European powers in their traditional export markets abroad. The years before the First World War saw the modest beginnings of the instrument of metropolitan expansion that would in a few decades come to dominate the world stage, the multinational corporation. Initially, the movement abroad by direct investment of these American firms was small and was restricted primarily to Mexico and Canada, a natural spillover of the internal growth of the American firms. Prior to the war the US remained a net debtor to Britain, and the number and scale of the US industrial firms ready to make the quantum leap to modern multinational status was limited. The world remained essentially a preserve of European, especially British, finance capital until the war and the economic chaos of the postwar recession weakened the British system, and the ensuing depression fractured it completely.

The post-Second-World-War era began with American industrial hegemony over the Western world unchallenged. Marshall Plan 'aid' dollars replaced the pound sterling as the medium of international exchange. Beginning with the search for new raw material sources the American multinational firms recommenced their global spread. Initially Canada was the forefront of the new class of borrowing country, but by the mid 1950s European reconstruction made the European market especially desirable. American investment, while continuing to flow into Canadian resources and manufacturing, in relative terms shifted increasingly to European final product markets. By 1963 the shift in emphasis became pronounced, but at the same time the symptoms of the incipient decline of the American system were evident.

European economic recovery especially after the mid-1950s was rapid and broad based. Economic resurgence behind common market tariff walls was accompanied by a government-assisted cartelization movement. Together with the even more phenomenal economic rebirth of Japan these developments spawned a system of competing corporate empires on a world scale as direct investment flowed from Europe and Japan into various resource hinterlands and even into the United States itself. For the US the sixties were increasingly bleak. Balance of payments problems resulting from the growth of competition abroad and the increase in military expenses to maintain global hegemony precipitated a series of currency crises. Each successive crisis was followed by an increasingly severe effort to impose the costs of empire on the captive satellite economies by stepping up the rate of repatriation of earnings and other devices to maintain or increase the American hold on foreign industrial structures while reducing the outflow of capital necessitated by such a hold. Finally in 1972 came virtual economic abdication as the US ceased to try to maintain the exchange value of the dollar. This abdication, coupled with a vast expansion of petrodollars in 1974, helped to shift the centre of the world monetary system increasingly towards Europe, while at the same time it became no longer amenable to control by any one power.

In very broad outline these are the major structural transformations of the world capitalist order of late. A much debated question has been Canada's position in these contemporary structures – whether it is best regarded as a small economy of the developed metropolitan type or a remarkably large and wealthy one of the colonial variant. Is it an industrial economy whose exports happen to be almost entirely primary products, or is it a staple-extracting hinterland that just happened to achieve large-scale industrialization? Its national income, industrial structure, and the foreign investments its own capitalists have undertaken on their own account point in the first direction, while the importance of the export of staples in generating national income, the derivative and dependent nature of its industrial structure, the overwhelming volume of foreign, especially American, investment in that industrial structure, and its assiduous cultivation of bilateral agreements with the US point in the second. The nature of the present structure can perhaps best be understood with reference to those of the past.

THE DEVELOPMENT OF THE HINTERLAND

New France and Newfoundland

Dependence on an external metropole is and has been a fundamental fact of Canadian economic and social life from the earliest days of white conquest and settlement. An accidental and largely unwelcome offshoot of the sixteenth-century scramble for New World gold, Canada grew very slowly in the seventeenth and eighteenth centuries as a fishing base and elaborate fur-trading post. These early staples of fish and fur fitted well into the logic of European overseas expansion in its primary phase. The fisheries, cultivated by the English in particular to provide a trade to drain Spanish bullion, for a considerable time contributed nothing to the development of the hinterland areas, Newfoundland in particular, apart from providing a pretext for the extermination of the island's indigenous population. What little settlement emerged in Newfoundland in the early centuries of the fishery was a casual and energetically discouraged byproduct of the fisheries. Genuine development, as opposed to the simple and seasonal looting of the immediate resource base, was absent. And of course the motivation behind the fisheries was inseparable from that of Iberian expansion in phase one, the quest for precious metals. Not until after the mid-seventeenth century, with the steadily growing displacement of the annual English fleet by a rising resident fishery, did the industry spawn stable settlement, and even then for another 150 years indigenous growth was harried and hampered by the efforts of the English fishing interests to maintain control. Moreover the growth of a resident fishery implied settlement on the periphery of the island and little more. Capital requirements were still furnished by British merchants who extended credit in advance of the catch, and the island's resident fishing industry remained inextricably tied to the metropolitan capitalists by the chain of debt that the system engendered.

This chain of debt-bondage was the first instance in Canadian history of what became the normal pattern. The staple-producer relies on markets in the metropole to pursue the process of staple extraction. Commercial credit extended in the fisheries was the original form of that investment. Because the producer was indebted to the merchant, and thus the hinterland economy to the metropole, production patterns remained set. More production of the staple was required to settle the debt, and current receipts almost never sufficed to settle past debts. The debt grew, and so did the need for yet more staple production to try to pay it off.

The French fur trade, especially in its early years, also fits into the phase one pattern. A luxury-commodity trade which discouraged large-scale settlement and any genuine self-sustaining development, it did however induce some more concrete results than the early fisheries. The early fur trade was the preserve of French mercantile monopoly corporations, charged with governmental and colonizing as well as trading functions and sponsored purely by private capital. While a class of indigenous fur merchants did slowly emerge and at one point played a substantial role in the prosecution of the trade, the control of distribution of furs and the importation of merchandise and credit by the metropolitan monopoly largely nullified any significance such a development could have on local progress. And with the destruction of the Huron Indian trading and agricultural system by the English allies, the Iroquois, the character of the fur trade was changed and metropolitan domination reinforced.

The new wave of French expansion into the Americas after the 1660s saw a much more active role of the state both in the direct establishment of bona fide governmental institutions to replace those exercized formerly by privately owned corporations, and in the state subsidization of commerce, industry, and government abroad. As the French fur trade was forced to reach ever deeper into the continent, great fixed-capital outlays in the form of military posts and garrisons were required to protect commercial routes and suppress competition. A new agricultural settlement policy to replace the Huron supply system followed. Some short-lived industrialization efforts which might have helped the development of a local bourgeoisie were also made; but these waned quickly in the face of metropolitan disapproval, and the colony relapsed to the status of fur-trapping hinterland, albeit with a considerably augmented population.

The France–New France colonial relation brought capital imports to the hinterland that were of greater relative importance than at any subsequent point in Canadian history. And the link between capital flow and the commerce in furs was nearly absolute both in the private and the public sectors.

Commercial credit extended by La Rochelle, Bordeaux, and other merchant companies involved an unbreakable chain of debt and dependence. The merchant houses of the metropole established branch houses or local commission merchants in the colony to negotiate the movement of furs to France. The same companies in turn were intermediaries for the return flow of manufactured goods to the colony at fixed terms of trade. The high profits, if somewhat erratic, of the fur trade helped discourage capital from entering other pursuits. Furthermore, half of the profits went back to the metropole directly as the share of the French partners; while of the profits that accrued to local agents, those not reinvested in the trade were spent in France on commodities to be imported to the colony. The very success of the fur trade and the resultant tie-up of capital therein ensured that such commodities would never be produced in New France itself. The chain of short-term debt guaranteed, just as in the fisheries, the simple reproduction of past production patterns.

The resulting balance-of-trade deficit of New France, the direct consequence of the inflow of commercial credit and the reinforcement of the fur-extracting bias of the economy, had to be covered on capital account in three ways. The least significant was the private investments in the colonial resources and industries, other than commercial credit in the fur trade, undertaken by French capitalists. Apart from a couple of timber establishments and the early ventures of French entrepreneurs in the 1660s (industrialization efforts which were subsidized by the government), these private investments were negligible. Second were the fairly sizeable imports of capital by clerical establishments. Much of the clerical expenditures were linked directly to the fur trade – while the clergy may not actually have traded in furs with the Indians as some accused them of doing, they certainly recognized the critical link between the fur traffic and their Christianizing mission and, apart from disputes over the debauchment of Indians with brandy, actively encouraged the trade. Furthermore, the clerical establishments exported considerable sums from their colonial revenues for investment in France, which would at least partly offset the favourable capital-account effects of their import of funds. And, finally, a substantial amount, as much as one-third, of clerical expenditure on public goods in the form of hospitals and educational establishments came from government subsidies.

The inflow of capital in government account was by far the most important offset to the trade deficit. Much of this capital was also inextricably linked to the fur trade. Military expenditures, the largest item, were prompted directly by the extension of the trade into the interior. Much of the funds for civil administration were so directed as well, as the colony for all of its history was ruled by speculators who robbed the public purse with impunity to divert funds into their fur-trade interests or related commercial pursuits. The colony thus became a haven for either the upstart bourgeois or the bankrupt aristocrat to make or repair his fortunes in the commerce in pelts.

Part of the state subsidies, it is true, found their way into industrial development. But the only large-scale industrial ventures of the French period were the forest and ship-building industries and iron-mining and smelting. None of these ventures had bona fide roots in the colony to permit any spurt of development. In both cases the industries relied on American technique, French government subsidies, and a military market supported by the French Crown, which market was in turn linked to the fur trade. Relying upon external capital and American technique, derivative from and dependent on the staple trade, these industries in a real sense were the prototype for future Canadian industrial history.

In New France even the circulating medium depended on the fur trade. The specie sent in on government account in the early years flowed out again, often on the same ship. To counteract the adverse effects of the balance-of-trade deficit draining circulating medium out, the colony used fiat issues of currency of various sorts by the military authorities or the civil administrators, or both, with no coordination between them. To further complicate the monetary situation, merchants' bills of exchange and fur-trade company certificates with a value fixed in terms of fur were also circulated. All of the currencies were derivative from the fur trade, directly in the case of fur certificates, and indirectly in the case of military 'ordonnances' to finance the building of infrastructure in the interior to protect trade routes, merchants' bills issued by the wholesale houses who dominated the import of merchandise and export of furs, and the issue of civil authorities to cover the deficit left by the shortage of French appropriation for the colony or the yield of its tax on fur exports. The government issues were theoretically restricted to the amount of the annual subsidy from the French Ministry of Marine, and were required to be redeemed annually in bills of exchange in France, which bills in turn were redeemable in specie in France. In fact escalating expenditures in the colony, coupled with a reduction in appropriations for the colony in France when financial difficulties caused by war beset the metropolitan government, threw the colonial finances into chaos. A steadily growing supply of irredeemable paper fed the wartime inflationary process in the dying days of New France. The result was a unique state of international indebtedness for Canada. For the only period of its history an enormous paper debt was owed to the colony from the metropolis. The subsequent repudiation of this debt added to the already enormous economic problems of the wartime economy. Commercial dislocation and conquest by the British destroyed the already weak Canadian commercial class and led directly to the hegemony of a group of newly arrived British merchants.

There was little or nothing inherent in the structure of the colonial relation between France and New France to permit sustained local capital formation and the development of a vigorous local capitalist class. Domination by
metropolitan merchants inhibited accumulation, and the profits of the fur
trade kept the attention of local merchants restricted to short-term investments within that trade. While France after the mid-seventeenth century undertook a program of colonial expansion based on the search for industrial and
other raw materials and the creation of a system of sugar plantations, Canada
remained confined to the pattern of development typical of the earliest phase
of European expansion – looting the surface for luxury commodities with
little or no intensive, even if dependent, local development.

British North America, 1763-1867

Phase two of European expansion, albeit with many retrograde elements deriving from an early dependence on furs, was ushered into Canadian development
by the British Conquest. With the active collaboration of the British military
authorities, Anglo-American and British commercial capital quickly supplanted
French and Canadian capital in the still dominant fur trade. French and Canadian capital had been weakened by the ravages of inflation and plundering by
officials during the war, by the flight of French capital after the war, and by
the obviously superior commercial and financial connections the British merchants had with the new metropolis.

Initially little seemed to have changed, apart from the different nationality
of the commercial élite. Capital entered the colony in the form of commercial
credit accompanying commodity flows – furs out and general manufactured
merchandise in. Substantial amounts of British government funds moved in
on military account and to subsidize the establishment of Loyalist settlers
after the American Revolution. Industry was almost totally lacking, capital
accumulation on any significant scale was restricted to the fur trade, and specie
coming into the colony flowed out almost immediately to cover the balance-
of-trade deficit.

However the effects of the shift of metropole from France to the more dynamic industrial metropolis of Britain were not long in manifesting themselves.
While the American Revolution led to a northward migration of the fur-trading
capital formerly strong in New York, a migration that would have tended to
confirm the colony's traditional role, other forces were at work to transform
its role. As Britain industrialized, its demand for imported foodstuffs rose.
Rising world grain prices led to an expansion of Canada's wheat exports. During the declining years of French rule a sporadic export trade in grain had
begun; with the dawn of the British era wheat-growing for external markets

became generalized throughout Quebec, and Ontario (Upper Canada) witnessed the opening of its agrarian frontier for grain cultivation. As well, after the American Revolution the locus of the British West Indies trade moved north to Nova Scotia. Halifax especially grew as an imperial entrepôt and British export-import firms set up branches there. New Brunswick became the new centre of the imperial mast trade, with other types of timber exports showing a rising importance. In fact, near famines often resulted in the province as the existing manpower began servicing the British demand for colonial timber. British timber-dealing houses moved directly into the province, providing capital and direction for the exploitation of the forests. The fishing industry underwent a great expansion, responding to both the eclipse of the French fisheries and the blocking of American competition.

For several decades the inflow of external capital retained essentially the same pattern as during the French régime. Commercial companies in the import-export trade accounted for a sizeable sum in the form of commercial credit to finance the inflow of manufactures and outflow of staples. Rather than establishing branches, metropolitan houses generally extended such credit to Canadian factors or agents, but branch houses were certainly not unknown. On government account came funds for public works, subsidies for administration of the colony, and military subventions. After the initial Loyalist influx, subsidies to immigrants by government ceased and were partly replaced by capital carried in by Loyalists themselves. While the bulk of the inflow of settlers from the US was made up of impoverished families attracted by free land, some of the Loyalists carried considerable wealth with them.

In Nova Scotia the flow of funds on military account was the foundation of early development. War meant prosperity, a prosperity which terminated in crisis whenever peace broke out. During times of peace the cream of Halifax's mercantile community would gather in a local coffee house and denounce the government, calling for 'loud war by land and sea.' In addition to military account, piracy ensured a steady influx of specie, again inextricably linked to a state of war. Nova Scotia was also remarkable for providing the first instance in British North America of government debt privately held abroad. The colonial government had begun to issue 'bounty certificates,' promises to pay subsidies to certain people who undertook specified agricultural or other improvements. These certificates were usually obtained by fraud, voted by the Halifax merchants who controlled the Assembly to individuals who owed them money, and then re-acquired by these same Halifax merchants at heavy discounts. Eventually yielding par value, most found their way into the hands of the leading merchant-financier of Halifax who retired to England to direct colonial affairs from there, still retaining in his hands the bulk of the province's public debt.

In New Brunswick, which received apart from government a much smaller military account, the inflow of British money largely took the form of commercial credit for the timber trade that grew during the Napoleonic wars. Prince Edward Island was completely in the hands of a few absentee proprietors whose quit rents were supposed to have formed the basis of government finance. In fact little flowed in for this purpose and no money for improvements came in until 1825.

After the War of 1812, the patterns of Canadian development shifted. Prior to the war, British North America's existence independent of the US was always tenuous; after the war there was little doubt as to where its short-term and indeed medium-term future lay. The border with the US was sealed and the colonies' dependence on Britain confirmed. At the same time the nature of the British metropolis underwent a radical change. The old mercantile-colony system quickly dissolved in the face of a rising tide of industrial expansion which burst asunder the commercial restrictions of the old empire to search for worldwide hegemony. New raw materials came in demand: cheap food to nourish the quickly growing industrial proletariat and timber as a construction material, ship-building material, and industrial fuel. British capital flowing abroad belonged not only to governments or commercial houses; private long-term capital exports became an established and steadily growing phenomenon. The human waste created by the factory system and by the deliberate destruction of Irish and Scottish peasant farms to create capitalist agriculture to feed the metropolis flowed to the overseas colonies along with capital. Some of the early emigrants carried their not inconsiderable personal wealth, but most of the well-to-do moved on to the US. At the same time three British controlled and financed land companies developed, and these did funnel some funds into the province for improvements. But the companies' expenditures were small, and their existence in two cases was very brief.

For British North America the new international order implied two contradictory tendencies. On one hand, British demand for colonial staples, wheat and wood in particular, continued to escalate, carrying with it a precarious prosperity in some of the resource-rich areas and a reinforcement of dependence on the metropolitan market. On the other hand, their protected position within the empire was sacrificed by Britain's rush to multilateralism in trade and by the rapid development of other resource hinterlands within the British nexus.

To develop the new export staples, major works of commercial infrastructure were required in Canada for the first time. British long-term capital in the form of purchases of public debt, effected through the intermediary of British private banks, came to the province of Canada to finance such works, especially canals in the era before 1840.

The year 1835 was a watershed in the history of external investment in Canada. That year the government of Upper Canada converted its debt from one denominated in currency to one denominated in sterling with the express purpose of conducting its future borrowings in Britain, on the premise that such a move would free Canadian funds from long-term investments and make them available for other undertakings, notably commercial investments. Along with the British funds came American investment on a significant scale for the first time in Canadian history. Major works of infrastructure like the Welland Canal, other navigation companies, and even a couple of short-lived banks, were the outgrowth of American direct investments, while some American money even entered the field of commerce with the establishment of import-export firms in Montreal. These ventures however were minor in comparison to the growth of other commercial establishments.

While British commercial houses were still active and prominent, as the process of commercial capital accumulation proceeded in Canada, the British houses' commission merchants and agents gradually ceded place to Canadian wholesale houses who dealt with British firms on a more equitable footing. With the evolution of a Canadian capitalist structure geared to the provision of short-term commercial credit came the development of an indigenous banking system. These banks would stand behind local merchants, from whose capital they generally grew, discounting their bills and issuing notes, thus rectifying the old problem of specie shortage resulting from persistent trade-balance deficits. For the first time a paper currency existed backed by the general worth of Canadian wholesale merchants rather than by periodic subventions from imperial treasuries. The development of banking and the growth of Canadian commercial capitalism were inseparable, and both were ultimately linked to the imperial trade system. The banks' chief role was the short-term financing of the movement of staples to Britain and the flow of manufactures back to Canada. They played virtually no role in financing agricultural development or in public or industrial finance.

By the late 1830s and early 1840s the contradictions inherent in the diverging tendencies of the period – the growing dependence on the British industrial system for marketing colonial staples on the one hand, and the abolition of formal imperial ties on the other – became absolute. The British financial stake in the colony, especially in light of the fact that the British government had financed directly most of the construction of the canal system, was very large and very precarious. The rebellion of 1837 led to near bankruptcy of the province of Upper Canada and an inability to float further loans in Britain, while the essential waterways system was still incomplete. The financial condition of the province caused near panic among the private banks in Britain who had marketed the province's public debt and caused a lot of anxiety in British government circles. The solution was quite simple – by joining the bankrupt upper province to the solvent lower one, and spreading the burden of debt repayment over both, Canadian credit could be restored. And the new united province of Canada had no trouble raising the necessary funds to complete the canal system: it was a precedent noted well for the future.

The end of the old system of colonial preferences precipitated economic collapse for the Montreal commercial community, and their reaction to the crisis is worth noting, for it set the pattern for much to follow. In the course of three days in 1849 over 1000 people, the cream of the Montreal commercial and financial community, signed a manifesto calling for annexation to the United States. The rationale behind such a policy was stated clearly in the manifesto: 'The proposed union would render Canada a field for American capital into which it would enter as freely for the prosecution of public works and private enterprise as into any of the present states.' The manifesto called explicitly for Canadian development to be predicated on the spillover of the industrialization process then in train in the northeastern United States. It stressed the necessity of the US market for engendering investment to effect a recovery, which American investment would then alleviate the high rate of unemployment. American capital would flow in for railway building as well. Political stability would be enhanced by the effects of the union, and hence provide a more suitable climate for the investment of foreign and domestic capital. The return of prosperity would inflate the value of the land in which much of Canada's elite measured their 'wealth,' and it would help induce more migration and stem the outflow of population. While annexation never occurred, most of the desired results came about in one form or another.

As the old colonial system disintegrated, the North American colonies were forced to assume certain governmental functions themselves. Fiscal independence and the ability to regulate financial institutions, until then inhering in the Colonial Secretariat in London, were soon ceded to the colonies. Fiscal 'responsibility' meant simply that the colonial government became responsible for its own debts. It is thus scarcely surprising that 'responsible' government was foisted on the colonies by Britain over the vehement objections of the leading colonial businessmen who saw in 'responsible' government a diminution in borrowing power in Britain and the threat of being made to account for already existing debts. And inside Canada pressure began to mount for closer commercial ties with the US to find an industrial metropolis whose demand for Canadian raw materials would offset the loss of the formerly protected British market. The transfer of the commercial nexus from an almost exclusively British orientation in favour of increasing the flow of raw produce to the US manifested itself in both of the key staples of the era. While Canadian grain generally continued to find British markets, it increasingly moved via New York rather than Montreal. At the same time the British demand for Canadian timber fell as the Age of Steam and Steel dawned in Britain, while American demand for Canadian lumber as a building material in the opening of its western agricultural frontier and the industrialization of the east grew apace. The result of the shift in the orientation of the forest industry was to replace British commercial capital invested in the Canadian industry with American direct investment in saw mills and timber limits, shifting the relations of production from merchant–independent proprietor to capital–wage labour.

However, the shift in commercial orientation of the economy did not engender any diminution in British capital invested in Canada. Quite the contrary. Under the aegis of the Act of Union and especially at the time of the negotiation of a reciprocal lowering of raw material tariffs with the US, British capital poured into the province to support the dawn of the railway age. Railway promoters seized control of the government apparatus to use state revenues to support railway-building, both directly through subsidies and 'loans' and indirectly via the guarantee of securities sold by the promoters in Britain. While commercially the colony moved further from the British nexus, financially the power of the British investment houses, especially the Barings and Glyn, Mills, had never been so great.

Nor was the investment of British capital restricted to government or corporate debt earmarked for railway purposes. As the Canadian economy slowly matured from the exceedingly primitive pioneer structure typical of the very early decades of the nineteenth century, efforts to develop a local financial system proceded apace. In the evolution of these institutions the response of the British financier was the all-important consideration. The first trust and mortgage loan company in Canada, established by the mercantile community of Kingston in 1843, stated in its charter that a crucial objective of its formation was to facilitate the influx of British money. Exactly the same consideration underlay both the formation of the Toronto Stock Exchange in 1853 and the passage of the first Canadian companies act introducing the general principle of limited liability in 1850. British capital was invested in the shares of some of the early commercial banks of the province in addition to the British commercial long credit that was essential to the early banks' discounting activities. An experiment with 'free banking,' that is, small banks of deposit and issue, was abandoned in 1855 precisely because British capital was afraid to invest in such a presumably unstable banking structure.

Nonetheless railway finance was and remained the single most important link between British finance and the Canadian economy. The railway projects tied the Barings in particular more closely to the province than to any of their other clients, such that the Canadian political apparatus became little more than an overseas administrative arm of the private bank. The power ceded by the Colonial Office in Whitehall got no further than Lombard Street, there to stay for the rest of the century. The power of the bankers' was enormous and frequently exercised. In 1851, at the bankers' request, the province passed an act agreeing that the public debt would not be increased without prior consultation with the Barings and Glyn, Mills. To aid the democratic decision-making process, the Barings prevented Canadian securities from being quoted on the British Stock Exchange lists until the act was passed.

The Barings and Glyn were financial agents to the government of New Brunswick and Nova Scotia as well, though so much of their resources were tied up in Canada they could lend but little to the other provinces. Nonetheless some debts did exist. In fact debts to the Barings were about the only thing the British North American colonies had in common before Confederation. These debts in the Maritimes were largely the result of railway finance (and frauds as well), and provoked the same kind of direct interference by the British financiers in the political process there as was typical in Canada.

There were other major external sources of capital for the Atlantic region. Newfoundland remained the direct fiefdom of the London fish peddling interests. After 1825, for the first time the group of noble and ersatz nobel proprietors who ruled Prince Edward Island from afar allowed a few coins to make their way into land improvement – a paltry investment repaid many times over in rising rents. New Brunswick timber stands remained the happy hunting ground of British commercial houses: the American influx in the province was not as dramatic as in Canada – in large measure because the British government had simply ceded a substantial piece of New Brunswick timber lands directly to the New England lumber barons. In Nova Scotia the external investments were diverse. The great British commercial houses retained substantial agencies there even after the repeal of the Navigation Laws eliminated a large measure of Halifax's special position in the British West Indies trade. Halifax banks took a place in the long credit system in moving the imperial trade. The flow of funds on military account to Halifax remained substantial, and the natural resources of the province attracted the interest of overseas investors. The Nova Scotia gold rush of the 1850s drew in British and American funds; and the great Cape Breton coal fields were firmly in the grasp of the British-controlled General Mining Association, with a monopoly to 1857 granted by the British Crown.

The interior of British North America submitted to an exceedingly archaic mode of control. The power of the great chartered trading monopolies was a history-book phenomenon in the mid nineteenth century. Yet the western regions were controlled absolutely by the Hudson's Bay Company, an absolute government with military and fiscal as well as monopolistic commercial powers. The gold rush of the 1850s in British Columbia tore that part of the Hudson's

Bay Company fiefdom from it as a wave of individual American prospectors plus a battery of American gold dealers and assorted commercial and transportation interests swept the area. Still British finance and investment, in the form of Hudson's Bay Company subsidiaries in the transportation and commercial spheres and the sale of government bonds in London to finance the building of infrastructure, continued to dominate the economic structure.

Canada was by far the most important colony from the point of view of British investment. Fiscal policy in the province was inseparable from railway finance. In 1858 and 1859 an economic crisis struck the province, and the response set a crucial precedent for the future. The crisis was met in part by concessions to foreign capital whose vagaries by this time had a powerful effect on the state of prosperity of the Canadian economy. With the British-controlled railway system teetering on the verge of bankruptcy, tariffs were raised to augment government revenues. The minister of finance stated baldly that the purpose of the fiscal changes was 'to protect those parties in England who have invested in our Railway and Municipal bonds.'

Canadian interest in the importation of industrial capital began to manifest itself in this era. Businessmen's organizations with a number of objectives had begun to manifest themselves. Some were protectionist; all were in favour of rapid development. In Upper Canada the leader of the principal 'protectionist' bloc saw industrial development as synonymous with the importation of foreign manufacturing capital. While some business organizations called for the raising of tariff walls to stimulate local capital formation, he called for lowering of the tariff between Canada and the US to force British manufacturing firms to migrate to Canada, from which they would be better able to export to the United States. In 1866 tariff reductions were decided upon, one purpose of which was to encourage an influx of foreign industrial investments by reducing production costs in the province.

The American Civil War led to an economic boom in the province of Canada, and its close precipitated a commercial and financial crisis from 1864 to 1866. In Britain investors, already worried about the threat of American invasion of Canada, which would in all likelihood be followed by a repudiation of the Canadian public debt, saw railway earnings plummet and the lines facing bankruptcy once more. A financial crisis broke out in Britain early in 1867 complicating even further the delicate problem of colonial finance. The Barings and the Glyns were called upon for more interim financing for the province and fretted openly about the possibility of repayment.

Railway security issues were impossible, and even a government issue in 1866 was only partly saleable at a very substantial discount. A time of grave crisis when the traditional economic structures were proven untenable required imaginative leadership and political acumen to find a solution that would augur well for the future; both of these qualities were conspicuously absent from the ranks of those who found an expedient to temporarily salvage the provincial credit.

Dominion of Canada 1867-1914

Confederation followed logically from the 1840 union of the two Canadian provinces, which widened the tax base and thus assured the repayment of colonial debt. The result was to attach the revenues of the Maritime provinces to the empty treasury of the province of Canada. Both the British private banks and the Canadian financial élite and railroad promoters pushed avidly for the scheme as the sole means at hand for restoring the province's sagging credit. London finance was quick to give its assent to the new system of public credit. Less than six months after Confederation the new dominion placed a major loan in Britain without difficulty; six months previously dominion bonds had been only partly saleable at heavy discounts.

Railway finance proceded apace. A few scattered instances of British direct investments in branch factories also occurred. Some British capital flowed into natural resources, especially petroleum in southern Ontario, and in general the inflow of capital revived somewhat. However these movements ground to a halt with the crisis of 1873 and the ensuing Depression. To reactivate the flow some other policy was required. Like a conditioned reflex Canadian governments responded to crises by efforts to cultivate the approval of foreign investors. What was new however was the type, the scale, and the role of the new investments in the Canadian development process.

There are two principal routes, with some minor variants, that an economy can follow on the road to industrialization. Manufacturing industry can grow up 'naturally' from a small scale, even artisanal mode of production when capital accumulation is a largely internal phenomenon based on the reinvestment of the firm's own profits. A second path implies direct development to large-scale oligopolistic enterprise where outside capital is invested to facilitate its expansion and where the state takes an active, direct role in its growth. The outside capital required could come from commercial capital accumulation, from the state, or from foreign investment. The first path, if successfully followed, would lead to the emergence of a flourishing and independent national entrepreneurial class. The second may or may not; it may simply reproduce the conservatism of commercial capitalism in a new guise, the development of inefficient non-innovative, and backward industrial structures with a penchant for dependence on foreign technology, foreign capital, and state assistance.

In Canada during the formative years of the Confederation era, both paths of development were available. A string of small industrial establishments, catering to local markets, growing through reinvested earnings without outside capital, dominated a number of manufacturing fields – agricultural implements, meat-packing, much of secondary iron and steel, wool, boots and shoes, among others. These industries were largely, though certainly not exclusively, located in small urban centres and linked to the prosperity of surrounding agricultural areas.

On the other hand, the chief metropolitan centres of Canada witnessed another pattern of evolution as the wholesale merchants who grew to prominence in the staple trades began to reach back to control production. Iron and steel, cotton, and sugar-refining in particular came under their control. There also emerged large-scale textile and woolen factories which quickly eclipsed the artisanal ones, and industries like railroad rolling stock with obvious links to the commercial sector of the economy grew up in this era. These industries had several salient characteristics. Their scale of production had to be large from the outset by virtue of the technology they utilised, their markets had to be widespread to cover their heavy fixed costs, and they relied on outside capital and assistance, from accumulated merchants' capital, from foreign investment and technology, and from the state.

Apart from the Patent Act of 1872 (which stipulated that for a foreign patentee to maintain his rights he had to ensure that manufacture of the patent took place in Canada within two years of the patent being granted, an act whose importance became evident at a later period), the chief forms of state intervention were the National Policy tariff of 1878-9 and a subsequent set of iron and steel subsidies and further upward tariff revisions. While the tariff of 1878-9 was a fiscal instrument designed specifically to deal with the crises of the 1870s its long-term effects were far-reaching.

A number of capitalist interests pressured for the high-tariff policy. Among domestic interests the wholesale merchants in the iron and steel, textile, and West Indies trades used the tariff wall to invest in primary iron and steel, cotton and woolen mills, and sugar refineries, often with British partners. The petroleum industry of southern Ontario, in a state of crisis and overloaded with British creditors and investors demanding a return, joined the pro-tariff ranks. The British capitalists and their Canadian junior partners in the Cape Breton coal fields did likewise.

Among small-scale industrialists in Ontario a split emerged. A very wide range of small-scale manufacturing interests fought the tariff, seeing in it an impetus to monopoly, which would quickly squeeze out the small producer, and a tax on a wide range of crucial industrial raw materials, especially primary iron products and coal. At the same time a large group who had benefitted from the artificial protection to Canadian industry that the American Civil War engendered, faced with renewed competition at the end of that war – a competition made more serious by depreciation of the American exchange rate and the beginnings of a long-term downward movement of prices which squeezed profit margins – responded by opting for protection. The split in the ranks of small-scale producers, with one group allying temporarily with Montreal commerce, and the British investors in other key sectors on the tariff issue carried the National Policy.

The objectives of the tariff were much more than the protection of existing industries, guaranteeing returns on already existing British industrial investments, or the provision of a climate for commercial capital to shift to industrial investments. Many industries in fact opposed and were crippled by the high duties. The tariff was explicitly intended to attract American and British industrial investments into Canada. During the tariff debates, a Conservative Senator declared, 'To secure the success of manufactures we must endeavour to encourage the manufacturers and capitalists of Great Britain and the United States to establish workshops in the Dominion.' Yet perhaps the most important objective was the most traditional of all – to raise revenue especially in light of the major railroad projects being contemplated. The tariff revenue could be poured into promoters' pockets as a subsidy to construction. The minister of finance declared that if the tariff surplus were as much as anticipated, 'We will not from the day to the finishing of the Canadian Pacific Railway require to go to the English market except to replace those liabilities which matured.' Indirectly the tariff revenues guaranteed the repayment of government debts contracted earlier for railroad purposes. The immediate effect of the tariff was that Canadian public securities in London immediately rose to the top of the colonial list.

While a brief boom coincided with the new fiscal policy, by 1883 recession hit again, and the new large-scale industrial capacity, especially sugar-refining, iron and steel, and cotton faced collapse. Apart from new tariff increases, an iron and steel subsidy system, and a spate of new borrowings in London, there was little scope for government action. The period from 1873 to 1896, except for the 1879–83 revival, was one of very slow growth: the population was not growing, the western areas were largely empty, and few foreign branch plants were responding to the high tariff wall. But the world revival of 1896 brought a secular boom to Canada as well. The transformation of the world economic order after that date had four main characteristics: 1/ it gave a new importance to raw material hinterlands with rising staple prices and industrial demand; 2/ it witnessed the renewed flow of financial capital from Europe, especially Britain, to the new and old raw material hinterlands of the empire, formal and informal; 3/ it also witnessed the transformation of the industrial base of the Western world with the old age of steam and steel giving way to the era of electricity, the chemical industry, and the internal combustion engine; 4/ the importance of the new industries meant a shift in the locus of world industrial power. Despite Britain's continued commercial and financial dominance, it was in the US above all where the new industrial system matured.

In Canada these trends manifested themselves dramatically. The staple frontier expanded rapidly in the West; the industrial base did likewise in the East; and a flood of immigrants provided both farmers and workers whose falling real incomes built the new prosperity for the Canadian commercial and financial élite. British portfolio investment was an essential building block for the new structures, and there was little the Canadian business and political élite would not do to encourage its influx to sustain the enormous program of railway development, to finance land settlement, to fund all levels of government, to float public utilities, and even for a brief atypical period to purchase industrial bonds to support a merger wave. In the name of maintaining the confidence of British finance, strikes were broken, provincial statutes threatened with disallowance and sometimes even actually disallowed, and the social efficacy of liberal democracy itself was publicly challenged by at least one eminent banker. The dominion government showed an unseemly haste to undermine and subvert the small amount of financial independence it had been ceded at Confederation by agreeing to disallow or repeal all laws that would impede or inhibit the British coupon-clipper from receiving the just reward of his great labour on behalf of Canadian economic development. The Dominion further pledged to the imperial financial élite Canadian troops for the war of colonial annexation in South Africa. In exchange for Canada's pledging financial fealty and despatching the troops, federal government securities were admitted in London to the much coveted Trustee List, whereby English trust funds could for the first time be invested in them. The Liberal finance minister who negotiated the arrangement could not restrain himself from crowing in the House of Commons that 'this action of the British government in coming to the assistance of Canada will be worth in actual cash every cent that it costs to send Canadian troops to South Africa.'

The results of the influx of British capital were several. The transportation system, public utilities, and financial institutions that were built up with the aid of British capital were confirmed in both their dominant position in the economy and in their Canadian ownership, private while solvent and public after bankruptcy; the impact of British finance capital reinforced the propensity to staple extraction for imperial markets; and the Canadian economy was bequeathed a huge burden of fixed-interest debt that had to be met out of the proceeds of rapid resource extraction for export to earn the foreign exchange required to repay the British loans.

Capital formation under Canadian control reinforced these patterns. Canadian banks drained funds out of the industrial centres of the eastern provinces and the agricultural (mixed-farming) areas of Ontario, formerly the staple frontier, and shifted the funds to the Canadian West. Both Maritime industrialism and the Quebec industrial entrepreneurs who had built up local industries in small urban centres underwent secular decline. The Ontario mixed-farming areas were depopulated and food production there underwent a relative decline. On the other hand the new staple-extracting areas flourished as a single cash crop frontier as the Canadian banks poured funds into financing grain movements for export, and Canadian insurance, mortgage, and trust companies drew funds out of the east or from abroad to channel into mortgage lending on the prairies. The result of the movement of capital into staples was to create a vacuum in the financing of industry, government, and other long-term investments that foreign capital had to fill.

The Canadian banking and monetary system of the period reflected well the structure of dependence on external finance. The reserves of the banking system, instead of being held in specie or in government of Canada notes, were held largely in the form of call loans in New York on the supposed rationale that the money there could be liquidated on demand for use in Canada when required. In fact the call loans in New York rose steadily and in times of crisis or need for more liquid funds it was the call loan business in Canada that contracted. As to government notes, these were scrupulously limited in issue to avoid provoking the ire of the Canadian chartered banking cartel. The result was to block off another potential source of finance for the government and force it to rely ever more heavily on external borrowings to finance the infrastructure it was building. As to those notes that were issued they were backed by a reserve of gold or British government securities, while the chartered banks had no reserve ratio at all.

A booming agricultural frontier should aid the industrialization process in several ways. It should provide cheap food under conditions of rising productivity for the industrial proletariat. It should generate surplus income for investment in industrial capital formation. And it should provide a market for the products of the industrial sector. In fact in Canada the new agricultural hinterland produced grain for export to imperial markets primarily, at the same time draining off funds and helping to underdevelop the mixed-farming areas producing foodstuffs for local consumption. Bread prices in Canada during the 'wheat boom' were higher than bread prices in Britain made from Canadian grain. Even flour was imported into the prairies from other parts of Canada or abroad. As to surplus income, the flow in fact moved the other way – from the industrial East to the agrarian West. The only aid to industry provided by the agricultural frontier was a market, a protected market for Eastern industry, while farmers sold their goods on international markets subject to the depredations of Canadian financial and commercial intermediaries as well as the vagaries of world grain prices. And much of the impetus to industrialization benefitted the American industrial system that was dominating an ever larger proportion of the Canadian industrial process.

American industrial capitalism entered Canada in four principal forms. In the pre-Confederation era came a flow of American technology via the theft of patents: American patterns and industrial designs were blatantly copied, often from imports which had an already established market. At the same time there came a migration of American industrial entrepreneurs who shifted bodily north of the border. The distilleries of Ontario, the sewing machine factories, foundries, and other parts of the secondary iron and steel industry, and especially the agricultural implements industry, were largely the products of one or both of these movements. After the Patent Act of 1872 which forced the American inventor to find a Canadian agent or establish a branch factory to retain his patent, and after the National Policy tariff of 1879 which cut American firms off from the Canadian market, the pattern changed. Instead of a flow of entrepreneurs and unattached technology which could be easily integrated into the Canadian economy, there came a movement of licensed affiliates dependent on a parent firm and controlled by an American parent, or joint ventures of American and Canadian capital around American product lines. There came as well a movement of direct investment in the form of full-fledged industrial branch plants. The new pattern carried with it a structure of industrial dependence that grew over time, a dependence that clearly could not be measured by any calculations of the value of foreign direct investment alone, there often being no flow of capital accompanying dependence by patent affiliation.

At first the licensed ventures existed in and returned royalties to their American parents in a number of scattered fields. But after the new prosperity following the 1896 recovery, a distinct pattern emerged. The new industries of the second industrial revolution – chemicals, automobiles, electrical apparatus, mining machinery, etc. – almost to the last firm entered Canada in the form of licensed ventures of American parents. These new industries were the growth industries of the future. And although there was often little if any direct American investment in them the patent relationship ensured their dependence and that innovation in technique and product line would be contingent upon decisions taken in the US. Canadian financial and commercial capitalists often invested in the industries based on American technology. During the National Policy boom of 1879 to 1883 the Canadian commercial and financial élite had allied with British capital and technique to make large scale investments in sugar refining, cotton, primary iron and steel and other industries of the earlier epoch of industrialization. With the coming of the second industrial revolution they did the same with American capital and technique.

American direct investment grew steadily with the boom of the 1896-1914 period. Initially branch plants were established to regain markets lost behind the high tariff. Subsequently new forces came into play. The growth of the American national firm spilled over into Canada; tariff rates in Canada rose; the expansion of the Canadian market attracted new entrants; and the growth of the British Empire itself during this period made a Canadian location for an American firm all the more attractive. With Canada's growing exports of staples, further incentives to the migration of American capital existed. The American giant cereal mills moved in to process Canadian grains for export, and, secondarily only for the domestic market, increasingly displaced small local mills. Meat-packing too felt the effects of the expansion with American refrigeration techniques entering Canada in the form of branches of the giant American firms. A range of sophisticated metal products followed.

In resources industries the steady inflow of American capital into forests and mines accelerated. In part this increase in the rate of investment simply reflected the growing shortage of cheap, easily accessible resources in the us. In part it reflected the tendency of Canadian commercial capitalism, especially the banks and railways, to foster rapid extraction of primary products for export rather than encourage secondary processing. And in part it was a result of the actions of the provincial governments, starved for revenue, who responded to their rising expenditure liabilities by encouraging the rapid exploitation of royalty-yielding natural resources. In a few cases some effort was made to force some initial processing of the resources in Canada, with pulpwood export duties, threatened but not effected nickel duties, lead bounties, and a renewed iron and steel bounty system. The result, when the policies were effective, was to substitute some American direct investment in processing industries for American direct investment in resource industries.

The one major exception was the primary iron and steel industry whose foundations went back to the mid-nineteenth century but whose early financial career had been precarious. The old industry had been British-controlled, but its obsolete equipment and plant were idle when the boom began at the end of the century. The industry revived under specific conditions. The railway-building orgy that led to the opening of the western staple frontier guaranteed a home market, and Canadian commercial capital responded. American techniques were adopted. A sea of government largesse, federal, provincial, and municipal, was heaped upon the precocious infant. And the industry was built up and directed by American entrepreneurs in conjunction with Canadian commercial capitalists and British portfolio investment. These Americans were refugees form the big squeeze J.P. Morgan was then imposing on the American industry, which eliminated many of the small entrepreneurs who migrated north without any corporate strings attached. Like the agricultural implements and distilling industries in an earlier period, this industry, although totally derivative, had no corporate linkages and therefore grew to independence. From the time of the Forges of St Maurice during the French régime to the true foundation of the industry in the early twentieth century, the pattern of development of primary iron and steel showed a remarkable persistence. External capital, state subsidies, American technique, and commercial demand – either derivative from the fur trade and the military posts required to defend it as in the French régime or derivative from the wheat trade and the railways needed to move it as during the late years of the British régime – these factors in conjunction with local commercial capitalists built and maintained the industry.

The Canadian economy since the First World War

The years 1912 and 1913 saw the spectre of chronic recession hanging over the Canadian economy: world wheat prices plummetted, the overextended railroads faced bankruptcy, and a merger movement of industry, financed by British capital, came to a sudden halt with a drastic liquidation threatening. The war, however, brought respite. An enormous industrial expansion in the East occurred based predominantly on imperial munitions requirements; the western grain frontier revived again as high wheat prices encouraged inefficient and overextended farming, and for a while the railroads looked solvent. War however only delayed the crash that was inevitable after the rush of development of the preceding decade. The railways began to collapse as early as 1917; the postwar recession forced nationalization of two of the systems. The banking system was salvaged only by a postwar continuation of the wartime manna of government fiat issues. The merger wave fell apart, and grain prices fell catastrophically.

The war and its aftermath also eroded considerably the ability of Canada to raise loans in Britain. The British economy entered a long era of crisis, and investors who had already felt the bite from the postwar crash were reluctant to re-enter the Canadian loan business. More and more portfolio capital had to be raised in the US, and the flow of American direct investment continued to grow with a wave of takeovers of industries, especially automobiles, electricity, and the like, that had formerly operated as joint ventures and licensed ventures affiliated to American oligopolies. By as early as 1921 the structure of ownership that has continued to prevail to the present day was firmly in place. Canadian capital controlled the competitive, low level of technology sector, especially consumer non-durable goods. Canadian capital was solidly in control of the primary iron and steel industry whose capacity had been augmented enormously by its role in the massive blood bath in Europe during the war. The agricultural implements industry, while most of it was Canadian-controlled, nonetheless had a substantial American interest, as did the agri-business sector, milling, and meat-packing. In the smelting and refining of non-ferrous metals, especially where new electrical techniques were required, in petroleum-refining, in automobile, electrical apparatus, and chemical manu-facturing American capital was solidly entrenched. Yet Canadian policy re-mained predicated on the need for even more foreign investment, especially American direct investment, to sustain the process of economic growth.

One enigma immediately emerges from the posture struck by the Canadian ruling clique in the postwar period – why they chose to pursue the policy of industrialization by invitation vis-à-vis the American corporate system. The experiences of the war had pointed in another direction. War had cut Canada off from external capital. The war had been financed internally by a massive redistribution of income from the poor to the rich. A flood of paper currency caused rapid inflation of incomes of the rich while wages and farm incomes were held down. The redistribution thus built up enough great fortunes to provide an internal market for bond issues to aid the process of war finance, the burden of repayment of which could be spread over the population at large by the steep tariff and excise duties on consumer goods. Domestic financ-ing was not only adequate for the massive internal economic expansion of the war but also for Canadian exports of capital to finance the war effort abroad. At the same time in the postwar period no great commitments to build infra-structure on the level of the prewar investments were necessary.

The decision to continue to foster the inflow of foreign capital, especially direct investment, was the result of several factors. The chronic postwar reces-sion caused panic in financial circles in Canada, and the conditioned response to recession was to try to alleviate the short-run problem by increasing the long-run problem, by importing more foreign capital to offset the crisis caused by an over-reliance on foreign capital in the prewar period. Furthermore an organized and militant labour force in Canada entered the political scene for the first time as a factor of immense importance, and the possibility of con-tinuing to finance expansion by a squeeze on working-class incomes was con-siderably circumscribed. The Canadian capital market before the war had been thoroughly integrated with that of New York, especially via the activities of the Canadian banks in Wall Street; the war had meant a temporary interrup-tion and when it ended the normal flow of funds was renewed as quickly as possible. A Canadian entrepreneurial class, small and weak though it had been, no longer existed to all intents and purposes – the least-cost, least-risk pattern of industrial development by a junior partnership role had already been well rehearsed. The pending collapse of the British Empire was obvious to all, and the need for a new metropole to replace Britain was widely appreciated. All of these factors, coupled with the 'natural' expansion of American big business typical of the era, determined the development pattern that was followed. American investment thus grew steady during the decade of the twenties while British investment fell absolutely and relatively. The inflow continued into the Great Depression as the proven device of high tariff walls was used once more. The success of the new tariff of 1932 was registered immediately in an increase in the number of American branch plants in Canada, an influx encouraged in the hope that, at least in part, it would offset the virtual cessation of domestic private net investment during the Depression. It would further provide the foreign exchange earnings to help settle the staggering burden of fixed interest payments due to Britain as a result of past borrowings: interest and dividend payments during the Depression combined with falling prices of staple exports to absorb 25 per cent of total foreign exchange earnings.

During the Second World War, as in the First, the private inflow of capital was replaced by a massive outflow in loans and grants to allied economies to finance their war effort; at the same time output surged ahead. However, with the return of peace, the traditional patterns were quickly resumed. The 1950s saw the dawn of a long boom, fed by American investment, primarily in Canadian natural resources, though the flow of investment into manufacturing plant also accelerated. The investments in the resource industries were encouraged by a number of factors. By the mid 1950s the American government deemed twenty-nine industrial raw materials as likely to be in short supply in the US in the near future, if not already. For twelve of them Canada was regarded as the major source of supply, not only by virtue of availability but also security. In one other case Canada was classified as the major supplementary source should the leading producer fail to fill US political or economic needs. And the list of commodities discussed did not include forest products or energy where US reliance on Canadian products was accelerating rapidly. The boom in resources in the 1950s was led by investment in Alberta oil and gas. US capital poured into forest products on an unprecedented scale. And in the 1960s American interest in hydroelectric power production and fresh water supplies in Canada led to the emergence of a number of grandiose schemes for their development. The flow of investment also reflected Canadian policy. Tax concessions to foster rapid resource depletion were built into the fiscal structures of all levels of government. As to manufacturing, the structure of foreign, especially American, investment began to change. Instead of investments in branch plants for the production of American product lines, simple horizontal extensions of the American firm, or vertical integration via investments in the production of raw and semiprocessed materials to meet the needs of the American parent, the conglomerate merger phenomenon began to dominate the movement of American capital across the border. A growing number of Canadian businesses were absorbed by American firms intent on diversifying their interests to spread risks and profit-taking over a large number of product lines and enterprises.

The consequences of the assiduously cultivated tightening of the American hold have been several and far-reaching. Commodity trade patterns have been increasingly twisted into a north-south basis with a substantial part of it taking the form of intracompany transfers. Of this trade, the Canadian subsidiaries and even the independent sectors export raw and semifinished products, while Canada imports finished products from the US. The only significant manufactures exported from Canada are automobiles and parts, exported to the US by the completely American-controlled Canadian branch plants of the large automobile producers, and armaments exported under the Defence Production Sharing Agreement. Both these exports represent efforts to transfer the locus of part of the production of American firms to their Canadian subsidiaries. Both were a modern variant of the old game of inducing a northward flow of American industrial capacity by commercial policy. With tariff increases contrary to international law and with preferential tariffs anathema under the new postwar American rules of the game, the bilateral discriminatory arrangement necessary to induce the movement had to take these other forms. Both also had the effect of making two of the largest sources of employment in Canada directly dependent on the whims of the American State Department and thus involved, much as had the resource-alienation policy, an implicit guarantee of good political behaviour on the part of the Canadian government.

The industrial structure that exists in Canada today, apart from exhibiting the greatest degree of dependence of any in the world, for the same reasons is notoriously inefficient and non-innovative. The pay-off from the Patent Act of 1872 and all its successor legislation has been very powerful. After the Patent Act and again after the National Policy tariff of 1879 patents granted to Canadian residents fell absolutely. As a percentage of total patents issued, those granted to Canadian residents for the next hundred years exhibited a secular decline. And the current Canadian record of patents granted to its own residents is one of the worst in the world. Technological backwardness and lack of industrial research in Canada are self-reinforcing.

While the industrial structure has been increasingly pulled into the American orbit, even to the extent that American anti-trust legislation bears a powerful influence on its organization, the capital market has done likewise. As the American balance of payments crisis deepened in the 1960s with a deterioration of the balance of trade and an increased outflow on capital account to maintain the military infrastructure around the world, the American government responded by a series of measures to try to improve the capital account by twisting the patterns of private investment. In 1963 a 15 per cent interest equalization tax was imposed to cut back on the amount of portfolio borrowing being done in the US by foreign governments and firms. Canada begged for exceptional status and it was granted, almost automatically. The intent of the tax was to cut back the long-term portfolio capital outflow while, it was hoped, leaving intact the flow of direct investment abroad. At that time there could be no question of curtailing the outflow of funds on military account. Two years later more drastic measures were tried – the 'voluntary' guidelines which pressured American multinational firms to cut back on their export of capital, to do a larger share of their long-term borrowings abroad, to repatriate short-term assets held abroad, and to step up the rate at which they repatriated earnings from their foreign affiliates. With its own balance of payments crisis looming as an immediate consequence of the American action, the Canadian government again begged exemption. It was granted, but for a price. In return for its privileged access to the American capital market, giving it unrestricted ability to pawn its natural and industrial resources, Canada had to peg the level of its foreign exchange reserves and relend any surplus above an agreed figure to the US. The agreement to peg the reserves was bad enough, effectively pre-cluding as it did any independent monetary policy in Canada; to the extent that any was possible before, it vanished thereafter. But, more important, the guidelines gave the American government the power to dictate the investment policies of a large part of the manufacturing and resources sector of the econ-omy. In 1968, in exchange for further exemptions from the new mandatory guidelines, the Canadian government made what was, even for it, a catastrophic concession. It froze the already perverse pattern of international capital flows into the status of an officially sanctioned and enforced pattern. US funds flow into Canada on long term to take control of resources and businesses, while the foreign exchange is automatically relent to the US on short term. Canada thus officially agreed to continue to borrow back at long term what it lent at short term. Finally in 1971 came the New Economic Policy, a new program of subsidizing exports, curtailing imports, abdication of previous trade agree-ments, and sundry other methods to repair the crisis. Again Canada begged exemption, and it secured only partial satisfaction. Just how much sovereignty and wealth was bartered away in the corridors of power in Washington remains unknown.

For the private capital market the effects of American domination have been marked. The growth of wholly owned branch plants has caused a rela-tive shrinkage in the volume of shares traded on the stock exchanges, especially in the already weak category of industrial shares. Canadian equity investment flows through its financial institutions to the US. In Wall Street too Canadian banks do over half the call loan business that keeps the American stock jobbers going. The result can only be to impede the marketing of new issues by inde-pendent companies in Canada. Precisely the same considerations hold with respect to corporate bond issues in Canada, impeded by a limited and illiquid market at the same time Canadian financial institutions carry large portfolios of American bonds. This twisting of the capital market which facilitates the trend to industrial dependence is in fact an outgrowth of a historical process of evolution as long as, if not longer than, the pattern of industrial domination itself.

CANADIAN INVESTMENT ABROAD

At the same time that the Canadian economy provided the leading example of a capital 'borrowing' country in all the various possible forms – commercial credit, portfolio capital in government loans, utilities and the like, direct investment in manufacturing and resources – it also undertook the export of capital in its own right, making short- and long-term investments in the metropolitan economies as well as seeking its own hinterlands to dominate.

The flow of capital from Canada to other countries began in the French régime. Fur-trade fortunes accumulated in the colony often returned to France in the form of investments, especially in land. While some of this outflow was the 'natural' result of the return of the fur traders themselves to resume or begin residence in the metropolis, some of it constituted a flow of unaccompanied long-term capital, over and above simple remittances of profit to the French partners in the business. The Church in Quebec also made long-term investments in France from its earnings from land in the colony. And most substantial of all were the massive sums plundered from the public purse and the population at large by government officials who remitted these earnings to France for investment there.

The early years of British rule witnessed an export of capital in several directions. Accumulations by wholesale merchants in Montreal and Halifax sustained investments in the United Kingdom, including at least one case of investment in the British asset of the era that carried the highest rate of return – the purchase of a seat in the unreformed House of Commons. As in the French régime, a major objective of early merchants in British North America was to make as much money as quickly as possible in the colonies and to subsequently retire to the metropolis. Typically the very few Canadian wholesale houses that entered the timber trade to Britain had to establish a British branch house, but the British branch often evolved into the head office of the concern.

As their roots in the colonies became firmer, other external investments attracted the merchants' attention. While New York capital was being invested in the Welland Canal system, Montreal capital found its way into the equity of the Erie Canal. Canadian banks by the 1830s were solidly established in exchange speculation in New York; Maritime wholesale houses extended long credit to the West Indies followed in 1837 by the creation of a joint-venture of Halifax and London capital in the establishment of a bank in the West Indies, the first of a long series.

Towards mid-century, and especially after the negotiation of a reciprocal lowering of raw material tariffs between British North America and the US in 1854, Canadian banks grew in importance in financing international movements of produce in Chicago and expanded their role in New York. As well, Canadian railway investments in the US began on a large scale.

The decades between Confederation and 1896 witnessed a slow but steady growth in Canadian activity in the US and the Caribbean, but with no major innovation apart from a few industrial branch plants. After 1896 however major structural changes occurred. Canadian banks and insurance companies spread across the Caribbean and into Latin America. Great utility promotions involving Canadian direct investment also dotted the area. In the US the Canadian banks and railroad investments multiplied; the banks by that time had become indispensable for the operation of Wall Street stock jobbers. They were joined by large insurance company portfolio investments in American utilities and by direct investments by Canadian firms in the secondary iron and steel industry.

There was a major distinction between Canadian investments in the Caribbean and South America and those in the US. Those in the Caribbean and South America were aggressive enterprises, involving substantial economic control and imposing a large net draining of funds on the areas concerned. Those in the US were rentier-type investments, or were geared to facilitating long-distance trade, or to call money operations in Wall Street. They thus represented a substantial drainage of funds from Canada to the US. The Latin American investments helped perpetuate the area's colonial status: the American investments helped perpetuate Canada's colonial status. The contrast is sharp between Canadian banks' drainage of deposit money out of the Caribbean to Canada and their drainage of deposit money out of Canada to the US. It is equally strong with utilities – Canadian direct investment and control of major operations in Latin America on the one hand and Canadian portfolio investments in American promotions in the US on the other. The Bank of Nova Scotia's portfolio investment in United Fruit Company bonds neatly summarizes the relations for all the areas concerned.

With the decline and fall of the British Empire, Canadian investment abroad in the underdeveloped world began to shrink in importance. The banks remained in place, as did the insurance companies, but the utility and railroad operations abroad dwindled. But as the Canadian hold on the underdeveloped areas declined, the volume of investments in the US in the form of railway extensions, portfolio investments by financial institutions, and bank activities, grew. The Canadian investments in secondary iron and steel in the US were eclipsed by the growing hold of the US secondary iron and steel industry in Canada. However, among industrial investments, partnerships with American racketeers during the prohibition era permitted a number of respectable old Canadian breweries and distilleries to lay the basis for further growth in the US. The post war period accelerated these trends as the Canadian capital market grew increasingly integrated into that of the US, both by virtue of the 'natural' growth of the banks and financial institutions and as a result of conscious government policies on both sides of the border.

The proliferation of multinational corporations in the period since the mid 1960s had its Canadian representatives as well. The Canadian Pacific Railway had evolved into a modern conglomerate, albeit still firmly rooted in transportation and communications. The banks' importance in Europe and beyond, either by themselves or as part of multinational bank consortia, was another development of the period. A few mining operations began, renewed, or strengthened themselves abroad. The creation of a badly misnamed Canada Development Corporation in 1972 was the federal government's response to the request of Canadian big business for public money to assist their international development. But despite a few spectacular successes, which because of their roots in the old established banking and transportation sector represent the exceptions that prove the rule, Canadian participation in the multinational scramble has remained necessarily feeble. And those cases where participation has occurred in sectors other than finance and transportation may well reflect the fact that expansion within Canada is blocked by the already existing American hold; hence the aspiring Canadian multinational is forced to move abroad, unlike the American which moves as a result of its internal growth.

CONCLUSIONS

Canadian dependence on foreign capital has deep historical roots. From the beginning of white exploitation of its natural resource base external capital in one form or another has been invariably an adjoint of its development process. The types of 'foreign' investments changed as the metropolitan economies developed and as their economic objectives vis-à-vis the hinterland economies altered. Commercial credit and loans or subsidies from metropolitan governments to the colonies dominate the early, preindustrial relationships based on looting of the surface resources. With the coming of the industrial age in Britain, larger scale, longer term commercial investments, plus long term loans to finance the construction of infrastructure to move industrial raw materials and foodstuffs from the colonies to British markets, became typical. As the nineteenth century drew to a close, Canada became an open field for British portfolio investment prompted directly or indirectly by the search for more raw materials and foodstuffs for the imperial market, and for American direct investment prompted by the growth of an internal Canadian market and the rise of American oligopolies. In time the second source of foreign investment displaced the first completely.

The relations between Canada and the two great metropolises of recent history bear in some ways a striking resemblance. During the golden age of British finance capital, the note issue of the dominion government was linked to its holdings of British government securities, and until the First World War virtually all of its coinage was struck in Britain. Its financial and banking institutions were in many ways linked to those of Britain through the flow of funds to the colony. British law reigned supreme in many fields. Not only was the dominion's political power directly circumscribed and ultimately subject to British judicial review, not only did legislators tremble at the prospect of inciting the ire of the lords of high finance, but statutes in the dominion explicitly acknowledged the ultimate rule of British finance. Canada eagerly participated in the imperial wars and zealously sought bilateral preferential arrangements with the metropole.

As the balance of world economic power shifted to the US, drawing Canada into its orbit, similar relations emerged. The Canadian capital market and its financial institutions became directly tributary to those of the US. Canadian governments pledged financial fidelity to the stars and stripes to maintain and reinforce the tributary relation, subjecting the Canadian financial system to direct US rule. American law entered Canada along with its capital just as in the heyday of the British empire. Canada directly profited from, as well as participated in, the imperial wars. And large parts of its industrial base survive only by virtue of bilateral preferential arrangements with the metropole.

It is tautological that a capitalist economy and the society built upon it takes its orders from a capitalist class. And it is certainly an unassailable proposition that economic power is unevenly distributed among the various capitalist economies of the world. It follows that every 'small' capitalist economy is susceptible to a degree of outside direction of its development process. However the degree to which the Canadian capitalist class not only has bowed to pressures from abroad but has deliberately and earnestly set out to induce those very pressures to which it has bowed results in a difference in kind in its external relations, rather than just in degree. It makes the Canadian experience approximate much more closely that of a Third World neocolonial economy than that of a small Western European economy. The level of its national wealth and the extent of industrialisation, albeit dependent and derivative, are superimposed on a set of social relations and economic structures that are essentially neocolonial. The typical neocolonial economy, when measuring its poverty and the degradation of its people against the shameful abundance and waste of the Canadian social system might well retort that it would give a great deal to achieve Canada's hinterland status. So, it seems, would the Canadian ruling class, for as long as they have something left to give.

NOTE

The principal sources from which this paper is derived are two works by the author: *The History of Canadian Business, 1867-1914*, two volumes (Toronto: James Lorimer and Co. 1975), from which the Canadian material from the 1850s to the First World War is taken in summary form; and a preliminary draft, 'Economic History of Canada.' Full footnote references will be available in these books.

R.O. Matthews

The Third World: powerful or powerless?

Observers of the contemporary world disagree profoundly over the influence of the small, underdeveloped countries that make up the Third World. On one hand, there are those writers who, following in the tradition of power theory, find the image of the small state as a pawn on the chessboard of world politics inadequate. Such a view, for example, cannot explain the evident ability of Cuba, Egypt, and Yugoslavia to ward off the close embrace of their all-powerful enemies, or the failure of the United States and the Soviet Union always to have their own way against their small neighbours. As Henry Kissinger expressed the problem so paradoxically, power has never been as great as it is and yet less useful.[1] Strength has in some sense been undermined, while weakness has become an asset.

For other observers, however, the developing countries of the Third World are nothing but puppets or appendages of the capitalist metropolitan centres. Tied to international markets in the West and dependent on governmental and private capital flows from the developed countries, the Third World relies upon and is wholly responsive to the interests of the capitalist powers. Any effort to break away from this straightjacket is likely to be dealt with by force or by a variety of economic sanctions. Thus, it is argued, the recent overthrow of the Allende régime in Chile was the result of a carefully orchestrated blockade by US private and government interests: US banks closed off all lines of credit; the Export-Import Bank refused to grant any new loans or to extend guarantees; the World Bank and the Inter-American Development Bank, under pressure from their major contributor, likewise denied Chile any credit; and finally, Kennecott prevented Chile from selling its copper to France and other West European countries. The resulting dislocation contributed significantly to Allende's downfall.[2]

Thus the countries of the Third World are variously portrayed as independent, sovereign states which wield considerable influence on the great and even the superpowers of today;[3] and as lifeless puppets, manipulated and exploited by their masters in the boardrooms of Wall Street and the corridors of power in Washington. Both these images, in my view, reflect part of the truth, but neither contains a totally accurate view; and so, after sketching the principal outlines of these two models, I shall attempt to suggest another perspective which combines elements from each of the other two.

A MODIFIED POWER-POLITICS MODEL

For many years the power-politics paradigm dominated international relations. It was assumed that all states, driven by an urge for power or by a sense of insecurity, were engaged in a continuous struggle with each other. Periods of peace resulted from a temporary balance which matched force (usually defined in terms of military capability) with equal force. In such a Hobbesian world small states had to depend for their security upon the distribution of power in a particular situation, the national interests of the major powers, and a measure of good fortune.[4] The small states (weak by definition) did have some room for manoeuverability but, for the most part, had to take advantage of situations created by the great powers. Their independence and even their very survival depended in the last resort on external factors.

This view of small states as pawns in the world of power politics ran into considerable difficulties even as early as the 1950s. As they attained independence, the new states of Asia and Africa resisted all efforts by both theorists and statesmen alike to be fitted neatly into one of the then two opposing camps of East and West. Not willing to sacrifice their newly won freedom, many of these states adopted a stance of nonalignment, which initially meant the refusal to permit the presence of foreign troops and the establishment of foreign bases on their territories. Theoretically, this development was explained as movement from a tight bipolar to a loose bipolar world. In the latter configuration, small states could survive outside the two blocs and could even exercise influence on the superpowers by carefully playing one side against the other.[5] The ability to blackmail either or both superpowers by threatening to change camps, or to shift from one camp to nonalignment, or from nonalignment to outright allegiance to the other camp, derived in large part from the existing configuration of power. This influence certainly involved considerable skill on the part of the small state's leadership – something that not all small powers possessed. But in the last analysis their influence grew out of special circumstances over which they had little control. In that sense, their strength or power was not permanent but temporary. Once the rivalry of the great powers eased, the new status of the small state would inevitably fall.

But are conditions in the contemporary international system similar to those that existed in all past systems characterized by bipolarity? In fact, analogies with the past seem to have little relevance for the present. Observers of the world scene have been struck by the consistency with which small states managed to ward off threats and pressures by the great powers and to secure concessions as well. If Castro could set up a communist régime in Cuba under the nose of his American enemy, if Nasser could nationalize the Suez Canal despite the open opposition of Great Britain and France, and if North Vietnam and the Vietcong could keep the largest military force ever known in history at bay in Southeast Asia, then surely small states were not as weak as the traditional theories of international relations suggested. Nor could their real power be explained solely in terms of the precarious balance of power and the intensity of the Cold War. If great powers were no longer 'all-powerful' and small states could exercise power out of all proportion to their capabilities, the security-politics model would have to be revised or modified. The essence of power had, in some sense, changed. It was to this paradox of the strong small power and the impotent great power that several authors addressed themselves.[6]

All of these writers share in common a more sophisticated understanding of the notion of power. A state's power had traditionally been measured by its military capabilities. A great power was therefore one which had the greatest number of battalions, the most sophisticated weaponry, and the most advanced economy to sustain a long and bloody war. Ultimately the rating of any state in the pecking order was determined by its ability to wage war. To attain the rank of great power a state had to engage successfully on the battlefield with an already acknowledged great power. Japan won its honours against Russia in 1905-6, while the United States acquired recognition by its victory over Spain at the turn of the century.

While power was employed in a relative sense - the ability to wage war against another state - the tendency was always to use it as a measure of a state's assets or capabilities. In the nuclear age the superpowers (a term coined at the end of the Second World War to set off the Soviet Union and the United States from the other great powers) were therefore those who possessed the ultimate weapon, the ability to deliver it, and, more recently, the ability to sustain a first strike and still inflict unacceptable damage on one's opponent. All too easily observers began thinking of power as a possession, a set of tangible and intangible assets. In this way the states of the world were ranked. Those at the top were designated as the superpowers; below them were the great and then the middle powers; and at the bottom were the small powers, who were actually powerless in the face of the middle, great, and superpowers.

The only way to account for the 'paradox of power,' or what we have described as the power of the weak and the relative impotence of the strong, is to distinguish between force or capabilities, on one hand, and power or influence, on the other. Used in this way, power is not a possession to be weighed and measured but a relationship. A state has power over another state to the extent that it can oblige the latter to do something that it would not otherwise have done or, alternatively, refuse to do what the latter would have it undertake. Thus a state may indeed be strong; it may have the greatest arsenal history has ever witnessed; and yet, for numerous reasons, it may not be able to translate this force or potential into actual power. Force should therefore not be mistaken for power; they may not, as several authors suggest, be even closely correlated with one another.[7]

But why have the mighty states not had their own way? Why are they usually described not as being in their glory but rather like Gulliver hobbled by a network of Lilliputian strings or like Baudelaire's albatross 'immobilized by its own weight'?[8] It is the emergence and impact of nuclear weapons which is most frequently mentioned as the primary explanation of this development. While these weapons have added a destructive capability unequalled in the past and thus further widened the gap between the superpowers and the rest of the world, the very potency of these weapons has, paradoxically, inhibited their use and increased the dangers involved in open warfare between the superpowers. Conflict has thus been shifted from a military to a paramilitary, political, economic, and psychological level. Even in their relations with small states the superpowers are reluctant to intervene militarily for fear that counterintervention by the other nuclear power may escalate the conflict to catastrophic proportions. To the extent that the superpowers are unlikely to resort to force other sources of power are greatly enhanced, such as the possession of scarce raw materials, an advantageous geographical location, a population with resourcefulness and ingenuity, and sincere, hard-working statesmen. In such a world the small states can fend for themselves and even exercise considerable influence.

Another restraint on the behaviour of the great powers (a term which hereafter denotes superpowers as well) is the presence and operation of the United Nations. The very existence of the world organization alters the way all states, in particular the great powers, behave. In a positive manner the General Assembly performs the function of an old-fashioned town meeting where the great and the small, the strong and the weak, can voice their views equally. An aggressive or threatening act by a great power will be brought to the attention of other states as well as to the great power's own public. Concerned with its world reputation and constrained by local opinion at home a great power will undertake controversial activities only if it is seriously provoked or if its vital interests are endangered.

The United Nations serves not only as a continuous forum for debate but constitutes also an embryonic world community. At least in theory all states are considered equal and, as such, exercise the same influence within the UN system. It has thus been argued that international organizations act as equalizers, moderating the excessive influence of the great powers and giving support to the weaker ones. This role of the United Nations as legitimizer and protector of the nation-state, however small, is strengthened by an enhanced and more vociferous nationalism. Notwithstanding claims that the nation-state is obsolete, the intense attachment to it, particularly in the Third World, and the willingness to fight to protect it against foreign intrusions, cannot be easily dismissed. The effective result is that territorial conquest or simply military invasion is now regarded as illegitimate and likely to be fiercely resisted.

In a world in which military force is therefore no longer as usable as it was in the past, in which domestically and internationally public opinion is mobilized and employed as a restraining influence on the behaviour of great powers, and finally where the nation-state has become in some sense sacrosanct, the small, weak state is in effect transformed. In Klaus Knorr's words 'as resort to military force has become hemmed in by a number of restrictions and discouraged by a variety of costs, including the risk of mutual destruction on a monstrous scale,' other bases of international influence are given greater relative importance.[9] Some of these other sources of power, such as economic assistance and technological skills, are distributed as unevenly in the international system as military capability. But others are as available to the small as to the great power. To the extent that these latter sources are given prominence, small states can exercise considerable influence on their environment. This view is best illustrated by quoting from one of the most recent and influential textbooks in international politics. In concluding a chapter on 'Power as the Capacity to Act,' Donald Puchala wrote: 'With traditional styles of persuasion by coercion or threatened coercion substantially undermined in contemporary international politics, the older 'iron-steam-steel' pathway that led England, Germany, and other powers to political influence in past eras is becoming a dead-end. The mass armies and navies, the wielding of huge explosive might ... are no longer directly related to political influence. On the contrary, essential international political resources today are such factors as highly astute, highly competent, and highly sensitive and perceptive statesmanship; capacities for self-awareness, both physical and intellectual; and reputations for sincerity and world-mindedness rather than narrow-mindedness.'[10] If this analysis is accurate, that is, if 'mind rather than muscle is the key to contemporary international political influence,'[11] then clearly this view of small states as at least potentially great must receive our closest attention and perhaps our open endorsement.

A RADICAL MODEL

Both the security-politics model and its revised version focus on the sovereign nation-state as the principal unit of analysis. Whether small or large, weak or strong, developing or developed, a state is assumed to be ruled by a government which, on the basis of its own calculation of national interest, formulates and carries out domestic and foreign policy. Geographical location, the actual distribution of power in the international system, and the policies of other states may set limits on what any one given state can hope to accomplish. But the policies it adopts are a reflection of its own needs and goals, modified at some point in anticipation of the likely response of other actors. Whether a state is able to attain its objectives will depend ultimately on the resources available to that state and on the ability of its government to mobilize those resources and to translate them into influence. Though power is perceived as a relational concept, its primary source lies in the state itself and its peculiar properties.

Another model of international politics has been evolved by theorists starting from an entirely different perspective. The concern of these writers lies in explaining the slow rate of economic growth in the less developed countries, in providing a revisionist history of the Cold War and an adequate explanation of the basic roots of American foreign policy, and in developing the theory of monopoly capitalism to reflect more accurately contemporary reality. In contrast to the image of international politics as involving a green baize table on which billiard balls of differing sizes career against each other, they view the world as a single system, divided into two groups or blocs of states but tied together at the same time by a complex network of capital movements, technological transfers, trade flows, human migrations, and value transplants.

Hierarchically organized, this system is composed of a few countries at the top, which are variously referred to as the rich, the developed, the West, the North, the metropolis, and the centre, and the mass of proletarian nations at the bottom, described often as the poor, the underdeveloped, the South, the periphery, or the satellite.[12] The system or network of flows in money, skills, goods, people, and ideas is structured in such a way that the poor nations have little choice of the direction and impact of their contacts with the international environment. The logical consequence of what Gunnar Myrdal describes as the 'enforced bilateralism' inherited from the colonial period, the external relations of the Third World are to a large extent limited to the linkages established with their former metropolitan powers, altered in part since independence with complementary links to other parts of the industrialized West. While it is true that Third World nations are increasingly aware of their common interests and thus frequently meet and, to a certain degree, even trade and communicate with one another these relations are insignificant by comparison to their well-established ties with the West. Links through communications and transportation, trade and aid, technology and values, all tend to flow in a vertical direction, from bottom to top, or vice-versa. The structure of the system is thus feudal in character: the few rich countries at the centre maintain a wide range of ties with each other and with the many poor countries along the periphery, while the latter are relatively isolated, cut off from each other, and dependent on the centre for a window on the world.

This system is characterized not only by the direction and form of its established relations but also by the unequal impact of these relations on the two blocs of countries in the system; in short, movements in goods, money, people, and ideas do not benefit equally the various parts of the system. Those at the top of the structure profit at the expense of those at the bottom. For example, a system which involves the exchange of primary products for manufactured goods is essentially unequal. As exporters of minerals and agricultural commodities, the demand for which fluctuates wildly and has grown only gradually, and importers of manufactured and capital goods, the prices of which have risen rapidly, the countries of the Third World face a growing trade gap. A tariff structure in the Western countries which increases the barriers to be scaled in proportion with the degree to which a good is processed, an aid program which ties the granting of any assistance to the purchase of the donor's goods, the ability of the multinational corporation to administer prices of imports and exports to suit its over-all, global needs – these features of the international trading system all weigh heavily against the less developed countries. Even though the advanced industrialized countries of the West (except the US) have now put into effect a general preferential tariff scheme, agreed upon in principle at New Delhi in 1968, the end result has not altered the previous situation by which the surplus value generated by low wages paid in the periphery was transferred from the less developed countries to the rich nations. As long as the latter retain control over technology, research, and the most advanced industrialized processes, the present vertical division of labour will not disappear but will shift upwards along the processing ladder.

Similarly, it is argued, the movement of capital, particularly in its most modern embodiment as the multinational corporation, influences adversely the poor countries of the Third World. While initially the investment by a foreign corporation in a developing country may have a positive influence on the latter's balance of payments, in the long run that same investment will actually siphon off surplus value through accumulated payment of royalties, dividends, and fees for technical and management contracts, as well as for patents and trade marks. In addition to its negative impact on a country's balance of payments, it is argued, foreign investment distorts and stunts the growth of the local economy, discourages exports and increases imports, often employs capital intensive technologies in countries faced with serious unemployment, prevents the development of a local research and development capacity, and, finally, creates false needs through advertising that can only be satisfied by the enterprise's own products, establishing a style of living which becomes a source of envy and imitation, with all the obvious consequences for the local culture and way of life.

Foreign investors and multinational corporations do not operate in a vacuum. They are openly assisted by their home countries. The home country, for instance, guarantees the initial investment against all political risks; it encourages host governments through the promise of aid to create a favourable climate for foreign investment; and it threatens (as indeed by law the United States government is compelled) to cut off aid when a recipient country nationalizes foreign investment without adequate and prompt compensation. Thus, through their assistance programs, the industrialized countries cooperate closely with private economic interests and facilitate their penetration of the Third World. Without such aid the system of international capitalist economic relations could not survive.[13]

Intergovernmental aid agencies also act as instruments of Western domination and control. In contrast with the expectation of the power theorists that international organizations serve as protectors of the small state and its interests, the radical school contends that such institutions as the World Bank, the International Monetary Fund, the Inter-American Development Bank, and the European Development Fund, are controlled by and used in the service of the rich, developed countries. As the major contributors to the budgets of these institutions, and by means of their voting strength, the industrialized countries are able to impose their interests and their values on these organizations and on their operations in the Third World. This 'control by rich countries of action directed to poor countries' has been defined in a recent study of influence patterns in international organizations as 'collective colonialism.' These organizations have assumed 'some of the burdens formerly carried by the colonial administrations ... They have spread the financial burden more widely, altered the symbolism of colonial rule by making the administration of these services consistent with accession to formal sovereignty by the recipient country, and even eased the transition for some individuals from the old to the new colonialism by providing many jobs for former colonial administrators.'[14] International organizations apparently do not reduce the difference in power between great and small nations; instead they are manipulated by the rich to serve their interests in maintaining a system of domination.

The migration of people and the exchange of ideas and values are closely interrelated. Taken together they too reflect the exploitative nature of the present system of relations between the Third World and the West. It is the foreign adviser in a Third World country or the local national returning from a tour of study abroad who imports new ideas and new standards. Through technical assistance, scholarship programs, and other mechanisms the Third World is introduced to a wide range of consumer products, to the high standard of living to which most Westerners are accustomed, to techniques and approaches appropriate to a developed economy, in short, to a distinctive way of life which often clashes sharply with existing local conditions.

The consequences of these movements for Third World countries are extremely harmful. On one hand, there are the many citizens of developing countries who, having travelled abroad to acquire a technical or professional education, having thus tasted the 'finer' things in life or grown accustomed to work with certain levels of technology, then find it impossible to return home.

In admitting them as immigrants, however, the West drains off the most highly skilled and most badly needed personnel from the Third World and effectively undermines the intended purpose of its training programs. On the other hand, those who do return find that their new ways and expectations conflict with indigenous practices and values. They soon discover that they often have more in common with the managers of foreign corporations and foreign banks than they do with their old friends and former communities. The new élite thus loses the local basis for its identity and imitates foreign ways at great cost to itself and to the nation. Even after independence, as Frantz Fanon so clearly saw, the national bourgeoisie will act as a 'transmission line between the nation and a capitalism ... which today puts on the masque of neo-colonialism.' It will identify 'itself with the Western bourgeoisie, from whom it has learned its lesson'; it 'will have nothing better to do than to take on the role of manager for Western enterprise, and it will in practice set up its country as the brothel of Europe.'[15]

The focus of this model is therefore on a system of relations which is characterized by a vast inequality of wealth and power between its various parts, by a division of labour which perpetuates and strengthens that inequality, and by a structure which isolates Third World countries from each other and ties them firmly to capitalist centres in the North. Indeed, it is often emphasized that the poor countries of the South are not just weak, underdeveloped, and, in some cases, small. In a very real sense, they are not sovereign entities at all, but merely satellites or appendages of the capitalist centres of North America and Western Europe. The formal granting of political independence was but an illusion. It has not resulted in the transfer of power from the metropolis to a new indigenous leadership committed to locally determined goals with sufficient internal resources to carry them out.

Even long after independence, foreigners continue to play an important role in the determination of the new state's goals, either through direct participation in the decision-making process (a 'penetrated system' in James Rosenau's words) or, indirectly, through the indigenous élite (the lumpenbourgeoisie or the comprador class) which serves as a bridgehead for external interests. In either case, the new states often lack the means with which to implement their objectives and policies. Faced with a military threat, for instance, they are forced to rely on their own inadequate forces, the general protection offered by international organizations, or, as is often the case, on a security alliance with a Western power. Economically, these same states depend for most of their foreign exchange on the sale of a single or several primary commodities to Western markets, the receipt of capital for investment in development programs or simply to cover the recurring costs of the administrative budget, food aid to tide them over a prolonged period of drought, and technical assistance to organize and manage government, run private businesses, and staff schools and institutions. Concerned with their own political survival, the local élites come to lean more on external than on internal support and resources. Thus, it is not simply that along with all other states the Third World state has lost its outer hard shell, what John Herz has called its 'impermeability'; the shell simply does not exist except in theory. The gates or barriers that traditionally control or regulate the role of international actors and the influence of external interests in domestic affairs are wide open.

The small, underdeveloped state of the Third World is thus powerless. This conclusion derives not only from the fact that the developed, industrialized countries of the West possess many more of the ingredients or instruments of power than the Third World states, whether taken individually or collectively. Even in that limited sense, the power balance is heavily weighted in the former's favour. But the powerlessness of the Third World state stems also from the nature of the system of relations within which it operates. The radical model underlines the obvious reality that power arises not only from 'something found inside' a country but that it is also 'built into the structure in which two countries are placed.'[16]

The original contribution of the radical model is that it points to not just any system as a source of power or as a restraint on a state's freedom, but to the economic system, one in which the principal actors are often nongovernmental and the linkages thus transnational (rather than international). The new states of Africa and Asia achieved formal political independence after the Second World War but remained tied to an economic system of established trade and capital patterns which both exploited them and left them with no effective short-term alternative to their present status. Although military means have declined in importance as an instrument of state power, the metropolitan powers were able to retain effective control over their former colonies through the subtle manipulation of this economic system – a process referred to by Kwame Nkrumah and other Third World leaders as neocolonialism. In this new process private actors (businesses with investment interests in the Third World, banks, insurance companies, import-export firms, foundations) work in partnership with their governments. In the short run, the interests of these private groups and their governments may conflict, but it is often felt that in the long run their goals tend to complement each other. The 'invisible blockade' imposed by private corporate and banking interests together with the US government against a recalcitrant Allende régime illustrates this point in a most telling fashion.

Dependent upon either a single capitalist state or a group of them (such as the EEC, the World Bank complex, or the numerous consortia set up to coordinate all forms of aid extended to a particular recipient nation), the Third World has effectively no choice. The system, which ties a developing country tightly and inseparably to a specific set of relations, thus acts as a constraint on that country. It is as a severe limitation on the choice of alternative courses of action that the system constitutes a source of (negative) power.

CONCLUSION: TOWARDS A NEW PERSPECTIVE

Both these models are firmly rooted in the reality of everyday experience. On one hand, the success of the oil-producing countries in securing higher royalties from the international oil companies and effective participation in their operations clearly indicates that not all Third World countries are helpless in the face of the seemingly all-powerful multinational corporations. The recent recognition of the Palestinian Liberation Organization, not unrelated to the rising star of the Arab countries, suggests that this economic strength can also be translated into diplomatic and political credit. Equally impressive, on the other hand, is the unmistakeable dependence of many Francophone states in Middle Africa for their very survival on the economic, military, and political support of France. The overwhelming influence of French citizens, French corporations, and the French government on the affairs and life of most of Francophone Africa is easily discerned by even the most casual observer.

But these two illustrations also underline an obvious weakness in both models. The Third World (or for that matter the notion of the small state) embraces a wide diversity of states, with varying capacities, based on different levels of economic growth, different political capabilities and ideologies, and unequal resource bases. Thus to speak of all Third World countries as either powerful or powerless is not particularly useful. Some are obviously more influential than others – a difference that results from distinctive qualities adhering to separate sets of states. In this regard it has become common to refer to a Fourth World which consists of those twenty-five countries that the third UNCTAD conference in Santiago designated as the least of the less developed countries (LLDCs). Located primarily in Africa, and in some instances now faced with a catastrophic drought, these countries are dependent upon the good will and other more worldly motives of external powers. They are indeed the proletarian or underprivileged nations of the world. In sharp contrast with the LLDCs are the oil-producing countries of the Middle East, Africa, and Latin America, which have coordinated their policies and demands and thus achieved a more favourable return from their natural resources as well as a measure of influence in world politics. In between fall a number of semi-industrialized states, such as Argentina, Brazil, Turkey, and Israel, which have benefitted from a relatively high rate of economic growth and succeeded in exporting semiprocessed and manufactured goods. Finally, the vast majority of the Third World has improved its standard of living but remains closely tied to the West. What influence these countries wield is more usually in regional affairs than on the world stage.

In the same way that it is useful to clarify the concept of the Third World (or the notion of the small state), it is also helpful to consider the Third World, both as a whole and in its various parts, not as all-powerful or as totally power-less but as in some sense embracing elements of both. Returning to the two illustrations cited above we can easily see that there are limits to the influence of the oil-producing countries as well as opportunities for the LLDCs to exer-cise influence. The OPEC nations have discovered that control of oil is a blunt weapon that can harm some of their interests (for instance, in maintaining the friendship of non-oil-producing countries in the Third World or in keeping the world economy on an even keel) as well as promote others. And while these countries have secured larger returns from the exploitation of their own re-sources, they are still forced to share a large proportion of profits from the over-all process with the oil companies. The companies' control over the differ-ent stages of processing, transporting, and distributing the crude oil leaves them with a significant part of the profits.[17] By contrast, the LLDCs are not left entirely helpless. They too can acquire some influence if only through com-bining with other Third World countries at UNCTAD, benefitting from Nigeria's strong leadership of the Associated and Associable states in recent negotia-tions with the EEC, or from the 'collective legitimization' that the UN General Assembly accords to such notions as decolonization, the right of all states to a reasonable level of development, and the principle of full permanent sovereign-ty of every state over its natural resources and economic activities.[18]

In short, both models contain elements necessary for a complete under-standing of the Third World, but neither one alone is sufficient. On one hand, the modified power-politics model points to the strengths and opportunities available to small states. On the other, the radical paradigm underscores the weaknesses of Third World countries and the real limits or restraints on their manoeuverability that result from the international system in which they operate. Each thus complements the other and acts as an antedote to the blind spot in the other's vision. What emerges then from this study is the need to construct an alternative perspective that transcends the limitations of each of these models and yet capitalizes on the dynamic insights of both. Although it is clearly beyond the scope of this paper to investigate the creation of an entirely new model, it would be useful to outline some of the essential ingre-dients of such a perspective, the fundamental aspect of which will be the bar-gaining capabilities of Third World countries.

The indispensable working unit in international relations will remain for some time the nation-state. Even radical writers ascribe an autonomous reality to the poor nations, though that autonomy is severely circumscribed. This does not of course mean that people cannot simultaneously possess multiple loyalties – to their ethnic group, their class, their region, their nation-state, and even to the Third World. Nor does it argue that individual Third World countries will not find it useful, indeed necessary, to coordinate their actions with other states on a functional and/or regional basis. It simply refers to the obvious reality of the state – however small, however poor. It is, however, necessary to take into account the diversity of the states within the Third World. The ability of any given state to bargain and its choice of strategy will obviously depend on its particular assets – whether it is semi-industrialized, the owner of a key resource, strategically located on the geopolitical map, and so on.

As in traditional international relations theory, the state thus remains the principal actor in this perspective. But one can no longer pretend that it is a monolithic unit or that it is the sole actor of any political importance. On one hand, the representatives of the state, the government, are often divided; different ministers or departments may adopt substantially different positions on a question under debate. Interstate bargaining may thus involve a coalition of forces that crosses national frontiers, with governmental agencies in a developed country, for instance, linking up with the developing countries against other branches of its own government. On the other hand, it is impossible to dismiss the importance of nongovernmental actors (private financial interests, the multinational corporation) that participate directly in, or seriously affect, national and international political processes. The bargaining process is further complicated because the interests of these private groups in the developed as well as in the developing countries do not always coincide but may even conflict with the interests of their own government.

At the same time the Third World country must operate within a system or series of systems (political, economic, diplomatic, and military) which sets limits to what it can hope to attain. Its influence is not boundless but restricted by the needs, aspirations, and capabilities of other states – both within and outside the Third World – and by a system the characteristics of which have been determined in the past and are likely to change only very slowly in the future.

In order to attain their over-all objective of maximizing economic and political benefits in their relations with the external world, the Third World countries must choose among three broad options or strategies. The selection of one of these will vary from state to state depending on its level of development, its available resources, its strategic location, and its internal political régime. At one extreme a country may choose to assert national control over all its resources and economic activities, reorient its trade towards the socialist bloc, refuse all aid (at least from the capitalist states) – in short, to cut its ties with the international capitalist system in which it is presently entrapped. This is the option of self-reliance; internally, it involves the creation of a socialist pattern of production and distribution; externally, a reduction in dependence on external aid, trade, and financial relations with the West. Often, however, dependence on the West is simply replaced with another form of dependence on the socialist bloc. Thus while relations within a country are reorganized, those with the outside world are not substantially altered.

At the other extreme a developing country may decide to ally itself closely with a capitalist country or group of countries (as the eighteen Associated States have done with the European Community). As loyal ally, the developing state may expect to attain an assured and even a preferential access to the markets of the rich countries; to secure maximum allocations of aid; to receive diplomatic support for its international objectives; and, finally, to obtain military protection against domestic and foreign enemies. The LLDCs may in fact have little choice but to accept this strategy, while others may select it as the most likely to assist them in the pursuit of their developmental aims.

In between these two extremes of isolation from the West and total dependence there exists a range of alternative solutions. Underlying all of these is the belief that although Third World countries cannot expect to attain the unfettered freedom of the first model they need not accept the passivity to which the second model condemns them (when the hope of revolution is abandoned). Once aware of their present predicament and of the need to alter it, and confident about their chances of success, developing countries will seek to renegotiate old arrangements and establish new and more favourable ones. Any agreements these countries may enter into with the developed world (states, enterprises, etc.) are not unalterably fixed beforehand but are subject to negotiation. In effect, there exists a bargaining space within which a settlement can be reached. Where exactly equilibrium will be established – or, in other words, the extent of the gains likely to be extracted from the West – depends ultimately on a number of factors. These include the kind of Third World country engaged in the bargaining process, the assets it can bring to that process, its ability to coordinate its demands and policies with those of other regional or functionally related states in the Third World, the quality of information it can acquire about the operation of the international system, and the needs, expectations, and assets of its opponent(s), and, finally, the success with which it can promote or profit from discord within the West, or between the East and the West.

If the average Third World country in its relations with the West is faced with some space in which to bargain, that is, if it does have the luxury of choice, it would be useful to illustrate this in its relations with both the multinational corporation and the developed states. In need of additional capital, technology, and management skills to supplement its own internal resources, a developing nation is not restricted either to accepting a foreign investor on his own terms or to receiving no capital, technology, or skills at all. Alternatives such as management contracts, loans on the capital markets of Europe and North America or from donor countries, technical and marketing agreements, and joint ventures are available and have been resorted to on an increasingly large scale as a substitute for direct foreign investment. Confronted by an existing corporation which actively resists any change in its operating policies, the Third World country can nationalize or expropriate the corporation's holdings or threaten to do so in an attempt to induce the enterprise either to sell or to renegotiate its concession. Admittedly, in the short run this may involve certain power costs to the Third World country. The resulting uncertainty for potential investors or creditors may make it very difficult for it to attract new investment or to obtain new loans. In the long run, however, this uncertainty should be replaced with the recognition that the Third World is not an object to be played with and exploited at will, but a *cooperative adversary* prepared to negotiate an arrangement of mutual benefit to both sides. The Third World does need capital, technology, and management skills, but foreign investors continue to require ready access to markets, new sources of raw materials and semiprocessed goods, and an adequate rate of return on their investment. The Third World therefore does not come to the bargaining table with an empty hand, but with cards whose quality will vary considerably depending on the player at the table and the skill with which he plays. If this hand is played well, the Third World country should be able to extract additional benefits from foreign investors.

Similarly, in their relations with the developed states, on both a bilateral and multilateral basis, Third World nations need not accept their present position without a struggle. At the 1974 UN Special Assembly Session on Raw Materials and Development the member states approved a Declaration on the Establishment of a New International Economic Order and a Programme of Action by means of which to carry it out. Though this action represents only a symbolic victory at present, it does draw attention to the disparities of income distribution in the world, indicates the kinds of change necessary to remove this inequity and to formulate new international norms of behaviour, which the great powers can ignore but not without some cost. Of course, simple appeals to the better nature of the Western world are not likely to produce change on a significant scale. The Third World can no longer rely solely on such large and heterogeneous organizations as the Conference of Nonaligned States, the United Nations, and UNCTAD. Developing countries must organize on functional lines (according to different commodities or different issues) or on a regional basis (such as the Andean Group have) so as best to exploit those assets they have in common in negotiation with the rich countries.

And what are some of these assets? What is it that gives certain countries a 'good hand'? What are their sources of power? Some states, for example, are still considered important for strategic purposes by both the United States and the Soviet Union. Thus the US may be willing to pay something either to obtain naval bases, overflight privileges, satellite tracking stations, and the like, or to exclude the Soviets from the same advantages. Similarly, the West may be prepared to support a friendly régime on the brink of collapse with financial aid, military assistance, or an agreement to reschedule debt repayments. Cold War tensions may have lessened but the essential conflict has not yet given way to a real détente. In addition to benefits derived from exploiting the Cold War conflict, the developing countries are likely to be wooed by Western nations for their support at future international conferences dealing with such matters as pollution, population, narcotics, and the international monetary system. To the extent that they can coordinate their stance before such conferences and that the Western states are divided, the Third World states should be able to secure definite gains from the West.

But perhaps most important of all, the Third World controls a large share of certain key raw materials without which the developed Western world would have difficulty in maintaining its present standard of living. The OPEC nations have shown how concerted action by the producers of a single commodity can increase their revenues and, by the threat of withholding an urgently needed resource, extract other concessions not directly related to the particular resource and its price. Already a number of other producers (in bauxite, copper, coffee, tin, etc.) are attempting to duplicate this success. Whether these raw-material producers will attain the spectacular results of OPEC depends ultimately on several factors, including the ready availability of substitutes, the ease or difficulty of obtaining the cooperation of all or most producers, the vulnerability of these producers to retaliatory action by the principal consuming nations, and the strategic importance of the product in question. Given improved knowledge of market conditions and the political will to cooperate, some of these producer groups should be able to extract increased economic benefits. Even if the gains achieved are relatively small by comparison to those of the oil producers, the positive effects for these other producers may still be extremely significant.

It is of course very easy to exaggerate the potential influence of Third World countries and their ability to alter the biased international economic order. It is therefore important to keep in mind the limits on their influence that the great powers and the international system together exert. It is just as possible, however, to err on the other side and to adopt a deep-rooted pessimism that condemns the Third World to the passive resignation to its present fate. In observing the Third World, it is quite impossible to ignore the new mood expressed by leaders of developing countries at the UN Special Assembly on Raw Materials and Development, the most recent conference of Non-aligned States at Algiers, and the various world conferences on food, population, and the environment. This mood combines a growing awareness of the worldwide inequities, a total disillusionment and frustration with the West and its past efforts to help the Third World, and a confident expectation (warranted by OPEC's successes)[19] that through individual and concerted action by developing countries this situation can be changed. If these efforts fail to achieve their purpose, poor nations may, as Robert Heilbroner suggests, be driven to such despair that they are prepared to resort to nuclear blackmail in order 'to remedy their condition.'[20] But whatever the most likely scenario, we can assume with assurance that the old period of acceptance, of belief in a global harmony of interests, of widespread hope that international organizations, the law of comparative advantage, and the good will of the developed world will somehow introduce the Third World to prosperity and progress – this period of so-called *partnership* – has come to an end and in its place is emerging a new era of *confrontation.*[21]

NOTES

I am grateful to my colleague G.K. Helleiner for his critical comments on an earlier draft of this article.

1 *A Troubled Partnership* (New York 1965), 18
2 For such an argument, see Elizabeth Farnsworth, 'Chile: What was the U.S. Role?' *Foreign Policy* (Fall 1974).
3 The first model (the revised power-politics model) focuses generally on small states rather than specifically on Third World nations, which are here defined as the developing countries of Africa, Asia, and Latin America. But since most authors writing in this context refer to small states as a residual category which includes all states other than the great powers, a category which embraces almost all Third World countries, there should be no problem in contrasting the two models as they apply to the underdeveloped states of the Third World.
4 See Hans Morgenthau, *Politics Among Nations* (New York 3rd ed. 1962), 295. In his study of small states in international relations, *The Inequality of States* (Oxford 1967), David Vital has adopted a similar position.
5 In this regard Arnold Wolfers has written: 'The mere belief on the part of one great power that it would suffer a serious loss if a weak country with which it was dealing shifted either from one camp to the other or from alignment to neutrality gives the weak country a far from negligible coercive asset, sometimes called the power of blackmail.' *Discord and Collaboration* (Baltimore 1962), 112. See also Robert Keohane, 'The Big Influence of Small Allies,' *Foreign Policy* (Spring 1971).
6 Among the many authors one could list, the following are the most prominent and most frequently cited: James Eayrs, *Fate and Will in Foreign Policy* (Toronto 1967); Stanley Hoffman, *The State of War* (New York 1965) and *Gulliver's Troubles* (New York 1968); Henry Kissinger, *The Troubled Partnership*; Klaus Knorr, *On the Uses of Military Power*

in the Nuclear Age (Princeton 1966); and Donald Puchala, *International Politics Today* (New York 1971).

7   See Eayrs, *Fate and Will*, 71 and Puchala, *International Politics Today*, 193

8   Eayrs, *Fate and Will*, 76

9   *On the Uses of Military Power*, 171

10 *International Politics Today*, 196. See also Eayrs, *Fate and Will*, 86.

11 Ibid.

12 In this world system it is not always clear where the socialist states fit and how they influence relations between the poor and the rich nations. Most authors in this perspective tend to treat the socialist world as a residual category. See, for example, Robin Jenkins, *Exploitation* (London 1971), 208-9.

13 See Theotonio Dos Santos, 'The Contradictions of Contemporary Imperialism,' *Social Praxis*, I, no. 3, 230-1.

14 Robert Cox and Harold Jacobson, eds, *The Anatomy of Influence: Decision Making in International Organization* (New Haven 1973), 424

15 'The Pitfalls of National Consciousness – Africa,' in R.I. Rhodes, ed., *Imperialism and Underdevelopment* (New York 1970), 305, 306

16 Johan Galtung, *The European Community: A Superpower in the Making* (London 1972), 38. It is not quite accurate, however, as Galtung suggests it is, that liberal-power theorists exclude the system and its structure as a source of power, though it is true that they deal with it inadequately. Particular reference might be made to Robert Rothstein's work, *Alliances and Small States* (New York 1968), in which he has described the impact of different systems on the security and independence of small states. It is in the existing system, one in which 'Great Power relationships have neither sunk to war nor risen to peaceful cooperation,' that small powers can exercise considerable influence. But such manoeuverability is impossible, he argues, 'in conditions of Great Power war,' 'substantive cooperation,' or 'in a balance of power system' (246-7).

17 One report compared Saudia Arabia's revenues from oil in 1974 (estimated at $17 billion) with Exxon's earnings for the first half of the same year ($21.3 billion). Slightly more favourably for the oil companies, the same report noted an OECD study that had broken down 'the mid-1974 composite selling price of oil products in Europe of $24 per barrel' and which showed that two-fifths accrued to the producing countries, one-quarter to the companies for costs and profits, and about one-third to the consuming nations in the form of taxes. See J. Stork, 'Oil and the International Crises,' *Merip Reports*, no. 32 (November 1974), 14.

18 The term 'collective legitimization' was first coined and explored by Inis Claude in an article in *International Organization*, which was later reproduced as a chapter in his *The Changing United Nations* (New York 1967), chapter 4.

19 Many of the non-oil-producing countries in the Third World took vicarious pleasure from OPEC's success even though it meant increased prices for their own oil and oil-based imports. See, for example, the speech made by Julius Nyerere on New Year's Day, 1974, to the diplomatic corps in Dar es Salaam.

20 *An Inquiry into the Human Prospect* (New York 1974), 43

21 For a similar assessment of the Third World mood, see G.K. Helleiner, 'Standing up to the World: The New Mood in the Less Developed Countries,' *Development Dialogue*, no. 2 (1974).

C.B. Macpherson

Liberalism and the political theory of property

Property has always been a central concern of political theory, and of none more so than liberal theory. And nothing has given more trouble in liberal-democratic theory than the liberal property right. I shall suggest that the trouble it has given, both to liberal-democrats and to most of their critics (at least those critics who want to retain the ethical values of liberalism), is due to all of them having stayed within a historically understandable but unnecessarily narrow concept of property. I shall argue that a change in the prevailing concept of property would help to get liberal theory out of its main difficulties; that the change which I shall suggest is legitimate; and that it leaves a theory which can still properly be called liberal. I shall be speaking mainly of post-Millian liberalism, the liberalism of the twentieth century: to emphasize this I shall generally call its theory 'liberal-democratic theory' (which I take to have started with J.S. Mill and T.H. Green).

The central problem of liberal-democratic theory may be stated as the difficulty of reconciling the liberal property right with that equal effective right of all individuals to use and develop their capacities which is the essential ethical principle of liberal democracy. The difficulty is great. For when the liberal property right is written into law as an individual right to the exclusive use and disposal of parcels of the resources provided by nature and of parcels of the capital created by past work on them, and when it is combined with the liberal system of market incentives and rights of free contract, it leads to and supports a concentration of ownership and a system of power relations between individuals and classes which negates the ethical goal of free and independent individual development. There thus appears to be an insoluble difficulty within the liberal-democratic theory. If, as liberal theory asserts, an individual property right is required by the very necessities of man's nature and condition, it ought not to be infringed or denied. But unless it is seriously infringed or denied, it leads to an effective denial of the equal possibility of individual human fulfilment.

The difficulty was inherent in the liberal theory at least as soon as it had any concern about equality. One way out was proposed by Rousseau, who argued that the property right that is required to permit the realization of the human essence is not the right of unlimited individual appropriation, but a limited right to as much as a man needs to work on. The essentially human property right, being thus limited, would not contradict the equal right: everyone could have it. But Rousseau's (and Jefferson's) way out was no way out. For the market society, to operate by free contract, required a right of individual appropriation in amounts beyond that limit. And by the nineteenth century the possibility of a society consisting entirely of worker-owners could no longer be seriously entertained. A proletariat existed, as Mill and Green saw.

It was the fact that it did exist, and that its condition of life was a denial of humanity, that made sensitive liberals, beginning with Mill and Green, seek some other way out. They did not find one, nor could they have done so from their postulates. For they assumed the need for an unlimited exclusive individual property right, and equated it with the property right which is essential to the very nature and condition of man. So they were back with the basic contradiction.

Liberal-democratic theory has not yet found a way out of this difficulty. I have argued elsewhere[1] that the difficulty could be traced to the deep-rootedness of what I called the possessive individualism of the liberal theory, a set of assumptions about man and society which proved incompatible with democratic aspirations but which could not be given up as long as society was to rely on market incentives and institutions. Alternatively, I have suggested[2] that the difficulty could be stated as an incompatibility between two concepts of the human essence both of which are present within liberal-democratic theory – a concept of man as consumer, desirer, maximizer of utilities, and a concept of man as doer, as exerter and developer of his uniquely human attributes. I do not wish to retract or abandon either of these analyses, but I want now to propose a theoretically simpler statement of the central difficulty, which may point the way to a simpler resolution of it.

The difficulty, I suggest, is not that a liberal-democratic society, in order to have any prospect of achieving its ethical goals, must infringe and thus narrow an individual property right which is derived from the very nature of man. On the contrary, the difficulty is that the individual property right which liberal theory has inferred from the nature of man is already too narrow. What is needed is to broaden it. When this is seen, the old difficulty disappears. I shall argue that we have all been misled by accepting an unnecessarily narrow concept of property, a concept within which it is impossible to resolve the difficulties of any liberal theory. We have treated as the very paradigm of property what is really only a special case. It is time for a new paradigm, within which we may hope to resolve difficulties that could not be resolved within the old.

I shall suggest that property, although it must always be an individual right, need not be confined, as liberal theory has confined it, to a right to exclude others from the use or benefit of something, but may equally be an individual right not to be excluded by others from the use or benefit of something. When property is so understood, the problem of liberal-democratic theory is no longer a problem of putting limits on the property right, but of supplementing the individual right to exclude others by the individual right not to be excluded by others. The latter right may be held to be the one that is most required by the liberal-democratic ethic, and most implied in a liberal concept of the human essence. The right not to be excluded by others may provisionally be stated as the individual right to equal access to the means of labour and the means of life.

Let me argue first that there is no logical difficulty about broadening the concept.

The concept of property, like all concepts, has been shaped by theorists. Political concepts are generally shaped by theorists who are not simply grammarians or logicians but who are seeking to justify something. The most solid basis on which to justify an institution or a right is to derive it from the supposed essential nature and needs of man – to show that man, to be fully human, requires that institution or that right. The theorists who have shaped the concept of property have generally done this. And, no matter how much they might insist that man was a social animal, in the end they had to come down to the individual human being. So, the concept of property had to be based on the individual: property could only be seen as a right of an individual, a right derivable from his human essence, a right to some use or benefit of something without the use or benefit of which he could not be fully human. The very idea of property, therefore, is the idea of an individual right.

A second general proposition, which would scarcely have to be stated here were it not for the fact that current common usage appears to contradict it, is that property is a right, not a thing. It is an enforceable claim to some use or benefit of something (and sometimes, but not always, to its disposal): it is not the thing itself.

The source, and the transience, of the opposite current usage deserve some notice here. Ordinarily today we refer to a house, a plot of land, a shop, as a piece of property. We advertise in the newspapers 'properties for sale' and 'properties to let.' What the advertisement describes as being for sale or for rent is the building and the land it stands on. In fact what is offered, and what constitutes the property, is the legal title, the enforceable right, to or in the tangible thing. This is more obvious in the case of a lease, where the right is to the use of the thing for a limited period and on certain conditions, than in the case of an outright sale, but in both cases what is transferred is an enforceable claim. Yet we still speak of property as the thing itself. How did this current usage originate, and how long is it likely to last? If we look back over a few centuries we can see that the usage changed as (but some time after) the reality changed, and that the reality is changing again so that we may expect the usage to come full circle.

Down to the seventeenth century in England, and later in Europe, it was well understood that property was a right in something. Indeed, in the seventeenth century, the word property was often used as a matter of course in a sense that seems to us extraordinarily wide: men were said to have a property not only in land and goods and in claims on revenue from leases, mortgages, patents, monopolies, and so on, but also a property in their lives and liberties. It would take us too far afield to try to trace the source of that very wide use of the term, but clearly that wide sense is only intelligible while property per se is taken to be a right not a thing.

And there were good reasons then for treating property as the right not the thing. In the first place, the great bulk of property was then property in land, and a man's property in a piece of land was generally limited to certain uses of it and was often not freely disposable. Different people might have different rights in the same piece of land, and by law or manorial custom many of those rights were not fully disposable by the current owner of them either by sale or bequest. The property he had was obviously the right in the land, not the land itself. And in the second place, another substantial segment of property consisted of those rights to a revenue which were provided by such things as corporate charters, monopolies granted by the state, tax-farming rights, and the incumbency of various political and ecclesiastical offices. Clearly here too the property was the right, not any specific material thing.

The change in common usage, to treating property as the things themselves, came with the spread of the full market economy from the seventeenth century on, and the replacement of the old limited rights in land and other valuable things by virtually unlimited rights. As rights in land became more absolute, and parcels of land became more freely marketable commodities, it became natural to think of the land itself as the property. And as aggregations of commercial and industrial capital, operating in increasingly free markets and themselves freely marketable, overtook in bulk the older kinds of moveable wealth based on charters and monopolies, the capital itself, whether in money or in the form of actual plant, could easily be thought of as the property. The more freely and pervasively the market operated, the more this was so. It appeared to be the things themselves, not just rights in them, that were exchanged in the market. In fact the difference was not that things rather than rights in things were exchanged, but that previously unsaleable rights in things were now saleable; or, to put it differently, that limited and not always saleable rights *in* things were being replaced by virtually unlimited and saleable rights *to* things.

As property became increasingly saleable absolute rights to things, the distinction between the right and the thing was easily blurred. It was the more easily blurred because, with these changes, the state became more and more an engine for guaranteeing the full right of the individual to the disposal as well as use of things. The state's protection of the right could be so much taken for granted that one did not have to look behind the thing to the right. The thing itself became, in common parlance, the property.

This usage, as we have seen, is still with us today. But meanwhile, from about the beginning of the twentieth century the preponderant nature of property has been changing again, and property is again beginning to be seen as a right to something: now, more often than not, a right to a revenue rather than a right to a specific material thing.

The twentieth-century change is twofold. First, the rise of the corporation as the dominant form of business enterprise has meant that the dominant form of property is the expectation of revenue. The market value of a modern corporation consists not of its plant and stocks of materials but of its presumed ability to produce a revenue for itself and its shareholders by its organization of skills and its manipulation of the market. Its value as a property is its ability to produce a revenue. The property its shareholders have is the right to a revenue from that ability.

Secondly, even in the countries most devoted to the idea of free enterprise and the free market, a sharply increasing proportion of the individual's and the corporation's rights to any revenue at all depends on their relation to the government. When the right to practise a trade or profession depends on state-authorized licensing bodies and on judicial interpretations of their powers; when the right to engage in various kinds of enterprise depends on legislative enactments and administrative and judicial rulings; when the right to a pension or social security payments and the like depends on similar rulings; and when the earnings of a corporation depend more on the government contracts it can get, and on the legislation favourable to its own line and scale of business than on the free play of the market: then the idea of property as things becomes increasingly unrealistic.

Property for the most part becomes, and is increasingly seen to be, a right. It is the right to an income, not only from material assets and the use of one's energy, but also from one's skill (or one's ability to join others who have skill) in manoeuvring in the market and in establishing and maintaining an advantageous relation with government. We may conclude that, in spite of current common usage, property is likely once again to be seen to be a right, not a thing.

A third proposition may also be asserted. Inasmuch as the concept of property is the concept of an enforceable claim – an individual claim that will be enforced by society – property is the creation of society, that is in modern times, the creation of the state. Property is, as Bentham said, entirely the work of law.

These three propositions are, I think, all that can be asserted of property as such. Property is a right not a thing. It is an individual right. It is an enforceable claim created by the state.

What I would now point out is that none of these propositions, nor all of them together, require that property be an individual right to exclude others from the use or benefit of something. Property as an individual right not to be excluded from the use or benefit of something meets these stipulations equally well. Exclusiveness is not logically entailed in the concept of property as an individual right needed to enable men to realize their human essence as moral or rational beings: a right not to be excluded from something is as much an individual right as is the right to exclude others. Both kinds may be created by society or the state, and neither can be created otherwise. Both meet the essential requisites of property, in that both are enforceable claims of individuals to some use or benefit of something. An individual right not to be excluded from something held in common is as much an individual property as is the right to exclude.

How, then, did the idea that property is an exclusive right get so firmly embedded as it has done in the very concept of property? It goes back a long way, although it was not so firmly established in pre-liberal theory as it was from Locke on. From Plato to Bodin, theorists could talk about common property as well as private. Common property could be advocated as an ideal, could be attributed to the primitive condition of mankind, could be held to be suitable only to man before the Fall, or could be recognized as existing alongside private property in such forms as public parks, temples, markets, streets, and common lands. But most of the concern was about property as an individual exclusive right. Whether the theorist opposed it, as Plato did for his guardian class, or supported it, as Aristotle and the medieval theorists did within limits, it was property as *meum* and *tuum*, my right to exclude you, that they were mainly concerned with.

Why should these early theorists, who were familiar enough with common property not to think it a contradiction in terms, nevertheless generally have taken property to mean an exclusive right? When we recall that they were deriving property from human needs and the human condition it is not difficult to see a reason for their treating property as an exclusive right. Given their postulate about human inequality they needed to do so. Slaves and serfs they regarded as not fully human, not naturally capable of a fully moral or rational life. These lower ranks therefore did not need, and were not entitled to, a property right, exclusive or otherwise. But citizens, freemen, those above the level of slave or serf, those who were capable of a fully human life, did need a property right which would exclude those others. They had to have an exclusive right. And since they were the only ones who needed a property right at all, the property right as such was taken to be the exclusive right. Strictly, of course, the exclusion of the lower orders did not require that property be taken to be the right of each individual to exclude every other individual within as well as beyond the propertied upper orders. But it did require that property be a right to exclude, and this is very easily generalized into an individual right to exclude all others.

This derivation of an exclusive right from the nature of rational man obviously ceases to be valid when all men are asserted to be naturally equally capable of a fully human life. And this is the assertion made by liberal theory, from at least Locke on. How, then, could the liberal theorists still see property as only an exclusive right? They could, of course, assert intelligibly enough that each individual needed an exclusive right to a flow of consumable things which would enable him to live. But it had never been merely a property in consumable things that theorists of property had sought to justify by derivation from human needs. The theory of property had always been a theory of rights in land and capital.

Once the natural equal humanity of all men was asserted, the derivation, from human needs, of an exclusive right in land and capital required another postulate. The additional postulate was found by the first generation of liberal theorists, in the seventeenth century: it was the postulate that a man's labour is his own. On this postulate the labour justification of property was built, and it had the effect of reinforcing the concept of exclusiveness. The labour of a man's body, the work of his hands, was seen as peculiarly, exclusively, his. So the right to that with which he has mixed his labour is an exclusive right. This was the principle that Locke made central to the liberal concept of property.

The labour justification of individual property was carried down unquestioned in the liberal theory. Even Bentham, scorning natural rights and claiming to have replaced them by utility, rested the property right on labour. Security of enjoyment of the fruits of one's labour was the reason for property: without a property in the fruits and in the means of labour no one would have an incentive to labour, and utility could not be maximized. Mill and Green also held to the labour justification. 'The institution of property,' Mill wrote, 'when limited to its essential elements, consists in the recognition, in each person, of a right to the exclusive disposal of what he or she have produced by their own exertions, or received either by gift or by fair agreement, without force or fraud, from those who produced it. The foundation of the whole is the right of producers to what they themselves have produced.'[3] Similarly Green: 'The rationale of property, in short, requires that everyone who will conform to the positive condition of possessing it, viz. labour, and the negative condition, viz. respect for it as possessed by others, should, so far as social arrangements can make him so, be a possesser of property himself, and of such property as will at least enable him to develop a sense of responsibility, as distinct from mere property in the immediate necessaries of life.'[4] So the derivation of property in things from the property in one's labour stamped property as an exclusive right from the beginning of the liberal tradition.

Our question, how could liberal theorists regard property as only an exclusive right, is now answered: they did so by deducing property in things from the property in one's labour. In doing so, they created a new difficulty. For the derivation of the property right from labour was added to – it did not replace – the derivation from the needs of man. It was still, for Locke, the individual right to life that made property necessary; the labour expended merely justified particular appropriations. And for Green it was man's essence as a moral being that required that each should have the property without which he could not fulfil his moral vocation: labour expended was simply an additional requirement. Unfortunately, the added derivation of property from labour conflicted with the more basic and continuing derivation from the human essence.

The derivation from labour, as we have seen, was only needed when, and because, the liberal postulate of natural equality displaced the pre-liberal postulate of natural inequality. But we have also to notice that it was only needed when and because a moral case had to be made for putting every individual on his own in a market society, for letting the allocation of incomes and wealth be done by the market rather than by a political authority. If the market was to do the job of inducing people to work and allocating the whole product, men had to be given the right to alienate the use of their labour. A man's labour, his own exclusive property, had to be made an alienable property: the right to its exclusive use had to be made something he could sell. And whenever there was not enough free land for everyone, the man who had none had to sell the use of his labour. Those who had no land lost the right to the product of their labour. They lost also the possibility of their labour entitling them to a property in what they had mixed their labour with. They lost, therefore, the effective right to that which they needed in order to be fully human.

In short, in the circumstances in which the labour derivation of the property right was developed, the exclusive property right derived from labour became a denial, for many, of the property right derived from their essential human needs. As soon as a property in things is derived from an exclusive right which is at the same time an alienable right (that is, the right to or property in one's labour), the damage is done: property as a right needed by all to enable them to express their human essence is denied to many.

I have argued that the narrow concept of property as an individual right to exclude others from the use or benefit of something became the paradigm of property for historical rather than logical reasons: in the pre-liberal era it was the postulate of natural human inequality that required exclusiveness; in the liberal era it has been the postulate that a man's labour is his own. Each postulate was, in its time, needed to justify and support the prevailing or desired system of productive relations – slavery or serfdom in the earlier period, the free competitive market system in the later. But, by whichever postulate the narrow paradigm was reached, it led to a denial of property as a right to what is needed to be human.

What are the prospects of liberal-democratic theory now moving beyond this narrow paradigm? The market system is no longer freely competitive, and it is acknowledged not to be an adequate *system*, as witness the myriad government interferences with it and partial takeovers of it that all liberal-democratic societies have deemed necessary. But the monopolistic corporate structure with government patchwork which has become the twentieth-century version of the market system is still supported by the supposed sacredness of the exclusive individual property right. And its sacredness rests on no firmer basis than the acceptance of the narrow paradigm of property, that is, on the equation of individual property with exclusive property, an equation which never had any logical standing (except as applied to consumables).

It is surely now time to recognize that the concept of property as the right to exclude others is unnecessarily narrow; that its acceptance as the paradigm of property stands in the way of any rethinking of liberal-democratic problems; and that the assertion of the need for the exclusive right now works against the realization of liberal-democratic goals. If liberal-democratic societies are to be the guarantors of rights essential to the equal possibility of individual members using and developing their human capacities, the individual property right that is needed is not the exclusive right but the right not to be excluded from the use or benefit of those things (including society's productive powers) which are the achievements of the whole society. And the latter right does not contradict, but includes part of, the former, as will be shown in a moment.

Property, as the individual right not to be excluded from the use or benefit of the achievements of the whole society, may take either or both of two forms: 1/ an equal right of access to the accumulated means of labour, that is, the accumulated capital of society and its natural resources (with a consequent right to an income from one's work on them); or 2/ a right to an income from the whole produce of the society, an income related not to work but to what is needed for a fully human life.

Some questions arise when this new paradigm of property, as the individual right not to be excluded, is proposed.

First, is such a new concept of property legitimate, or is it so contradictory of everything property has always meant as to be an improper forcing of the very concept of property? I suggest that it is legitimate, on two grounds. 1/ As already noticed, from Plato to Bodin 'property' was not confined to an exclusive individual right: that confinement is a modern phenomenon – an invention of the liberal seventeenth century. 2/ The new paradigm of property, now proposed, is not wholly contrary to the confined liberal concept of property as an exclusive individual right. It does not contradict, but subsumes, as much of that exclusive right as is consistent with the liberal-democratic ethic. For it does include an individual exclusive right to consumables (though not an individual exclusive right to accumulated social capital and parcels of natural resources). This is evident from the definition of property as the right not to be excluded. For that right consists, as we have seen, in either or both a right of access to the means of labour (and consequently a right to an income from work on those), or a right to an income unrelated to work. In either case there is a right to an income, that is, a right to a flow of consumables, and it is assumed that this includes consumables which can be enjoyed only as exclusive property.

A second question arises: is the acceptance of this new paradigm of property consistent with twentieth-century liberal-democracy? There are already some indications that it is: that liberal-democratic societies are moving away from the concept of property as exclusion. Practice is moving faster than theory. The theorist may not have seen it yet, but the businessman is perfectly accustomed to looking at property as the right to an income not necessarily related to work, that is, not derived from one's own exclusive labour. And the politician is coming to see that the right to an income has to be regarded as a right to a share in the annual produce which is increasingly the creation of technology rather than of current labour.

It is true that all the operations of the welfare state, and all the talk of a guaranteed annual income unrelated to work, amount at most to a right to some minimum share in the means of life. They do not amount to a concept of property as a non-exclusive right of access to the means of labour. That concept of property is only clearly consistent with a socialist society. But the individual right of access to the means of labour becomes less important as the need for productive labour decreases. At the theoretical extreme of a fully automated productive system powered by non-human energy there would be no problem about access to the means of labour, for there would be no need for labour (in the sense of productive work that has to be induced). Every move towards that limit reduces the importance of access to the means of labour.

That is not to say that there will be no political problem left as the need for induced labour diminishes. On the contrary, it is to say that the economic problem which has been central to the liberal tradition will become purely a political problem, a problem of democratic control over the uses to which the amassed capital of a society is put. That is a problem that can be tackled with the concept of property as a right not to be excluded, but cannot be handled with the narrower concept of property as an exclusive right.

A third question remains: would a liberal-democratic theory which embodied the new concept of property still be in any significant sense a liberal theory? That depends, of course, on what you put into liberalism. If you insist that it must mean all the market freedoms – not just consumers' choice, and the freedom of the independent producer, but freedom of capitalist appropriation (with which liberalism was largely identified in the eighteenth and nineteenth centuries) – then clearly a political theory built around the new concept of property could not be called liberal. But if you take liberalism to be essentially an assertion of the right of all to full human development (as Mill and Green tried to make it), then a political theory built around the new concept of property is eminently qualified as a liberal theory. I argue simply that a new, less historically inhibited, paradigm of property would not destroy but would liberate the essential liberal-democratic theory.

NOTES

This article is to appear in *Property*, ed. C.B. Macpherson (New York: Lieber-Atherton), forthcoming.
1 *The Political Theory of Possessive Individualism, Hobbes to Locke* (Oxford 1962)
2 'Democratic Theory: Ontology and Technology' in *Democratic Theory: Essays in Retrieval* (Oxford 1973)
3 *Principles of Political Economy*, Book II, chapter 2, section 1
4 *Lectures on the Principles of Political Obligation*, section 221

Monika Langer

Merleau-Ponty: the ontological limitations of politics

In political life as conceived by Merleau-Ponty there is no place for Utopians, cynics, and forecasters of doom. On the basis of his philosophical analyses, Merleau points to the ontological ineradicability of a certain minimal violence which makes Utopia impossible and euphoria unfounded. Cynicism is precluded by the fact that there is already an 'intercorporeal communication' in which 'encroachment' *can* be enrichment. Likewise, despair is ruled out because it becomes evident that the violence which has gradually *established* itself in politics *can*, in fact, be eliminated, since it is not of ontological origin. Merleau's insight that violence has both an ineradicable and an eradicable dimension, therefore, goes 'hand in hand' with his attempt to articulate the necessary conditions for a politics of minimal violence. Such a politics maintains a lucid awareness of *in*eradicable 'intrusions' in political life, while trying to eliminate that violence which is eradicable. In order to appreciate Merleau's view of the political realm, it is necessary to comprehend what he means by the ontological ineradicability of a certain measure of violence. To this end, a synopsis of his phenomenological ontology must be presented.

The central theme of Merleau's entire phenomenological ontology is his notion of incarnate subjectivity, the idea that to be human is to be carnal. Merleau rejects the traditional mind/body dualism, the Cartesian notion that the mind is in the body like a pilot in his ship. For Merleau, the human being *is* a *living body* – not a mind 'tied' to a body, not a 'soul' animating what is essentially inert matter. Although he is not a pantheist, Merleau rejects any radical dichotomy between the human being as incarnate subjectivity and the world. He insists, instead, that these imply one another. To be human, yet not 'worldly' is, according to Merleau, utterly inconceivable; equally incomprehensible is the notion of a world radically divorced from any human experience. Merleau contends that incarnate subjectivity and the world share a common texture – namely, *flesh* – which makes the primordially present to one another: 'the presence of the world is precisely the presence of its flesh to my flesh ... I "am of the world" ... '[1] The flesh of the world and the flesh of human subjectivity has *pores*, is porous, permeable. Through their flesh, human subjectivity and the world continually permeate one another and are transformed.

Merleau argues that all forms of human coexistence are based on the perceptual realm. An investigation of violence in political life must therefore take into account Merleau's descriptive analysis of human perception. In his *Phenomenology of Perception*,[2] Merleau shows that, even at the simplest level of perception, the human subject 'invades' the object which he perceives. He not only incorporates and transforms aspects of the perceptual world, but also continually deposits and encounters vestiges of himself there. In perception, the perceiver 'enters into' the perceived and takes up his place there. In looking at a landscape painting, for example, his gaze goes out to it, 'invades it.'

The painting beckons the perceiver and, as his body responds to its hues, he situates himself through his eyes within the scene, 'inhabits' it, 'sees' and lives it from *within*, as Merleau puts it. Just as the subject 'goes out' to the object, so the object 'enters into' and becomes part of the subject. Merleau cites the case of the blind person to illustrate the manner in which the 'worldly' becomes transformed into the bodily subject. The blind person, in learning to use a cane, makes of it a prolongation of his body – or, since he *is* his body, of himself. He touches, feels his way, perceives his surroundings, with the stick. It becomes incorporated into his bodily spatiality as 'an organ' in which various sensibilities converge.

By the mere fact of perceiving in the world, the human being structures that world, transforms it, gives it a human shape. In perception, the human being and the world continually elicit and respond to modifications in one another. Merleau insists that there is already a 'dialogue' at the most basic level of perception. The perceived world 'speaks' to the incarnate subject, and the latter 'replies' at a prereflective level – the level of the *'bodily cogito.'* Bodily movements, for example, tend to expand or contract in response to surrounding hues: reds call forth broad sweeps of the arms, blues bring them closer to the sides.[3] The human being and the world are in primordial communication through their *flesh*. The incarnate subject finds himself always already situated *in* the world. He can never assume the position of an 'absolute spectator' who would enjoy an instantaneous, all-embracing grasp of the whole world as spread out before him. To be an incarnate subject is to have sensibilities; to have sensibilities is to be perceptive; and to be perceptive is to be perspectival. The perceiver necessarily perceives the world from a certain perspective. He is, himself, limited to a single perspective at a time. He cannot, for example, see all sides of a cube simultaneously; he can never grasp it from all possible angles in 'one fell swoop.' Perception, moreover, requires that the perceiver be *'present'* to the perceived in such a way that the two are neither too close nor too far apart. If perception is to take place, the perceiver cannot coincide with the object of perception, but must establish an 'optimal distance' between it and himself. Although the object is 'porous,' it is never absolutely transparent; it has a certain 'density,' an opacity, an 'inexhaustible core' which lends itself to unending exploration. Perception, of its very nature, is always open-ended, incomplete, perspectival, and ambiguous. It inevitably involves a certain interaction which rules out any clear-cut boundaries between the human perceiver and the perceived world. As a perceiving being, the incarnate subject cannot be an enclosed, self-contained entity.

The perceived world is always already the repository of human activities. Merleau describes the human body as 'spontaneous expression,' and explains that 'all perception, all action which presupposes it, and in short every human

use of the body is already primordial expression.'[4] Expression necessarily involves some measure of objectification, and objectification always implies a
certain distancing. Consequently, in that primordial dialogue between the incarnate subject and the world, of which Merleau speaks, the human being
everywhere encounters the 'expressed' – namely, the vestiges of human activity. The world, in fact, is always already a *cultural* world. The perceptual
world consists not only of 'nature,' but also of other people, and the perceiver
finds himself in dialogue not only with 'natural' objects but also, and *primarily*, with other human *subjects*. These subjects, as incarnate subjectivities, are
co-perceivers. They open onto a common world and the perspective of each
'slips into' and complements, the perspectives of the others. Through their
flesh, they 'invade' one another in a manner analogous to that between the
human subject and the 'natural' world, earlier explained.

Although dialogue, of course, is not restricted to verbal communication,
this kind of expression perhaps best illustrates the structure of subjectivity.
When a person speaks, his listener does not decode or translate the words, as
if they stood for a thought which is itself inaccessible. The listener lends the
speaker his ear, and the speaker extends his verbal and nonverbal gestures to
the listener. The speaker's thought is immediately 'taken up' by the listener
in so far as speaker and listener are 'present' to each other. Although human
beings have an 'inexhaustible core,' they are not inaccessible subjectivities because, as flesh, they are permeable. In so far as they have sensory functions
and fields, incarnate subjects are already open to others and in primordial
communication with them. According to Merleau, expression and what is expressed are always ultimately inseparable.[5] Expression is located neither in the
speaker nor in the listener but in that dynamic relationship *between* them, in
that ceaseless activity whereby they 'inhabit' one another. Such 'inhabiting'
connotes simultaneously 'invasion' and 'intimacy,' *encroachment and enrichment.* It is in dialogue that perspectives merge, complementing and circum-
scribing one another in ways not entirely foreseeable.[6] Since expression involves objectification, it invariably escapes the speaker who is expressing and
encroaches on another's field. That which is expressed becomes 'sedimented'
and forms part of the cultural world within which other human beings must
orient themselves. By virtue of being flesh, human beings are not self-contained
units divided from one another and free in the isolation of that self-enclosed
existence. Rather, the permeability of their texture dictates that human subjects inherently participate in an undivided existence, such that each influences, and is influenced, by the others. Freedom cannot exist in abstraction
from this common life in which all share. Since to be human is to be expressive, and to be expressive is to be engaged in communication, the human subject requires others as partners in dialogue. Only in such human coexistence

can freedom or fulfilment be found. Freedom, therefore, is inseparable from that violence which consists in the kind of encroachment described above. The latter is *ontological* because it characterizes the very *being* of incarnate subjectivity, as *flesh*. It is this sort of encroachment which, according to Merleau, constitutes the background of all political life.[7]

Merleau's firm rejection of euphoria in political life now becomes comprehensible. It has emerged that there is a kind of violence inherent in the human condition as such. This elemental violence permeates all forms of human co-existence, from the simplest level of human perception to the most complex modes of human interaction. Human beings, obviously, do not cease to be incarnate subjectivities when they enter the political realm. Consequently, the simultaneous opacity and permeability which characterize the carnal cannot be transcended in political life. Given the ontological origin of violence, it becomes 'a law of human action' and 'a fact of political life' that human beings encroach, or intrude, upon one another.[8] To condemn all violence, therefore, is to '[put] a curse upon the world and humanity – a hypocritical curse, since he who utters it has already accepted the rules of the game from the moment that he has begun to live.'[9] *No politics will ever be able to get rid of that violence which has to do with humanity's fundamental way of being in the world.* Actually existing régimes tend to mask this ontological encroachment with talk of a future Utopia or with the claim that they have, in fact, already eliminated violence.

No matter how they may otherwise differ, political régimes usually adopt as their goal the minimization of violence or, perhaps, the preservation of a freedom from conflict which they believe themselves to have achieved. Merleau is prepared to agree that the minimization of existing violence is definitely desirable. He is concerned, however, to stress that violence can never be absolutely eradicated because it is of ontological origin, and that a Utopia is therefore an idle dream. Merleau thinks that, despite any claims to the contrary, no existing régime has managed to eliminate *all* eradicable violence.

Western democracy (or Western liberalism), for example, is a politics which prides itself on its ostensible lack of violence, its 'clean hands,' its humanism. In reality, argues Merleau, it is an abstract élitism in which the powerful profess allegiance to a 'heaven of principles' and humanist values – 'Freedom,' 'Truth,' 'Justice,' 'Equality' – to divert attention from the violence perpetrated daily by their hands.[10] This violence may take the form of military suppression, or it may veil itself in more subtle forms: the manipulation of opinions through propaganda, the stalling of actions in parliamentary procedures, the banning of any serious opposition, and, of course, the perpetuation of a repressive régime in which the majority are forced to labour for the profit of the property-owning minority. Western democracy refuses to recognize its manifold forms of violence and blinds its members to them by pretending to be a system in which all are ultimately rulers and none are slaves – a system in which there is a rule *by*, of, and for 'The People.' Its claim to be a non-repressive system is fundamentally dishonest, not only because it disclaims its own eradicable violence, but also because it fails to take cognizance of the real *in*eradicable residue of encroachment in all human relations as such.

Soviet communism likewise masks its violence – this time, in 'the dictatorship of objective truth.' All opportunities for critical appraisal and lucid opposition are effectively blocked by a party élite which claims to be the mouthpiece of history itself, and thus both immune from error and unburdened by all responsibility. Like Western liberalism, Soviet communism is, in fact, a 'cruelly hierarchical society' which ceaselessly recreates exploitative relationships not only within but also outside its own borders.[11] Instead of being eliminated, eradicable violence is perpetuated, while *in*eradicable encroachment, once again, is not even recognized.

Speaking from the distance peculiar to 'the *philosopher*' who lives simultaneously 'everywhere and nowhere,'[12] Merleau is able to view Western democracy against the background of Soviet communism and vice versa without becoming entrapped in the mystifications and hypocrisies of either. Unlike the forecaster of doom who gives way to despair, or the cynic who dismisses all political involvement as ineffectual and useless, Merleau declares that that violence which goes far beyond ontological intrusion in existing régimes *can* be diminished and ultimately eliminated. The failure of Soviet communism and Western democracy to do this prompts Merleau to ask himself what other political form could be conceived which would accomplish the task. He detects the beginnings of an answer in Weber's 'New Liberalism' which, if elaborated, would provide the necessary conditions, the political infrastructure, for an *effectively* human society.[13] Such a liberalism would be a politics of minimal violence – that is, a politics that would minimize and eradicate all violence except that ontological encroachment which cannot, in fact, *be* eliminated in so far as it is inherent in the very permeability of incarnate subjectivities to one another and to the world. It is necessary, therefore, to examine briefly Weber's view of political life before turning to a consideration of its elaboration in Merleau's own thought.

According to Weber, 'politics ... means striving to share power or striving to influence the distribution of power, either among states or among groups within a state.'[14] There is already a violence in the making of, and obedience to, laws. The modern state controls the means of political organization; it monopolizes the legitimate use of physical force within a certain territory. The political leader, the leading statesman, must take 'exclusive personal responsibility for what he does,'[15] and that responsibility is *not* the same as purely moral responsibility. In the politician, responsibility must go hand in hand with 'passion' and a 'sense of proportion' or 'perspective.'[16] The politician must be devoted to politics, but that devotion must be 'genuinely human conduct,' and this, in turn, requires detachment. Absolutely crucial for political life is a '*distance*' towards things, towards others, and towards oneself.[17] According to Weber, all action, but especially political action, is interwoven with tragedy because 'the final result of political action often, no, even regularly, stands in completely inadequate and often even paradoxical relation to its original meaning.'[18] Nonetheless, the politician must assume responsibility for that final result. Political action requires 'inner strength,' because 'the decisive means for politics is violence,' and 'from no ethics in the world can it be concluded when and to what extent the ethically good purpose "justifies" the ethically dangerous means and ramifications.' Only 'a political infant' fails to appreciate 'the ethical irrationality of the world,' the fact that 'it is *not* true that good can follow only from good and evil only from evil, but that often the opposite is true.'[19] The 'absolute ethics of the gospel,' (which is an 'ethic of ultimate ends') commands: 'Resist not him that is evil with force.' Such an ethic 'does not ask for "consequences" ' but 'leaves the results with the Lord.'[20]

If the proponent of an 'ethic of ultimate ends' is forced to look at 'bad results' stemming from his 'good intentions,' he takes the position that 'not he but the world, or the stupidity of other men, or God's will who made them thus, is responsible for the evil.'[21] In the political arena, however, it is imperative that one take account of people *as they are*, not as one might wish them to be, and that one not burden others with the consequences of one's actions in so far as they are foreseeable. For the politician, precisely the reverse of the ethical commandment quoted above holds: ' "Thou *shalt* resist evil by force," or else you are responsible for the evil's winning out.'[22] If one adds to this the realization that the politician finds himself in a world which is already 'evil,' then it becomes clear that he cannot abstain altogether from the utilization of force. As Weber reminds us, 'the tasks of politics can only be solved by violence.'[23] It should not be concluded that an 'ethic of ultimate ends,' which takes responsibility *only* for the *intentions* motivating an action, and an 'ethics of responsibility,' which shoulders the consequences, are 'absolute contrasts.' Rather, they are supplements which achieve unison in the politician who 'measures up' to the realities and challenges of political life. Such a one is, in Weber's eyes, 'a hero.'[24]

In his *Adventures of the Dialectic*, Merleau discusses Weber's notion of politics and points out that the novelty of his liberalism lies in its recognition of history as 'the natural seat of violence,' and in the realization that 'truth always leaves a margin of doubt' and that it can never exhaust the reality of the past or present. This is due to the inherent *ambiguity* of historical 'facts,' the

'Vielseitigkeit' which Weber (and Weberian Marxists) appreciated so well.[25] For Weber, history is not a closed system, but rather, 'the advent of meaning' which excludes absolute knowledge and ultimate guarantees. Merleau stated that Weber appreciated the need to 'live history' and to engage in discussion with one's opponents. Weber's liberalism 'admits that all politics is violence ... It recognizes the rights of its adversaries, refuses to hate them, does not try to avoid confronting them ... ' To 'live history' means to invent, via 'creative choice' in the present, 'what will later appear to have been required by the times.'[26]

Merleau declared that 'certainly Weber's politics will have to be elaborated' and noted that 'it is not superficial to base a politics on the analysis of the political man.'[27] In order, therefore, to understand Merleau's further elaboration of New Liberalism, I propose to turn to an analysis of the political being in Merleau's work. I shall consider, first, the specific situation of the Occupation and Resistance in France in the 1940s. My reason for choosing this particular situation is that it provides a singularly clear contrast between those who practised extreme violence (Hitler and the collaborators) and those who 'measured up' to the demands and challenges of political life (notably, the members of the Resistance). It is in the analysis of such a particular situation that the distinguishing mark of the *genuinely* political being – namely, *political virtù* – emerges most clearly. Since Merleau's proposed politics, like Weber's, is a *new* liberalism, it requires a special kind of political being for its realization. This political being, as already noted, is the 'hero.' In the course of history, it has been possible at various times to catch glimpses of such heroes. The Occupation and Resistance period in France provided one such example. Since this particular situation also lent itself to mystifications about the nature of political life in general, it will be necessary to turn thereafter to a less situation-specific discussion of the *genuinely* political being.

Political life under the German Occupation of France caused both 'heroes' and 'wretches' to stand out with singular clarity. Hitler provides the prime example of the latter – the embodied antithesis of political virtù in every respect. There is little doubt that both his intentions and his actions were barbaric. Hitler's monstrous disregard for others was coupled with an outrageously tyrannical 'twisting' of events. His lack of judgment, prudence, foresight, and comprehension are too well documented to require further elaboration. The invasion of Russia and the refusal to comprehend Germany's losses provide the most blatant examples and testify to his recklessness, his ruthlessness, and his pathological inflexibility. Power-hungry and filled with racial hatred, Hitler rigidly refused to listen to his ministers' advice: once he had made up his mind to invade the USSR, absolutely nothing could dissuade him. He considered himself virtually omniscient and omnipotent. Ruthlessly and irresponsibly he

sent battalion after battalion to certain slaughter in the hope of self-aggrandise-
ment. 'Even if he had won,' says Merleau, 'he would have remained the wretch
he was.'[28]

Since it seemed probable that Hitler *would* in fact triumph, the Resistance
members manifested great courage in opposing him. Those who resisted were
flexible enough, and had sufficient foresight, to allow *human* considerations
to 'speak' to them.[29] They were not afraid to risk their lives in their opposition
to barbarism. They understood that barbarism must be destroyed because it
precludes the necessary conditions for genuine humanism. 'No enslavement is
more apparent than that of an occupied country'; those who resisted realized
that such domination can be combatted only through recourse to 'revolutionary' – that is, self-suppressive – violence.[30] Such violence is 'progressive' in so
far as it contributes significantly to the elimination of all eradicable violence –
itself included. The members of the Resistance did not hesitate to 'dirty their
hands,' but they did this in a *just* and *humane* way – neither ruthlessly nor
recklessly. Their justice was a *revolutionary* justice, one which bases itself on
the calculation of a future whose signs can already be detected in the present.
They had the courage to 'look their victims in the face,' and to assume 'historical responsibility' for their actions – yet they did not allow themselves to
become 'paralysed.' They appreciated what was humanly valuable within the
present possibilities, and set about the task of bringing this into existence.[31]

The members of the Resistance were present to others and to their times.
However, that particular time encouraged some illusions which, if retained
after the times change, could undermine political virtù. Despite the fact that
Hitler and the Resistance members were diametrically opposed, the former's
lack of a *lived* distance was at the centre of those illusions which had the potential to weaken political virtù. In Hitler's case, of course, the distance he placed
between himself and others was so vast that they became mere objects to be
tyrannically manipulated or eliminated – one need only think of the horrors
of reducing human beings to bars of 'soap.' The members of the Resistance,
on the other hand, tended to reduce the 'lived distance' so radically that they
became prone to illusions concerning the nature of political life in other-than-
crisis times. It should be kept in mind, in the subsequent discussion here, that
within the unnatural conditions created by foreign domination this collapse of
'lived distance' was not negative *per se*. Nonetheless, illusions were fostered
when the specificity of that situation was overlooked, when relationships à
propos the Resistance movement were generalized into 'truths' about political
life as such. Merleau captures the essence of this illusion in his article, 'The
War Has Taken Place': 'The war was not over before everything had already
begun to change – not only because of man's inconstancy but also because of
an inner necessity. Unity had been easy during the Resistance, because rela-

tionships were almost always man-to-man ... the Resistance offered the rare phenomenon of historical action which remained personal ... It is only too obvious that this balance between action and personal life was intimately bound up with the conditions of clandestine actions and could not survive it. And in this sense it must be said that the Resistance experience, by making us believe that politics is a relationship between man and man or between consciousnesses, fostered our illusions of 1939 and masked the incredible power of history which the Occupation taught us in another connection. We have returned to the time of *institutions*. The distance between the laws and those to whom they apply is once more apparent ... and once again the good will of some resumes its class features which make it unrecognizable to others. We must again worry about the consequences of what we say, weighing the objective meaning of every word ... This is what we did during the Occupation when we had to avoid any public gesture which might have "played into the hands of the occupying forces." But among friends at that time we had a freedom to criticize which we have already lost.'[32]

The Occupation made it impossible to consider freedom any longer as a property of self-enclosed individuals. It was only too obvious that each person's 'freedom is interwoven with that of others by way of the world.'[33] Under the Occupation, peacetime differences among French people were forgotten or suspended; the mere fact of being compatriots generated fraternity. Understanding flourished among those who were caught in a common palpable enslavement and united by shared fears and hopes. This was particularly true among members of the Resistance. Since safety dictated that the underground groups be of limited size, members were constantly and closely 'in touch.' The inherent dangers of clandestine action made for tremendous solidarity. Especially within the Resistance, the isolation of bourgeois individualism was replaced by the experience of working together to overcome concrete obstacles to freedom.

However, this cooperation in the pursuit of a common goal – the liberation of France – was not a genuine paradigm of political life as such. The alternatives were too clear-cut, the obstacles too unambiguous, cooperation and agreement too easily attained. Good and evil seemed to be singularly well defined. Evil found its locus in 'the enemy,' the absolute 'other' – namely, the Germans, the collaborators, the Vichy régime. Since personal life was largely abrogated, there was a collapse of the usual distinctions between 'interior' and 'exterior,' between 'self' and 'others,' between 'being' and 'doing,' between 'reality' and 'appearance.' Consequently, the inevitable violence in all human relations was obscured. The more Resistance members lived almost exclusively a common life, the less they remembered the built-in encroachments of political life – the inherent ambiguities, the misunderstandings, the interferences and intrusions. The absolute distance between French and Germans, and the utter lack of distance among the French themselves, made for distortions and created illusions about the nature of political life. Consequently, it is necessary to consider the less situation-specific aspects of political life and political virtù as outlined in Merleau's article, 'A Note on Machiavelli.'[34]

Virtù in political life designates a way of living with others which, while definitely precluding opportunism and oppression, nevertheless necessitates a wise and humane exercise of violence with respect to other people and 'the times.' Merleau argues that political beings are born into a cultural tradition which presents them with the 'givens' of a situation. This situation 'solicits,' but does not *determine*, responses. Though rooted in a certain cultural context, the political being is 'free' to structure that context in any of various ways – but structure it he must. He alone decides whether to remain within the confines of choices already outlined in the past, whether to 'take up' the tradition and 'carry it forward,' or whether to strike out in altogether new directions on the basis of those conditions which the past holds out. But whether he decides to reject or accept those institutions created by his forebears, he cannot avoid situating himself with reference to them. Merleau insists that events 'converge,' that there *is* a direction to history which, while not prefigured in things, emerges within the web of human relations. The past, retained in human institutions, exerts a certain 'weight' on the present – it is *not* the case that everything is equally possible at every moment. And yet, that which is humanly possible within the given 'field' of action never precludes the improbable, the remote. Nevertheless, the detection and utilization of present opportunities demands a presence to one's time. Such virtù involves comprehension, wisdom, prudence, flexibility, courage, and skill. Since political beings are actors within the world rather than spectators situated above it, and since history at any given moment is always open-ended, there can be no omniscience, no definitive acquisition, no absolute guarantee. In political life, no human being can assure any other that a certain course of action will bring about a certain result. The 'virtuous' political being acknowledges that 'what he calls the course of events is never anything but its course as he sees it.' He assumes responsibility for seeing it in this way, 'since in acting he has engaged others and more and more the fate of humanity.' He realizes that 'whatever his goodwill, man undertakes to act without being able to appreciate exactly the objective sense of his action; he constructs his own image of the future which has only a probable basis and in reality solicits that future so that he can be condemned for it because the event in itself is not unequivocal. A dialectic whose course is not entirely foreseeable can transform a man's intentions into their opposite and yet one has to take sides from the very start.'[35]

Decisions and actions inevitably intervene in history as already constituted.

Merleau insists that structuration is a form of exploitation. Hence there is an inescapable violence in the 'making' of history. The *form* which that violence takes distinguishes the 'adventurer' or the 'tyrant' from the political being who practises virtù. The adventurer and the tyrant are opportunists. They 'twist' events to suit their personal advantage; and what distinguishes the one from the other is merely the *degree* of oppression that is exercised in gaining that advantage. He who practises virtù, on the other hand, is present to 'the character of the times,' and adapts his actions in keeping with that character. Such a person has the wisdom to discern 'what is humanly valuable within the possibilities of the moment,' to realize that sometimes what seems 'virtuous' or 'good,' if adopted, will lead to its opposite; while that which appears to be 'vicious' may prove the lesser 'evil.' He does not demand unequivocal choices, unambiguous situations. Realizing the inevitable absence of absolute guarantees, he is courageous enough to take risks – yet he shows prudence in discriminating among various risks. He continually questions and reassesses his situation; he is flexible in adapting his actions to changes in 'given' conditions; yet he is neither rash nor reckless. He does not delude himself into thinking that decisions can be made once and for all, that the past can dictate the present; nor does he attempt to divorce intentions from consequences and means from ends. He assumes responsibility for both. He does not allow himself to become short-sighted; neither does he disregard the present in favour of some utopian future. He develops great skill in avoiding the extremes of paralysis and ruthlessness which become dangerous temptations when the 'lived distance' between human beings is destroyed.

He who practises virtù, in being present to his times, is thereby present to others in so far as those others are not only part, but also co-creators, of his times. He is aware that, in allowing particular meaning-structures to emerge or recede, he contributes to the 'shaping' of a 'field' within which others must situate themselves. He takes cognizance of the fact that his projects 'intermesh' with those of others, that they may divert these or be diverted, altered, thwarted by them. If he allows the 'lived distance' between himself and others to collapse, if he identifies his own life too immediately with theirs, then the 'virtuous' person runs the risk of empathizing to such an extent that the very idea of encroaching on others horrifies and paralyses him. He becomes caught in the terrible dilemma of being a party to violence by default because he shrinks from engaging in it more directly. Alternatively, if he allows the 'lived distance' between himself and others to become too great, he runs the risk of recklessness because he has removed himself from an appreciation of what violence means in the context of others' lives. True virtù requires a refusal either to become hardened to violence or to mask it. Virtù recognizes the inevitability and ubiquity of an ontological encroachment but does not consider this to justify either quietude or barbarism. The 'virtuous' human being accepts the need to exercise at least a minimal violence with respect to others and his times; yet he does not allow himself to become an oppressor. He who practises virtù 'seeks harmony' with himself and with others 'in a living dialogue' which 'accepts ... incoherence and conflict with others as constants'; yet he does his best to reduce these to the ontologically based minimum.[36]

Such, then, is Merleau's view of political life as seen through his consideration of the 'virtuous' political person. Merleau insists that if the eradicable violence which characterizes present political régimes is to be eliminated, if a politics of strictly ineradicable ontological domination is to be realized, then 'the remedy we seek does not lie in rebellion, but in unremitting *virtù*.'[37]

NOTES

1 *The Visible and the Invisible*, trans. Alphonso Lingis (Evanston 1968), 127
2 Trans. Colin Smith (New York 1962)
3 Ibid., 209ff, 319ff
4 *Signs*, trans. Richard C. McCleary (Evanston 1964), 67
5 *Phenomenology of Perception*, 391
6 Merleau is concerned to point out that even the most intimate of all relations, the love between two human beings, involves elements of violence: 'Could one conceive of a love that would not be an encroachment on the freedom of the other? If a person wanted in no way to exert an influence on the person he loved and consequently refrained from choosing on her behalf or advising her or influencing her in any way, he would act on her precisely by that abstention ... If one loves, one finds one's freedom precisely in the act of loving, and not in a vain autonomy. To consent to love or be loved is to consent also to influence someone else, to decide to a certain extent on behalf of the other. To love is inevitably to enter into an undivided situation with another ... the perspectives remain separate – and yet they overlap. To the very extent that it is convincing and genuine, the experience of the other is necessarily an alienating one, in the sense that it tears me away from my lone self and creates instead a mixture of myself and the other.' *The Primacy of Perception*, ed. James M. Edie (Evanston 1964), 154-5
7 *Humanism and Terror: An Essay on the Communist Problem*, trans. John O'Neill (Boston 1969), 109
8 Ibid.
9 *Humanism and Terror*, 110
10 Ibid., 180
11 Ibid., 102; *Signs*, 264, 265
12 *Signs*, 130
13 Maurice Merleau-Ponty, *Adventures of the Dialectic*, trans. Joseph Bien (Evanston 1973); 9ff, 29
14 *Politics as a Vocation*, trans. H.H. Gerth and C. Wright Mills (Philadelphia 1965), 2. Weber defines the state as 'a relation of men dominating men, a relation supported by means of legitimate (that is, considered to be legitimate) violence' (p. 2). A word of caution: For the purposes of this paper, I have simplified Weber's position as well as Merleau's elaboration of it. This should not blind one to the complexities involved (for example, Weber's notion of *power*); nor should it obscure the very real differences between Weber and Merleau (one might consider the question of élitism in this regard, for example).

15 *Politics as a Vocation*, 20
16 Ibid., 41, 55
17 Ibid., 41, 42
18 Ibid., 43
19 Ibid., 43, 47, 49
20 Ibid., 46, 47
21 Ibid., 47
22 Ibid., 47, 46
23 Ibid., 52
24 Ibid., 54, 55
25 *Adventures of the Dialectic*, 9, 29
26 Ibid., 26ff
27 Ibid., 28, 29
28 *Humanism and Terror*, xxxv
29 Ibid., 40, 41
30 Merleau-Ponty, *Sense and Non-Sense*, trans. Dreyfus and Dreyfus (Evanston 1964), 142; and *Humanism and Terror*, xviii, 1
31 *Humanism and Terror*, 33ff. I have purposely refrained from discussing Merleau's position regarding the Moscow Trials. The issue goes beyond the scope of the present paper.
32 *Sense and Non-Sense*, 151
33 Ibid., 142, 147
34 *Signs*, 211-23
35 *Humanism and Terror*, 64
36 Ibid., 187
37 *Signs*, 35

Keith McCallum

Domination and history: notes on Jean-Paul Sartre's
Critique de la Raison Dialectique

'History is not an *in-itself*, governed like the physical world by causal laws, but is a totality to be understood' – this, according to Merleau-Ponty in *Adventures of the Dialectic*, is the only hypothesis for an adequate comprehension of the historical process.[1] Merleau-Ponty and Sartre became estranged, but the philosophic method of treating the past pervading the younger man's thought is also present in the *Critique de la Raison Dialectique*.[2] The basic experience for each of them at the time of writing these works was that of a struggle for survival on a global scale: a hunger-ridden world, devastated by colonial wars and by interimperialist rivalries, defined their common situation. Domination originates in a world in which human life remains precarious, in a world in which there is not enough for all, in a world in which each person sees his neighbour as the Other to be enslaved or annihilated. In such a situation, consciousness is forced back upon itself by a world of inhuman enmity, material pressure, and improbable existence from which it is as incapable of abstracting itself as it is of reducing itself, from which it is not able to find any transcendental refuge. In such a situation, consciousness discovers itself as the concrete individual caught up in a terrifying universe of violence and mutual slaughter who is implicated by all the forces of history. He is no longer the epistemological observer who is autonomous from, or external to, that which he observes; he is the 'grouped or communal individual' who experiences his own being as it comes back to him mediated by a social milieu and a time-sequence stretching from the primitive tribe to present-day society.[3] The real question for him is not directed to a metaphysical abstraction but to the human being's actual existence in this world: how is it possible to think about domination within the whole of history so that domination becomes comprehensible in all its concreteness?

The essence of this philosophy of history was most clearly formulated by Marx himself in *The Eighteenth Brumaire of Louis Bonaparte*. 'Men make their own history,' he wrote, 'but they do not make it just as they please; they do not make it under circumstances chosen by themselves, but under circumstances directly encountered, given and transmitted from the past.'[4] Unlike dogmatic Marxism, whose practitioners dissolve man into nature as one more of its objects governed from the outside by a priori mechanical laws, truly conceived dialectical thought grasps the practical rationality of human beings making their own history. If for the dogmatic Marxists human beings were controlled by the finality of much vaster developments in nature, man is now situated in that sector of being in which he is neither a passive vehicle nor an unconditioned creator: human history.[5] The dogmatic Marxists transposed humanity into the realm of the dialectic of nature where it was reduced to nothing more than an inanimate object considered as the focal point of reactions; now the dialectic does not have any foundation unless it derives from the individual (not, of course, visualized as the *solitary* individual, but comprehended in the *totality* of his conditions and relations as a *totalization* in process of *retotalization*) who is able to experience it in terms of his own *praxis*.[6] The dogmatic Marxists made authentic knowledge dependent upon the blindness of natural necessity without further reference to the living 'logic of action' of human beings; now men as the 'subjects of history' are at one with the knowledge they have of themselves and recognize in it the product of their own intentional and conscious collaboration. The dogmatic Marxist world as a pure materiality held together by suprahuman natural-scientific laws was unable to account for itself; now there is no understanding of the historical process except *for* somebody who makes the effort to understand it by reconstructing from individual *praxes* collective realities and practical ensembles which have a dialectical intelligibility.[7]

The foundation of the dialectic as a method on the ground of history does not lead to an irrationalist relativism. This dialectical thought is no abstract negation of reason in its strict philosophical sense; it must not be confused with a vague humanistic psychologism or historicism which enshrines the relative by positing a given being, man, as the measure of all things. In the flux of time and circumstance, one thing maintains itself: the rigorous critical awareness of the mind which refuses to accept this idolatry of the essential qualities of man as a genus. It holds each of its formulations about human beings as temporarily relative to a particular phase of the historical process, and, by continually criticizing itself, moves towards a truth that is always coming-to-be. Man is *not* yet in his concrete existence the realization of the genus man in a world where a configuration of specific historical forces made up by the various hostile groups, interests, institutions, et cetera, have crippled the growth of potential human capacities. This philosophy of history is in reality nothing but the development of the partial insights that any human being who attempts to understand himself in the contemporary world must have of his past and his present. As Merleau-Ponty formulated it in *Adventures of the Dialectic*: ' ... dialectical thought is always in the process of extracting from each phenomenon a truth which goes beyond it, waking at each moment our astonishment at the world and at history. This "philosophy of history" does not so much give us the keys of history as it restores history to us as permanent interrogation. It is not so much a certain truth hidden behind empirical history that it gives us; rather it presents empirical history as the genealogy of truth. It is quite superficial to say that Marxism unveils the meaning of history to us; it binds us to our time and its partialities; it does not describe the future for us; it does not stop our questioning – on the contrary, it intensifies it. It shows us the present worked on by a self-criticism, a power of negation and of sublation, a power which has historically been delegated to the proletariat

... Knowledge is rooted in existence, where it also finds its limits. The dialectic is the very life of this contradiction. It is the series of progressions which it ac- complishes. It is a history which makes itself and which nevertheless is to be made, a meaning which is never invalid but is always to be rectified, to be taken up again, to be maintained in the face of danger, a knowledge limited by no positive irrationality but a knowledge which does not actually con- tain the totality of accomplished and still to be accomplished reality and whose ability to be exhaustive is yet to be factually proved. It is a history-reality which is judge or criterion of all our thoughts but which itself is nothing else than the advent of consciousness, so that we do not have to obey it passively but must think it in accordance with our own strength.'[8]

Consciousness acts in history and is not simply 'the reflection of an external social being, but a singular sphere where all is false and all is true, where the false is true as false and the true is false as true.'[9] The experience of the ambigu- ity of history occasions a new and complex rationalism which distinguishes this mode of thought from that of all sceptical relativists and positivists. As such, its 'relativism beyond relativism' implied that dialectical rationality alone makes the particular form of human self-estrangement embodied in the rela- tion of domination and subjection comprehensible. But while these aspects seemed to commit the new rationalism to recomposing the intelligibility of the historical process in which human beings came to be coerced and manipu- lated, others seemed to indicate a different type of orientation. Merleau-Ponty himself always rejected any interpretation of historical experience in terms of too precise an extrapolation. Moreover, he recoiled at what he referred to as Sartre's 'cursed lucidity' – a calculated abstention from sharply circumscribed concepts was characteristic of his later phase.[10] Here, there is a parting of the ways: Merleau-Ponty categorically disclaims philosophical system-building since it must necessarily 'explain' the inexplicable, eliminate the ambiguities of the world and distort its truth. Abstraction, universalization, formal sys- tematization, these fatally underestimate a human reality ambiguous in its very structure. Sartre, on the other hand, does not wish to deny the ambiguity of lived experience but to develop its latent contradictions into a coherent philosophy of concrete existence: to elaborate those notions, categories, and other instruments of thought whereby the domination of man by man in the historical process may be conceptualized intelligibly.

Sartre's *Critique de la Raison Dialectique* was published in the early 1960s during the Algerian Revolution, the consolidation of the Cuban Revolution, the politicization of the civil-rights organizations in the United States, the escalation of the Vietnam War, and the worldwide development of the anti- imperialist movement. That these circumstances should have come to corres-

pond to a substantive change in the pure ontological-phenomenological conceptions of *Being and Nothingness* which came out in 1943; that he should
have come to be concerned not with the world of solitary individual existence
but rather with how men act in history once the practice of human beings has
been socialized into group behaviour – such eventualities are not at all surprising especially when it is realized that Sartre's terminology of praxis and overt
class conflict now seems starkly consistent with the day-to-day lived experience of the period. In view of the successful overthrow of several corrupt political systems, in view of the ominous reality of violent struggle on a collective
scale, Sartre is obliged to recognize that man does not submit to a fixed and
permanent human nature, but that he makes his own history. The ambiguity
which exists in the fact that, after the challenge to reactionary régimes on different fronts, the totalitarian organization of human existence does not fall
apart but appears to be given new strength – such an ambiguity persists in the
new conception. However, it persists as a historical fact, not the experience of
an immutable ontological condition which permeates the entire Being of man.
Domination is conceived as fundamentally a historical phenomenon. If human
beings are 'dominated,' they must be dominated *by* something, as a result of
certain historical factors which circumscribe the scope and degree of their
freedom. Likewise, the 'suppressibility of domination' is an intrinsically historical phenomenon which envisions the provisional suppression of the dis-
torting societal fetishes and ideologies in certain real and determinate situations. In his new philosophy, Sartre understands this process-character of the
development of human freedom as manifesting itself only in a *practico-inert*
world of *serial dispersion and scarcity*; that is to say, a world in which each
sees his neighbour as the Other to be subjugated or destroyed. Sartre defines
his philosophy of history in terms of a doctrine which is founded on scarcity
as 'the lived relation of a practical multiplicity with the materiality environing
it and within it.'[11] Scarcity is the negation of human multiplicities in exterior-
ity by matter which in turn becomes internalized in the negation of the Other
by each Other. It is the ultimate foundation of history as the struggles of social
groups and classes that must act in a situation where 'there is not enough for
everyone.' In other words, it is only because everyone in the 'milieu of scarcity' is for the others a 'supernumerary' or an 'anti-man' that history has developed the way it has for mankind. Sartre maintains that this presupposition
cancels the basis of pure ontology according to which human existence is determined by the perpetually identical ontological structure of man. In philosophy
the transcendental-ontological concepts which traditionally aim at forms of
Being have abstracted from the concreteness of human existence. Sartre's
philosophical analysis is a strictly historical one in the sense that it comes
to grips with the ontic-empirical world: examples of the efforts to liberate

men from the 'milieu of scarcity' do not simply illustrate abstract and meta-historical conceptions, but comprehend the prevailing concreteness of the *realité humaine*. In so far as Sartre's dialectical rationalism is a philosophical doctrine, it is a realistic doctrine: it does not hypostatize the specificity of historical existence into metaphysical and ontological characteristics. Sartre's 'historicism' thus insists that man's freedom is limited, not by the ontological concept of the *En-soi-Pour-soi,* but by his specific sociohistorical context which prescribes the content and range of his 'choice.' Human freedom, as Sartre sees it, remains bound up with the toil, misery, material pressure, and enmity of the 'world of scarcity.' For, in the concrete historical reality, man's existence is organized in such a way that his liberty is wholly 'dominated' and nothing short of a qualitative change in the material structure of society can give back to him the development of his freedom.[12]

Here, Sartre's 'historicist' philosophy represents a considerable methodo-logical advance since the prevalent tendency has been to subordinate the irre-ducible character of historical existence to a preconceived schematization that is given a counterfeit supersensible reality. Here, too, his new conceptual instru-ments are less the expression of metaphysical abstraction than of a further concretization which never forgets the particularity of events and personalities; however, such thinking remains committed to reconstructing the dialectical intelligibility of the ongoing historical process as a whole (something the dog-matic Marxists could not do on their mechanistic-determinist assumptions, be-cause for them, the concepts only 'reflect' a changing set of circumstances and thus lack any genuine theoretical validity).[13]

Although the argument of the *Critique de la Raison Dialectique* is complex, its main outlines may be summarized in the following manner. Sartre starts from the concrete individual, not conceived in his isolated practical determina-tions, but grasped manifold in the totality of his conditions and relations as a totalization in process of retotalization who experiences himself in terms of his own praxis. Next, Sartre demonstrates how the freedom of the grouped or communal individual is inextricably tied up with his situation in the 'milieu of scarcity' in which each is for others an Other to be reduced to the state of a thing and how all attempts to suppress violence and domination in human re-lations can only be provisional in such material and historical circumstances. In the last part of his book, Sartre analyses the metamorphoses of the fused group which as the dissolution of serialized Otherness raises itself above this primitive level of distrust, hostility, and enmity only to finish by falling back into it.

For Sartre, man's freedom becomes subject to the tribulations of the 'anti-dialectic' when the actions of an individual escape from him and he is made unfree, inert, and passive by the Other who sees him as an enemy to be exploited or liquidated in a practico-inert world of serial dispersion and scarcity. This 'inert practicality' of society is the blind activity of human beings embroiled in the immediacy of concrete daily existence. Everyone is for the others an Other who threatens to deprive him of the minimum necessary for survival. As against this original threat of usurpation by the Other and in an effort to master the uncontrolled operation of social forces, human beings are compelled by the presence of an external adversary to form their own active and conscious fused group. The fused group, in which dispersed individuals come together, is constituted by the common praxis of a multiplicity of human beings, each of whom incarnates its unity by undertaking to transform the situation of impotent serialization and oppression shared by all in the direction of a common goal. However, precisely because it wants to realize its goal of a liberated society, the fused group also eventually must undergo a dialectical reversal: it must protect itself from disintegration in a world of scarcity and struggle by relapsing into serialized organization. Here, Sartre returns back to where he first started his analysis. The gradual degradation of the fused group into the petrified inertia of an institution gives rise to a sovereign (that is, the State or the Leader) who guarantees the practical unity of the group. But at the same point he raises the possibility of the suppression of domination and manipulation when the fused group is shown to be the most effective means of achieving a victory over scarcity even if it can only be provisional in present material and historical circumstances.

It remains to explicate this whole development of Sartre's thought by clarifying some of the basic concepts of the *Critique de la Raison Dialectique*.

Sartre's *Critique de la Raison Dialectique* begins from the individual who does not simply exist as a solitary monad in a world of monads, but exists only in so far as he 'totalizes' himself within the whole of his conditions and relations as praxis: 'praxis ... is a passage of objective to objective through internalization. The project, as the subjective surpassing of objectivity towards objectivity, and stretched between the objective conditions of the environment and the objective structures of the field of the possibles, represents *in itself* the moving unity of subjectivity and objectivity, those cardinal poles of activity. The subjective appears then as a necessary moment in the objective process.'[14] This 'impulse towards objectification' applies to each moment of a man's life and resembles what in *Being and Nothingness* was referred to as the project. The latter (that is, *Pour-soi*, consciousness, *Cogito*) also characterizes the human being who is 'going beyond a situation ... by what he succeeds in making of what he has been made.'[15] However, in *Being and Nothingness*, this realization of intentional action was hypostatized into the ontological form of the subject as such and detached from the specific historical context in which alone it might have become one of the preconditions of the possibility of freedom.

It is true that man finds himself thrown in the midst of a pregiven situation which degrades him into a thing, but this situation has been absorbed by the ever-transcending power of the 'Pour-soi' to a point where it appears to be irrelevant and cancels itself.[16] In contrast, the praxis or totalization identical with the human being of the *Critique* always occurs, not in some absurd and illusory world of prostration and failure interpreted in terms of the free activity of the 'Pour-soi,' but through the mediation of quite real and determinate historical conditions. My praxis or totalization gives rise to a practical field structured around me which reveals the intractable inertia in material objects and other people that opposes my future end. In other words, human freedom does not create a different world at any moment and in any situation, but can be debased by the organization of society to such an extent that it all but ceases to exist. By the same token, totalizing praxis does not involve only my negation of the things surrounding me with the reworking of them towards an end performed by that negation, but is the experience of a 'curse of matter' which turns my actions or their results against me to the advantage of the ends of the Other who makes it impossible for me to realize freely my being.[17]

In the concrete historical reality, the transcendental liberty of the 'Pour-soi' thus becomes necessarily dependent on the world in which it manifests itself and upon which it tries to act. If *Being and Nothingness* was concerned to restore consciousness to itself as freedom by demonstrating the formal ontological relation between being-for-itself and being-in-itself, in the *Critique* Sartre devotes all his efforts to establishing the 'hierarchy of material mediations' by which this relation is made impotent in a world of inorganic inertia by other praxes. In order to concretize his new conception of human freedom, Sartre's analysis orients itself, not to the *Pour-soi* in relation to the *En-soi*, but to the practical activity of human beings which in its objective reality enters the materiality and time of things to be thwarted by the passive totalization of its own praxis in the world of the inert. This disintegration of totalizing praxis into the dead inertia of matter that turns my action against me and deflects it toward the ends of another reveals the brute reality of unfreedom which constitutes social reality. However, in *Being and Nothingness* the human being (as an ontological lack or emptiness striving to satisfy itself) was identified with the series of negations, or rather 'free acts' by which he continually created himself and his world.[18] Moreover and most important, the entire series of these negations occurred in a world abstractly characterized as *contingent* where the very origin and life of human freedom was traced back to its *facticity* (man's ever lacking coincidence with himself).[19] In the *Critique* this whole process is translated into the concreteness of need, the resistance of the world to human beings is now understood and evaluated in terms of scarcity: ' ... scarcity – whatever form it may take – dominates all praxis ... One must understand *both* that man's inhumanity does not come from his nature – that, far from excluding his humanity, his nature can be understood only through it – *and yet* that, as long as the sway of scarcity is not yet ended, there will be *in each man and in everyone* an inert structure of inhumanity which, in short, is nothing other than the material negation in so far as it is interiorized.'[20] Scarcity as the negation in man of man by matter is the basis of our understanding of the inhuman in human history. It is the negative unity of interiorized scarcity which is re-exteriorized for us as the conflicts of social groups and classes. In this sense, it implies that human freedom is determined, not by the ever-transcending 'Pour-soi,' but by specific historical forces which shape human society. Objectification of human praxis takes place only within a multiplicity of dispersed individuals acting separately in a common situation of scarcity: that is, in a world in which each person poses a threat for the Others to be controlled or eliminated. For scarcity is the material *contingent datum* of the world in which I must live; it is the global sociohistorical framework which conditions and estranges my actions even in their very conception.[21]

This characterization of the 'réalité humaine' provides the fundamental terms which guide the subsequent development of the argument. To begin with, the identification of the human being with the inhuman milieu of hostility, enmity and constant exercise of violence permits Sartre to discard his concept of the absolute freedom of the 'Pour-soi' which had been presented in *Being and Nothingness*. There it was because the autonomous 'Pour-soi' freely 'created' himself and his world at any moment and in any situation that every obstacle encountered on the way served only to exemplify the perpetual liberty of man. It was in this sense that, even in a situation of utmost determinateness, human beings were perfectly free to change their conditions. If a human being lived in a state of actual exploitation, enslavement, and oppression, it was only because he had 'chosen' this state and continued to posit and consent to all the constraints which society had placed upon him. In *Being and Nothingness*, 'exploitation,' 'oppression,' et cetera, emerged and existed only for the 'Pour-soi' who made them part of his own free project and, ultimately, was 'responsible' for them.[22] However, this erroneous notion of the free realization of the 'Pour-soi' is cancelled in the *Critique* by the attempt to comprehend the real grouped or communal individual as he is reduced to a thing in a world of inertia. In Sartre's interpretation of the sociohistorical sphere, it is the lived fact of serial dispersion and scarcity, not the transcending activity of the 'Pour-soi,' that is indispensable for understanding enslavement and repression in all their forms.[23]

Sartre's human beings are not the free and autonomous masters of their own destiny: they are subjected to a thoroughly reified material necessity, or as he puts it, 'conditioned' by the omnipresent danger of starvation, by external pressures, by violence, by group hostility. Indeed, scarcity is shown to have controlled not only the primitive life of food-gathering tribes, but the whole temporal sequence down to the contemporary world. Human beings have always been pitted against each other ('serialized') and it is this otherness ('alterity') which makes everyone see his neighbour as somebody who is to be exploited or destroyed.[24] True, in Sartre's analysis, human beings raise themselves above this intolerable set of circumstances by forming an active and conscious unit (the fused group), but it cannot have a durable basis in the 'milieu of scarcity' and ends up falling back into the inert. Human freedom thus grasped is not the absolute freedom of the creative subject as such, but what man possesses or lacks within the global sociohistorical context of scarcity and struggle.

Secondly, from the identification of the human being with the frightening and tyrannic world of scarcity and serialized sociality proceeds a quite different conception of man's responsibility for himself than had been suggested in *Being and Nothingness.* Following Heidegger's existential ontology, human freedom and responsibility had been understood to have arisen only with man being 'thrown' into the midst of a pregiven situation. Man discovered himself existing in a situation which he himself had not created, and this situation could be such that it handicapped the freedom of the 'Pour-soi.'[25] In *Being and Nothingness* Sartre illustrated this phenomenon by several different examples: the independent existence of the Other who usurps the world of another human being; the enthralment of the Ego to the standardized commodities of the market society; the dehumanized interchangeability of persons.[26] But the constant transcendence of the 'Pour-soi' beyond every one of its contingent situations necessarily gave an illusory quality to the Ego's *Geworfenheit* (being thrown into) an environment not his own; it came to be assimilated to the *projet fondamental* which posited, as its own free choice, all obstacles, limitations, and restrictions on its liberty. For it was once again a matter of the absolute freedom of the 'Pour-soi' which was and remained autonomous in the most determined situation. My contingent situation became 'mine' to the extent that I 'engaged' myself in it. Everyone was able to accept or reject his condition; everyone enjoyed a degree of freedom from the necessities of life.[27] However, in the *Critique* Sartre abandons this atemporal notion of man's full and unqualified responsibility for his own being. He no longer tries to revive a universal and abstract morality, but acknowledges the fact that, in the empirical reality, man is not free to be 'responsible.' If values are the mere manifestation of human existence under the 'reign of scarcity,' it is unavoidable that they are often masks to conceal systems of exploitation and repression.[28] Sartre himself wrote on one occasion: 'A moral attitude appears when technical and social conditions make a positive behaviour impossible. Morality is an ensemble of idealistic tricks which help you to live in the way the lack of techniques and resources compels you to live.'[29] It is the persecutors and executioners of the status quo who are 'humane' and urge all of mankind to emulate their exemplary conduct. Behind a semantic moralism lurks an ideology which offers itself as a most convenient justification for the guardians of the established social order. Moreover, Sartre insists that exploitation and repression is itself rooted in the material structure of society in so far as it has scarcity for its ultimate foundation. The achievement of a genuine normative ethics implies a qualitative change in this structure: it requires a more rational organization of the relations of production which is the very precondition for the abolition of scarcity and the creation of a liberated society.[30] To be sure, human beings who have conferred upon matter (*matière ouvrée*, 'worked matter') its malignant potentiality may be still categorized as 'responsible' for what subjugates them, but such categorization does not transcend the content and substance of their concrete existence. In Sartre's interpretation of the socio-historical sphere, human freedom and responsibility splits apart into two separate moments: the first, in which human beings, by their totalizing activity and work on the outside world, invest matter with a kind of 'surplus-value' or 'stored human energy'; and the second, in which that 'energy' comes to life and is used against them forcing a temporary abdication of their liberty (what Sartre calls the *practico-inert* or *counterfinality*).[31] Man is no longer literally and actually free to create his own being at any moment, but is humiliated in the exteriorized world of inertia by the passive totalization of his own praxis. As such, he is not the absolutely and perfectly free master of self-responsible choice, but must make that which made him by recognizing and seizing the necessity of liberation from a world of scarcity, misery, toil, and hunger.

Thirdly, human freedom lies, not in the ever-transcending activity of the 'Pour-soi,' but rather in its cancellation, in its collapse into the inertia of inorganic matter. In *Being and Nothingness*, man as free being for-itself, was identified with the series of negations by which he 'made' himself and his world. The whole series of these negations were essentially parts of the 'project fondamental' that is man's life: human beings existed as the perpetual realization of their possibilities; they always went 'beyond' their situation towards a future end; they continually strived for some definitive mode of being.[32] This existentialist formula was derived from the Hegelian notion of human experience as a negation of existing being, as an ontological lack (*manque*) endeavouring to complete and fulfil itself. But this ontological lack, which was identical with the very being of the creative subject, was not a lack of something that would vanish upon attainment of its full reality. It functioned only to indicate the fundamental fact that man's actual situation never coincided with his possibilities. In other words, the 'project' in its futile and self-defeating attempts to make the *Pour-soi* an *En-soi* and, vice versa, was forever doomed to an inescapable frustration and failure.[33] On the other hand, since the essential frustration which characterized the 'human enterprise' was operative as the very being of the 'Pour-soi,' it was also the ultimate basis of man's freedom. Human freedom existed only in so far as man 'engaged' himself in his contingent situation which in turn, because it was a pregiven one, prohibited him from ever coinciding with his own possibilities.[34] Sartre's identification of the opposites (human freedom and frustration, self-responsible 'engagement' and contingent determination) was not consummated via a concrete analysis of the dialectical process of history, but via an a priori ontological definition of man's existence. It is true that the development of the subject through its negation into self-consciousness seemed to be a process, but this process-character was obviously undialectical. For after each 'engagement' the 'Pour-soi' was haunted by its feeling of frustration and continued to move only in a closed circle. Moreover, the ontological concept of the 'Pour-soi,' which subsumed quite different historical actors (serf and landlord, wage-earner and capitalist, white-collar employee and intellectual) under its 'projective' activity, reduced their very concreteness to a mere manifestation of a transtemporally simultaneous and structurally identical universal essence of man. It thus contradicted its own argument that 'existence creates the essence.'[35] In the *Critique* Sartre no longer avails himself of the ontological shortcut, but conceives the revolutionary goal of a liberated society in terms of the whole historical process. The ego forfeits its peculiar quality of being 'Pour-soi,' set off from and against everything other-than-the ego, and it seeks the reality of its freedom in and through the complex mediations of history. Sartre had previously described the activity of the 'Pour-soi' as man's absolute freedom over himself and his material world; now the 'curse of matter' becomes the force which cancels all the 'subjectivist' paraphernalia of free choice, autonomous activity, and morality. 'Matter' becomes this overpowering force by virtue of the fact that it turns my actions or their result against me to the advantage of the ends of another who directs them toward his own ends.[36] In Sartre's interpretation of the sociohistorical sphere, man is not free, is not his own project, but discovers himself degraded into a thing by the materially structured processes of the practico-inert or counterfinality as one praxis exercised among others at the same time: 'Man is still the man of need, of praxis, and of scarcity. But, in so far as he is dominated by matter, his activity no longer derives directly from need, although that is its fundamental basis. It is awakened in him from without, by processed matter as the practical requirement of the inanimate object. Or, if you prefer, it is the object that designates its man, as he of whom a certain behaviour is expected.'[37] This proposition implies that man's 'choice of being' does not remain the same in all situations, but may be circumscribed to such an extent that it all but disappears: it is weakest and fragile where man is most thoroughly 'dominated' by the inert, where he is least master of his destiny. For example, in situations where he has become a reified 'thing,' where the materialized practice of the Other has stolen his freedom from him, his 'Pour-soi' has been superseded by the passive activity of quasi-physical objects (such as in a factory assembly line). In this situation, the worker's freedom continues to exist as a 'dead freedom' or exercise of 'dead possibilities,' but has been reversed and used against him by the factory owner.[38] True, Sartre says that the worker who feels powerless when submerged by the capitalist machine process and separated from all other workers is the predominant type in a world of violence, enmity, and material pressure, but he may be able to recover his freedom momentarily in certain propitious physical and historical circumstances. So it is precisely at this point, where man exists almost exclusively as a thing, where his activity is essentially overwhelmed by things, that the possibility of liberation arises for him – although it cannot be a lasting liberation in a world of scarcity and struggle.[39]

Here Sartre's philosophical analysis reaches its centre: it is the existence not of the free 'Pour-soi' but of the victim of reification that points toward the real establishment of the 'realm of freedom.' Ever since the reflexive *cogito* of *Being and Nothingness* has acknowledged its degradation by other praxes in a material world of inorganic inertia, his philosophy has forsaken the transcendental ontological realm and moved within the ontic-empirical world. In the *Critique*, Sartre constantly emphasizes not the ontological structures of interiority of the 'Pour-soi' in relation to the 'En-soi' but the totalizing action of human beings which extends itself outside into the history and materiality of things to be acted by the passive totalization of its praxis as one praxis among others in a practico-inert world of scarcity and serialized Otherness.[40] Sartre writes: 'From the moment when impotence becomes the truth of practical power and counter-finality the profound meaning of the end pursued, when praxis discovers *its* freedom as the means chosen everywhere to reduce it to slavery, the individual suddenly discovers himself in a world in which free action is the fundamental mystification. He no longer knows freedom except ... as propaganda of the rulers against the ruled. But one must understand that this experience is no longer that of the act, that of the result become concrete; it is no longer the positive moment in which one *does*, but the negative moment in which one is produced in passivity by what the practico-inert field has done with what one has just done.'[41] The quasi-totalization of a multiplicity of praxes by the inert is not the same, for Sartre, as the activities of the solitary 'Pour-soi' condemned to an eternal ontological frustration and failure, but is the experience of the 'curse of matter' in which my action is reversed and used

against me to the advantage of the ends of the Other who deflects them towards his own ends. If things dominate human beings and are insurmountable
obstacles for them, it is only because they are not purely passive, but are ' ... like
a passive activity, a materialized practice, the practico-inert, sustained and
sealed by other praxes.'[42] Domination is not a permanent and inevitable ontological characteristic of the human being as such; it is a humiliation which
praxis suffers through the praxes of others in a practico-inert world of serial
dispersion and scarcity. For domination is something historical, not metaphysical or ontological. By the same token, since domination is a state of affairs
which comes to men from men on the basis of determined material circumstances, it is conceivable that the reified subject may provisionally overcome
his sociohistorical vulnerability by the invention of collective acts and collective units.[43]

The philosophical analysis of the practico-inert world of serial dispersion
and scarcity now provides the framework for the interpretation of the metamorphoses of the group. In the *Critique* we have seen that, according to Sartre,
any group which comes into being through totalizing praxis in a world of scarcity and struggle must end up by falling back into serialized Otherness and the
practico-inert. To him, the fused group exists as the moment of perfect freedom when each grouped or communal individual recognizes himself in the
common praxis of all. However, the fused group cannot have a durable basis
due to its existence in the 'milieu of scarcity' and inorganic inertia. On the
other hand, since the freedom of human beings remains intact, but has been
secretly stolen from them, it must be possible in a certain definite situation
for necessity to reconvert itself into liberty. For example, the unity of the
practical ensembles or modes of totalization, instead of being an external cohesion forced upon the praxes of atomized individuals by the material world as
the negation of man by man, would appear as interiorized and produced in all
by each and in each by all in the creation of a shared end. This would be the
praxis of the grouped or communal individual who liquidates the serialized
otherness encompassing him as a means towards realizing the shared object of
all.[44] ' ... The group constitutes itself on the basis of a need or a common danger, and defines itself by the common objective that determines its common
praxis. Yet neither the common need, nor the common objective can define
a community, unless the latter makes of itself a community by feeling individual need as common need, and by projecting itself, in the internal unification
of a common integration, towards the objectives that it produces as common.'[45]
Sartre's constant emphasis is on the fused group as the only way to the liberation of mankind, but he insists that those physical and historical circumstances
favourable to its emergence in the world of the inert must be analysed closely.
He mentions in this connection the following: a threat to the vital interests of

each member of the group; geographical nearness; a tradition of solidarity in the face of other hostile groups that will constitute the 'structural nucleus' of the group. If the imminent danger cannot be eliminated except by the unity of all, and the determinate sociohistorical conditions are opportune, each of the individuals concerned catalyses the seriality around himself and acts as he wants everyone else to act. Each person totalizes all others at the same time as they totalize him in the dissolution of serialized alterity through the communalization of praxis. Reification of human praxis itself thus turns into liberation as the reappropriation of necessity as necessity of freedom by the fused group.[46]

But if the fused group is to realize its goal of a liberated society, then it must necessarily protect its internal cohesion against disintegration by making itself inert. When its members came together *in struggle* to defend themselves against an enemy, they experienced a profound sense of urgency. However, the danger, which the group produced itself to fight, may evaporate in time, and the temptation is to return to the former molecular life of serial dispersal. Now at this point the group interiorizes the external menace in the *oath* that exercises sovereignty and juridical power over each of the members. Each pledges his own death should he weaken the unity of the group by betraying it. Each affirms the power of each over all others as well as becoming a guarantor of group unity himself.[47] Fear of the enemy no longer serves to guarantee group unity but is in its entirety displaced by *Fraternity Terror.* This conception of terror expressed in the violence both against the 'selves' and against the adversary as 'structures of the revolutionary group' would appear to substantiate Merleau-Ponty's criticism of voluntarism, but Sartre would only like to account for the lived experience of the concrete life-and-death situation that is the 'hot' moment of the group-in-fusion. Moreover, Sartre suggests that the terror itself ultimately fails in the progressive 'cooling down' and institutionalization of the group. In spite of the attempts on the part of the fused group to forestall an eventual breakdown and to preserve itself from within, the latter relapses into a serialized dispersal which weighs down the active freedom of each of its members with a complete inertia.[48] The fact that for the group to be effective and cope with a diversity of tasks in the 'milieu of scarcity' means that it must differentiate itself into *specialized functions* and *subgroups*: ' ... with structure or organization, the group became itself a grouping of subgroups, and in psychological terms the problem of maintaining group unity may be stated as the difficulty of making every member feel his place in the whole and realize the way in which his own perhaps limited technical responsibilities are on the contrary indispensable to the group effort and remain, as in the group-in-fusion, an omnipresent center.'[49] The specialized subgroups, each with its own inertia, discipline, and social hierarchy, have come to acquire an organization or apparatus, but all have a tendency to become uninformed about the activities of other subgroups and separated from them by mutual antagonisms.[50] In describing the coordination and integration of the serialized partial praxis, Sartre makes reference to a supreme organism, a *sovereign* (for example, the state or the leader) which incarnates the unity of the group by virtue of its monopoly of juridical power as the *institutionalized group*. The sovereign institutionalized group appears when ' ... powerlessness and imperative terror and inertia, are reciprocally established. The institutional moment, in the group, corresponds to what might be called systematic self-domestication, that of man by man. The end is, in fact, to create men such that ... they are defined in their own eyes and among themselves by their fundamental relation (mediated reciprocity) to institutions.'[51] The practical unity of the group is only brought about by a sovereign third party that not only retotalizes the multiplicity of serialized ensembles, but also preserves them in their passive serial dispersion by circumventing all efforts at regroupment. Consequently, in Sartre's analysis, the state manifests itself only as the mediation of the sovereign third which guarantees the unity of the group by determining that its members have no more than serial relations between them. This demystifying identification of the state is designed to understand the process in which bureaucratic institutions emerge by embodying the 'reified' lives of their members.[52]

According to Sartre, other forms of reciprocity between the mediator (*tiers regulateur*) and the group may become possible, for it is true that the free activity of the fused group at the moment of revolutionary apocalypse represents the only authentic model of 'voluntary cooperation' – in spite of its material determination. Sartre has recognized this freedom by laying stress on the significance of the maturity of consciousness during periods of revolutionary élan. If the fused group as the model of free and liberating human relations cannot have a stable and lasting basis, several concrete historical factors have to be considered: 1/ the scarcity of productive forces and the constant menace of hostile groups; 2/ the inorganic inertia, resistance, and complexity of the practico-inert or counterfinality. This in turn discloses a world which is at the same time the very negation of totalizing praxis since it forces the fused group to become inert and complex as it organizes specialized functions and subgroups to cope with tasks of increasing complexity and scope.[53] For Sartre, this certainly does not imply that the suppression of domination, scarcity, violence, bureaucracy, and the state should be seen as ridiculously 'utopian.' But it does imply that in a world in which three-quarters of humanity suffers from malnutrition and two-thirds is on the edge of starvation, in a world in which inter-imperialist conflicts and antagonisms intensify from day to day, enmity to one's fellow man continues to be a 'formal law of the dialectic' in the historical process. It is thus understandable that the possibility of abolishing the inhuman in human history once and for all remains almost inconceivable under present-day conditions.[54]

NOTES

1 Maurice Merleau-Ponty's *Les aventures de la dialectique* (Paris 1955) has been translated as *Adventures of the Dialectic* (Evanston 1973) by Joseph Bien. The quotation is from p. 69 of the English translation where Merleau-Ponty discusses Georg Lukács' book *Geschichte und Klassenbewusstein* (Neuwied und Berlin 1968). The latter has been translated as *History and Class-Consciousness: Studies in Marxist Dialectics* by Rodney Livingston (London 1971). Cf. in this context p. 10 where Lukács argues that 'concrete totality is ... the category that governs reality.'

2 The beginning section of Jean-Paul Sartre's *Critique de la Raison Dialectique* (Paris 1960) has been translated by Hazel E. Barnes as *Search for a Method* (New York 1968). Selections from the *Critique* can also be found in *The Philosophy of Jean-Paul Sartre*, ed Robert Denoon Cumming (New York 1965), 415-83.

3 On this see R.D. Laing and D.G. Cooper *Reason and Violence: A Decade of Sartre's Philosophy 1950-1960* (London 1964), 15, 16f, 148.

4 *The Eighteenth Brumaire of Louis Bonaparte* in Karl Marx and Frederick Engels, *Selected Works* (Moscow 1968)

5 For a critical view of dogmatic Marxism, see Andre Gorz's pertinent remarks in his article 'Sartre and Marx,' *New Left Review*, 37 (1966), 35

6 Nicos Poulantzas, 'La Critique de la Raison Dialectique de J.P. Sartre et le Droit,' *Archives de philosophie du droit*, X (1965), 104, misinterprets this point when he criticizes Sartre for his concern with the 'solitary' individual. See also his 'Vers une théorie marxiste,' *Les temps modernes*, 240 (1966), for a critique of Sartre's 'historicism' from a structuralist viewpoint, 1052-82. Cf. Gorz's vigorous defence of Sartre's position against the structuralists in 'Sartre and Marx,' 37.

7 Ibid., 36-7

8 56-7

9 Ibid., 40

10 See, for example, Merleau-Ponty, *La visible et l'invisible* (Paris 1964), recently published as *The Visible and the Invisible*, ed. Claude Lefort, trans. Alphonso Lingis (Evanston 1963).

11 Sartre, *The Philosophy of Jean-Paul Sartre*, 433

12 For a critical view of Sartre's own 'abstractness' from the irreducibility of the historical process, see Henri Lefebvre, 'Critique de la critique non-critique,' *La nouvelle revue marxiste*, 1 (1961). It seems to me, however, that Lefebvre overdoes the subject of Sartre's alleged inability to grasp the historical moment in its uniqueness.

13 Cf., above all for this aspect of Sartre's thought, the chapter entitled 'Sartre and History' in Frederic Jameson's comprehensive study, *Marxism and Form: Twentieth Century Dialectical Theories of Literature* (Princeton 1970); cf. also George Lichtheim, 'Sartre, Marxism and History' in *The Concept of Ideology* (New York 1967).

14 Sartre, *Search for a Method*, 97

15 Ibid., 91

16 Herbert Marcuse develops this theme through an analysis of the existentialist Sartre's notion of absolute freedom in his 'Existentialism: Remarks on Jean-Paul Sartre's L'Être et le Néant,' *Philosophical and Phenomenological Research* VIII (March 1948). In what follows his critical points on Sartre's exaggeration of capacities of the human subject in the earlier ontological-phenomenological treatise are assumed to be valid.

17 Gorz, 'Sartre and Marx,' 43

18 Marcuse, 'Existentialism,' 312-13

19 Ibid., 315

20 Sartre, *The Philosophy of Jean-Paul Sartre*, 438

21 Gorz, 'Sartre and Marx,' 43-4

22 Marcuse, 'Existentialism,' 320-1

23 *Critique*, 221-3

24 Cited in Lichtheim, 'Sartre, Marxism and History,' 302

25 Marcuse, 'Existentialism,' 314
26 Ibid., 323
27 Ibid., 314-15; 321-3
28 Wilfred Desan, *The Marxism of Jean-Paul Sartre* (New York 1966), 244-9
29 Cited in ibid., 245
30 Ibid., 245-6, 248
31 Jameson, 'Sartre and History,' 236-7
32 Marcuse, 'Existentialism,' 313
33 Ibid., 315
34 Ibid., 315-16
35 Ibid., 324
36 See Jameson's discussion of Sartre's evaluation of matter in 'Sartre and History,' 237-40.
37 Sartre, *The Philosophy of Jean-Paul Sartre*, 454
38 Jameson, 'Sartre and History,' 246
39 Gorz, 'Sartre and Marx,' 46
40 Ibid., 41-2
41 Cited in ibid., 42
42 Ibid., 43
43 Ibid., 44
44 Ibid., 46
45 Sartre, *The Philosophy of Jean-Paul Sartre*, 465
46 Gorz, 'Sartre and Marx,' 46-7
47 Jameson, 'Sartre and History,' 254
48 Ibid., 254-5
49 Ibid., 270
50 Gorz, 'Sartre and Marx,' 49-50
51 Sartre, *The Philosophy of Jean-Paul Sartre*, 479
52 Gorz, 'Sartre and Marx,' 50
53 Ibid., 51
54 Ibid., 45-6, 51-2

Ato Sekyi-Otu

Form and metaphor in Fanon's critique of racial and colonial domination

Man is born free; and everywhere he is in chains.

JEAN-JACQUES ROUSSEAU

The black is not a man ...

The black is a black man.

FRANTZ FANON

I

'Et véritablement il s'agit de lâcher l'homme.' That Fanon's metaphor for what is to be done – 'and truly what is to be done is to let man out'[1] – is so programmatically minimal, almost prepolitical in its very conception of the emancipatory project, is the profoundest disclosure of the singularity of his critique of domination. For what does this metaphor signify? Not the eschatological inauguration of the realm of human freedom but the violent release of man's humanity in a truly cosmogonic moment. How could it be otherwise for one who experienced domination 'in its immediacy'[2] neither as a tragic excrescence of human self-development nor as a perennial scar upon the human condition but as a contingent and systematic segregation of 'my brother, my sister, my father' from 'the universality inherent in the human condition.'[3] Normal men when they call for the transcendence of domination speak in the name of liberty. Their point of departure is Man: 'Man is born free; and everywhere he is in chains.' For this reason the dehumanization to which the heterogeneous modes of domination reduce men is seen, from the perspective of normal crittiques of human bondage, to be irreducibly connected with human phylogenesis and generic human experience. Normal critiques of domination are sustained by a latent ontology and historiosophy of social being.

In this sense, the critique of domination is generically an epic story of human being defined by tragedy. However macabre the plot, however deformed the profile of man that emerges, there is little doubt left that the story concerns generic man, that the state of bondage is still a human condition, and that the object of coercion is irreducibly a human subject. Marxism, the greatest and the most elaborate of all critiques of domination as epic narrative, not only makes explicit, under the aegis of a thoery of alienation, how it is that domination is 'rooted in the nature of human development'[4] but also insists that the genesis of this story is to be found in human *activity*. That is what Lukács meant when he proclaimed the inalienable possibility of detecting, beneath the coercive icons of social experience, 'a trace of human activity,'[5] the fateless causality of the human deed. It is because Marxian theory apprehends domination as the consequence of an 'activity of alienation,'[6] it is because it proceeds from a science of dominated man which, however extraordinary, is the science of normal man and his generic activity, that it would deny the transcendence of alienation and domination the status of a *creatio ex nihilo*, an absolute and catastrophic negation of the existing world. The revolutionary act is thus no more than an explosive *anamnesis* of human agency, repressed but never obliterated: it is, in Marx's own words, 'a confession, nothing else.'[7]

It is to a heterogeneous universe of discourse that Fanon's critical vision summons us. He was not and could not be the epic chronicler of the human world, depicting for us the promise and tragedy of man's generic self-development, the conflicts and agonies rendered ineluctable by humanity's iniquity, infancy, and immaturity. If Marx's account of alienation and domination constitutes a 'dialectical teleology'[8] linked to an ontology of human activity, its historical degradation and immanent recovery, Frantz Fanon's portrayal of the colonial experience as racial domination plunges us, so to speak, *in medias res*. The genre to which the Marxian theory belongs is the narrative;[9] Fanon's representation of reality is, by contrast, dramaturgical.

We need not see this as a congenital idiosyncracy of Fanon's imagination. To be sure, the young Fanon entertained aspirations for dramatic writing and wrote some unpublished plays.[10] But it is also true that in its supreme political expression articulated in *A Dying Colonialism* and *The Wretched of the Earth*, Fanon's aesthetic sensibility was motivated by the historical consciousness, by that understanding which accords a privileged place to 'the phenomena which disclose the historical formation of men' (les phenomènes qui rendent compte de l'historicisation des hommes).[11] Fanon's vision of time as a virgin field of open possibilities, his refusal to encase the self-understanding and political imagination of postcolonial man in the 'secure anchorage'[12] or 'materialized Tower of the Past';[13] his very understanding of the past as 'an invitation to action' and therefore dependent, as Soyinka would say, 'on the sensibility that recalls it,'[14] – this regulative attitude to the temporal dimension of political experience is inseparable from the historical consciousness. But this sensibility whose vocation is the narrative illustration of men's acts of self-constitution, development, and world transformation was called upon to commit itself to a task of irrevocable immediacy: the dramatic representation of a universe in which human universality and agency as such, to say nothing of their translucidy and optimal realization, have been not so much repressed and forgotten but radically banished and obliterated.

Thus Fanon's project of a representation of reality the 'architecture' of which is 'rooted in the temporal' because 'every human problem must be considered from the standpoint of time'[15] is arrested at its very foundations where it confronts its intransigent limits in the ahistorical principle which governs the colonial experience. Race, the regnant principle of 'this narrow world' is the tomb wherein the historical consciousness is interred alive. From an aesthetic preference for chronicling the vicissitudes of human desire, expression, and action, for depicting the local histories of human being and human doing, Fanon's imagination was constrained to undertake the dramatic description of a 'state of being' cursed with the inhuman stamp of race. For race, Fanon understood, is a category extrinsic to man's specifically human relations and political existence. It is, of all mediations between man and man and the world, the most useless, sterile, and insignificant; the least revelatory of what a human being does, to say nothing of who he is; a description of man signifying nothing. As an axial principle of a relation of lordship and bondage, race has the perverse singularity of lacking any *a priori* connection with human activity, any intrinsic significance in the matrix of man's worldly engagements, any inner bond with the coercive roles and relations of which men, beyond their biological existence, sheer humanity, and the ineluctable cycle of birth, senescence, and death, are inescapably the authors. To be dominated in the name of race was for Fanon to suffer the violent usurpation by 'what is contingent' of the privileged place of 'what is important' and endemically problematic for human existence.[16]

Fanon was not the first to have grasped the primal crime of racial domination: the fact that its constitutive principle is a denial of man's universality, historicity, and political being. He was the first to have faced the awesome consequences of this unsettling insight by developing a philosophical critique of domination adamantly attentive to the contingency and singularity of its subject matter and therefore insistent on its inassimilability to any general theory of human bondage as a tragic consequence of human action and intercourse. There was unavailable to Fanon a critique of domination based on a fundamental ontology of human existence or on any general historiosophy, sociology, or psychological explanation of human experience: in short, any critique of domination whose point of departure is human universality and historicity.

It was for this reason that this humanist, this devotee of the universal who could proclaim that 'all forms of exploitation are identical because all of them are applied against the same "object": man,'[17] would, in his definitive 'psychopathological and philosophical explanation of the *state of being* black' repudiate the paradigmatic accounts of domination offered by Hegel, Marx, Freud, and Sartre. That is why it is a facile misreading of Fanon's motives to ascribe this conceptual repudiation to the fact that Hegel, Marx, Freud, and Sartre were European, inescapably 'Others' for all the critical character of their vision, and inevitably committed to a Europocentric representation of human experience.[18] To be sure, Fanon experienced with Césaire the congenital crisis of the black intellectual, the fact that every interpretive act of his, every act of self-understanding, hence of self-transcendence, is executed under the categorial rubrics of European thought; all his sayings, his 'no' no less than his 'yes' are caught within the coercive circle of alien words: this is *his* hermeneutical circle, the vicious circle which is at once the symbol of colonial alienation and nemesis of the revolutionary imagination. But if Fanon learned from Césaire the fugitive circumspection for the traiterous snares of Europe's words, he also relished with him the cunning possibility of transcending their coercive and alienating power by placing them at the service of revolutionary utterance and the non-repressive conversation of the nascent postcolonial nation. This attitude to European thought and language which he called 'dialectical'[19] forbade any simplistic or phobic rejection of their interpretative categories.

It was therefore not because of their Euro-centrism, manifest or veiled, but because of their putative universalism that Fanon rejected the conceptions of human bondage in Hegelian social philosophy, Marxism, psychoanalysis, and existential phenomenology as inapplicable to *l'expérience vécue du noir*. For beyond their conceptual debate in the matters of determinism and voluntarism, methodological individualism versus holism, the differentiation or collapsing of ontology and history, these schools of thought understand the phenomena of domination and alienation not as absurd contingencies but as the manifestations of causal relations unleashed by generic human desires and actions and, therefore, accessible to an explanatory interpretation of their genesis, temporal vicissitudes, and immanent transformations. Even when history is frozen by the transcendental concepts of existentialism into 'temporality', domination retains its meaningful character as necessitated by the intentional history of human activity and intercourse.

It is just his availability of historical meaning which, Fanon suggested, is occluded by an experience of domination based upon the race principle, rendering a 'regressive' inquiry into its phylogenesis a problematic enterprise. The missing link in the temporal architecture of Fanon's critique of domination is the past, not as the *locus* of determinism but as the foundation of causal relations constituted by human activity. Thus his commitment to an analysis of 'the black-white relation' rooted in the temporal amounts to an accusation of the present 'in terms of something to be exceeded,' that is, the future.[20] Given the radical contingency of race as a principle of domination, this accusation of the present and vision of the future must be denied that necessitarian anchorage in past human deeds and that logic of historical immanence which distinguishes the *humanist* critique of domination.

The formal preeminence of 'lived experience' (*l'expérience vécue*) in Fanon's discourse, then, does not coincide with the phenomenological 'reduction' of sociohistorical causation, nor with the existentialist program of rescuing the human world from the taint of determinism. It is a testimony not to the transcendental freedom of generic man's 'lived experience' but rather to the extraordinary opacity in which *l'expérience vécue du noir* is shrouded, rendering impossible the enterprise of the historical consciousness which is the narrative reconstruction and deciphering of causal relations created by men's deeds. For the Marxian language of causality is, paradoxically, committed to the view that the autonomous, mysterious, and coercive character assumed by these relations is the work of human subjects; that 'all reification is a forgetting,'[21] that the translucidity of human deeds may be impaired but never irredeemably interred. And the narratival form of Marxian discourse is inseparable from this privileged refusal to regard the experience of heteronomy as a *state* of being inaccessible to a historiosophical interpretation.

Black Skin, White Masks, Fanon's first work, contains an anguished endeavour to reclaim for the critique of racial domination this humanist interpretation of human bondage as man's self-incurred agony. We see Fanon valiantly struggling to transcend, on the level of critical theory, the reification which is the *primordial* foundation of the colonial experience, to rediscover the origination of reified relations in human activity, and so to re-unite causality with human agency: 'Man's tragedy, Nietzsche said, is that he was once a child. None the less, we cannot afford to forget that, as Charles Odier has shown us, the neurotic's fate remains in his own hands.'[22] This effort to breathe humanity into the inhuman principle of the colonial condition, to recover the banished reality of human agency, testifies to the irrepressible power of Fanon's humanism. It also explains his conceptual explorations of Hegelian-Marxian, existentialist, and psychodynamic interpretations of human coercion and alienation. What this exploration reveals, then, is not a philosophic indecision or eclecticism, as many of Fanon's interpreters suggest, but a rebellious attempt on the part of the humanist imagination to compel 'an absurd drama'[23] to yield decipherable frâgments of universal human significance in spite of its heterogenesis: 'it is a story that takes place in darkness, and the sun that is carried within me must shine into the smallest crannies.'[24] For not to endeavour this sisyphean labour of extracting a universal, human meaning would be a supine prostration of the imagination before the fatality of the race principle, a phenomenalistic endurance of the instantaneous and the contingent as timeless realities refractory to the power of transcending thought and action. Fanon did not intend the 'absurd drama' of the colonized to be staged in the 'theatre of the absurd.' Repressed but never destroyed, submerged under the imperious necessity of the descriptive form,[25] the impulse for epic narration maintains a tabooed existence in Fanon's imagination: as the archetypal genre for the representation of man's historical being, historical suffering, and self-transcendence, the narratival form serves as a foil for depicting a universe emptied of the premise of a shared humanity, shared activities, and shared sentiments; the temporal vicissitudes of these bonds of reciprocity; the tragic possibility of their mutation into chains of bondage; and the fragile promise of recovering, through time, their primordial purpose.

II

It is through a series of conceptual differentiations that Fanon attempts to establish the formal and substantive heterogeneity of the critique of racial domination. He is concerned to show us what the colonial experience is *not* by juxtaposing it to other, universally significant modes of human bondage as interpreted by various traditions of social thought. These exercises in definition by negation culminate in a comparative analysis of Hegel's celebrated epic of interhuman recognition and domination in the *Phenomenology of the Mind* and the colonizer-colonized relationship.[26] Although this is the last of Fanon's conceptual differentiations in *Black Skin, White Masks*, its status may be regarded as teleological, for the argument of the 'Negro and Hegel' is latent in the distinctions he draws earlier between his universe of discourse and Sartre's, Freud's, and Adler's accounts of coercive human relations. The same argument may be said to be the Archimedean point of Fanon's divergence from the Marxian theory of domination in the first chapter of *The Wretched of the Earth*. In short, Fanon's insistence that the pathological desires and conduct of colonized men 'have only an extrinsic relationship'[27] to psychodynamic classifications; his thesis that 'in the Weltanschauung of a colonized people there is an impurity, a flaw that outlaws any ontological explanation';[28] his inversion of the explanatory categories of the Marxian theory of alienation and domination such that the hierarchy of cause and consequence in the Marxian dialectic is transformed:[29] all these may be regarded as thematic modulations of Fanon's brief confrontation of his critique with the Hegelian paradigm of interhuman recognition and domination.

The regulative principle of Hegel's phenomenology of human interaction, including the relation of mastery and bondage, is *reciprocity*. By sketching 'a pure conception of recognition' according to which two human consciousnesses 'recognize themselves as mutually recognizing one another,'[30] Hegel established reciprocity as the transcendental ideal of human intercourse – a norm of complementarity which is ontologically prior to the dialectic of domination and emancipation. In the words of Jürgen Habermas, what is dialectical in the Hegelian theory of interaction 'is not unconstrained intersubjectivity itself, but the history of its suppression and reconstitution.'[31] Hegel suggests, then, that the relationship of mastery and bondage, the emergence of 'the aspect of disparity' in the encounter being consciousness is but a deformed epiphenomenon of the primordial structure of reciprocity.

But if domination is the ineluctable tragedy of human intercourse, if it is necessary for what Kojève called 'anthropogenesis,'[32] this domination succeeds in rupturing not the generic bond of reciprocity but its specific pure form of complementarity. It is the transcendental status of the norm of reciprocity which establishes the possibility of a mutual transformation of the roles of master and slave in the course of their career. If the violent struggle till death institutes the dominance of the consciousness that showed contempt for mere life, the dependence of the master on the subjugated consciousness for 'the truth of his certainty of himself,' together with the slave's 're-discovery of himself by himself'[33] through the very act of coerced labour, reconstitute the impaired bond of reciprocity in a dialectically transformed manner. Reciprocity is therefore the transcendental norm of human interaction and the dialectical irony which attends its degradation into the relation of domination and subordination.

Is it possible, after we have unveiled 'the rational kernel in the mystical shell,'[34] to transpose Hegel's notion of the dialectic of domination and emancipation to Fanon's phenomenology of the colonial experience? Can any dialectical process – the ironic unfolding of the epic of lordship and bondage – be counted on to redeem the relations of colonizer and colonized man? Although Fanon did not pose the problem in exactly the same language, he did address himself to its essence, and we can interpret his reflections as providing a negative answer to our question. For Fanon understood the relation of domination he described not as a phenomenal expression, a 'moment,' of an anthropologically necessary social process but as a contingent experience extrinsic to man's sociality and developmental history. The alienated relations of colonizer and colonized did not constitute for him a tragic deformation of an intercourse which was in its genesis human and humanizing, an original structure of reciprocal recognitions whose fundamental norms would be recaptured in a cunning return of the repressed; rather, he saw coercion and alienation as the inescapable corollaries of a primordial violence which inaugurated and forever sustained the relations between the colonizer and the colonized.

'The Negro and Hegel' does not elucidate with unambiguous cogency the nature of this 'existential deviation' from the inner vicissitudes of human sociality. Fanon appears to have missed the complex interplay of the transcendental and the dialectical as the dual logic of Hegel's theory of interaction. He does not recognize the important fact that what Habermas has identified as the dialectical aspect of Hegel's paradigm – namely, the suppression and reconstitution of unconstrained intersubjectivity – owes its possibility to that which is antecedent to repressive interaction: the transcendental imperative of complementarity predicated upon the premise of a common humanity. In this Fanon probably followed a tendency in Kojève's interpretation of the *Phenomenology* towards suppressing the ontological priority of non-repressive interaction to the emergence of lordship and bondage, and therefore towards collapsing these two strictly distinguishable moments and seeing violence, domination, and inequality as coeval with 'anthropogenesis.' Thus the overarching significance of the category of reciprocity in Hegel's social philosophy is not lost on Fanon: 'At the foundation of Hegelian dialectic there is an absolute reciprocity which must be emphasized.'[35] But what he does not recognize is the transcendental status of this reciprocity, that is to say, its logical priority to the life and death struggle. And so Fanon one-sidedly interprets Hegel to have understood violence as that which makes possible 'the creation of a human world – that is, of a world of reciprocal recognition,'[36] as opposed to that which leads to the development of man's social experience in a dialectically transformed manner.

The result of this conceptual confusion in Fanon's reading of the *Phenomenology* is that he sometimes suggests as the grounds for the inapplicability of the Hegelian paradigm the fact that the historical emancipation of the black slave was accomplished without his violent struggle. Thus Fanon writes: 'There is not an open conflict between white and black. One day the White Master, *without conflict*, recognized the Negro slave.' Again: 'Historically, the Negro steeped in the inessentiality of servitude was set free by his master. He did not fight for his freedom.' An emancipation proclamation suddenly prompted 'the machine-animal-men to the supreme rank of *men*.' The consequence? 'The upheaval reached the Negroes from without. The black was acted upon. Values that had not been created by his actions, values that had not been born of the systolic tide of his blood, danced in a hued whirl round him. The upheaval did not make a difference in the Negro. He went from one way of life to another, but not from one life to another.'[37]

It will be noted that the import of these passages foreshadows the argument for revolutionary violence in *The Wretched of the Earth*. There, Fanon's earlier protest that the former slave 'can find in his memory no trace of the struggle for liberty or of that anguish of liberty of which Kierkegaard speaks'[38] will be given a political restatement in the vision of revolutionary violence as that which creates in the consciousness of colonized man '*une image d'action*,'[39] an archetypal experience of action. But deriving as they do from a one-sided interpretation of Hegel, the passages just cited from *Black Skin, White Masks* cannot be regarded as providing an adequate foundation for a justificatory theory of revolution. In his attempt to locate the concrete historical genesis of the black condition, Fanon takes as the point of departure what is actually an *epiphenomenon* or secondary fact: the emancipation of the black slave in a manner that would, according to Fanon, only reinforce his heteronomy.

An adequate justification of revolutionary violence based on Hegel's social philosophy must proceed from a critical comparison of his transcendental ideal of human intercourse with the structural characteristics of the relations between whites and blacks. Such a comparison must not only show how inadequate the historical fact of the emancipation was to the requirements of authentic human liberation, but, more fundamentally, it must indicate in what respects the primal encounter between blacks and whites was radically dehumanizing. If Fanon could show this encounter to be extraordinary, even as an experience of domination, he would establish the justification for a revolutionary project whose significance would be equally 'extraordinary' (*impor-*

tance inhabituelle):[40] a revolutionary project entailing not simply a *transition*, immanently possible, 'from one way of life to another' but a *leap* 'from one life to another.' What must the structure of interaction be and what must the experience of domination consist in to necessitate this catastrophism in the philosophy of revolution?

There must, *ab initio*, be absent from the structure of interaction the premise of a shared humanity and with it the ideal of reciprocity upon which the possibility of an eventual exchange of roles, hence the possibility of freedom from the reification of roles, is predicated. In spite of his misleading interpretation, presented in the main body of the text, concerning the function of violence in Hegel's theory, a lengthy footnote in 'The Negro and Hegel' indicates Fanon's intuitive grasp of the differentiating characteristics of racial domination. 'I hope I have shown that here the master differs basically from the master described by Hegel. For Hegel there is reciprocity; here the master laughs at the consciousness of the slave. What he wants from the slave is not recognition but work.

In the same way, the slave here is in no way identifiable with the slave who loses himself in the object and finds in his work the source of his liberation. The Negro wants to be like the master.

Therefore he is less independent than the Hegelian slave.

In Hegel the slave turns away from the master and turns toward the object.

Here the slave turns toward the master and abandons the object.'[41]

The import of this comparative analysis of Hegel's master-slave paradigm and the structure of black-white relations has not been fully appreciated by some of Fanon's interpreters. Thus Renate Zahar reading Fanon's concept of violence as 'implicitly derived from Hegel through the philosophy of Sartre' writes in *L'oeuvre de Frantz Fanon*: 'Colonialist domination and enslavement are a new historical form of the relationship between master and slave analysed by Hegel.' Without paying due attention to the problematic nature of Fanon's debt to Hegel, Zahar could then charge Fanon with leaving out of his account 'the element in the Hegelian theory which alone makes the emancipation of the slave possible: the process of material labour,' and substituting for it 'the political process of emancipation through violence.' From the perspective of Zahar's Marxifying Hegelianism, Fanon woefully neglects 'the economic derivation' of the colonial experience of alienation.[42] On the other hand, Irene Gendzier appears to see in Fanon's analysis a narrow economism which substituted, for the condition of the Hegelian slave, 'the economic exploitation of the servant.'[43] According to this thesis, Fanon 'may have been reflecting on the utter disdain in which the white master held the black servant, a disdain so totally destructive that it seemed to obviate any consideration of the servant, save as a labour-producing machine.' Gendzier offers no textual evidence for the view that Fanon's archetype of colonized man was modelled on the situation of the black servant. Nor does she seem to understand that the unredeemable character of the work of Fanon's 'slave' is a derivative phenomenon: where domination does not represent the tragic deformation of an original experience of reciprocal recognitions, the labour of colonized man must be reduced to a crassly instrumental and economic status; it can no longer be the privileged medium for the rehumanization of a dehumanized interaction.

Thus it was not ignorance of the ontological significance of human work, or the 'non-philosophic sense'[44] in which Fanon supposedly understood the terms labour and recognition that led him to deny the emancipatory possibilities of work or to see nothing immanently redeeming in the existence of colonized man, but an agonizingly critical insight into how widely the black-white relation departs from the norm of reciprocity which governs the Hegelian paradigm of human interaction and domination. For, ultimately, what drives Hegel's master to an 'existential impasse' consisting in his involuntary dependence upon the dominated consciousness and makes possible the self-transcendence of the slave is the prior insertion of both in the same human world of reciprocal recognitions, their participation in a dialectic of identity and difference which establishes the exchange or mutual transformation of roles as a structural possibility. In Fanon's scheme, by contrast, prior to all economic exploitation, servile toil, and social inequality, presiding over these compelling facts as *secondary* phenomena is the primal crime of the colonial experience: the radical violation of the premise of a common humanity and, with it, the rupture of reciprocity in the interaction between the colonizer and the colonized.

Although this crucial insight into the heterogeneous patterns of Hegel's master-slave nexus and the colonizer-colonized relation is intimated in *Black Skin, White Masks*, it is in the first chapter of *The Wretched of the Earth* that Fanon, without mentioning Hegel, definitively establishes the ground for his departure from that ontological paradigm. In contradistinction to the dialectic of complementarity which regulates the Hegelian model, Fanon identifies the structural logic of the colonial relationship of domination as 'Aristotelean.' 'The zone where the natives live is not complementary to the zone inhabited by the settlers. The two zones are opposed, but not in the service of a higher unity. Obedient to the rules of pure Aristotelean logic, they both follow the principle of reciprocal exclusivity. No conciliation is possible, for of the two terms, one is superfluous.'[45]

This passage provides the key textual evidence that any interpretation of Fanon's critique of the colonizer-colonized relation as a 'reflection on the *dialectics* of domination' after the manner of Hegel's theory is in serious error.[46] For the dialectical character of Hegel's analysis consists precisely of the fact that it accords the experience of reciprocal recognition an ontological priority to the phenomena of violence and coercion. It is because Fanon denied the colonial condition any ontological foundations, it is because he disengaged it from the tragic vicissitudes of universal social experience, that he saw 'absolute violence' as coeval with the 'first encounter' between the colonizer and the colonized. In Fanon's critique of racial domination all ontological categories are obliterated by an insistence upon the radical contingency of a historical event: foreign occupation.

III

This indeed is what distinguishes the Fanonist attitude to ontology and history from Marxism. For Marx did not *repudiate* an ontological explanation of human coercion: he transcended ontology by dialectically incorporating it into a historiosophical theory of human development, self-alienation, and emancipation. Marx replaced the idealist ontology of the reciprocal recognition and tragic confrontation of consciousnesses with a materialistic ontology *and* historiosophy of human activity and 'activity of alienation' or alienated labour. This tension between ontology and history, which Marxian theory maintains, establishes human self-alienation and bondage neither as transhistorical constants indelibly inscribed into human experience, nor as chance occurrences radically contingent and devoid of phylogenetic significance, but as historical manifestations of men's practical activities and intercourse between themselves.

Of this dialectical connection between human productive activity and the development of coercive social and political phenomena, Marxian theory regards the structuration of class relations as the summary expression. Class relations – the alienated and exploitative relations of men to the mode of production – epitomize the transformation of men's practical activities into structures of domination. The point that needs to be underscored here is the causal dependence of class division and coercion upon the dialectic of social labour: the idea, in short, that class is a *product* of alienated activity.[47] 'Master' and 'slave' do not owe their assymetrical roles to political accidents; nor are these roles *prior* to the elaboration of the relations of coerced labour and exploitation; they are constituted by alienated productive activity. This point was clarified by Herbert Marcuse over four decades ago: 'It is not a case of a "master" existing first, subordinating someone else to himself, alienating him from his labour, and making him into a mere worker and himself into a non-worker. But nor is it a case of the relationship between domination and servitude being the simple consequence of the alienation of labour. The alienation of labour, as estrangement from its own activity and from its object, already *is* in itself the relationship between worker and non-worker and between domination and servitude.'[48]

Thus bourgeoisie and proletariat, the antagonistic classes of capitalist society, are seen by Marx as antithetical members of a social totality created by human activity; they are the 'positive' and 'negative' sides of a contradictory reality. As formulated in *The Holy Family*: 'The propertied class and the class of the proletariat represent the same human self-alienation.'[49] Class relations may therefore be said to epitomize the 'passion' of human activity. By the same token the possibility of emancipation from a reified and coerced existence is rooted in the dialectical structure of the class relation itself. Only the class whose coerced work sustains the fabric of the alienated world, the class upon whose very 'passion' the mark of activity is indelibly stamped, is privileged with the capacity to decipher the secret of capitalist society and, hence, to transform it. That class is the proletariat. But the entire salience which Marx accords class as the epitome of the experience of domination and the epicentre of revolutionary transformation is a function of his overarching ontology of productive activity.

Altogether different is Fanon's interpretation of the structure of the hegemonic relation in the colonial world. From the central premise of the role of violence and forceful *occupation* as the constitutive feature of the colonial experience, Fanon drew far-reaching conclusions with regard to the relevance of Marxist analysis. Beneath the coercive social relations of the colonial world, Fanon uncovers not the tragic history of human practical activity, but a primordial reification of roles, a structure of power relations based upon the bastard principle of race. And this disclosure impels Fanon to call for a revision of the structure of causation in the Marxian explanation of domination: 'The originality of the colonial context is that economic reality, inequality and the immense difference of ways of life never come to mask human realities. When you examine the colonial context in its immediacy, it is evident that what parcels out the world is to begin with the fact of belonging to or not belonging to a given race, a given species. In the colonies the economic substructure is also a superstructure. The cause is the consequence; you are rich because you are white, you are white because you are rich. This is why Marxist analysis should always be slightly stretched every time we have to do with the colonial problem.'[50]

It is evident that Fanon's revisionism is much more serious than his tame call for a stretching of Marxist analysis would suggest. It embraces, in fact, nothing less than a logical inversion of the relation between base and superstructure, the economic and the political or relations of production and power relations, material conditions and consciousness, social reality and ideology: in brief, the principal categories of historical materialism. It may perhaps be more accurate to characterize this exercise in categorial revision not as an inversion of cause and consequence but as a disclosure of their reciprocal and circular co-implication. Thus between class, race, and power there pertains not a unidirectional causal relationship constituted by productive activity and relations but a circular relationship of ascribed, imposed, and reified roles.[51]

By the same token, the ways in which human collectivities, colonizers and colonized, perceive themselves and each other are not so much ideological prisms masking relations of production, but are unmediated structural aspects of the power relations of the 'colonial context.' Hence, the ideology of colonial domination, racism, is *consciously* entailed by it, and may even be said to exercise a significant role in the structure of social relations. It is for this reason that Fanon calls that ideology the '*primary Manicheism*':[52] primary because it is neither 'a superadded element'[53] nor the falsifying prism through which men's practical activities and relations emerge distorted or through which, in Marx's words, 'men and their circumstances appear upside down as in a *camera obscura.*'[54] Ideology is here not the mask of reality but its emblem. Thus racism, Fanon allowed, is 'not a constant of the human spirit,' nor is it 'fundamentally determining.' But neither is it 'a mental quirk' or a 'psychological flaw.' Although Fanon would sometimes suggest a historical-materialist explanation of racism in a humanist opposition to biologistic and psychologistic explanations, and would argue for the historical contingency of racism upon the structure of capitalist society,[55] his definitive interpretation suggests that the historical contingency of racism is a special contingency: in other words, that racism is a functional requirement of colonial domination as a historical phenomenon *sui generis*. Obeying 'a flawless logic,'[56] racist ideology reflects the 'totalitarian' organization of roles established by the 'first encounter' between the colonizer and the colonized and the institutionalized 'racialization' of 'their existence together.'

In its primary Manicheistic structuring of human relations bearing no intrinsic connection with human activity and historicity, the politics of race proscribes *time* as a dimension of human experience – time as 'the room of human development.'[57] What is in question here is something far more fatal to human experience than the Marxian critique of the degradation of time which is the direct consequence of the quantitative and qualitative alienation of the workers' time in the service of surplus value. At stake in the colonial world is nothing less than a people's consciousness of the possibility, granted by their autonomous relation to a shared community of time, of beginning something all their own, of disturbing the silence of the world with the poetry of their public deeds, of reversing the timeless fatality of things by re-arranging their material and moral circumstances. For the colonized, time and history are effaced by that totalitarian collusion of political force and racist ideology which segregates them to a decreed *space* of action, motion, and expression maintained by pervasive signs against transgression. The domination of colonized man is depicted by Fanon as being primarily and archetypically an experience of spatial coercion, constriction, and confinement.[58] Leon Damas, a colonized poet had written before Fanon: 'They have stolen the space that was mine.' In Fanon's hands the poetic accusation is turned into a regulative political metaphor evoking 'the geographical layout' of 'this narrow world, strewn with prohibitions:' 'a world divided into compartments, a motionless, Manicheistic world, a world of statues: the statue of the general who carried out the conquest, the statue of the engineer who built the bridge; a world which is sure of itself, which crushes with its stones the backs flayed by whips: This is the colonial world. The native is a being hemmed in; apartheid is simply one form of the division into compartments of the colonial world. The first thing the native learns is to stay in his place, and not to go beyond certain limits.'[59]

From this confining world no historical action can emerge, only pathological dreams of 'action and aggression,' of possession and vengeful freedom. To Fanon's colonized man is denied that retributive cunning of reason which makes dominated man in the Hegelian-Marxian epic the privileged agent of history. Disavowing every historiosophical theodicy of human bondage, Fanon faced the terrifying consequences of his phenomenological attention to 'the colonial order of things' experienced 'in its immediacy': 'the colonizer makes history; his life is an epic, an Odyssey. He is the absolute beginning: "This land was created by us." He is the unceasing cause: "If we leave, all is lost, and the country will go back to the Middle Ages." '[60]

Aimé Césaire whose great poem *Return to My Native Land* was probably the source of Fanon's spatial metaphors and topographical imageries was the first to suggest the fatal bond between the experience of spatial oppression and the utter paralysis of action: the relation between coercive space, alienated time, and the estrangement of colonized men from history – from participating in 'everything expressed, affirmed, freed' in their own land.[61] Because historical action is the monopolistic privilege of the colonizer, the colonized are incapable of being 'actional'; they are condemned to 'reactive' and mimetic behaviour, defence mechanisms, envious dreams of taking the colonizer's place.

In the name of *lived experience*, Fanon resolutely refuses to credit colonial domination with offering the colonized an apprenticeship in the labour of universal history. As Amilcar Cabral, following Fanon, would argue, colonial domination entailed nothing less than 'the negation of the historical process' of the colonized people.[62] Paradoxically, it is precisely because Fanon and Cabral accepted the Marxian theory of universal history and the primacy which Marxism ascribes to class antagonism and action as the motive force of social and cultural transformation that they regarded the colonial experience as representing a structural deviation from *human* history. They argued that colonial domination, based as it is on a race structure of power, imposes on the colonized a homogeneity of condition and engenders, beyond all differentials of situation and nuances of behaviour, a *negative* identity of experience. Thus the colonial order of things presents itself as 'a coherent whole' (*un ensemble cohérent*), not in the Marxian sense of a dialectical totality constituted by the historical mediations of antagonistic relations to productive activity, but as a simple, *unmediated*, 'undifferentiated whole.'[63] The reified form in which the colonial reality *appears* as an undifferentiated monopoly of force in the hands of the colonizer and an undifferentiated loss of power on the part of the colonized is, Fanon suggests, its *essence*. To view the colonial reality in this manner is not because of the poverty of the phenomenalistic eye ignorant of more fundamentally determinative relations with all their 'internal contradictions,' nor is it 'out of simplemindedness or xenophobia,' but because every colonizer maintains, with reference to the colonized, 'relations that are based on force' sustained by a Manicheistic, racist ideology.

From this perspective, the totalitarian homogenization of situation symbolized by the experience of spatial confinement and segregation negates the primacy of class division based upon the exploitation of labour time as the definitive characteristic or constitutive feature of racial and colonial domination. In the words of Chinua Achebe, the white man 'came and levelled everybody down.' Neither Fanon nor Cabral confounded this externally imposed homogeneity of condition or negative totalitarianism of misery with a positive equality of situation or *classlessness*. To put it metaphorically, they recognized that the infernal world of the damned is a polycentric system of unrelieved destitution and treacherous privilege, hopeless despair and desperate hope, servitude without illusion and servitude wearing the mask of mastery. But they insisted upon the priority of the unmediated structure of racial dominance to every structure of class relations among the colonized. Thus while the phenomenological critique of the colonial experience refuses to submerge the reality of class formation within the colonized collectivity under the mystique of what Marx derided as 'universal fraternization and brotherhood,'[64] it nevertheless refrains from categorizing the colonial reality definitively as a *class society* from which *one* determinate social group, because of its specific relation to productive activity, must necessarily emerge as the privileged agent of historical transformation.

In this refusal to define the colonial order as a class society, the Fanonist perspective accords with Anthony Giddens' insistence on maintaining 'the Marxian emphasis upon the *explanatory salience* of class as central to the notion of class society.' Giddens writes: 'A class society, in Marx's writings, is not simply a society in which there happen to be classes, but one in which class relationships provide the key to the explication of the social structure in general.'[65] In fact the explanatory salience of class in Marxian theory, it may be recalled, is inseparable from Marx's theory of the alienation of man from his fellow man engendered by the alienation of productive activity. Having tacitly accepted the conceptual foundations of the Marxian theory of class, Fanon could not endow class formation constituted by the race structure of power, that is by an altogether passive and contingent principle, with any salient, sociohistorical and transformative significance. *This* mode of class formation, in short, may not be confounded with that manifestation of the cunning of historical reason which wreaks tragic suffering even as it transforms and renews human existence. Sustained by an indiscriminate intercollectivity of reified relations, a 'Manicheistic' dichotomy between the place of the whites and the place of the blacks, the social structure of colonialism is revealed as an aberrant form, a fatal digression from the plot of human history. It is from a similar perspective that Cabral, in response to those in quest of the class that constitutes the historical agent in the colonial world and the anti-colonial revolution, insisted that: 'Here a distinction must be drawn between colonial history and our history as human societies; as a dominated people we only present an ensemble vis-à-vis the oppressor ... What commands history in colonial conditions is not the class struggle. I do not mean that the class struggle in Guinea stopped completely during the colonial period; it continued but in a muted way. In the colonial period it is the colonial state which commands history.'[66]

No one emerges unscarred from the collective agony of racial coercion. No one escapes the colonizer's totalitarian and monopolistic appropriation of the spaces of action and expression, of the very meaning of being human, of truth, beauty, and virtue: his uncontestable right of being a pure subject commanding without listening; narcissistically presiding over a monologic universe; seeing without being looked at; the authoritarian principle of action never acted upon; secure in an inviolable tower of being consecrated by the capricious grace of race. Sartre who, in his preface to *The Wretched of the Earth* and elsewhere, would sympathetically misinterpret Fanon's inferno as if it were an exemplification of his own dismal and macabre picture of human intercourse, has given us an inimitable portrait of the colonizer's monopolistic privilege stressing its frightful transgression of the boundaries of historical time and its tyrannical veto against the principle of interhuman reciprocity: 'for the white man has enjoyed for three thousand years the privilege of seeing without being seen. It was a seeing pure and uncomplicated; the light of his eyes drew all things from their primeval darkness. The whiteness of his skin was a further aspect of vision, a light condensed. The white man, white because he was man, white like the day, white as truth is white, white like virtue, lighted like a torch all creation; he unfolded the essence, secret and white, of existence.'[67] Fanon evoked the 'absurd drama' of collective subjection to this totalitarian world which denies black humanity a right of entrance into the privileged and guarded spaces of the colonizer and, at the same time, any free spaces of their own to act, invent, and define themselves, thus confronting the colonized with a pathogenic struggle between fascination and taboo: 'the white world, the only honorable one, barred me from all participation. A man was expected to behave like a man. I was expected to behave like a black man – or at least like a nigger. I shouted a greeting to the world and the world slashed away my joy. I was told to stay within bounds, to go back where I belonged.'[68]

The spatial dichotomy between the 'settlers' town' and the 'natives' town' is but a physical representation of this repressive dialectic of appeal and prohibition: 'this hostile world, ponderous and aggressive because it fends off the colonised masses with all the harshness it is capable of, represents not merely a hell from which the swiftest flight possible is desirable, but also a paradise close at hand which is guarded by terrible watchdogs.'[69]

IV

Such is 'the state of being' of colonized man: a reified existence in a confining space guarded by 'these inspectors of the Ark before the Flood.' Having learned from phenomenological ontology that human freedom is intimately connected with man's living and acting in space, with the spatiality of his embodied consciousness;[70] that freedom *is* 'the open dimension of each consciousness'[71] in its affective, expressive, and practical activity, Fanon portrayed the colonial condition as an extreme experience of spatial closure, a condition wherein men are, in Fanon's words, 'besieged from within by the colonizer'[72] in all their fundamental relations to the world. I said that Fanon derived this preoccupation with human spatiality from existential phenomenology. But, as in all his philosophical debts to this and other schools of thought, he *politicized* the concept of spatiality by giving it a non-ontological explication. He understood that based as it is on a structure of racial dominance, the repressive spatialization of existence in the colonial world radically diverges from the structuring of 'lived space' or 'hodological space'[73] in which existentialist ontology locates the contours and possibilities of human action and self-transcendence in the presence of other men. For the constitutive principle of *this* structuring of space imposed by the occupation is nothing less than the segregation of black humanity from 'the usual conception of man.'[74] Colonized man is segregated to 'a zone of nonbeing, an extraordinarily sterile and arid region'[75] from which nothing germinates or originates, in which all autonomous action and responsibility are paralysed.

In 'Racism and Culture,' Fanon posed the following question: 'but the men who are a prey to racism, the enslaved, exploited, weakened social group –

how do they behave? What are their defence mechanisms?'[76] It is in terms of a pathology of lived space whose etiology is the experience of political force that Fanon portrays the reified and reactive conduct of colonized men: their perfervid endeavour to gain a right of entrance (*droit de cité*) into the privileged universe of the colonizer, to seek 'incorporation into a group that had seemed hermetic.' Fanon explains: 'there is a psychological phenomenon which consists in the belief that the world will open to the degree that the frontiers are broken down.'[77] But this thrust to transgress the totalitarian boundaries of the colonized condition is a sisyphean enterprise doomed to futility. Sisyphean because the colonizer's privilege was never established by the power of human activity but imposed by the speechless violence of racial conquest; futile because the colonized cannot attain this privilege without abolishing the colonial condition itself. The obsessive quest for a 'white destiny' is a double error to the extent that it at once confirms the colonizer's monopolization of human worth and because it seeks to break up this monopoly established by violence and ascription with ineffectual proofs of achievement.

Black Skin, White Masks portrays in detail colonized man's futile attempt to breach the segregation of his being and the reification of his role through deracialization and assimilation. For the mute violence of racial conquest that established 'a world where words wrap themselves in silence,'[78] colonized man substitutes proficiency in the colonizer's language as certificate of participation in a common universe of expression and meaning, a shared symbolic space – in short, a political community. He seeks to disengage the colonizer's language from the logic of domination not by placing it at the service of revolutionary utterance as Fanon would suggest in *A Dying Colonialism*, but by lending affirmative value to its original status: to the world view of which that language is at once the articulation and foundation; to its monological right to talk the shared and distinctive humanity of the colonized out of existence; to its systematic structuring of 'ways of seeing and thinking that are essentially white.' A 'pejorative judgement with respect to his original forms of existence,'[79] a disintegration of the cognitive bonds of his indigenous community, is the inevitable consequence of this imaginary participation in the symbolic space of the colonizer.[80]

But no fantasy, according to Fanon, can upset 'the chain of command' forged by violence; no mimesis of communication can transform the speechless relation of lordship and bondage. From the moment that an *evolué* is praised for his 'communicative competence' and entire array of cultural acquisitions *in spite of his race*, the original Manicheism is re-instated as the only honest foundation of the relations between the colonized and the colonizer. From the moment that a European speaks 'pidgin' to a black man and classifies him automatically as a 'pidgin-nigger-talker,' he obliterates, through this monstrous collapsing of subject and predicate, any possibility of the shock of recognition granted by men's mutual *poesis* of their identities through their words and deeds. Thus the fragile chance of interhuman dereification which is the moral promise of the communicative encounter is destroyed by the 'paternalistic structure'[81] and the essential monologism of speech in the colonial world. Hannah Arendt has written eloquently of the 'revelatory quality of speech,' the self-disclosure of the human agent through his words and deeds.[82] Fanon insists that colonized man, intent on 'revealing himself through his language,' that is, his acquired linguistic competence, only succeeds in disclosing his radical loss of subjectivity. Speech is here an 'internal siege,' a coercive phenomenon articulated through an obsessive ritual of self-inspection and phobic anxiety over inviting the stereotypic judgment of the dominant 'other.' The speech 'acts' of colonized men are inescapably *reactive*; they are compulsive anticipations of the terror and shame of collective reification. Fanon concluded that 'the first action of the black man is *reaction*.'[83]

That is why Fanon understood colonized man's singular 'problem of language' as symptomatic of his total situation in the world. The paradigmatic character of 'our relation to language' has been stressed by Heidegger time and again: 'if it is true that man finds the proper abode of his existence in language – whether he is aware of it or not – then an experience we undergo with language will touch the innermost nexus of our existence.'[84] For Fanon the linguistic experience of colonized man epitomizes his alienated attempt to break the coercive reification of racial roles, an attempt to open up a closed universe which merely perpetuates 'the infernal circle' of domination and fails abysmally to interrupt 'the rhythm of the world.' Language, which Heidegger has called the 'house of Being,' is in Fanon's colonized universe a house of bondage.

But this failure of language to breach the silence of violence and tyranny, this futility of the attempt on the part of the black *evolué* to demolish the alliance between language and domination – this structural impossibility of what Habermas has called 'linguistic intersubjectivity' – is itself derivative of a more fundamental and, so to speak, pre-communicative 'impairment of ... human relations.'[85] Fanon locates the pathogenesis of repressive and anti-dialogical communication in 'the collapse of the antennae with which I touch and through which I am touched.'[86] There can be no institution and experience of shared meanings, no intersubjectivity of understanding, 'for it is precisely the opening of oneself to the other that is organically excluded from the colonial situation.'[87] The closure of communicative relations between colonizer and colonized is a phenomenal manifestation of an affective refusal of the human quality and inexchangeable individualities of black men and women. It is in their very corporeality, their skin, that black colonized men and women experience the reification of their being.

The centrality which Fanon accords the experience of the body and the affective relations which are its superstructural manifestations reveals his debts to existentialist philosophy and Freudian psychoanalysis. But he departed from the psychologism and methodological individualism of Freudian theory, as well as the ontological realms in which the existentialist account of human embodiment is situated, and translated both perspectives into a critical theory of affective relations whose foundations and significance were transindividual and political. For the black skin is not simply a contingent or accidental form of human corporeality which constitutes man's centre of reference, perception, expression, action, and desire in a world inhabited by other men, and which is therefore the primal medium of the universal *individual* experience of subjectivity and alienation. The flesh is here an indelible sign of a collective role imposed by power relations, the visible emblem of a Manicheistic arrangement of human situations. The reification of colonized man's being is experienced with oppressive immediacy in the degraded flesh. ' "Dirty nigger!" Or simply "Look, a Negro!" I came into the world imbued with the will to find a meaning in things, my spirit filled with the desire to attain to the source of the world, and then I found that I was an object in the midst of other objects.'[88]

It is from this tyrannizing impersonality of the flesh perceived as racial property that colonized black men seek an escape. But in so doing they again lend support to the very Manicheism which condemned their flesh to an indiscriminate degradation and their being to a collectivized racial 'essence.' The belief that 'everyone of us has a white potential'[89] carries with it an obsessive desire for denigrification or 'lactification' – the desire to 'throw off the burden of that corporeal malediction' which is the fact of blackness. The overvaluation of whiteness which this desire expresses is described by Fanon as an 'affective erethism.'[90] And its most tangible form is the passion for interracial sexual unions: 'out of the blackest part of my soul, across the zebra stripping of my mind, surges this desire to be suddenly *white*. I wish to be acknowledged not as *black* but as *white*. Now – and this is a form of recognition that Hegel had not envisaged – who but a white woman can do this for me? By loving me she proves that I am worthy of white love. I am loved like a white man.'[91]

Although Fanon devotes two chapters of *Black Skin, White Masks* to the phenomenon of interracial sexuality as an exemplification of 'affective erethism,' he did not regard sexuality to be causally determining or as providing an explanation of the black-white relation. To begin with, he denied that the 'racial drama' is enacted in the recesses of the unconscious wherein the Freudian drama of desire is located:[92] distorted passions and alienated desires were not to be explained through a reconstruction of forgotten wishes but to be subjected to the ethical criticism of 'moral consciousness'[93] compelled by an un-concealed relation of power to don a mask of whiteness. Moreover Fanon insisted that sexual phenomena are to be given 'considerable importance' if one wanted to understand the racial situation 'not in its totality' but psycho-analytically, that is, 'as it is experienced by individual consciousnesses.'[94] It is therefore the moral-political and exemplary significance of interracial sexual-ity that interested Fanon. And that is what makes his analysis of sexuality far more important than a mere autobiographical and confessional document of his own relations with white women. It may be said that Fanon understood the compulsive craving for white flesh to be evidence of a displacement and fundamental estrangement of what Edmund Burke, in his acute appreciation of the 'sentimental bases' of political community called the 'public affections.'[95]

In their obsessive aspiration for incorporation into the very being of the white colonizer, the colonized rupture their affective bonds with each other and their community. So that to the estrangement of self and community en-gendered by the appeal of the colonizer's word is added the political alienation bred by fascination with the colonizer's flesh symbolising the exogenous charac-ter of the passionate feelings which are the metarational springs of political obligation, the 'value-building superstructure,' and the 'entire vision of the world' that sustain political existence. Ayi Kwei Armah has captured the poli-tical significance of alienated eros in *Why Are We So Blest?* 'Love, a fusion, a confusion, of the self with an other self. With terrifyingly different, *other*, selves, a terrifying case of love. A loss of identity, the beginning of wild erring journeys for the soul dissolved.'[96] Thus the alienated consciousness of the black skin and the imperious appeal of the white skin herald the ruin of com-munity, the violent death of the body-politic. This is what Césaire meant when he described colonized men as forming a 'strange crowd which does not gather,'[97] a collectivity of dissonant hopes and fears bereft of a moral bond made flesh.

V

What can this passionate embrace of the white world, this desire for a 'new way of being,' engender in the interaction among the colonized themselves if not obsessive mutual comparison, depreciation, and self-exceptionalism – a pathological project of individual ascendancy founded upon an illusory ap-proximation to 'the essence of the white man' and the domination of fellow colonized man? The wish to be 'closer to the white man' and to be 'distanced from the black' instigates a morbid will to repressive power, a desire 'to lord it over this niggertrash as an, unchallenged master.'[98] It is evident to Fanon that 'the permanent preoccupation with drawing the attention of the white man, the anxiety to become powerful like the white man'[99] should make of the colonial experience not 'a school for democracy,'[100] as Rupert Emerson's curious understanding of dialectics would have it, but an apprenticeship in authoritarian behaviour and politics: 'the Negro is comparison. There is the first truth. He is comparison: that is, he is constantly preoccupied with self-evaluation and with the ego-ideal ... Every position of one's own, every effort of security, is based on relations of dependence, with the diminution of the other. It is the wreckage of what surrounds me that provides the foundation of my virility ... The Antillean is characterized by his desire to dominate the other.'[101] Reduced to an object by the Manicheism of racial dominance, colonized man sees another colonized man as an object, a mere instrument enabling him to realize his 'subjective security.' Thus each colonized man becomes 'an isolated, sterile, salient atom with sharply defined rights of passage.'[102]

This profound insight into the pathogenesis of authoritarian relations and coercive individualism among the colonized is first presented in the seventh chapter of *Black Skin, White Masks*, entitled 'The Negro and Recognition.' It is the second part of this chapter, 'The Negro and Hegel,' which, I have argued, defines the fundamental pattern of the colonizer-colonized relation as founded upon a norm of irreciprocity and so provides genetic explanation for the structure of aspirations of colonized men and their mutual relations with each other. Just as the fundamental thesis of 'The Negro and Hegel' is restated in 'Concerning Violence' – the first chapter of *The Wretched of the Earth* – so Fanon's argument with regard to the genesis and structure of social hierarchy, status politics, and class consciousness among the colonized in *The Wretched of the Earth* is an elaboration of his analysis of authoritarian relations in his first work. In short 'the logic of social hierarchy'[103] within the colonized community, Fanon suggests, is derived from the 'Aristotelean' logic of 'reciprocal exclusivity' which governs the primary relations of the colonizer and the colonized. The former is a desperate imitation of the latter's patterns of monological and coercive relations.

It is in this context that the peculiarities of Fanon's attitude to class formation and class consciousness in the social structure of the colonized world is to be understood. The ethical, 'subjectivistic,' and accusatory accent of Fanon's analysis of class relations makes sense only from the vantage point of his entire critical phenomenology of the colonial experience. From this perspective, every particularism in the face of the essentially 'undifferentiated' structure of racial subordination – in the face of what is 'a mass relationship'[104] – appears to be, at best, a futile and unrealizable endeavour to share the colonizer's position, at worst it is a traiterous aspiration which Fanon does not hesitate to castigate as 'le "démerdage," la forme athée du salut.' For Fanon, then, class formation and class consciousness among the colonized are founded not importantly upon endogenous productive relations, but upon *ressentiment*, status aspirations, unproductive acquisitiveness, and the impulse to establish in relation to fellow colonized men the authoritarian 'narcissism'[105] which is the colonizer's privilege. In so far as it engenders an unshared understanding of a shared condition, class consciousness may be said to mask colonial reality and is therefore a false consciousness; it substitutes for the real world of absolute coercion and confining spaces of action, what Ayi Kwei Armah calls a 'pretended world' of infinite mobility and possibilities available to all who can proffer material and intellectual proofs of liberation from the cave of the 'damned.'

Of this pathology of class formation – pathological because it lacks an intrinsic connection with the historical development of the human species through productive activity – the 'national middle-class'[106] is singled out by Fanon for special examination and execration. The indeterminate nature of the relation of this 'class' to productive activity, hence the questionable character of its qualification to be called a 'class,' let alone a 'bourgeoisie' in the Marxian sense, is reflected in Fanon's shifting nomenclature. He refers to members of this 'class' interchangeably as the 'élite'; 'colonized intellectuals' or 'native intellectuals'; 'a kind of class of affranchised slaves, or slaves who are individually free'; 'the national bourgeoisie'; a 'caste'; 'a bourgeoisie of the civil service.'[107] I have noted that Fanon did not categorize colonial society as a class society precisely because of his adherence to the Marxian conception of class as a creation of productive activity and relations, and his denial that colonial relations are constituted by the historical dialectic of social labour. We can now understand Fanon's terminological vacillation in the matter of the 'national middle-class' and his unwillingness to honour it unambiguously with the historical title of *bourgeoisie*. For: 'under the colonial system, a middle-class which accumulates capital is an impossible phenomenon.'[108] Again: 'The absence of any analysis of the total population induces onlookers to think that there exists a powerful and perfectly organized bourgeoisie. In fact we know today that the bourgeoisie in underdeveloped countries is non-existent. What creates a bourgeoisie is not the bourgeois spirit, nor its taste or manners, nor even its aspirations. The bourgeoisie is above all the direct product of precise economic conditions.'[109]

Thus the *contingent* character of its formation and its inescapable dependence upon an exogenous and superordinate structure of power and ideology disqualifies the native middle class for the historical vocation of a creative bourgeoisie. The condemnation of the colonized 'bourgeoisie' is therefore not 'laid down by the judgment of history' as is the Marxian critique of the bourgeoisie: Fanon accuses the colonized 'bourgeoisie' not of historical obsolescence but of 'precocious senility.'[110]

Such a critique of class unanchored in a fundamental ontology and historio-sophical theory of man's productive activity, self-alienation, and immanent emancipation is inescapably indeterminist and must oscillate between absolute condemnation and moral exhortation. Beneath Fanon's astringent critique of the native 'bourgeoisie' is the injunction that it is its 'bounden duty to betray the calling fate has marked out for it, and to put itself to school with the people';[111] that, given what Cabral called 'the fundamentally *political* nature of the national liberation struggle,'[112] it can and ought to 'repudiate its own nature in so far as it is bourgeois' and transform its fruitless particularism and that of other social groups into a political consciousness, into 'a consciousness of social and political needs'[113] shared by a nascent community.

· But of such an indeterminate negation of class relations congenitally deformed by the constricting structure of racial and colonial domination, the whole vision of revolutionary decolonization must provide overarching meaning. Through the same hermeneutic of experience which summoned colonized men to descend into the real depths (*véritables Enfers*) of their condition beneath the mask and veils of their desires and aspirations, the revolutionary act of decolonization must be rendered 'intelligible' and 'translucid to itself' (*translucide à elle-même*).[114] The critical imagination of the anti-colonial revolutionary must now embrace as an awesome privilege the very contingency of the 'racial drama': to it is supremely given the power to articulate an indeterminist vision of a community of men who, condemned to being a subhuman species, 'an indistinct mass' of racialized objects, 'totally irresponsible only yesterday,'[115] transmute this reified homogeneity of their condition into a public world of historical agents no longer seeking a plenitude of being from alien eyes; their consciousness no longer fixated to the contingent fact of race, but filled henceforth with 'human things' and intent on creating through their shared deeds, words, and vows, 'a prospect that is human because conscious and sovereign men dwell therein.'[116] With such a vision of self-creation, Fanon's imagination is restored to its original humanistic vocation by making a formal leap from the 'absurd drama' of the colonized to the epic of historical action as he reconstructs the immense decision of a people 'to tell a story about itself and to make itself heard (*de se raconter et de dire*).'[117]

The qualitative difference between the fatalistic universe of the 'racial drama' and the created world of postcolonial man cannot be articulated in terms of a dialectical logic of immanence whose metaphoric expression is the Marxian description of revolutionary violence as 'the midwife of every old society pregnant with a new one,' and which recoils from the vision of revolutionary transcendence as a *tabula rasa*.[118] The transcendence of the colonial condition is for Fanon a cosmogonic act, precisely what the Marxian conception suggests – a '*table rase*' upon which 'a new history of Man' is to be inscribed.[119] The humanization of 'the "thing" which has been colonized,' the 'minimum demands of the colonized' that their denied and masked humanity be released cannot, it seems, be accomplished without 'a whole social structure being changed from bottom up.' In this Fanon's vision concurs with so different a thinker as Plato who, because he knew the infernal caves of human bondage, was the first to have suggested the metaphor of the 'clean slate' as the epistemological distinction between revolutionary political artistry and ordinary reform.[120]

Today 'the critical theory of society,' whether oblivious to the ontological and historiosophical foundations of the Marxian critique of domination or in spite of them, has asked if the epistemological principle of revolutionary praxis as immanent or 'determinate negation' was not 'too tied to the notion of a continuum of progress' and if a true vision of transcendence, unembarrassed by the 'idealistic core of dialectical materialism,' ought not shamelessly to commit itself to 'the scandal of the qualitative difference.'[121] According to Max Horkheimer, 'the doctrine of midwifery degrades the revolution to mere progress.'[122] Are we to say in the light of these interrogations that the Fanonist vision, in its insistence on an 'extraordinary' change that is 'willed, called for, demanded,' and in its imagination of what Césaire called 'the undared form,' is more radical than the Marxian perspective? No matter. Other images of human bondage, other metaphors of emancipation.

NOTES

1 Frantz Fanon, *Black Skin, White Masks*, trans. Charles L. Markmann (New York 1967), 11
2 Fanon, *The Wretched of the Earth*, trans. Constance Farrington (New York 1966), 32. I have amended Farrington's rendition of Fanon's 'dans son immédiateté.'
3 *Black Skin, White Masks*, 255
4 Karl Marx, *Economic and Philosophic Manuscripts of 1844*, trans. Martin Milligan, ed. Dirk J. Struik (New York 1969), 118
5 Georg Lukács, *History and Class Consciousness*, trans. Rodney Livingstone (London 1971), 184
6 Marx, *Economic and Philosophic Manuscripts*, 116, 119
7 *Writings of the Young Marx on Philosophy and Society*, trans. and ed. Lloyd D. Easton and Kurt H. Guddat (New York 1967), 215
8 István Mészaros, *Marx's Theory of Alienation* (London 1970), 114-19
9 See Fredric Jameson, *Marxism and Form* (Princeton 1971), 205. In this sense Stanley Edgar Hyman in *The Tangled Bank* (New York 1974) exaggerated the centrality of 'the dramatic form' in Marx's work.
10 Renate Zahar, *L'oeuvre de Frantz Fanon* (Paris 1970), 6. For Fanon's allusions to the dramaturgical character of his subject matter see *Black Skin, White Masks*, 145, 150, 188, 197
11 *The Wretched of the Earth*, 174
12 Ibid., 175
13 *Black Skin, White Masks*, 226

14 *The Wretched of the Earth*, 187; Wole Soyinka, 'The Writer in a Modern African State'
    in Per Wästberg, ed., *The Writer in Modern Africa* (New York 1969), 19
15 *Black Skin, White Masks*, 14
16 *Toward The African Revolution*, trans. Haakon Chevalier (New York 1967), 18
17 *Black Skin, White Masks*, 88
18 As suggested by Francis Jeanson in his 1965 postscript ('Reconnaissance de Fanon') to
    Peau noire, masques blancs (Paris 1965), 221-2; Irene Gendzier, *Frantz Fanon: A Critical
    Study* (New York 1973), 53; R.M. Lacovia, 'Frantz Fanon: A Rehabilitation of our
    Living Dead,' *Black Images*, 1, 3, 4 (Toronto, Autumn and Winter 1972), 47-62; and
    Dennis Forsythe, 'Radical Sociology and Blacks,' in Joyce A. Ladner, ed., *The Death of
    White Sociology* (New York 1973), 213-33
19 *A Dying Colonialism*, trans. Haakon Chevalier (New York 1967), 90, n 8
20 *Black Skin, White Masks*, 15
21 Max Horkheimer and Theodor W. Adorno, *Dialectic of Enlightenment*, trans. John
    Cumming (New York 1972)
22 *Black Skin, White Masks*, 12
23 Ibid., 197
24 Ibid., 29
25 According to Georg Lukács: 'Description is the writer's substitute for the epic signifi-
    cance that has been lost'; see 'Narrate or Describe' in *Writer and Critic*, ed. and trans.
    Arthur D. Kahn (New York 1971), 127
26 G.W.F. Hegel, *The Phenomenology of Mind*, trans. J.B. Baillie (New York 1967), 229-40;
    Fanon, 'The Negro and Hegel,' in *Black Skin, White Masks*, 216-22
27 Ibid., 215. For other instances of Fanon's critique of psychodynamic categories, see
    ibid., 93, 116, 141, 150-3, 225; cf. *Toward the African Revolution*, 81; and Paul L.
    Adams, 'The Social Psychiatry of Frantz Fanon,' *American Journal of Psychiatry*, 129, 6
    (December 1970), 809-14
28 *Black Skin, White Masks*, 109-10
29 *The Wretched of the Earth*, 32
30 *The Phenomenology of Mind*, 231
31 'Labor and Interaction: Remarks on Hegel's Jena Philosophy of Mind,' in *Theory and
    Practice* (Boston 1973), 142-69; *Knowledge and Human Interests* (Boston 1971), 56-63
32 Alexandre Kojève, *Introduction to the Reading of Hegel*, trans. Jame H. Nichols, jr
    (New York 1969), 3-30
33 Hegel, *The Phenomenology of Mind*, 239
34 This is the famous metaphor with which Marx announces his transformative appropria-
    tion of the Hegelian dialectic: see *Capital*, 1 (Moscow 1971), 29.
35 *Black Skin, White Masks*, 217
36 Ibid., 218
37 Ibid., 217, 219, 220
38 Ibid., 221
39 *The Wretched of the Earth*, 33
40 Ibid., 29
41 *Black Skin, White Masks*, 220-1
42 Zahar, *L'oeuvre de Frantz Fanon*, 86-7, 29
43 *Frantz Fanon*, 26
44 Ibid.
45 *The Wretched of the Earth*, 31-2
46 As suggested by Trent Schroyer, *The Critique of Domination* (New York 1973), 97.
    Cf. Howard P. Kainz, 'A Non-Marxian Application of the Hegelian Master-Slave Dialectic
    to Some Modern Politico-Social Developments,' *Idealistic Studies*, 3, 3 (September 1973),
    285-302. Kainz does not mention Fanon's work, but he suggests as exemplifications of
    the Hegelian paradigm, 'colonial emancipation' and 'Negro emancipation in the United
    States' (294-5, 296-7). Yoweri T. Museveni commits violence against the text by citing

Fanon's description of the logic of the colonial relationship as 'Aristotelian' to support the *antithetical* claim that 'there is a dialectical relationship between the existence of the settler and the "native" ': see 'Fanon's Theory on Violence: Its Verification in Liberated Mozambique' in N.M. Shamuyaeira, *Essays on The Liberation of Southern Africa* (Dar es Salaam 1971), 2.

47 This point is underscored by Bertell Ollman, *Alienation: Marx's Conception of Man in Capitalist Society* (Cambridge 1971), 205-14
48 Herbert Marcuse, 'The Foundations of Historical Materialism,' in *Studies in Critical Philosophy* (London 1972), 38-9
49 *Writings of the Young Marx*, 367
50 *The Wretched of the Earth*, 32
51 Compare Leo Kuper, 'Race, Class and Power: Some Comments on Revolutionary Change,' *Comparative Studies in Society and History* (September 1972), 400-21
52 *The Wretched of the Earth*, 40
53 *Toward the African Revolution*, 36
54 Marx and Engels, *The German Ideology*, ed. R. Pascal (New York 1968), 14
55 See in this regard: *Black Skin, White Masks*, 86-8, 202; *Toward the African Revolution*, 18, 40
56 Ibid., 40
57 Marx, *Wages, Price and Profit* in Marx and Engels, *Selected Works* (Moscow 1970), 219. Cf. Marx, *Grundrisse*, trans. Martin Nicolaus (London 1973), 708
58 It has been argued that *coercion* is a specific mode of human domination 'primarily associated with the human condition of being-in-space': See Michael Weinstein, 'Coercion, Space, and the Modes of Human Domination,' in J. Roland Pennock and John Chapman, *NOMOS 14: Coercion* (Chicago 1972), 63-80. Weinstein wishes to distinguish coercion as a fundamentally spatial experience from other modes of domination such as oppression and repression. But the 'totalitarian' character of racial and colonial coercion, according to Fanon, consists in the fact that it *entails* a whole range of experiences of unfreedom. At the hands of the Nazis, Europe got a taste of this totalitarian coercion which she has visited upon other peoples. The shock of this experience symbolized by the phenomenon of the occupation provoked one of the most moving accounts of human bondage employing the metaphor of space. I am referring to Simone Weil's depiction of the Nazi occupation under the guise of an interpretation of Homer: *The Illiad or The Poem of Force*, trans. Mary McCarthy (Wallingford, Pa 1962), especially page 8. Compare Merleau-Ponty's insistence in 'The War Has Taken Place' that 'the situation of an occupied country' was 'the prototype of an inhuman situation': *Sense and Nonsense*, trans. Hubert L. and Patricia A. Dreyfus (Evanston 1964), 148.
59 *The Wretched of the Earth*, 31, 41
60 Ibid., 4
61 Aimé Césaire, *Cahier d'un Retour Au Pays Natal* (Paris 1971), 34-5
62 *Revolution in Guinea* (London 1969), 82
63 Fanon, *Toward the African Revolution*, 82
64 *Class Struggles in France* (New York 1964), 44
65 *The Class Structure of the Advanced Societies* (London 1973), 132
66 *Revolution in Guinea*, 56
67 *Black Orpheus*, trans. S.W. Allen (Paris, no date), 7
68 *Black Skin, White Masks*, 114-15
69 *The Wretched of the Earth*, 42
70 Consider Martin Heidegger, *Being and Time*, trans. John Macquarrie and Edward Robinson (New York 1962), 138-48; Eugène Minkowski, *Lived Time*, trans. Nancy Metzel (Evanston 1970), 400; M. Merleau-Ponty, *Phenomenology of Perception*, trans. Colin Smith (London 1962), 98-147.
71 *Black Skin, White Masks*, 232
72 *A Dying Colonialism*, 92

73 Jean-Paul Sartre, *Being and Nothingness*, trans. Hazel E. Barnes (New York, Washington Square Press ed. 1969), 424-5
74 Yambo Ouologuem, *Bound to Violence*, trans. Ralph Manheim (New York 1968), 163
75 *Black Skin, White Masks*, 10
76 *Toward the African Revolution*, 38
77 *Black Skin, White Masks*, 21
78 Ibid., 229
79 *Toward the African Revolution*, 38
80 *Black Skin, White Masks*, 25
81 Ibid., 33
82 *The Human Condition* (New York 1959), 160
83 *Black Skin, White Masks*, 20, 36
84 *On the Way to Language*, trans. Peter D. Hertz (New York 1971), 57-8
85 Habermas, 'Toward a Theory of Communicative Competence,' in Hans Peter Dreitzel, ed., *Recent Sociology No. 2: Patterns of Communicative Behavior* (New York 1972), 123
86 *Black Skin, White Masks*, 33
87 *A Dying Colonialism*, 89
88 *Black Skin, White Masks*, 109
89 Ibid., 40
90 Ibid., 60, 152
91 Ibid., 63
92 Ibid., 150
93 Ibid., 194
94 Ibid., 160
95 *Reflections on the Revolution in France* (Harmondsworth 1970), 135. Cf. John O'Neill, *Sociology as a Skin Trade* (New York 1972), 72-4
96 Armah, Why Are We So Blest? (Garden City 1972), 139
97 *Cahier*, 33
98 *Black Skin, White Masks*, 26
99 Ibid., 51
100 *From Empire to Nation* (Boston 1966), 227
101 *Black Skin, White Masks*, 211-12
102 Ibid.
103 Edward O. Laumann et al., eds., *The Logic of Social Hierarchies* (Chicago 1970)
104 *The Wretched of the Earth*, 43
105 Ibid., 37, 122
106 Ibid., 122
107 Ibid., 35, 37, 48, 122, 142, 144
108 Ibid., 122
109 Ibid., 143
110 Ibid., 141
111 Ibid., 122
112 *Revolution in Guinea*, 85
113 *The Wretched of the Earth*, 162-3
114 Ibid., 29
115 Ibid., 74
116 Ibid., 163
117 *A Dying Colonialism*, 93
118 Lukács, *History and Class Consciousness*, 163
119 *The Wretched of the Earth*, 29, 255
120 *Republic* vi, 501a
121 Herbert Marcuse, *Five Lectures* (Boston 1970), 62, 69; *Counter-revolution and Revolt* (Boston 1972), 70; 'The Concept of Negation in Dialectic,' *Telos*, 8 (Summer 1971), 130-2
122 'The Authoritarian State,' *Telos*, 15 (Spring 1973), 12

Christian Lenhardt

Magic and domination

In the modern world the interplay between magic and domination seems to have waned, if not entirely ceased, because the magical basis of domination has been supplanted by 'rational creeds' (a phrase which raises problems of its own). It has been postulated that the prehistoric magical form of life was, in some respects, eminently modern; that is, primitive magical occultism and its institutional derivatives were in a sense shaped and supported by rational modes of behaviour. I am deriving this premise from such diverse sources as Fraserian anthropology, Weber's sociology of religion, and critical theory.[1] While these traditions of thought are on the whole independent of each other, they do converge on the notion that rational practice and irrational belief interpenetrate and sustain each other, making it impossible to segregate the irrational clearly and unequivocally by means of a simple historical criterion like the idea of progress through time. Looking back to the darkest age of primitive mankind, one still finds a belief-behaviour complex that is an amalgam of reason and myth. Magic is just such a complex. To deal with it under the heading of 'non-logical actions,'[2] as has been customary among positivists, is to miss some of its essential characteristics.

I shall not try to define precisely what it is that magic shares with purposely rational behaviour; rather, I shall simply assume that such hidden correspondences and dialectical relations exist. I realize that this assumption is hazardous, since the logical soundness of some of the theories about magic, especially Frazer's, has been much contested by anthropologists and philosophers of science;[3] but I hope the direction of the present inquiry will succeed in overcoming the more controversial issues surrounding the question of the quasi-rational character of magic *qua* mode of behaviour.

In this article I am interested in discovering the conditions under which magic was, in turn, politicized and depoliticized and in gaining some understanding of how these changes affected magical beliefs themselves. 'Politicized' and 'depoliticized' refer to the changing structural nexus between magic and domination in primitive and ancient societies. Why was it that sorcerers became powerful political figures and then gradually withdrew from the struggle for political authority? Can magocracy, the rule by the magician, be understood in terms of a framework of irrational supernaturalism, or are more complex hypotheses needed to explain it? These are some of the questions raised here. Since the historical data are unreliable, the answers will be conjectures rather than demonstrably certain.

To anticipate some of the salient motifs of the argument: It seems that the sorcerer was caught up in a dialectic of rationalization and mystification which pushed him in the direction of enlightenment while at the same time kept him imprisoned in his demonology. I shall show that the practice of magic necessarily produced its negation. However, since magic was being practised in an interpersonal, social framework, its self-transcendence towards empirical knowledge of causes and effects was seriously retarded. For under conditions of magocracy – that is, under conditions of socialized magic – the sorcerer's interest in domination of men militated against his interest in rational knowledge of object domains. It is not unreasonable to speculate that the tendencies towards enlightenment inherent in magic would have come to fruition much more directly and forcibly had magic sprung up in Rousseau's state of nature or some such imagined presocial condition. The fact that it was not practised *in vacuo* but in concrete primitive collectivities accounts for the deflection of its rationalizing dynamic. Being a *social* practice, magic transformed itself from an authentic aspect of occultism into a political ideology rather than into enlightenment and emancipatory science.

MAGIC, RELIGION, AND THE PERFORMANCE PRINCIPLE

The concept of magic can be defined as a rule-bound symbolic behaviour which is believed to be able to effect a purpose by prevailing upon a spiritual agency whose ways are unknown but not totally unpredictable.[4] Three modes of classifying magical phenomena can be distinguished: sociological, technical, and teleological. Under the heading of sociological classifications, the most important distinction may well be that between structural-functional diffuseness and the specificity of magic as a socially recognized form of behaviour. A technical classification would be, for instance, Frazer's influential distinction between homeopathic and contagious magic, where homeopathic magic refers to the mock enactment of a desired event, and contagious magic to acts in which a part (hair, excrement, finger-nail parings) of someone is destroyed in the hope of affecting the fortune of the person from whom that part stems (pars-pro-toto magic). A teleological classification, in its most rudimentary form, would be the distinction between imprecatory and supplicatory magic, or, simply, negative and positive magic.[5] The former typically consists of casting a spell upon an adversary; the latter seeks to obtain a positive good for the sorcerer or his clientele.[6]

It goes without saying that the sociological classification is the most important one for our purposes since it provides us with a ready framework for historical comparison. It can be assumed that the performance of magic, like other social functions, was widely dispersed in primeval societies. Only gradually did certain individuals gain recognition as public magicians.[7] This transformation may have been one of the first qualitative steps taken by man towards a social division of labour. Frazer speaks of a 'higher stage of savagery'[8] during which this centralization of magic was being achieved. Despite this tendency towards specificity, however, considerable residues of magical practice remained in the hands of dilettantes and ordinary people.[9] In any event, few, if any, historical records and anthropological field studies depict magical societies in which magical functions were not in the hands of specialists. This professionalization of sorcery rests on a number of tenets which, although analytically separable from the main body of magical superstition, constitute a system of political superstitions unto themselves. I shall return to this idea shortly.

One cannot properly appreciate the historical scope and significance of magic without reflecting on the affinity magic has with religion. Cultural historians have tended to think that religion is a higher stage of supernaturalism which does not share in the pragmatic spirit underlying magical rites. Religion is said to orient people to transcendent and other-worldly realms, whereas magic is said to be an aspect of people's mundane lives.

This way of separating magic and religion, however, is too simple. Max Weber understood the relation more clearly when he pointed out that religion also is originally this-worldly and rational. In fact, the breaking away of religious creeds from magical practice never succeeded completely. Both are outgrowths of the same interest in technical control over objective processes of nature.[10] From the point of view of Weber's theory of action, pragmatic goal-directed action and magico-religious ritual have essentially the same ends, except for the fact that those of the former are more routinized than those of the latter. But this difference is one of degree only.

Behind the conception of magic as a form of technical control lie certain assumptions about the specific nature of supernatural powers, as well as about the way they intervene in human affairs. The institution of magic presupposes a god or demon or occult power that can be made to serve human rational purposes. In its purest form, this subservience would be tantamount to duress or compulsion. More typical is the case of an amalgamation of extortion, supplication, and worship, which occurs when the divine spirit or agency is believed to be superior in strength so that bending its will to human purposes can only succeed on occasion and partially. But this is only a difference of degree which does not obviate the fundamental affinity magic has with religion, even contemporary religion. The prevalent mode of communicating with a god in most religions, including those that deem themselves non-magical, is prayer. Again, as Weber points out, the boundary between a magical formula and prayer is not well defined: 'In prayer, the boundary between magical formula and supplication remains fluid. The technically rationalized enterprise of prayer (in the form of prayer wheels and similar devices, or of prayer strips hung in the wind or attached to icons of gods or saints, or of carefully measured rosary bead counting – virtually all of which are products of the methodical compulsion of the gods by the Hindus) everywhere stands far closer to magic than to entreaty. Individual prayer as real supplication is found in religions that are otherwise undifferentiated, but in most cases such prayer has a purely business-like, rationalized form that sets forth the achievements of the supplicant in behalf of the god and then claims adequate recompense therefor ... The pervasive and central theme is: *do ut des.* This aspect clings to the routine and the mass religious behaviour of all peoples at all times and in all religions. The normal situation is that the burden of all prayers, even in the most other-worldly religions, is the aversion of the external evils of this world and the inducement of the external advantages of this world.'[11] Just as it is analytically and historically dubious to separate religion from magic, so it is incorrect to distinguish between gods and demons on the ground that only the latter are approached by means of magical rituals. Gods are also subject to human incantations, perhaps with the difference that the magical approach to these gods is more supplicatory and humble than the magical approach to demons.

In view of the pragmatic premises of magico-religious lore, clearly the institution of magic and the tenure of its practitioners are in principle subject to a crude criterion of success and failure. What happens when, as will inevitably occur in the long run, the thaumaturge fails to sway the divine power? Does not the status of the magician-priest depend on whether he can continually perform his magic with creditable results? It is natural to think that the professional failure of the magician would involve his removal from office. However, it turns out that since the structure of the situation is one of cognitive dissonance it allows for a greater variety of possible resolutions. To be sure, there must have been many instances where the magician was ousted or even put to death if he divined wrongly. Where this occurs with some regularity, magicianship will not be popular as a career. But there are several other ways of managing the situation of cognitive dissonance, which arises when delusional beliefs are exposed. It is possible, for instance, to shift the blame to the god or demon and abandon him in favour of another; apostasy is one way in which the magician can avoid a loss of charisma. Or it may be possible to blame the people themselves, if the culture has a concept of impiety. This allows the thaumaturge to explain the failure of the magical act in terms of divine wrath. To appease that wrath, new kinds of religious attitudes, such as expiation, and new religious acts, like sacrifice, will then become necessary; ironically these new attitudes and acts arrest the decline of sorcery. In short, the failure of magical acts does not automatically induce disillusionment with the magical world-view.

From what has been said so far it does not follow that magic and religion are one and the same. Of course, they do differ and there is a historical evolution from magic to religion. One can try to reconstruct the logic behind the transformation of magic into religion in terms of an elementary sociology of knowledge. If it is supposed that the thaumaturge is more interested in pre-serving his position than in the orthodoxy of any particular occultist world-view, then it becomes apparent that he must react to a crisis of his charisma in a predictable way. In view of the indeterminacy of a situation of cognitive dis-sonance arising from abortive magic (such as drought despite a rain dance, an omen disproved by actual events) – when an element of disbelief must surface – it stands to reason that the group of magical specialists would be inclined to disfavour certain dissonance-reducing strategies while trying to promote others. Above all, they will tend to defeat interpretations which call their own charis-matic powers into question. They will be prepared, however reluctantly, to sacrifice the coherence of the traditional belief-system by tolerating, if not ac-tively endorsing, an interpretation which might suggest, for instance, that not only they but all members of the tribal society are responsible for the demon's 'change of heart.' Thus they would be taking a first step away from magic towards a different conception of the occult. Quite possibly then, the great historical shift from magic to religion came about because it was in the *inter-est* of the sorcerers who were caught in a performance principle which they could not satisfy.

Such a transformation cannot and did not occur over night. It may there-fore seem quite odd – untenable, in fact – to assert that the thaumaturge had both an interest in, and an influence on, the elimination of the magical, quasi-rational components of his trade. It is evident, on the other hand, that in the long run the magicians as a social class could hardly fail to notice the benefits accruing to them from the transformation of magic into religion and the con-current transformation of magicianship into priesthood. To the sorcerer, get-ting rid of the underlying pragmatism of supernatural beliefs may have been equivalent to saving his job, possibly even his life.

I do not mean to suggest that in this instance sociology of knowledge ex-plains very much. It does, however, highlight the fact that the history of reli-gious beliefs, in so far as it can be viewed in evolutionary terms as a history from pre-animistic forms of supernaturalism to the so-called universal religions, is also the history of a prestigious and dominant class seeking to strengthen and perpetuate its hold on society. One cannot deny that the spiritualization of dematerialization of religion, which occurred over a span of several thousand years and which had the effect of making more and more tenuous the link between the divine realm and the pragmatic sphere of human labour and ac-tion, has rebounded to the advantage of the intermediaries between gods and men. Logically, nothing could have been more unnerving to the primitive thaumaturge than the performance principle to which he and his craft were subject, for he could never live up to it over the long term. The operational criteria of what constitutes success and failure in magic were too clear, too public, however keenly the sorcerer may have sought to render them private and vague. Any lapse of the magician's charisma and divining powers could be detected immediately. To say the least, then, religion was a welcome development for the magician.

THE IDEOLOGICAL BASES OF MAGOCRACY

Magocracy is a primitive political institution; yet the ideology of magocracy is complex indeed. For it is not just the belief of primitives in spirits that automatically results in magical kingship. A host of additional ideological conditions, combined with certain economic conditions, must be present for magocracy to become a viable institution. Among the most important ideological conditions are: (*a*) that all or most of the clansmen believe in the existence of supra-sensible powers (primal occultism); (*b*) that they consider these powers to be autonomous but subject to influence (primal belief in magic); (*c*) that they believe some clansmen have superior abilities to practise exorcism, augury, and the like (belief in the specialization of magic); (*d*) that they do not believe the art of the magician to be subject to a conclusive pragmatic test of success (belief in the arcaneness of magic); (*e*) that they deem magic to be of such great importance that its practitioners should be invested with generalized political authority (belief in élitist magic or magocracy). The average conception of primitive superstition is summarized by propositions (*a*) and (*b*). From them alone, no conclusions can be drawn as to the existence of magicianship as an office, let alone as to the unity of magicianship and kingship. In other words, the primal forms of belief in the occult and in magic, which together constitute primal superstition, are socially and politically inconsequential. What gives rise to political power is not primal superstition but various secondary ideologies which are superstitious in their own way. These are summed up in propositions (*c*) to (*e*). They do not predicate anything of the existence and mysterious behaviour of demons, or of the human ability to harness the occult to human designs. Instead they describe beliefs primitives have about the nature of their own species, beliefs which seem more rational than (*a*) and (*b*) without really being so.

Modern man is only too ready to accept the notion that some people naturally excel at performing a certain craft. In fact we are so inured to thinking in terms of professionalism and specialization that it does not surprise us to find that this same idea existed among prehistoric peoples, even though we would be disinclined ourselves to place sorcery alongside other skills like hunting and wood-carving. Nor were the primitives themselves fully convinced that hunting and sorcery could be subsumed under a category like craftsmanship. This shows up in the tension between propositions (*c*) and (*d*): mistakes the thaumaturge made were not always detectable. Primitive societies wavered between a public (discursively arrived at) testing of magical operations and arcane self-interpretations by the sorcerers of what they were doing. It was this vacillation which helped the magician's political strategy of seizing and holding power. There is another reason why proposition (c) may be misleading. As I pointed out before, it seems quite likely that the sorcerer was not merely one among many occupational specialists but was, historically, the very first. In this case, the office of the magician would not have been legitimated by a general belief in occupational specialization, but the magician would have been the test case for such a belief and he himself would certainly have been interested in propagating it. Despite these caveats it is not unreasonable to state that the concept of magic as a skill does not seem incongruent with the primitive world view, especially when we look at situations where magic has already become significant.

The notion of the investiture of the magician as king (e) rests, at least in part, on the substance of those primal attitudes towards the occult (a, b). We can assume that the emotional terror wrought by the demonic forces was so fundamental and pervasive as to make the collective management of fear the prime concern of the whole society, which was only too eager to hand this task over to the 'best man for the job,' endowing him with the power and political privilege to make decisions about the public good.[12]

I am trying to show that while the beliefs stated in propositions (c) to (e) may appear to us to be the expression of primitive 'rationality,' they are in fact as irrational as the superstitions concerning the preternatural (a, b). The skill of the magician is undemonstrable. His craft is not like the craft of the wood-carver who produces things visible to and appreciable by everybody. More often than not the magician practises his skill in secrecy, claiming victory over the invisible without public proof; or he defines the empirical manifestations of successful enchantment himself in order to be able to bring them into being at will.

The interminable controversy touched off by Frazer's *Golden Bough* about the sense, if any, in which magic is a rationalistic pattern of ideas and actions has been completely divorced from the sociological and political dimensions of the problem.[13] In this sense, the subsequent debate, however important it may have been for philosophy of science, was a regression behind the position attained by Frazer, who in retrospect stands out as an early sociologist of knowledge because he was interested above all in reconstructing the institutional context of magic. He was keenly aware that the magical domination, whether pragmatic or symbolic in essence, proceeded within a social framework of intersubjective domination of man by man. The form of this domination was autocratic, the magician being one of the first despots in human memory. Yet Frazer was not sufficiently interested in the origin of political society to follow up his own leads. If anything, he implied that it was the animistic belief in spirits (or pre-animistic *mana* type conceptions of the supra-sensible) that caused the differentiation between rulers and ruled in primeval societies. Our analysis has shown this conclusion to be false. Primal occultism and magic do not enjoin any particular type of sociopolitical formation. It is rather the superposition of functionalist, professionalist, and élitist ideologies upon primal superstition to which the origin of political domination must be traced. The belief in the preternatural agencies itself does not foreclose the possibility of a social group organizing itself along anti-authoritarian lines. Only when superstitious primitives begin to form superstitious conceptions of the *exercise* of magic itself will they confer a specialized function and ultimately power on the magician. Primal animism is politically indifferent. Therefore, magocracy must be viewed as an archetypal ideologization of human relations.

In effect, the setting up of magic in the role of a specialized pseudo-craft is a classic case of a differential ideology posing as consensus: while all believe it to be true, for some this belief is more beneficial than for others. Also, like all such ideologies, this one carries within it the seeds of fraud, for the magicians not only refuse to share what they know, but they also conceal from their public the conclusion to which some of them may well come after honest self-examination – that they know nothing and can effect nothing. At this point the monolithic ideology invisibly is transformed into the false consciousness of the many and the unadulterated manipulative quackery of power technicians. This latent charlatanism has been the constant accompaniment of political power from its magical beginnings.

It would be incorrect to pretend that although the two forms of superstition (occultism and political ideology) seem to have had different roots, they have remained separate and distinct throughout. It is precisely the subtle fusion of these two streams of false belief that has contributed to the longevity of the magician's rule and that of his historical heirs – the divine king, the sacerdotal functionary, and nowadays the technocrat. While the magician *emerged* as the standard-bearer of his peers in their campaign against fear, he quickly became the personification and representation of the occult in their midst. In due course he was thought to *possess*, or be possessed by, the *mana* of the ghosts. Not that he had a monopoly on such possession; the *mana* would also occasionally seize ordinary folk. But the magician enjoyed the privilege of being at one with the spirits more regularly and *ex officio*. This made him something more than the appointed agent of the people; possessing the *mana* meant strengthening his legitimacy by making it independent of notions such as stewardship or delegation of powers. Once in office, he was no longer the mandatory of his tribe but the mediator between it and the occult forces, and therefore part of his authority was derived from the latter. It is this ingenious strategy of politicizing magico-religious superstition and of spiritualizing political interest that cemented the position of the autocrat for centuries to come.

THE RESISTANCE OF MAGIC TO SCIENTIZATION

Why did magic have such a strong appeal for so long? Why was it not exposed as a fraud much earlier? Although it appears that ideal-typical magocracy is beset by inherent flaws – such as the pragmatic performance principle – causing it to seek new ideological foundations, it does contain elements that tend to stabilize it by disarming public scepticism and any serious inclination to disobedience. It is these elements that I will emphasize in this section.

Those who look upon magic as the 'bastard sister of science' (Frazer) argue that sooner or later the nonoperational nature of magic had to be discovered. The primitives, they say, were bound to realize that there was no connection between magical charms and a subsequent occurrence. Frazer, for his part, believes that it was the sorcerers themselves who had a sufficiently strong motive for substituting causal knowledge for superstitious belief. He writes: 'certainly no men ever had stronger incentives in the pursuit of truth than these savage sorcerers. To maintain at least a show of knowledge was absolutely necessary; a single mistake detected might cost them their lives. This no doubt led them to practice imposture for the purpose of concealing their ignorance; but it also supplied them with the most powerful motive for substituting a real for a sham knowledge, since, if you would appear to know anything, by far the best way is actually to know it.'[14] Note again the sociological accent of Frazer's approach to the question of magic. He reconstructs what he thinks is the logic of action of a social class. The behaviour of the magicians can be viewed as either instrumental or as self-defeating in terms of their overriding political goal of maintaining themselves in power. Rationality in this instance denotes the ability to select strategies of political self-preservation and discard strategies not conducive to that end. Where I disagree with Frazer is on the evaluation of various strategies themselves. In other words, what precisely would be considered a purposely rational course of action, given the two premises that sorcerers want to stay in power and are capable of choosing, if not the best, at least a workable alternative among a universe of possible means?

According to Frazer's hypothesis, the self-interested magician is inclined, out of concern for his stake in society, to forsake magical superstition for empirical knowledge. Regardless of its deficiencies, this argument is important in so far as it emphasizes that at the stage of institutionalized magic, in the darkest prehistory of mankind, knowledge was not sought for its own sake. It was not even sought for the sake of controlling nature, although this must have been the reason why primitives retained sorcerers in the first place. Viewed from the standpoint of the magician, the motive for the performance of magic was the domination of man and the perpetuation of social privilege. Frazer's statement also suggests (naively) that the thaumaturge, threatened with removal from office due to his lack of control over things, will actually choose the path of enlightenment. Why he would do so remains unexplained. Presumably it is because of a tacit premise that reason is a universally shared attribute of mankind and that therefore appeals to it have a better chance of being heard than does recourse to myth. If this were not the case, there would be no incentive for the shaman to acquire empirical knowledge because it would remain unrecognized as such and thus would in no way help him fortify his position. In fact, if he persisted in demystifying magical lore in the absence of universal reason, he would be doing so with the awareness that he was risking the security of his position even further.

In several respects, the institution of magic was less vulnerable than it appeared. The pressure towards transforming magic into science (or into religion) in order to preserve the socio-political *status quo* may not have been great.

First, if knowledge, whether empirical or mythical, is centralized in, and monopolized by, the magician, so are to some extent the criteria of distinguishing success and failure of his art. I say 'to some extent' because obviously his status ultimately depended on some sort of public consensus about the nature of good and bad thaumaturgy. And yet the magician is not the captive of the society in which he practices his craft; he may well succeed in redefining the purposes of that craft in terms more in accord with his capacities.

Second, another strategy whereby sorcerers were able to immunize themselves for some time against the scientization of magic was to dilute the element of time in causation. A man upon whom a spell is cast will always die; and it will always rain after a rain ceremony – perhaps not at once, but surely sooner or later. It is this element of time which in magic was held in suspension so as to make it difficult to state with certainty that the magician was *not* the efficient cause of an occurrence. However, the conviction that the quality of magic was related to the temporal distance between presumed magical cause and empirically visible effect must somehow have gained ground.

At this point, the attribution to the magician of an interest in causal knowledge begins to make some sense. For if good magic must seek to shorten the temporal distance between cause and effect, then the magician does indeed have a compelling motive for knowing something about the precise sequence of natural phenomena. For instance, he may have learned to understand cloud formations and, to avoid embarrassment, he would simply postpone the performance of his 'rain-producing' incantation until the signs were right. Similarly, he may have learned to diagnose health by looking into a person's eyes and, upon finding them sick, cast his spell on them. These considerations serve to support Frazer's argument as contained in the passage quoted above: There is indeed a motive for the magician to acquire operational knowledge of the necessary and sequential connection between natural phenomena, provided his public has achieved an intuitive understanding of the role of time in causation so that he can no longer confound them with long-distance magic but must produce instant results. I am not certain, however, that this trend towards proto-scientific knowledge has produced 'incalculable good to humanity,'[15] as Frazer claims. I will argue further on that the magician robbed himself of the chance of being the first scientist because he simply added the empirical insights he gained to his tricks, thus reducing them immediately to *arcana imperii* and stifling the emancipatory potential they had for prehistorical society as a whole.

Third, the thaumaturge cannily exploits the determinacy of natural phenomena governed by laws. He tends to insinuate himself into the laws of nature rather than try to accomplish what we would regard as unnatural. There is a stark stylization of this idea in the enigmatic film *Orfeo Negro*. In this film, the basis of the protagonist's charisma in the eyes of the slum-dwelling children is their belief that Orfeo, bus driver and mystagogue, makes the sun rise with his guitar and his song. This is perhaps one of the most archaic scenes in the entire literature of film. It is a representation of primal magical superstition at its purest (and, from our modern secularized perspective, at its most poetic). Nothing could show more clearly the relation both between magic and deceit, and between superstition and infantility, than this rite. In regard to our analysis of magic as domination, we see here an enactment of the literal everydayness of magic: it is the bringing about of a phenomenon of daily recurrence. (We also see that the successor to the magician is not only the scientist but the artist whose poetry is an outgrowth of the incantatory mumbo-jumbo, just like the physicist's formulas). There is a sense in which Weber was quite wrong to attribute charisma to the magician and then allow for a process of 'routinization' to set in when the charisma has spent its original force. The case of Orfeo and his youthful adulators, which I take to be archetypal, shows that the charisma of the magician has always rested upon his presumed ability to effect the *ordinary*, that which occurs as a matter of fact. From its very inception, magic has been a strategy of insinuating that human volition controls the ordinary and mundane aspects of the life-cycle. Never was there a sorcerer who set himself the task of preventing the sun from rising. Had he tried to define his office in these terms, the viability of his tenure would have been very precarious indeed.[16]

I have been suggesting some elements which may account for the persistence of magic despite pressures to transform it. As I pointed out, I do not believe that either the professional ethic of the magician, if any, nor the fact that he acquired relatively more causal knowledge in the pursuit of his craft led him to relinquish his hold and act as a demystifier of primitive society. Nor did the desire to stay in power necessarily require of him to choose knowledge over superstition, if he had both. He was more likely to try to reinforce magical beliefs as long as he could get away with it. If he acquired shreds of empirical knowledge by chance or methodical observation, he would not logically have to use them to *supplant* magical lore.

Typically, he would try to foster an idea of over-determination so that, for instance, the rise of the sun is seen to be due to both natural and subjective-magical causes. In any case, he could, by a multitude of devices, avoid public awareness of his redundance as a magician.

In sum, to imply that the magician is adequately motivated to substitute real for sham knowledge rests on a variety of auxiliary hypotheses, some of which seem to be dubious indeed. Frazer himself knew of no single instance where such a displacement had actually occurred, that is, where primitive occultism had given way immediately to a naturalist axiomatic *without* passing through a long interregnum of spiritualized occultism (religion).

SCIENCE AS DOMINATION AND EMANCIPATION

The interplay in the history of magic between an inchoate tendency towards scientization, on the one hand, and the simultaneous obfuscation and obstruction of science, on the other, gives us a glimpse of the ambivalent status science has had in the field of tension constituted by enlightenment and mystification. I have argued that from its beginning science bears the mark of ideology in the crude sense that the rise of science was attended by manifestations of class interest and status anxiety. There is, however, another deeper sense in which science has come to be viewed as ideological.

When science began to challenge traditional philosophy in the Age of Humanism, the newness of its quest was well understood in terms of the polemical contrast with the old metaphysics: science was to reveal, not the being or essence of things, but their laws of motion and interdependence. However, while science was asking new questions, it was asking them in the old spirit. First, it was asking them *intentione recta* – and was doing so with no more justification than scholastic ontology – and, second, it was asking them on behalf of the old classico-medieval ideal of truth. Science was to be the pursuit of a new kind of knowledge, but it was to be a *disinterested* pursuit, like speculative philosophy before it. It is this self-perception of science as a disinterested quest which eventually resembled ideology.

The first to realize dimly what science is all about was Francis Bacon, who

unwittingly gave the initial impetus to a reflexive theory of science by admitting that science was concerned with power. This admission was turned
critically against science by a tradition of metascience which has only recently
grown to maturity.[17] In general terms, it holds that science is founded on
abiding aspirations of the human species which are rooted in its constitution.
Among these, the interest in universal truth or certainty of knowledge is secondary. The primary human basis of science is the urge to render nature more
habitable by gaining control of it. The ideological quality of science consists
then precisely in its hypostatization of objective knowledge as an absolute
value.

Today the metascientific tradition is as radically opposed as ever to the
objectivistic self-understanding of science. In one of its most articulate forms –
the philosophy of Habermas – the metascientific critique postulates that the
only reflexively adequate conception of science is a transcendentally grounded
pragmatism which reveals the anthropological roots of science *qua* specific
form of cognitive ability of the subject.[18] Science springs directly from our
need for 'practical action' for which science is the only appropriate *organon.*
But while science is indispensable for accomplishing that purpose, it is ill suited
for other purposes. It cannot, for instance, aid us in achieving intersubjective
understanding of how to live and what social norms to adopt. Nor can it aid
us in questioning the rationale of extant prescriptive codes which are felt to
be repressive. In other words, it cannot emancipate us from the artefacts of
traditionalism and from contingent patterns of socialization. If we want to be
freed of those, we must call on different cognitive resources, such as argumen-
tative reasoning or 'communicative action.'

These are problems concerning the deep structures of cognitive acts that
are not immediately relevant to this study, which deals mainly with the rather
unsubtle issue of the repressive use of science in magical society. There is,
however, a way in which our thoughts on the origins of science in magic affect
the discussion of a transcendental theory of science; they may reveal a more
complex relation between scientific control and emancipation than meta-
critiques of science have so far postulated. This relation, however, has not
been constant over time. In particular, I think that the reduction of science to
practical action in the specific sense just defined, though appropriate to the
analysis of modern science, may not be germane to the description of primitive science. There may have been a time when science was not a linear uni-
functional response to the human need to control natural environments.

To repeat, it is doubtless difficult not to agree with the idea that science is
unifunctionally oriented to extending man's domination of nature. For several
centuries at least, people have stopped expecting science to rid them of the
oppressive influence of false beliefs, idolizations, and prejudices to which they

may be subject. In other words, the development of science over the last 200 or 300 years has aided us immensely in discarding false hypotheses about regularities of natural phenomena; it has contributed immeasurably to improving the adequacy of our cosmology; and it has prepared the ground for progress in technology and for the general advancement of material culture. All of this is undeniable (though far from unproblematic). And to that extent, science in its innermost dynamic had indeed been the outgrowth of an interest in technical control. But this generalization does not apply to ancient science, especially the potential scientific knowledge of the thaumaturge operating perpetually on the brink of defeat. For him, science was a new and better tool for managing the problems of everyday life *and* a means of emancipation, for it enabled him to disconfirm the hypotheses of his magical cosmology.

The emancipatory anti-demonological element has completely disappeared from science. We do not believe any longer that future scientific discoveries will result in the displacement of occultism and remnants of false belief. This has become evident in the effect scientific discoveries have had for several centuries. There is no conceivable benefit which could accrue to the enlightenment of man from any additional progress in science. The succession of scientific paradigms (for instance, the rise of quantum mechanics or the displacement of Lamarckian evolutionary theory by Darwinism) has, to be sure, destroyed false perceptions, but in no way has it been accompanied by a sense of increasing freedom. The world is no longer populated by demons, whether one looks at it with the eyes of Newton or of Heisenberg. That is what makes science and its emphasis on progress appear redundant from the point of view of the philosopher or the critic. All the important victories science could win over superstition have now been won, or, if they have not, then science is not a suitable instrument for winning them. Classical physics was not a false belief, but at worst an erroneous theory. Therefore, supplanting it by, or supplementing it with, a more adequate theory is not an act of enlightenment, if by enlightenment we understand the dissolution of complexes of myth and occultism. All of this is entirely compatible with a transcendental critique of science, such as Habermas', which claims that science is man's way of looking at the world in a pragmatic attitude. This is not to say that science will not or should not undergo future revolutions. Nothing seems to be more certain than that science will remain harnessed to the concept of transforming the natural environment of man and presumably of improving the conditions of life. There is simply nothing else for it to do.

Science ceased to be a factor of enlightenment and emancipation a long time ago. I would go so far as to argue that even the most conspicuous historical case of 'emancipation' by science, that of the Copernican revolution in astronomy, is a highly dubious example. The old geocentric cosmology was wrong and, if retained, would have produced fewer discoveries than its rival. But it was not intrinsically oppressive. The reason its overthrow came to be regarded as a liberating development was that, in this instance, science (heliocentrism) tested and finally broke the shackles of its bondage to an institution, the Church, which was fundamentally hostile to any science and revolution at all. The Copernican revolution broke this spell, gaining autonomy *for science* which is by its very nature revolutionary. The Church adroitly withdrew from science entirely, leaving it to the new breed of seekers while continuing to claim authority over human souls; and science eagerly accepted what appeared to be a favourable compromise. As a result, the real battle of liberation from traditional authority was fought later in the eighteenth century, not by scientists, but by critics and other literary figures.

Already in Bacon's *New Organum* the debunking of various classes of idols has an artificial and élitist ring. It would not have been inappropriate to react to it with a shrug. For was this enlightenment? Strictly speaking it was not. Again this is not to belittle the salutary effect science has had and perhaps will have in the future. I merely contend that the transcendental grounds of science have not always been what they appear to be today. For a long time, science posed as the great liberator of mankind, and while it is possible to refute or moderate these claims in some crucial cases such as Bacon and Copernicus there remains the fact that they are not wholly unjustified. Modern science as the methodical attempt to objectivate in symbolic systems the processes of nature answers to our need for greater technical control. We do not think that science can fulfil our craving for freedom from false beliefs and occultist phobias. The science which is today the last word cannot be said to oppress us even though we *know* that tomorrow it will be exposed as an error. The science of today is not the equivalent of occultism with its Evil Eye and other diabolical claptrap.

In comparison with our contemporary science, the rudimentary science possessed by the prehistoric thaumaturge was truly emancipatory in theory because it was able to free the mind from superstitions which were not just false but oppressive by virtue of the fear and fatalism they inspired. In actual practice, ages intervened before this effect made itself felt. In fact, the surprising thing about naturalistic attitudes is not that they arose but that it took so long to acquire them. Part of the answer must necessarily lie in the sorcerer's ambivalence towards science. While he had some incentive to gain causal knowledge, his interest in science was too weak to override his class interest. Although he engaged in an elementary kind of operations research, he superimposed magical interpretations on it wherever possible. In this way, he stemmed the tide of science, his own brain child, which would otherwise have swept him away. Lest his status be eroded, he monopolized knowledge by keeping his 'findings' from public view.

The suppression of knowledge goes hand in hand with the suppression of people. The secrecy surrounding the nascent empiricism of the magician is a paradigm for all subsequent ideologies of domination which have stylized the idea of governance in terms of arcane principles of craftsmanship to which only the few can be initiated.

THE INSTABILITY OF MAGOCRACY

In an earlier section, I indicated that the magician-king was the more secure in his dominant position the better he managed to obscure the social origins of his office and to make people believe he had a divine mandate. Now, one of the problems for the survival of magocracy was precisely that the magical rulers could never entirely stamp out those pragmatic components in the thought of their followers which kept pulling them back into the orbit of a publicly enforced performance principle. In Confucian China, for instance, the king, though incarnate, was made responsible for the good issue of collective undertakings. If he failed to perform according to expectations, he was put to death.[19] The same practice obtained in other ancient civilizations and primitive cultures. For the people, the best way to determine whether the charisma of the magical leader was still intact was to look at what he was actually accomplishing on behalf of the community. Ritualized regicide, as practised in ancient China, points to the lingering on of the pragmatic attitude which had made the institutionalization of magocracy possible. This attitude is irrepressible. It threatens again and again to desacralize kingship the more the rulers try to leave all magical abracadabra behind. Regicide is the mental reservation of the early historical peoples vis-à-vis the idea of incarnation and personal charisma.

The *mana* attributed to the magician-king was a plausible hypothesis only as long as it produced results. Sustained bad luck was the undoing of magicoroyal authority. That is why in the long run magical kingship proved to be unstable, for nothing could have been less appealing to its incumbents than the idea of their heads being chopped off for mismanagement of worldly affairs. To survive, they had to extricate themselves from the confining, nay mortal, embrace of pragmatistic cultural beliefs. One way of achieving this was to transform magical into priestly kingship, which required a wholesale abandonment of magic for religion. In priestly kingship, for instance, the link between the royal charisma and socially useful action became more tenuous. No longer is the holder of power accountable in the same way to his followers as he was when he posed as a magician. Our discussion here returns to the transformation of magic into religion and the concomitant sociological changes which I touched on previously.

While it can be said that primitive charismatic authority benefited from the spiritualization of magic by becoming independent of periodic assessments in terms of pragmatic values, it is equally true that this transformation was a risk because it involved the preservation of the life of the thaumaturge at the expense of power. Would the people go along with a fundamental shift of their occultist perspectives away from magical pragmatism to a more spiritual form of religion? If so, would they not retain an attachment to pragmatism in some other form? In other words, in ceasing to be a thaumaturge and in becoming a priest, does the charismatic leader not abandon the field of political power to those who had always insisted that they can more reliably effect some of the things the magician was supposed to effect: to make crops grow, to increase the wealth of the community, to combat disease, and to defeat the enemy? The magician-kings had to take the risk that this might occur while hoping that it would not. The strategy failed. This at least is the conclusion we have to reach when we consider the very long run. Spiritualization of the magician's office did indeed result in an erosion of political power. On balance, sacerdotal functionaries gave up the place of political authority won for them by their magical predecessors. This had nothing to do with enlightenment among the many. On the contrary, the withdrawal by the priests from power went hand in hand with a heightening of mythical fervour and superstitious sentiments. Thus the belief in the supernatural did not abate; if anything, it became more complex in terms of the hypotheses sustaining it. And yet while pragmatism began to be rooted out in the religious sphere, it continued to be influential in the socio-political sphere where, finally, it became fully dominant only during the last 200 or 300 years of Western civilization. Viewed from a secular perspective, the emancipation of religious charisma from the constraints of an operational principle of performance was thus achieved at the price of a wholesale relinquishment of erstwhile claims to political domination.

In this respect, it is difficult to arrange the historical facts in anything resembling a logical sequence. Even Frazer did not pretend that his theory of the magical origin of kingship could replace all other explanations. Far from being a monist on this point, he thought that his theory was no more than an important aspect of a larger problem.[20] Not only were there multiple, culturally variable avenues to political power – such as the matriarchate, the patriarchate, magic, conquest – but in the course of time hybridization took place, which made it very difficult to sort out what may have been the original ingredients. According to B. de Jouvenel, the ancient magocracy was persistently challenged by the rise of a warrior caste.[21] The coming of the warrior marks an important way-station in the trend towards the secularization of politics, which took the form, at first, of juxtaposing the principle of military leadership (*dux*) to the traditional conception of political power based on sacred legitimacy (*rex*), and, later, of merging the two. As compared with the élitist conversion of magic into political ideology (magocracy), the new military aristocracy represented a demystifying principle. Their claim to political rule was clearly less ascriptive than the sorcerer's because their credentials were tangible: where often the magician had nothing to show for his divination and necromancy, they brought home loot; and although they may have kept the biggest share for themselves, they still managed to create an atmosphere of deference based on an operational idea of achievement, shared by the community as a whole. Thus it is that the warriors not only introduced a secular principle of social differentiation, they also insinuated themselves into the power structure of society, gradually eroding the political hold of the oracular magician. This tendency gained momentum when the magicians decided to redefine notions of the divine in terms of greater sublimity and inscrutability. While this made their lives as charismatic intermediaries between men and gods more secure, it paved the way for power-hungry experts who, unlike the new priests, were willing to subject themselves to hazardous appraisal by pragmatic publics.

THE FICTION OF BENEFICENT SORCERY

Let us return once more to Frazer. Frazer is at once perspicacious and naive in attempting to give a kind of universalistic, rational account of the functioning of magocracy. He, I think correctly, considers the functionalist aspects of expertise and achievement to be more crucial for building up a system of magocratic legitimacy than the charismatic aura surrounding the person of the magician, which is a derivative, albeit necessary, product in the development of supernatural beliefs. What Frazer fails to do is to demystify the notion of expertise itself. He writes: 'When the welfare of the tribe is supposed to depend on the performance of ... magical rites, the magician rises into a position of much influence and repute, and may readily acquire the rank and authority of a chief or king. The profession accordingly draws into its ranks some of the ablest and most ambitious men of the tribe, because it holds out to them a prospect of honour, wealth and power such as hardly any other career could offer ... The acuter minds perceive how easy it is to dupe their weaker brother and to play on his superstition for their own advantage. Not that the sorcerer is always a knave and imposter; he is often sincerely convinced that he really possesses these wonderful powers which the credulity of his fellows ascribes to him. But the more sagacious he is, the more likely he is to see through the fallacies which impose on duller wits. Thus the ablest members of the profession must tend to be more or less conscious deceivers; and it is just these men who in virtue of their superior ability will generally come to the top and win for themselves positions of the highest dignity and the most commanding authority.'[22] A careful reading of this passage shows Frazer to be arguing that 1/ ambitious men seek positions of social prominence; that 2/ the populace is gullible; that 3/ where magic contributes to the collective good its practitioners achieve social prominence; that 4/ ability is a prerequisite to the exercise of magic; that 5/ deceit is a prerequisite to the exercise of magic. Frazer goes on to suggest that when conflicts arise between knowledge and self-interest, as they necessarily must, the sorcerer is prone to suppress knowledge. The honest wizard who takes the failure of his charms to heart is rarer than the charlatan who improvises and covers up.

Frazer nonetheless sees nothing wrong with white-washing flaws like these. Rendering judgment on the world-historical merits, as it were, of magocracy, he writes: 'Many men who have been least scrupulous in the acquisition of power have been most beneficent in the use of it.'[23] From this bit of common-sense lore, he concludes that with the advent of the magician-king mankind extricated itself from savagery. In no time at all the real circumstances of the rise of magocracy are altogether forgotten, for only a few pages after he had pinpointed their 'unscrupulous character,'[24] Frazer speaks of the sorcerers as the 'ablest men' whose coming to power 'has contributed to emancipate mankind from the thraldom of tradition and to elevate them into a larger, freer life, with a broader outlook on the world.'[25]

I disagree with this world-historical verdict. The sorcerers had no pressing and unambiguous interest in dispelling the mists of occultism. Once sorcery had become a functionally specific and powerful office, the magicians forswore the emancipatory role they had been designated to play by reason of subjective intelligence and sagacity. They became guilty of repressive manipulation of knowledge. For to the extent that they intuited the fallacies of magical occultism they suppressed these intuitions in the interest of domination. They realized that they would be safe for a long time in keeping reason and superstition in some sort of operative balance. As a consequence of its prehistorical association with charisma, reason has been compromised for all times. For while freeing man from fear and uncertainty, reason has also served to perpetuate domination, thus being at once anti-magical and magical. The latest manifestation of this dialectical alliance can be seen in the fact that nowadays reason has acquired the quality of an aura: people defer to it without exactly knowing why. Today we seem to be stuck with an ideology of merit whose first propagandist may have been a magician. That ideology is no more credible now than it was ages ago. Its demystification, on a broad scale, is a task of education and critical praxis which is far from being universally recognized as important, let alone being accomplished.

NOTES

1 Notably the philosophy of culture in M. Horkheimer and T.W. Adorno, *The Dialectic of Enlightenment* (New York 1972).
2 For example, Vilfredo Pareto, *Treatise on General Sociology*, I (New York 1935), sections 182-215
3 Some of the relevant arguments, both for and against Frazer, can be found in: L. Thorndike, *History of Magic and Experimental Science* (New York 1923); E.E. Evans-Pritchard, 'The Intellectualist (English) Interpretation of Magic,' in *Bulletin of the Faculty of Arts*, University of Alexandria, 1 (1933), 282-311; B. Malinowski, *Magic, Science and Religion* (Glencoe 1948); J.H.M. Beattie, *Other Cultures* (London 1964); B.R. Wilson, ed., *Rationality*, (New York 1970).
4 In his desire to separate magic from religion, Frazer goes too far indeed in despiritualizing sorcery, arguing that wherever 'magic occurs in its pure unadulterated form, it assumes that in nature one event follows another necessarily and invariably without intervention of any spiritual or personal agency. Thus its fundamental conception is identical with that of modern science; underlying the whole system is a faith, implicit but real and firm, in the order and uniformity of nature.' James Frazer, *The Golden Bough*, I (London 1911), 220. I agree that the aboriginal sorcerer 'abases himself before no awful deity' (Ibid., 221). But this does not mean that we must rule out animistic or theistic conceptions as being non-magical *by definition*. On the contrary, to think of what the magician tries to enlist in his service in terms of some higher potency, be it of the *mana* type or of some anthropomorphic variety, is not necessarily to adulterate the concept of magic.
5 Evans-Pritchard and other scholars have preferred to speak of negative magic as witchcraft and of positive magic simply as magic.
6 Under the rubric of teleological classifications, and cutting across the imprecatory/ supplicatory distinction, one can further differentiate types of magic along functional lines. Without trying to be exhaustive, I would list as important: divination, health magic (including both black and therapeutic magic), love magic, weather magic, fertility magic, hunting magic, cathartic magic.
7 *The Golden Bough*, I, 244-7
8 Ibid., 246
9 Paradoxically, the remnants of diffuse magic seem to have survived longer than those of magic in its more 'modern' institutionalized form. In modern Western civilization, many traces of decentralized magic can still be found. See for instance the compilation of varieties of love magic practised in Europe as late as the beginning of this century, in Geza Róheim, *Animism, Magic, and the Divine King* (New York 1930), 96-104.
10 Max Weber, *Economy and Society*, II (New York 1968), 400ff
11 Ibid., 423-4. William Goode, *Religion Among the Primitives* (Glencoe 1951), gives a concise summary of the prevalent dichotomous view on the subject of magic and religion.
12 The link between fear and magocracy has to my knowledge not yet been systematically explored. Max Mueller and the so-called natural theories of religion have perhaps come closest to arguing for such a connection. See F.M. Mueller, *Physical Religion* (London 1891), and R.R. Marett, *The Threshold of Religion* (London 1914).
13 See note 3 above.
14 *The Golden Bough*, I, 247
15 Ibid.
16 'In the great majority of cases, everything happens as if the ritual gestures really did produce the effects expected of them. Failures are the exception. As the rites, and especially those which are periodical, demand nothing more of nature than that it

   follow its ordinary course, it is not surprising that it should generally have the air of
   obeying them.' E. Durkheim, *Elementary Forms of Religious Life* (New York 1965), 404

17 The history of this tradition of thought after Bacon is still somewhat obscure. No doubt
   Nietzsche and Pragmatism have a central place in it.

18 See his *Knowledge and Human Interests* (Boston 1971), and 'A Postscript to Knowledge
   and Human Interests,' in *Philosophy of the Social Sciences* (June 1973).

19 See, for instance, P.B. Fedele, 'Lo stato e la società nell'antica Cina,' in *Annali Later-
   anensi* (1951), 145-349

20 *The Golden Bough*, I, 332-4

21 *On Power* (Boston 1962), chapter 5

22 *The Golden Bough*, I, 215

23 Ibid., 216

24 Ibid.

25 Ibid., 218-19

Ben Agger

On science as domination

If the eighteenth century was the age of reason and philosophic agnosticism, the twentieth century is the age of science. The hope of Francis Bacon that science could control the universe instrumentally has come to fruition only in the last few decades. Enlightenment has become a total social and cultural force with the rise of industrial society and, specifically, with capitalism. Enlightenment, however, is not a strictly philosophic attitude anymore, if it ever was. It has become an approach to the common-sense realities of society, an uncritical, 'one-dimensional' acceptance of the authoritative *definitions* of reality. To be enlightened is to be aware of all of the compromises that one must make with 'reality' in order to survive.

This essay deals with aspects of the debate within Marxism on the critique of science: I want to contrast and compare the positions of Althusser, Colletti, and the Frankfurt critics on the status of science in Marxist theory. The central problematic in the dispute between Althusser, Colletti, and the Frankfurt School is the idea of the scientific nature of Marxism.

The Frankfurt critics (except Habermas) argue that science has become a mode of accommodation to the reality of capitalism. The scientific attitude has been translated into an uncritical, instrumental mode of everyday life so that it has become a reactionary force. Science has become, to quote Colletti, an 'institution of the bourgeois world.'

Western Marxism since about 1920[1] has, of necessity, belonged to what might be called the speculative tradition. 'Of necessity' is crucial. I suggest that Marxian theorizing has been denied any concrete political role and thus it has restricted itself to the critique of ideology. One-dimensional society, according to Marcuse, is a society closed both to effective political rebellion and even to criticism of its logic. The speculative tradition has tried to criticize the justifying theories of capitalism, especially its assumption that its own systemic reality is supremely rational. Reality is not rational but inhuman and exploitative. Speculative critique tries to poke holes in the illusion that we live in a truly rational society. In so far as science has been a mystifying force in the protective apparatus of capitalism, it too must be criticized.

Yet Marx is not to be overthrown as a theorist of the expropriation of surplus value from labour. He is only to be revised by analysing why the objective irrationality and inhuman quality of capitalism have not led to its collapse. Capitalism has developed superstructural mechanisms for hiding its economic dysfunctions. These mechanisms are to be found strictly on the level of the non-economic superstructure. They include all of the psychological forms of consumer fetishism and manipulated needs. One such mechanism for hiding economic dysfunction is an objectivist social science which is concerned only to give a piecemeal critique of these dysfunctions, not a fundamental and totalizing critique of domination. Critical theory accepts Marx's analysis of the economic base but adds to it the theory of a culture which has diverted the otherwise critical attentions of people. This is the sublation of Marx, not his simple negation. Critical theory says that science has itself become a mode of apprehending reality which contributes to obfuscating ideological claims.

In a very introductory form, I want to discuss Horkheimer's and Adorno's concept of enlightenment and science in the context of contemporary Marxism. It is their contention that the positive ideal of reason has been eclipsed by the overinflation of expectations about the capacity of reason to free us from mythic beliefs and our unconscious.[2] They contend that the modern capitalist world is damaged by the pervasive but unreflective faith in the powers of instrumental reason and the rational method. Their own position is hopefully rationalist in the sense that they support an untraditional and largely untried conception of reason – a reason freed from the instrumentalist ideology of the Enlightenment and no longer exaggerated out of proportion to its real powers. They do not oppose thinking and dialogue, nor do they wish to return to a mythic precivilization populated by dragons, beasts, and primal fears. They only wonder whether reason in its ideologically interested, scientific form – in other words *capitalist reason* – is anything but another form of mythology and irrationalism.

In the work of Horkheimer and Adorno, enlightenment stands for the demystification of the world through science. Rationality, an operational scepticism which assumes that the world can be fundamentally comprehended, is the *modus operandi* of enlightenment. Max Weber called rationalization 'the disenchantment of the world.' Enlightenment first presupposes that the world can be essentially understood through the methodical dissection of heretofore mysterious forces. Its second assumption is that things which can be understood can be controlled.

Rationality is the organizing principle which applies the demystifying insights of science to the ordering of an irreligious, liberal society. 'Enlightenment' for Horkheimer and Adorno does not need to be preceded by the definite article 'the.' *The* Enlightenment in the eighteenth century was a limited instance of the total instrumentalist outlook on nature which persists to the present day, even within mechanical Marxism. The rational society, in Weber's sense of rationality, depends upon the application of instrumental, technically exploitable knowledge to bureaucratic capitalism. Horkheimer and Adorno do not oppose this conception of enlightenment with prescientific mysticism or irrationalism but only question the authenticity of what passes for enlightenment today. As Horkheimer wrote in 1947, ' ... the denunciation of what is currently called reason is the greatest service reason can render.'[3] By seeing through the mythic, ideological function of the instrumentalist conception of science enlightenment could subvert its own bastardization.

This position on science has been attacked by Lucio Colletti and Louis Althusser as belonging to the reactionary nineteenth-century tradition of the romantic hatred of science. Colletti has likened Horkheimer's and Adorno's critique of science to Hegel's critique of common-sense thinking found in the *Phenomenology of Mind*. Hegel contraposed the common-sense objectivism of understanding to the reason of total idealist self-reflection. Colletti suggests that the Frankfurt School has accepted Hegel's glorification of idealist Reason against materialist science. He also charges Marcuse for being party to the 'annihilation of the world' allegedly found in Hegel's *Science of Logic*.

In fact, Adorno was radically anti-Hegelian, attacking Hegel for creating a metaphysics which was equally as uncritical of the present as science. From the original Frankfurt circle, only Marcuse harboured any sympathy for Hegelian idealism. Adorno felt that instrumental science and Hegelian metaphysics were both radically inadequate in the face of domination which defied 'rationalization' or explanation: science pretends that domination is eternal and necessary, idealist metaphysics pretends that domination can be spiritually transcended. Only a nonidealist dialectics, a negative dialectics, rids itself of this uncritical self-understanding shared by science and philosophy. Adorno felt that the undialectical, scientistic temperament of mechanical Marxists sold out Marx's notion of the dialectic. Horkheimer and Adorno contributed to reconstructing some of the themes of Marxism by applying their critique of science to the mechanical economism from the Second International onwards. Marxists were forgetting how to be dialectical. They believed that the revolution was in the cards, that revolution was guaranteed by the science which they used to analyse the transparency of capitalism.

The domination of nature is also furthered by instrumental science. Marcuse has envisioned a 'new science' which could 'play' with nature, not destroy it unthinkingly. At the very least, science has become one of the handmaidens of capitalist domination. It covers exploitation in the mystification of rational necessity and remains unaware of the harm it does when it thinks of nature and society as inert, exploitable objects. Ultimately, science is thoroughly undialectical.

Horkheimer and Adorno did not wish to replace dialectics with a gloomy philosophy phrased in totalitarian screams. But Adorno did not feel that Auschwitz represented only a temporary aberration perpetrated by Nazi gangsters. Fascism represented the ultimate decline of science into mythology. Fascism occurs when the subject runs away with the object, when the subject thinks of itself as omnipotent. Modern society shares some of the totalitarian aspects of Nazi Germany, especially the belief that we can engineer social problems out of existence. Ultimately, for the Nazis the problem of Jews was simply a problem of rational instrumentality.

Yet one must be dialectical, even if it means wearing a gloomy face. Dialectics is neither resigned to eternal fates, nor so omnipotent that it can exploit the object thoughtlessly. Adorno and Horkheimer felt that the deep imperfections of late capitalism could not be exorcised by a mechanical science of revolution. The Marxian dialectic had taken a turn for the worse.

Adorno's argument is not that objectivity is evil; rather that objectivity is one of the moments of the dialectic. A 'non-idealist dialectics'[4] will assign primacy to the object, yet it will recognize the contribution to the object by the thinking subject. Adorno conceived of the relation between subject and object to be a historical one, not fixed for all time. His critique of science was essentially that science presupposes an eternal, unchanging relation between subject and object. The historical direction of subject and object vitiates the attempt to create a transparent science of objects. Since the subject is not in control of the world, he cannot fundamentally understand it.

For Horkheimer and Adorno, science was the programmatic expression of the Enlightenment. The *philosophes* thought that the world could be understood and thereby controlled once God's epistemological primacy was undercut. Yet Horkheimer and Adorno claim that science came to be a lever of domination, control *over* the object, and not a truly preprejudicial source of reason and criticism. Horkheimer and Adorno hated science not because they found in it an essentially pernicious logic but because it was untrue to its emancipatory idealism. The novelty of their argument is that they did not locate the passage of enlightenment into myth and ideology originally in the eighteenth century, or even in Francis Bacon. They contended that 'enlightenment' has plagued us since the Greek myths were demystified. Homer's Odysseus was the first rational man, the first instrumentalist, yet he was as stunted by the *hubris* of enlightenment as Bacon or indeed the Encyclopedists. Horkheimer and Adorno did not feel that science was simply misused in technological applications. Science itself conceived as instrumental control dominates the object-world. The misuse of science only extended the logic of domination written into the purely instrumental conception of science. Science became ideology.

By 'enlightenment,' they mean to describe the attitude towards the world which presupposes a logical connection between knowledge and the instrumental control of nature and society. Enlightenment is an instrumental attitude to the object-world which attempts to control the world through methodical science and technique. 'Men pay for the increase of their power with alienation from that over which they exercise their power. Enlightenment behaves toward things as a dictator toward men. He knows them in so far as he can manipulate them.'[5] Enlightenment has been thoroughly transposed into a mode of purposive rationality, to use Weber's phrase. Enlightenment means getting things done.

Horkheimer and Adorno contend that enlightenment has become dogmatic and totalitarian. By replacing mythology, science became a new mythology because society was not ready yet to make use of science in an intelligent, humane way.[6] It has exorcised primitive beliefs from knowledge-constitutive activities by calling into question all beliefs. Yet enlightenment is itself a form of belief. Enlightenment becomes totalitarian when it decides to judge everything but itself by a standard of rationality.

Conservatism usually fights Marxism on the grounds of the eschatological and utopian dimensions of the Marxian *telos*. Yet it is Marx's utopianism which is the most valuable inheritance. Dialectical thinking shows how the present conceals possible forms of self-transcendence which can lead to a qualitatively different future. In Marx's view, science was to be not only a study of structural domination but also a mode of surpassing and reconstituting human history. Without the second interest, Marxism degenerates into another form of social science.

Enlightenment undermines Marxism when it fosters a belief in the strictly instrumental nature of Marxian science. Scientific Marxism assumes that the world out there can be looked at in a way which will reveal its true contour and being. Only then, after the science has held a mirror to material structures, can we change the world. But Marx implied that science and politics are the same type of activity: 'practical-critical activity.' We change the world by knowing it, we know the world in the process of its transformation. How can we believe Althusser's claim that the 'mature' Marx cleansed his science of practical, ideological interests?

Enlightenment according to Horkheimer and Adorno has reduced the world to a one-dimensional horizon of self-same objects: the radicalization of Weber's 'disenchantment of the world,' the *Aufhebung* of the world itself. The passion of living in a heterogeneous world of colours and textures is reduced to the epistemological relation between subject and object. Positivism is the most advanced form of enlightenment and the most barbaric in terms of what it thinks of metaphysical deviance. Some metaphysics at least fostered a sense of wonder and reverence, a sense of man being one creature among many. The Cartesian age has seen this wonder reduced to a disruptive source of superstition which is said to impede the rational progress of science. Even philosophy has been reduced to epistemology, namely, the study of how a subject can know an object.[7] Enlightenment is the contemplative relation of a subject to an object about which it becomes enlightened. The predicate of enlightenment is the mute object-world, denuded of its lively enchantment. The humanization of nature has resulted in the disenchantment of the subject who used to enjoy a 'human' relation to the environment and to things. Some Marxists talk about the correct science of reality, forgetting Marx's novel claim that the only form of science is our practical engagement with history and nature, not a distanced contemplativeness.

With the cool mien of enlightenment has come the sublation of passion which is chalked up to prescientific totemism and treated as archaic. Adorno characterized modern society as 'frigid,' equating sexual neuroses with societal neuroses. Both are the products of an internalized superego which totally disregards the id and its energy. Frigidity is our being frozen into objects, subjects of reification and the dispassionate science which rationalizes reification. Objectivism is devoid of passion. Science and its theory of knowledge are political agents in one-dimensional society, agents which hide domination in the myth of eternal necessity. Science remains in its uncritical relation to the frozen object; it does not freeze the object but only fails to thaw it.

Passion is seen as a disruptive factor which must be controlled if science is to do its work. The most elaborate attempt to purge passion from Marxism is that of Althusser who has buried the subject in a vast, structural world wherein human consciousness has no currency. The subject comes to have a chilled, hardened reality in a world wherein he is relegated to being a passive consumer of ideologies. Althusser's structuralism fears the subject's contribution to the revolution in the same way that science fears metaphysical contributions. Freud, for instance, was treated by the Frankfurt School largely as a 'prophet of gloom.'[8] Yet Freud's analysis of the deep structure of mind and species leaves us with a valuable concept which can combat the surplus-rationalism of the Cartesian ego: that of the uncontrollable, unpredictable 'id.' Enlightenment assumes that the invisible and nonrational is unenlightened and superstitious. Psychoanalytic science is an attempt to demonstrate that the nonrational is not necessarily destructive of the legitimate instrumental interests of science. Marcuse in fact envisioned a 'new science' which would defer to the legitimate needs of the erotic id. It would be absurd to reject all of the knowledge-constitutive claims of science, for some of the uses of science are beneficent and emancipatory.

Horkheimer and Adorno only resist the totalitarian consequences of enlightenment when it debunks all nonrational forms of knowledge. They were not irrationalists. They simply refused to equate instrumental control with enlightened progress. Bigger is not better. For them, reason had not yet been realized. They do not attempt to erect a new religion, based on the unrealizability of reason. Religion is as barren as atheism. They imply that we need a dialectical attitude which respects the mythic and erotic needs of the id but which does not make the irrational a new resource for ideological mystifications. Marx said that the goal of the revolution is to let people become truly human. He never said that the end of history would bring a new non-bourgeois sacrament such as the cult of the proletariat (or the cult of the id). The 'new man' is unimaginable by us now. Only at the end of history can we begin to wonder about the proper balance between rational self-reflection and Dionysian abandon.

To specify the forms of the future in terms of a Marxian science would be an act of enlightenment. It would entrap us with plans and maps. Freedom will respect the right of the future to present itself as it chooses. If freedom means a stronger id, so be it. Resisting the imperious needs of the id, stifled for centuries, would be as irrational as erecting a new religion of science. Science which was no longer beholden to strictly instrumental interests would respect the needs of the id and would at the same time try to enlarge and enhance the capacities of the ego to free itself from domination. The struggle against domination will go hand in hand with a new respect for the passionate unknowable. Freedom from the irrational would give birth to a society of robots, a perfect world for science. The last vestige of uncertainty would be eradicated, and with it all hope of reversing the logic of instrumental control.

Max Weber considered rationalization to be an instance of the disenchantment of the world. The task of modern social thought according to Horkheimer and Adorno is to re-enchant the world without giving up all the benefits of a potentially productive technology. This means restoring the stagnant dialectic between myth and science. Herbert Marcuse has tried to conceive of a science which would fulfil the 'play-impulse.' These hopes could be the bedrock of a technologically advanced society which does not denude nature of its charm and enchantment. Habermas has challenged Marcuse by arguing that the control of nature can only proceed under the interest of possible technical control, a logic fundamentally different from that of intersubjective discourse. Marcuse is hopeful that science and technology could be humanized and eroticized, while Habermas is sceptical about humanizing the fundamentally instrumental logic of science. Habermas would maintain that instrumental rationalization always disenchants the world; whereas Marcuse hopes to discover a logic of industry and science which respects the 'humanness' of nature.[9] Ultimately, Marcuse hopes to unite instrumental and aesthetic interests in terms of the 'aesthetic ethos.'

Rationalization is not an inexorable process, associated with all forms of industrial progress. Weber said that rationality was the application of the demystifying approach of science to organizing bourgeois industrial society. Rationality is dehumanization. '[Bureaucracy's] specific nature, which is welcomed by capitalism, develops the more perfectly the more the bureaucracy is "dehumanized," the more completely it succeeds in eliminating from official business love, hatred, and all purely personal, irrational, and emotional elements which escape calculation.'[10] Bureaucratization is the ultimate expression of operational rationality. 'Formal organization is the structural expression of rational action.'[11] Weber himself admitted that industrial society is becoming less rational with respect to the human costs of 'rational' progress. He was described by Gerth and Mills correctly as a 'nostalgic liberal,' an apologist for rationalization but also one of its existential victims. The disenchanted world is devoid of ritual and magic – necessarily so, some would say. But it is precisely the position of the Frankfurt critics, especially Marcuse, that we do not necessarily lose in technological productivity what we gain in the re-enchantment of non-human nature.

It is this ability to combine technological interests in the instrumental control of nature with a new logic of thought and speech which will undermine the disenchanting effects of technology. Marx was not a Luddite, for he was hopeful that the logic of technological domination would be reversed under a new order. Following Marx, none of the Frankfurt critics were Luddites in their own right.

Critical theory wants to conceive of a non-exploitative logic of production and social organization which will not destroy the productive forces of advanced technology. A Marxian metaphysics would re-enchant the world and society, but it would preserve the interest in emancipation. Re-enchantment without emancipation would issue in another form of conservatism. Ultimately, a Marxian metaphysics would not be very different from science itself.

Yet emancipation without a respect for the irrational would give birth to more liberal monsters; it would free men but not the world. The liberal dream is of a world which is thoroughly reduced to certainty. We can control what we can know. This was not Marx's dream. He wanted to write a poetry of society which was historically advanced enough to dispense with science conceived strictly as instrumental control.

Critical theory shares an interest both in emancipation and in the post-instrumental re-enchantment of the world. The end of history will not spell the end of unhappiness, but only of domination. A post-Marxian science will still need to be dialectical, ever alert to the dangers of hierarchy and corruption. Communism will not bring the death of the irrational. There will still be things we cannot understand or control, but these will not be problematic in a decent society. We will need a kind of mythology to cope with uncertainty and confusion, yet this will not be a mythology which will be party to domination. It will be the mythology of Marcuse's 'new science' and of gratified Eros. Mythic does not mean impossible. It refers simply to a sacred zone around our rational technology. There will in fact be no contradiction whatsoever between productive technology and this mythological sacred zone of the irrational.

Men could thus be liberated from the spuriously emancipatory ideals of instrumental science. The logic of instrumentality is the control of everything, even human freedom. A Marxian metaphysics would invent a new instrumentality which would be satisfied with modest successes.

Horkheimer and Adorno theorized that Marxism has been tainted by these spuriously emancipatory ideals. By freeing men from the theological order of the Middle Ages, we entrap them in an invincible order, that of science and its faith in instrumental control. Yet at least one could *choose* not to be a Catholic. It is difficult to choose not to be enlightened. With enlightenment we have lost all of our innocence.

Marxists erred when they thought it could be another form of social physics. Adorno in 1966 wrote that 'the attempt to change the world miscarried,' throwing us into critical self-reflection designed to reconstitute the basis of materialism. This has been rather like fighting enlightenment with enlightenment. No one wins. Not all of the critical theorists, however, wished to reconstitute materialism. Habermas has taken a rather Kantian turn with his distinction between science and critique. Habermas is far more optimistic than Adorno was about salvaging the logic of instrumentality.

Horkheimer and Adorno were sincerely concerned about saving Marxism from an unreflective theory of knowledge which would invalidate the humanitarian humility of Marx. By humility, I mean Marx's conception that we could not foretell the precise relation of theory to practice without falsifying the indeterminate meaning of the dialectic. The critique of science reminds us that science conceived as instrumental control is not an authentic substitute for dialectical thinking. Science must take on a new meaning at the end of history.

Currently, in Europe, Louis Althusser and Lucio Colletti are challenging the Frankfurt critique of science as being pre-Marxian romanticism with its idealist critique of positivism.[12] They maintain that Marxian theory is to be judged by a standard of scientificity, a standard of faithfulness to the 'mature' Marx's texts and their non-ontological spirit. This scientism, especially Althusser's, responds critically to the Hegelian impulse in neo-Marxism introduced in 1923 by Lukács. Allegedly, the critique of science is a popular form of Hegel's view that objectivity was a form of pernicious alienation. Colletti says that Marcuse's critique of science is taken directly from Hegel's 'annihilation of the world' contained in *Science of Logic*.[13]

The scientific nature of Marxism is to be judged by a standard of objectivity which resembles that of the bourgeois social sciences, found in Max Weber. Marx's theory allegedly eschewed any normative or ideological interests, attempting to see the world for what it was and is. Althusser calls this Marx's 'epistemological break' between ideology and science. Althusser's primary claim is that Marx's science transcended ideology after 1857 in the sense that it shed all the remnants of political humanism and historicism.

This conception of science is part of what critical theory has called the objectivist self-image of the natural sciences. It treats society as a natural phenomenon which can be understood under the logics-in-use of the natural sciences. Scientific Marxism ideally treats the laws of society in the same way as a physicist would treat the laws of motion.

Critical theory from Horkheimer's first programmatic statement of its aims has contraposed itself to what Horkheimer called 'traditional theory,' theory which worked within the nomological presuppositions of the natural sciences.[14] Critical theory has normative intentions which are not to be masked under the pretense of scientific objectivism.

Marxian scientism breeds a mechanical and undialectical attitude to theory and practice: do the science, and then engage in politics. 'Theoretical practice produces knowledge which can then figure as *means* that will serve the ends of a technical practice.'[15] Theory that reads off the laws of nature and society can be used instrumentally to inform practice; correct practice depends on correct theory in a linear way. Critical theory rejects this conception as undialectical; instead, theory and practice stand in a historical relation.

A scientistic Marxism commits the same error as bourgeois objectivism when it treats society as a thing. This robs men of their capacity to break through all objective mystifications, including science. A truly dialectical theory would recognize its practical insufficiency in bad times, not pretend that the transparency of society makes the revolution any easier to bring about.

My claim is that critical theory recognizes that Marx conceived of theory and practice in an inseparable dialectical relation. The Frankfurt critics were materialists in the sense that they accepted Marx's critique of political economy. Yet they have revised Marx's critique of capitalism to include a critique of science and culture, which together hide the economic base and its structural inequities by purveying the lie that the real is rational. Critical theory treats science empirically as an institution of the bourgeois world, one that protects the system from being revealed for what it is. Marx knew what it was; but his critique of political economy can only be reintroduced into critical theory once the critique of culture and science has done its work.

For Marx, these two levels of critique were united. But since the late nineteenth century, the relation between base and superstructure has changed. Global capitalism is still essentially the same as Marx imagined. Yet the system has developed ideological mechanisms for occluding its real nature. The whole apparatus of the manipulation of needs and of consciousness protects capitalism from objective economic crises, catalyzed by public recognition that the system is neither just nor efficient.

Thus, the critique of science has arisen not to challenge Marx's critique of political economy but only to recognize the changed relation between base

and superstructure. This is far from Hegelian idealism. Marx analysed the objective structures of political economy within which men lost their humanity.
He never intended to divorce the 'ontological' concern with alienation from
his structural critique of capitalism. He wanted to do just the opposite, to read
structural domination in the fates of people.

Marx would have been the first to admit that politically disengaged science
is hopelessly stale. Only the dialectic between science and praxis will bring a
qualitative change in history. The science itself says that capitalist reality contains the seeds of its own destruction. The dialectic is the capacity of the world
for self-change. Science without a dialectical self-image only reproduces the
contemplative forms of bourgeois empiricism. The intent of Marxian scientism
is perhaps salutary but it is nonetheless completely undialectical. In over-
reacting to the allegedly Hegelian heritage of Marxism, Althusser and Colletti
have undermined Marx's dialectic.

Scientism is logically inadequate in so far as it assumes that the more we
know about capitalism the better we can control it. The political efficacy of
science is strictly a historical question. The most effective thing to do today is
to criticize the cultural-scientistic superstructure and not to produce more
knowledge about capitalist economics. Marxian economics will only be absorbed and perverted unless it can break through the pervasive belief that the
real is rational.

The Frankfurt critics, unlike Marx, were pessimistic but not fatalistic; their
pessimism was warranted by the surprising capacity of capitalism to reproduce
itself through superstructural deceits. Capitalism is still based on the exploitation of labour; but now there are other levels of domination which make the
exploitation of labour a rather distant concern. Capitalism has strengthened
itself since Marx. Like everything else, critical theory has failed to change a
world which becomes stronger the more it becomes irrational.

The critique of science is an integral part of the critique of the cultural
formations of late capitalism which effectively divert the attention of persons
who might otherwise be radicalized by economic crisis and the personal suffering incurred thereby. Undialectical science is another weapon in the arsenal of
one-dimensional society. The demystification brought by science – once a useful counter to fear and myth – has become a shallow ideological defence of
objectivism and common-sense thinking against the threat of genuine critical
thought.

To suggest that Marxian science is of a different order and had a different
genealogy than natural science is to mystify language. I do not see that Althusser's science is any different from the natural sciences. Marx was engaged both
in the critique of ideology and in the analysis of societal processes. Both are
essential to Marxism. Scientized Marxism would fail to engage in the critique

of ideology, arguing that such a critique is a trivial concern which saps vital revolutionary energy. The critique of science has a part to play in the critique of ideology. We must first resist domination on the level of the superstructure. Otherwise, economic critique will be effortlessly absorbed into trade-unionist socialism and rendered harmless.

The claim that critical theory can remain within the critique of science is arguable. Has capitalism changed that much? This is an important question. There may be nothing else to do but to fight the one-dimensionality of the times on every front. The Althusser school would relegate the critique of ideology to Marxian humanism. But equating critical theory and Marxian humanism is wholly incorrect.[16] The thrust of Adorno's 'negative dialectics' was directed against the premature reconciliation of subject and object presupposed by Marxian humanism.

Althusser attempts to return to a literal Marx who understood the reality of capitalism. But capitalism has altered the relation between base and superstructure since Marx. To get to the base, we must first penetrate the ideological veil. I do not suspect that Althusser's elegant philology will be of much use in this regard. Even Colletti has rejected Althusser's literalism. Recently, he has made the turn away from Marx scholarship towards the politically concrete tasks set by Gramsci.[17] Althusser's *Reading Capital* is certainly not a helpful account of the changed reality of capitalism. If anything, it deifies Marx by remaining true to his every word. This is too much even for Colletti.

What is mysterious about the scientistic attack on the Frankfurt School is the notion that the critical theorists were and are Hegelians. In fact, except for Marcuse's earliest flirtation with Heidegger and Hegel, the Frankfurt attack on Hegel has been devastating. Hegel breaks off the dynamic of the dialectic by absolutizing idealism. No one saw this more clearly than did Horkheimer and Adorno. The critique of science has directed itself against all forms of idealism, including that of Hegel.

The whole of critical theory is an attack on idealism. But materialism must first analyse the strength of the superstructure before it attempts directly to reveal the structural irrationality of the base. The two levels of critique, united in Marx's work, have been severed. The critique of science is an attempt to return to the critique of political economy by piercing the superstructural veil. Science is one of the most important parts of the superstructure, not only for the evils that it brings upon technical processes but for the passivity which it reinforces by its uncritical compliance with the given object-world.

The self-understanding of science is idealist. By this I mean that science conceives of the object-world as exploitable by the subject. Non-idealist dialectics locates the source of dialectical tension in the world itself, not in the knowledge-constitutive activities of science. Critical theory charges science not only with eternalizing domination, but with being unable to see objective situations in terms of their potential for self-transformation. Science sees the world only in terms of its own self-interest, not in terms of the 'self-interest' of the objects. The interest of science is in dissecting reality and then controlling it. Science wants to dominate.

But *after* the revolution, science can and must be transformed. No longer will science be conceived only as an instrumental control-mechanism. It will instead be a 'new science' concerned to appreciate the world for its beauty. The critique of science, thus, is historically specific. There will come a time when science will be a celebration of the entire cosmos, not a subjective device for beating nature to death. This does not mean that we retreat into a pre-industrial shell, but that we stop thinking of nature as something merely to be put under a microscope.

Marcuse is as concerned with 'structure' as the Althusserians. 'One-dimensional society' is an instance of an over-determined structure. We only inveigh against the scientization of the dialectical categories of critical theory through a precritical epistemology which is a relic both of positivism *and* of Hegel's spiritualism. After the revolution, the categories of science will change in line with re-erotization of the body and nature.

The critique of science is forced upon us by the altered relation between base and superstructure. Critical theory is an analysis of the historical situation which usurps the critic's political potency. Critical theory tries to account objectively for its own being relegated to speculative critique. It does not glorify its detached critical role but only hopes to understand why capitalism has renewed its lease on life.

The debate within Marxism about science is useless. Marxism can no longer be restricted to task-oriented theory; as such, it can at best criticize capitalist economics. Yet to have any resonance, it should primarily operate on the level of cultural-critique so as to break through the idealist illusions of the capitalist superstructure. Domination has found new domains. To keep the precarious economic logic of capitalism protected and invisible domination has had to find new domains.

Marxism must be materialistic in the last analysis. The materialism of the critique of ideology, however, analyses one-dimensionality as the concrete structure within which critical theory is politically irrelevant. The *tristesse* of critical theory is born of the realistic assessment that late capitalism has developed new ways to cope with political and metaphysical deviance.

The 'critique' of critical theory aims to account for the closure of capitalist society, its repressive tolerance of deviance and opposition. I do not belittle Althusser's sentiment that he is for Marx, not against him. Too much bourgeois social science pretends to be Marxist when it hates Marx and fears the revolution. The Frankfurt School was no closer to Hegel than is Althusser. Yet its critical self-image has clashed with the scientism of Althusser. The debate has produced heat but little light: there can be no science for all time; sciences change as societies do.

The critique of science is forced on the Frankfurt critics by the objective impenetrability of capitalism. That capitalism appears impenetrable is precisely the fact which occupies the reflective efforts of the critical theorists. Its impenetrability is strengthened by one-dimensional ideology which says that the real is rational. The task of the critique of science is to reject this identity.

Meanwhile, it should not be embarrassing to belong to the speculative tradition in Marxism. Perhaps in the future we could reunite the two levels of critique, sundered since the Second International; only then can we talk of a 'science' of society without introducing another form of ideology. Until then, science remains a tool for translating nature and society into strictly instrumental qualities. To be unscientific now is to hope for the redemption of science. But science will be pure only when it is disengaged from the matrix of instrumental control, a disengagement which will come at the end of history.

Science is an ideology of false harmony, it pretends the peaceful coexistence of subject and object. Yet science is also critique. Critique can break through ideological science by bringing out its fullest possibilities: a way to interact with nature which is no longer threatening or destructive. Science thus transforms itself from serious critique to play. This will happen only through the fulfilment of Marx's original project: the total reconstruction of society, in part by a science which knows itself to be a form of *temporary* seriousness ready to give in to its fullest aesthetic possibilities once its message is transmitted. What message? That capitalism is not eternal.

What is science? It is a mode for rationalizing domination. But it is potentially an expression of what Schiller called the 'play-impulse.' Science can also see through the ideological illusions of a scientized, reified reality. This is the perplexing character of the argument. Science veils oppression in rational necessity and at the same time only a science which reveals the dogmatic interest of science can liberate science from its own repression. Science becomes play only by being scientific.

Science *before* the revolution is Althusser's version: rigorous objectivism. Science *after* the revolution is Marcuse's vision: the aesthetic ethos. In the meantime, science has to fulfil its paradoxical role, as ideology and as the critique of ideology. Capitalism is not created by science, but the 'emancipation' from objectivist illusions is one of the most important critical priorities.

The false reason and universalism of science must be rigorously denounced. If science forgets its playful, erotic nature it will succumb to the eternal rigour demanded of it by late capitalism: *rigor mortis* will set in. Only by being aware of its paradoxical function as domination and as freedom will the science of neo-Marxism retain its critical energy.

The debate over the nature of Marxian science is undialectical, while the 'nature' of Marx's science was historical. Before the revolution, science is true seeing; after, science will celebrate the truth. Marxian science transforms itself by recognizing the contradictory character of its nature: science as rigour preparing for its becoming fantasy and play. 'Dialectics is the self-consciousness of the objective context of delusion; it does not mean to have escaped from that context. Its objective goal is to break out from within.'[18]

NOTES

1 This is approximately the date on which Georg Lukács and Karl Korsch came on the scene; Georg Lukács, *History and Class Consciousness* and Karl Korsch, *Marxism and Philosophy.*
2 Max Horkheimer and Theodor W. Adorno, *Dialectic of Enlightenment*, 3; 'In the most general sense of progressive thought, the Enlightenment has always aimed at liberating men from fear and establishing their sovereignty. Yet the fully enlightened earth radiates disaster triumphant. The program of the Enlightenment was the disenchantment of the world; the dissolution of myths and the substitution of knowledge for fancy.'
3 *Eclipse of Reason*, 187
4 This phrase is taken from 'On Subject and Object,' private translation.
5 Max Horkheimer and Theodor W. Adorno, *Dialectic of Enlightenment*, 9
6 Max Horkheimer and Theodor W. Adorno, *Dialectic of Enlightenment*, 24; 'For enlightenment is as totalitarian as any system. Its untruth does not consist in what its romantic enemies have always reproached it for; analytic method, return to the elements, dissolution through reflective thought; but instead in the fact that for enlightenment the process is always decided from the start.'
7 This reduction is the precise theme of Jürgen Habermas' *Knowledge and Human Interests*
8 Cf. Martin Jay, *The Dialectical Imagination*
9 Jürgen Habermas, *Toward a Rational Society*, 81-122; Herbert Marcuse, *An Essay on Liberation*, 31-54
10 *From Max Weber*, ed. Hans Gerth and C. Wright Mills, 215-16
11 Philip Selznick, 'Foundations of a Theory of Organization,' *American Sociological Review*, XIII (1948), 25
12 Louis Althusser, *For Marx*; Louis Althusser and Étienne Balibar, *Reading Capital*; Lucio Colletti, *From Rousseau to Lenin* and *Marxism and Hegel*
13 *From Rousseau to Lenin*, 120
14 *Critical Theory*, especially the chapter entitled 'Traditional and Critical Theory'
15 Louis Althusser, *For Marx*, 171, fn. 7
16 Martin Jay, 'The Frankfurt School's Critique of Marxist Humanism,' *Social Research* 39 (1972)
17 Cf. Lucio Colletti, 'A Political and Philosophical Interview,' *New Left Review* 86 (July-August 1974) 3-28
18 Theodor W. Adorno, *Negative Dialectics*, 406

David Cook

Albert Camus' *Caligula*: **the metaphysics of an emperor**

Man is metaphysical in his very being, in his loves, in his hates, in his individual
and collective history.

MAURICE MERLEAU-PONTY

The world of Albert Camus is tragic. The human journey is marked by suffering. It is a journey the history of which has darkened the imagination, leaving only the paths of quiescent solitude or violence. The consequence is a blindness that is only relieved by coming to terms with the metaphysical.

The illumination of the metaphysical begins for Camus with the desperate choice that confronts the weary traveller of this century: the question of suicide. The individual contemplating death penetrates to the nature of being, and with this knowledge may again enter the realm of human action. The question of death precedes life, and its consideration must precede the introduction to Caligula[1] who meets the reader only after rebelling against suicide.

Suicide, which for many marks the end of the individual's consideration of life, is for Camus the beginning. *The Myth of Sisyphus* argues from that imaginary space where the individual draws back to view life and to reconstitute a world. It is a reflection on origins which may lead the individual back to the world or cause him to take his final leave.[2] Reflection on one's own death reveals the existential condition of life. The nature of reality is illuminated by mortality, which conditions the relations that are established with others and with nature. It is the exploration of the individual's relation with the world that unveils a dualism implicit in existence.

The first part of this dualism is the epistemological assumption that existence is unreasonable. Life has no a priori or absolute meaning. Death for Camus is inscrutable; it reflects the inscrutable nature of the universe. In the work of Sartre, by contrast, we find that death renders existence contingent. It is the individual's being which is robbed of its freedom by death, as happens to Ibbeita in the short story *The Wall*.[3] In *The Myth of Sisyphus* it is reason that is betrayed, and this betrayal illuminates the fact that the human condition cannot be rendered reasonable. As Camus simply states it: 'This world in itself is not reasonable.'[4]

Thus the individual contemplating suicide because life has 'lost its meaning' is enveloped in a more general dilemma facing the human mind. In fact, the claim of scientific rationalism to render existence reasonable, which suffices as a basis for life of most twentieth-century individuals, collapses into myths or into the poetic for Camus.[5] As he points out, within the context of an individual's experience the sensual relation to the physical world may be more meaningful than reducing nature to a technical aspect of a production process. But in neither case can existence be fully transcended by the categories of human thought. The drawing back from the world to consider suicide, in essence a philosophical bracketing of the world, illuminates its epistemological limitations which must be carried back with the individual when he returns to action in the world.

While Camus believed that the attempt to know the world will ultimately fail, the very attempt itself points towards a basic aspect of human nature. The individual for Camus is a creator of meanings. Camus rejects the view of man as primarily a creator of his material conditions. Camus goes further in his view of man as a creator of meaning to claim that humanity has always strived for absolute knowledge and complete unity in relations with the world. 'That nostalgia for unity, that appetite for the absolute illustrates the essential impulse of the human drama.'[6] Ontologically the individual desires to know life's complete meaning.

Therefore, *The Myth of Sisyphus* presents existence as defined by a contradiction: epistemology conflicts with ontology. The historical moment of this conflict in the twentieth century is called the absurd for Camus. The conception of the absurd is the fundamental proposition of Camus' metaphysics. It defines the task of philosophy, as well as of individual life, as being to preserve the dualism in existence rather than to attempt to resolve it. European philosophy for Camus is characterized by the failure to realize that this dichotomy cannot be transcended. As a result, Europe has witnessed philosophies that lead to intellectual suicide, if one asserts an a priori meaning in the world, or to murder, if one pursues an impossible unity that is forced on others.

At the end of each of these paths lies a solitude where even the awakened have nightmares filled with the haunting forms of a reality they do not comprehend. It is these paths of violence or solitude that form the setting of *Caligula*. It is here that the emperor attempts to find his way among the metaphysical ruins where humanity wanders.

'Men die; and they are not happy.'[7] This modest piece of ideology, as Camus calls it,[8] is the starting point of Caligula's exploration of the human condition.[9] It is the beginning of an imperial pursuit of happiness unto death. It is in addition the attempted metamorphosis of humanity from dreary discontent.

An individual's world can be upset for many reasons. For Caligula it began with the death of his sister and lover Drusilla. As Camus writes in the preface to the play, Caligula was 'a relatively attractive prince up to then' who becomes aware on the death of Drusilla 'that this world is not satisfactory.'[10] The dissatisfaction with the world is a crisis in meaning. Caligula can no longer explain the world he lives in; his reason fails him.

This failure is Caligula's introduction to the absurd. An introduction does not mean that Caligula has learnt all he needs to know about his new-found consciousness. He is ignorant of the limitations implicit in the absurd. The absurd becomes a compulsion to rebellion. It pushes the emperor into action; he gropes towards the heavenly city by making a hell on earth. His torment becomes that of the gods who are all powerful but know not where, or how, to employ their force. It is a frenzy of ever increasing terror to fill the chasm that has appeared in his existence.

Caligula's conclusions drawn from the absurd are striking. He defies the seemingly inscrutable universe. He announces that he will capture 'the moon, or happiness, or eternal life.'[11] His goal is that which does not exist, 'a desire for the impossible.'[12] The means by which he is going to realize his end 'is to be logical right through, at all costs.'[13]

We can observe from Caligula's reaction that his view of the absurd differs from the view expressed in *Sisyphus.*[14] Absurdity is not for Caligula the epistemological limitation in the understanding of reality; rather it reflects the conflicting ontological proposition. Absurdity results only to the extent that the individual has not pursued the 'desire for unity,' 'the nostalgia for the absolute,' to its conclusion. Humanity has failed because the individual has not followed human nature to the end.

Caligula's perception of the absurd is only partially a reflection of the existential, for the absurd has profound social implications. Humanity has not pursued its reason to its logical conclusion precisely because no one had the power to be strictly logical, to carry out the absurd. Caligula believed that fortune had presented him with the unique opportunity to realize human nature, for he was an all powerful emperor – the philosopher-king come to power.

The Roman world that Caligula creates is consequent on his ambition to find meaning through an unwavering adherence to his truth. He duplicates in the political realm the conditions he encounters in his own life. Thus death, which struck Drusilla for no apparent reason, is made to strike the patricians with equal randomness. Death also reduces all human activities for Caligula to an identical level – all are equally meaningless, 'everything on an equal footing: the grandeur of Rome, and your attack of arthritis.'[15] Following this logic Caligula elevates the market with its claim to equality to the first among equals. The idea that 'Treasury's of prime importance'[16] is carried to its logical extreme in Caligula's schemes, such as disinheriting all children,[17] or in compulsory visits of all citizens to the state brothel in order to balance the budget.[18] Through these actions the metaphysical condition of the individual is presented to each character. The absurd universe is translated into the absurd polity.

The universe created by Caligula is responded to in different manners by each character. Scipio, the poet, and Cherea, the leader of the rebellion against Caligula, attempt to find an accommodation with the philosophical challenge. Some, like the Roman patricians and Caligula's mistress Caesonia, watch with uncomprehending horror; others, like the liberated slave, Helicon, watch with detachment. These characters are participants in the metaphysical drama and serve as foils to the play's elucidation of the metaphysical condition embodied in absurdity.

For example, Camus' presentation of Scipio, the poet, is an ideal type of a strictly personalized interpretation of absurdity. Like Caligula, Scipio finds the world unreasonable, but he concludes that it can be 'explained' by means of the poem or myth. He accepts the limitation implicit in the absurdist concept of reason which rejects the universal power of rationalist thought to understand the world. Caligula's path of creating meaning through 'super-rationalism,' logic at all costs, is contradictory to Scipio's own experience of the natural world. 'The wavy outline of the Roman hills and the sudden thrill of peace that twilight brings to them,'[19] to quote Scipio's early poem, lends a 'provisional meaning' to the individual's relation with nature which is not transcended by scientific or religious categories.

Scipio also appeals to the individual's natural relation to the world in the last act of the play during Caligula's poetry contest on the subject of death. Scipio's poem 'Pursuit of happiness that purifies the heart, / Skies rippling with light, / O wild, sweet, festal joys, frenzy without hope!' is a lesson that can be derived from death only in the absence of a final transcendence.[20] The creation of meaning, then, rests on the lived experience of the individual and the individual's rebellion or reaction to the absurd. Scipio is a phenomenologist in his approach to the world.[21] Experience forms the initial constitution of meaning and the touchstone Scipio returns to.

While Scipio has understood the epistemological basis of absurdity that Caligula failed to grasp, his own inadequacies are aligned with an inadequate comprehension of the ontological. The lifestyle that Scipio portrays is very likely to end in a romantic mysticism or complete solitude.[22] This certainly is the path followed by Glahn in Knut Hamsun's *Pan*[23] who shares Scipio's sensual attachment to the world. Camus' characterization of Caligula, and more forcefully of Cherea, indicates that the constitution of meaning must involve others, in part because the very transcendence of the individual by God which can give rise to solitary relations is lacking.

Scipio finds it very difficult to decide whether to support Cherea's rebellion. In the Gallimard edition for the Pléaide based on Camus' 1958 text,[24] Scipio does not participate in the final assassination at all. This is certainly a logical outcome of the opening of the fourth act where Scipio is pressed by Cherea to join the rebels but refuses.[25]

Camus treats the characterizations of Scipio and Caligula as obverse reflections of each other. It is not without coincidence that Caligula was also a poet and frequently expresses sympathy with Scipio throughout the play.[25] There is some similarity as well in the glimpses we see of Caligula's past in the play, and in Suetonius' portrait of Caligula before his sister's death.[27] Scipio comes to represent Caligula's past in embodying the relations Caligula had before his ascension to power. Though Caligula may have experienced life in the same fashion as Scipio, his death indicates that he did not learn the lessons his past held out to him.

The events leading up to Caligula's assassination reinforce the metaphysical double-bind Caligula faces. Having experienced the reality of death, Caligula cannot return to his old world, nor can he advance in the new. His path is blocked by the false conclusions he has drawn from the fact of mortality. In moving from an existential limitation, the absurd becomes a social imperative for Caligula. His actions, reflecting his impossible goals, become boundless. His power, which was as absolute as any ruler's, becomes reduced to sheer violence. But even in a world where 'the living don't suffice to people,' and where Caligula takes 'ease only in the company of my dead,'[28] he does turn to the patricians for the aid the heavens have denied him.

The patricians as much as Caligula are faced with the necessity of rebellion. It was this fact that Caligula knew and accepted as part of a conscious response to the world. Caligula's own actions are the motivating factor in the rebellion, and its very success depended on Caligula's tolerance of the plot on his life.[29] We learn from Cherea that the tyranny was as much a metaphysical as physical threat to the Romans. As he points out, ' ... what's intolerable is to see one's life being drained of meaning, to be told there's no reason for existing. A man can't live without some reason for living.'[30]

But even in the dramatist's world a conscious rebellion is an uncommon occurrence. The patricians prove to be much more concerned with the threat to their physical lives and to their public images. The old patrician is an ideal stereotype of the individual's ability to translate the metaphysical challenge into traditional categories of little or no critical content. Caligula's reaction to Drusilla's death is explained away by the old patrician, 'Of course, for one girl dead, a dozen living ones,'[31] and, in the patrician's view, given time Caligula will realize this. It is not surprising, therefore, that the old patrician's motivation for joining the rebellion is not at all what Caligula had hoped for. 'He calls me "darling"! In public, mind you – just to make a laughing-stock of me. Death's too good for him.'[32]

To the extent that the old patrician is representative of the conspirators, Caligula's search for meaning through social interaction is brought to an abrupt check. Political activity for the patricians becomes associated with maintaining the status quo. Politics, much like death, is circumscribed for the patricians. There is no imagining of new worlds where the individual's nature is realized. These are empty concepts for the patricians. Their rebellion does not create meaning.[33] Their participation in the assassination only eliminates the manifestation of Caligula's tyranny. Caligula's last words, 'I'm still alive,'[34] are indeed true for the patricians. For the existential problems which gave rise to Caligula's rebellion have been left untouched. The patricians have learnt nothing.

Caligula himself began to realize that the Romans' rebellion was going to

be a failure. This placed his own actions in a very ambiguous light. His attempt
to establish meaning was in danger of becoming nothing but a highly calculated
series of murders. In the last act of the play Caligula makes a final appeal for
help by calling on the poets. As he remarks, 'I sometimes pictured a gallant
band of poets defending me in the last ditch.'[35] The appeal to the poets sheds
a final light on the inadequacy of Caligula's metaphysical position.

The poets, who are symbolic of all intellectuals, are called upon to provide
the illumination of absurdity which Caligula himself lacks. As we have seen
with Scipio, the poetic activity is able to point towards natural relations the
individual can develop with the world which do constitute a 'provisional meaning.' Thus the world's absurdity, its unreasonableness, is interpreted as a limitation and guide to individual action.[36] These limits are the relations with others
and with nature, which also reflect the individual's being. Sensuality, which is
the basis of beauty, is given a role in the political realm by marking the boundaries to the paths political actors choose and by giving the political actors a
glimpse of a future world implicit in political action.

Caligula rejects the poets, for his rule has negated their message. He has
chosen a path which attempts the impossible, and hence implicitly rejects any
limits to his action. Caligula's misinterpretation of the epistemological proposition of the absurd has its roots in Caligula's own past. He has cut off this
past, and in so doing has eliminated what tentative meaning he had found in
personal existence. As emperor he becomes the public personality par excellence. He comes to a realization of this fact near the end of the play in talking
with Caesonia: 'Wouldn't it be better that the last witness [of the past] should
disappear?'[37] But by this time it is too late; Scipio's world is banished. The
ontological desire for unity has turned into the negation of ontology through
the enforcement of a false unity on humanity. The solitary and the murderous
join. Caligula's world becomes that of the dead whose haunting presence
eventually takes the emperor himself.

Caligula's downfall can certainly be partly ascribed to his mistaken notion
that if the world is unreasonable then reason may be replaced by the consistent
application of a method. This is brought out in Camus' characterization of
Cherea, the one patrician who understands Caligula,[38] yet who responds to his
tyranny in a 'reasonable' way. Cherea's character shows traits of both Caligula
and Scipio, for he also is a writer. He may well be described as the older Scipio
that Caligula should have been.

Through Cherea, Camus gives the reader the rough outline of an individual
who does manage to live with the absurd. Cherea attempts to honour both
propositions of absurdity in living with the contradiction: ' ... what I want is
to live, and to be happy. Neither, to my mind, is possible if one pushes the
absurd to its logical conclusions.'[39]

The meaning Cherea has established in his existence is a fragile one. He is very much aware of the tension in the absurd which can undermine the security of a lifestyle. Caligula points out to Cherea that 'Security and logic don't go together,' to which Cherea responds, 'My plan of life may not be logical, but at least it's sound.'[40] The reader is not informed of how successful Cherea is in continuing his absurd life. We are told that Cherea planned to withdraw from political action after the assassination.[41] The consequences of this might very well have broken the balance in Cherea's world and led him into accepting one aspect of the absurd over the other.

Caligula was a play written by a young man, but a play that interested its author throughout his life. Camus added the last touches in 1958, two years before his death, for the performance at the Petit Théatre de Paris. However, the play's fascination for Camus cannot solely be explained by its dramatic success. For *Caligula* as a metaphysical drama is a metaphor of the human condition. It is true that Camus' philosophy may have failed to capture, in Merleau-Ponty's phrase, 'the metaphysical in man.' The past lay dormant in Caligula's memory, banished from his world just as society was put to flight by his tyranny. Yet Camus has succeeded in raising basic questions concerning human existence and in showing the force of man's answers.

NOTES

1 Albert Camus, *Caligula and Three Other Plays*, trans. Stuart Gilbert (New York 1958)
2 Albert Camus, *The Myth of Sisyphus and Other Essays*, trans. Justin O'Brien (New York 1955)
3 *The Wall and Other Stories* (New York 1948)
4 *Sisyphus*, 16
5 Ibid., 15
6 *Sisyphus*, 13
7 *Caligula*, 8
9 Ibid., vi
9 Camus' concern with 'happiness' is also shared by Herbert Marcuse. Despite the immense differences in the work of each thinker, especially in the use of psychological categories, there are many interesting comparisons between Marcuse's view of art and revolt and Camus' concern for the artist and rebellion.
10 *Caligula*, v
11 Ibid., 8
12 Ibid.
13 Ibid.
14 See page 203.
15 *Caligula*, 11
16 Ibid., 11. Camus treats the economy and market relations as a secondary theme in the play. It is clear that the market's claim to maximize happiness is false for Camus. The market society is another manifestation of the inadequate response to the absurd.
17 Ibid., 12
18 Ibid., 29-30
19 Ibid., 35

20 Ibid., 66
21 An interesting treatment of the phenomenological aspects of Camus' work is given by
    A. Nicolas, *Une Philosophie de l'Existence* (Paris 1964)
22 Albert Maquet's view of Camus in his *The Invincible Summer* (London 1958) , is typical of
    the interpretations which play down the philosophic for the view that Camus was a
    Mediterranean hedonist.
23 (New York 1972)
24 See Albert Camus, *Théâtre, Récits, Nouvelles* (Paris 1962), 108.
25 *Caligula*, 56
26 For example see Caligula's comments on Scipio's poem; ibid., 66 and 35-6
27 Suetonius, *The Twelve Caesars*, trans. Robert Graves (Harmondsworth 1957), chap. 4.
    Caligula was based on Suetonius' account. See the program notes for the 1958 performance
    reprinted on p. 1749 of the Pleiade.
28 *Caligula*, 68
29 See Caligula's discussion with Cherea at the end of act III.
30 Ibid., 21
31 Ibid., 4
32 Ibid., 19
33 The portrayal of Helicon, the liberated slave, also indicates that awareness of the world's
    absurdity is not assured if you are set free. Camus expanded Helicon's role in the 1958
    performance not unrelated, I believe, to the Algerian conflict.
34 Ibid., 74
35 Ibid., 66
36 There is for Camus another dimension to poetry which may be dangerous. The infinite
    metaphysical aspects of poetry can lead to nihilism. See Albert Camus, *The Rebel*, trans.
    Anthony Bower (New York 1956), 81-100.
37 *Caligula*, 70
38 See ibid., 58
39 Ibid., 51
40 Ibid.
41 Ibid., 20

Alkis Kontos

Domination: metaphor and political reality

For my friend José Antonio Nájera, after years of silence

Les yeux seuls sont encore capables de pousser un cri.

RENÉ CHAR

Think of Dante's *Inferno*. The mere utterance of the word conjures up fearful images in the mind. It is a place marked for eternity. Its boundaries have been drawn with authoritative precision and a merciless lack of ambiguity as to its awesome purpose. There it stands, a hierarchy of circles signifying a divine taxonomy of human sorrow permanently devoid of any hope for relief: an immutable structure erected to house the futile, remorseful laments of the imprudent. Domination, that singularly peculiar darkness of the mind, is our inferno.[1] This scandalous kingdom of darkness encircles humanity with inaudible ferocity. Domination roams the earth with indiscreet access, in myriad disguises. It perverts the intimacy of the bedroom; it erodes the meaning of the necessity of production in the factory.

Domination is a satanic thief. It robs the vibrant rhythm of the essential motion of life. It distorts and falsifies and then it imposes an embellished mirage upon the traces of its ruins. The kingdom of domination wants to engulf the world with its promised blissful sleep. But ultimately its political reality provides only a troubled sleep.

Unlike Dante's *Inferno*, ours is not a divine punishment but a human creation. It is a complex, labyrinthine drama enacted under an empty sky. Perhaps the prophetic rumours of that mad genius, Nietzsche, regarding the fate of God have been fulfilled. Or perhaps the sky is just silent. A divine withdrawal from human affairs may have been reached; remember the luminous mushroom of Hiroshima, the smoke of Auschwitz suffocating cries and whispers. Unlike Dante, we have no master poet to guide us, no loving Beatrice to mediate on our behalf. We are alone. And yet our inferno might not be permanent; its darkness could be made to recede, revealing the scarred face of humanity, elegant and beautiful.

Let us seek the contours and nuances of the architectonic structure of domination which history, that master pimp, imposes on life. Let us try to weave with lucid intelligence and imagination the thread that Ariadne denies us.

I

Writing in defence and praise of politics, Machiavelli insisted that political activity, when properly engaged in, denied by its very nature and purpose both purity of the soul and complete moral licence.[2] He perceived politics to be wrought with violence and fraud.[3] The political greatness he so admired was predicated upon the willingness to participate in the brutal, nasty side of political life. From this ensues Machiavelli's peculiar notion of noble 'dirty hands,' a notion he so painfully attempted to delineate by holding conscience in abeyance, a notion which would re-emerge with extraordinary vigour in the critical years of the birth and maturity of existentialism as a philosophic doctrine of action and commitment.[4] His political realism claimed force to be in the very heart of politics: force undergoes mutations but never does it disappear.[5] For Machiavelli, naked and swiftly delivered force is indispensable to the founding of a new order of things. The ugliness of violent politics can be disguised, even mythologized through subsequent glories; violence itself can be tamed into law; but it cannot be eradicated from the task of maintaining political power and social order. Politics and violence can maintain only a truce, never genuine peace.

Though Machiavelli saw politics and force inseparably interwoven, he, nonetheless, insisted on seeing more in politics than mere force and violence. The adumbration of a paradoxically heroic and ruthlessly calculating mood is visible in Machiavelli's passionate concern with the great political figures whose fierce and deadly struggle with Fortuna he examined and recorded, never reducing it to a mere selfish desire for power and fame, even when brutal and murderous.[6]

It is Hobbes who fully impoverished politics by reducing it to the function of policing society. Politics as *the* means to social order is a concept unequivocally voiced by Hobbes. Leviathan, that 'Mortall God,'[7] emerges through merciless deductions whereby the mechanics of motion and power prevail triumphantly. Machiavelli's ambivalence and ambiguity, occasional as they may have been, disappear. Under the austere, haunting images of the Hobbesian natural man, neither glory nor heroics can survive. Power and politics become one and the same and the only measure is self-interest, the supreme mover in the presence of violent death, the *summum malum*. Where self-interest is absent, indifference prevails.

In an extraordinary passage, Hobbes suggests that intentional denial or suppression of truth will occur if it is in one's interest. More clearly, Hobbes furnishes a cynical opinion as to why geometric truths are not disputed: it is so 'because men care not, in that subject [geometry] what be truth, as a thing that crosses no man's ambitions, profit, or lust.'[8] And if that truth were not to be so neutralized in terms of self-interest then, Hobbes informs us, men would immediately attack it in order to serve their own interest.[9]

Hobbes' notion of politics as power exercised in order to control individual conflicts does not assign to politics any positive, creative qualities. Politics is necessary but sterile. Politics authoritatively allocates or denies access to already established values; no new values are created. The procurement of obedience terminates the task of politics. Emphasis on power as the crux of politics does not stop with Hobbes. It reaches its negative culmination in Marx's insistence that the emancipation of humanity from alienation would also, of necessity, spell the end of politics. The notions of politics and power found in Machiavelli, Hobbes, and Marx created the intellectual context in which our age sought to identify and assign meaning and scope to political activity and thought. Inevitably power came to loom large in, indeed to preoccupy, our political language.[10]

If modern political thinking stresses power, classical thought was not oblivious to it. But politics proper, political life which testified to the uniqueness of humans as political creatures, was beyond power. Aristotle's claim that the polis is the appropriate domain of humans (only beasts and God had no need of the polis for obviously distinct reasons) is a claim made regarding the civilizing, humanizing role of politics.[11] Human beings are political creatures; or rather, they become human only when they are also political. To be social beings is not enough. Marx has effected a total transvaluation of the social and political categories at the expense of the latter, and, inevitably, the balance between them is lost.

Politics is coeval with the emergence of human society. It is inherent in collective, group life. Chronologically, politics is prior to political philosophy. Only later the distinction arose between factual political activity – concrete political arrangements and practices – and normative prescriptions about such activity and practices. What we describe and analyse is distinct from, but obviously related to, what we long for and advocate. Thus Hobbes might have been terribly accurate in what he described, but utterly wrong in ontologizing it.[12]

The necessary distinction between the *is* and the *ought* is not only sharpened by the theoretical possibilities of improving political life, but it is further intensified by the imminent danger of the corruption and deterioration of an existing political order. Political thinkers from antiquity on recognized the ominous possibilities of the misuse and abuse of that indispensable feature of politics, power. Fearfully they spoke of tyranny.

Perhaps Plato's *Republic* stands as a classic, complex, and exquisitely elegant presentation of the relation between philosophers and politics, wisdom and power. It is true that the philosopher can be killed by the anti-philosophical polis. The philosopher questions uncompromisingly; the polis responds with hemlock. Plato with subtle poetic irony re-evaluates the philosopher's fate in the polis and offers us the most powerful condemnation of the philosopher's temptation to seek the royal throne. If philosophers were to seize power, tyranny would ensue and philosophy would cease. Philosophy must castigate the polis but cannot rule it. Philosophers should not rule; they should educate. The delicate balance between thought and action, speech and command, can easily be broken. The philosopher must be cleansed of the youthful and resentful tyrant that lies dormant in him. The world, according to Plato (a point missed by most of his readers), would not be a better place if the philosophers were to become kings or the kings philosophers. The world would be a worse place. The kingdom of philosophy is of this world, but primarily of the mind.

Philosophy on the throne is tyranny, not philosophy. Therefore, in Plato's verdict, no final resolution exists between the desire to change the world and persecution by those who are threatened by such desire. Philosophers, true to their vocation, must live dangerously.[13]

Machiavelli may have believed that he was improving on Plato by insisting that not the throne but the king's ear be reserved for the political philosopher. From Plato's possible tyrant restored to educator, the philosopher becomes a counsellor, to be transformed into Hegel's historiosophic elucidator, and then into Marx's revolutionary, where the tension between thought and action, knowledge and cosmos, collapses in that strangely volcanic unity, praxis, which disguises more than it resolves the enigma of the human condition and the meaning and orientation of history.

If Plato knew of the imminent danger of philosophy lapsing into tyranny, Thucydides knew of might and its immanent ability to speak as right. However, the severity with which ancient philosophy criticized the mediocrity and anti-philosophical character of the polis should not obscure the fact that the philosopher in asserting an ideal did not abdicate his place in the polis and his concern with the daily actuality of his citizenship. Neither cosmopolitanism nor homelessness could extinguish the philosopher's awareness that between the ideal and the real the emergence of tyrannical rule could only deteriorate the life of the polis.

Tyranny is present today as it was in the past, but today its instruments are more effective in establishing and maintaining its cruel yoke.

Tyranny as a political concept can be inadequate and misleading when treated as the sole instance of human oppression and when the implicit assumption is made that in the absence of tyranny all is well politically. The juxtaposition of tyranny with domination indicates the constricted applicability of the former and exposes a serious misconception of political reality.

To insist on employing the concept of tyranny – or variants of it such as despotism or dictatorship – as the sole perverting phenomenon of political life is to regress in our political awareness and understanding. To insist on linguistic purity in the name of traditional categories is tantamount to the obliteration of the substance of political reality: social structure. Hence there is the need to differentiate tyranny from domination, for the latter captures best our modern political experience in the advanced industrial societies.

Politics takes place in society, in a specific, concrete structure. The characteristics of political institutions and of the sources of power and its exercise are greatly conditioned by the structure of a given society. Power and structure are reciprocally moulded until the basis of power is so concealed as to become almost invisible to the ordinary, casual observer of society. Power in a Greek polis of antiquity did not manifest itself through the same channels or in the same degree as in a Persian or Egyptian kingdom. Yet it was present in all three polities.

The fundamentals of social structure condition the character of a society's political life and expression not in a mechanical unidirectional mode but in a dynamic, interactive, and comprehensive way.[14] The patterns of legitimacy do not develop, nor can they be comprehended in a social vacuum. They are rooted in the very structure of society. Of course the beliefs and values of society play a vital role. The mentality, the personality, so to speak, of society permeates and is permeated by the concreteness of social structure. But it is the social structure that sustains the growth and quality of the self-images of society and world.[15]

Politics is not an autonomous activity. It springs from the plurality of social life and tends to enforce, promote, and protect what has received the sanction of the past. It legitimates the existing social order. Politics in this sense is conservative in mood, as is the legal system which formalizes the social structure. The language, definitions, and questions pertinent to the smooth functioning of society are well entrenched in the structural visibility allowed within the preestablished boundaries of property relations and social hierarchies. Any rupture of this frame of reference appears to be destructive and hence a threat. Critical scrutiny is not welcomed when it tries to expose the foundations of social existence.

Tyranny, from classical times on, has been generally perceived as the arbitrary abuse of power.[16] It is viewed as an episode in the normal functioning of politics. It disrupts the normal state of affairs just as a disease afflicts the healthy body. The status prior to the emergence of tyranny is presumed to be legitimate and appropriate. Elimination of tyranny would spell the restoration of the prior order of things, the return to the normal. Tyranny is an assault on such order, a violation of its purpose and procedures. A critique of tyranny entails an almost unavoidable tacit, if not explicit, acceptance of the legitimacy of the status *ante*. The sociopolitical structures prior to the tyrannical rule are affirmed and upheld without any re-evaluation. The moral condemnation of tyranny is inversely an encomium for what preceded tyranny. The evil of tyranny which must be combatted blinds us from seeing inadequacies and inhumanities in what passes as a normal, healthy state of the body politic. For example, John Locke, in his *Second Treatise*, clearly and vehemently objected to the tyranny of the rule of divine right. Yet any restriction of such rule, including its elimination, did not force or invite Locke to examine the inequities of his society.

To insist on an exclusive use of the concept of tyranny is to consolidate, strengthen, and then obscure the possible oppressive features of a social structure. Attack on tyrannical rule, necessary that it is, could be identical to protection of existing privileges rather than a genuine defence of humanity. The formalism inherent in the idea of tyranny pre-empts and prevents any serious and penetrating critique of society. The central social bond and bondage remain untouched and therefore unexposed.

The concept of tyranny, with all the ominous images that it evokes, is grounded in the assumption that tyranny as a phenomenon is highly visible. This is a valid assumption. The terror of tyranny cannot be disguised. Torture cannot be made appealing, cannot be sweetened. The arbitrary cruelty of tyranny cannot be hidden from its victims. It is the visibility of tyrannical rule that generates the belief that tyranny is a political anomaly and that non-tyranny is logically the normal state of affairs. The irrational cruelty of the tyrant tends to suggest the reasonableness and decency of a society freed from tyranny. Tyrannicide suggests more than liberation from tyrants; and yet it means only the removal of tyranny. Here lies the mental deception. The grotesqueness with which tyranny assaults and violates law and order, life and property, does not demand of its opponents that they scrutinize the concrete meaning of these notions. Society, naked, with its privileges, mutilations, pitiless suffering, eleemosynary guilt, is never forced to confess its crimes.

The formalist nature of the concept of tyranny impoverishes it seriously. This does not mean that it should be discarded as a political category. After all, the phenomenon of tyranny is not yet obsolete. The usage of the term tyranny should not prevent us from the urgent and indispensable need to examine critically the social context of politics, for a politics divorced from its social aspects is a fallacy which serves the interests of those whose privileged status is well protected by political power.

Tyranny as a paradigm of negative politics has a place in the political vocabulary. But neither conceptually nor as an actual phenomenon can it have a meaningful place in political thinking without an indication of its precise significance and severe limitation. That the term tyranny has become interchangeable with other forms of faulty political order indicates not so much a careless use of terminology, but rather the tension between the narrowness of the concept itself and the complexity of modern methods of social control. That a social thinker such as Hannah Arendt, who demands linguistic clarity and purity, would study totalitarianism not as an advanced form of tyranny but as a novel mode of political control and degeneracy, indeed a uniquely modern phenomenon of control and destruction[17] in the face of which tyranny pales, should suffice to demonstrate that our task is to articulate accurately our political predicament. And this can be done not by ignoring society, the locus of politics, but by courageously and somberly unveiling the real structure of our social existence, the stage upon which the drama of politics is enacted daily.

That politics cannot be dissolved fully into the social structure is evident enough. Any attempt to do so can only lead to pathetic and ridiculous intellectual pronouncements. But it is equally true that, factually, politics is born from the societal womb which marks its role. This does not render politics passive, but it does reduce it to subservience.

Politics as the active concern with the public affairs of a community should not allow us to neglect that it is a political issue to determine what constitutes public affairs at any given time. A society that renders everything political is impoverished; so is a society that ignores or denies the vital significance of political life. The human spirit demands both the light of the public ambience and the silence of solitude and privacy. Insistence on collapsing this interplay of speech and silence, of public and private, amounts to the impoverishment of human existence.[18] The freedom to be political corresponds to the equally necessary need for freedom from politics. These two freedoms to be meaningful must presuppose a society where politics itself has been restored to its active, humanizing task and not to a mere wielding of power.

Political rule might always run the risk of becoming tyrannical. However, historically, politics in its supposed normal state of affairs has been progressively in the service of domination. Oppression in general and domination in particular are not inherent qualities of politics, but they are central aspects of its history. Therefore those who wish the emergence of a free human society should not seek the abolition of politics per se but the eradication of politics as oppression and domination. And this is itself a political act, an act of liberation, which must be guided by the solid understanding of the complexity of the forces of oppression and domination. Indignation and passionate longings are not only inadequate but also irresponsibly dangerous. It is the paradox of politics to be capable of both freedom and oppression. The dignity or inhumanity of politics stems from its social foundations. Refusal to recognize this is either the result of naiveté or hypocrisy.

II

All oppression is control over others for the exclusive benefit of those who exercise it. In intention, at least, it must be so exclusive. Any deviation from this exclusivity is either unavoidable or unintended. Certainly no oppressor seeks to benefit his oppressed with anything that might endanger his rule of oppression. Domination, compared to all other modes of oppression, is unique in that the dominated remain oblivious of their domination. The establishment and maintenance of domination is effected on psychological grounds: the dominated internalize the external social structure, which achieves a re-orientation of their energies, desires, and perceptions. The world of the dominated is a falsified reality that has been granted the semblance of the natural, which in turn grants it an aura of rationality and legitimacy.

The semblance of the natural, the pretensions of autonomous consciousness, and the absence of a forceful crushing of the will characterize best the condition of domination and differentiate it from the nightmare of totalitarianism and the grand metaphor of Orwell's *1984*.[19] Totalitarianism relies on externally imposed terror and fear. It isolates and forces submission; it is never internalized. The master is always external to the self. A conflict exists between my will and his. At worst a surrender is effected, a defeat which does not propagate any delusions about my actual condition.

Orwell's *1984* portrays not the victory of totalitarianism but its inability to achieve total control of thought, expression, and experience. Orwell's pessimism stems from his awareness that once total control is sought an irreversible historical process is set in motion which generates the bizarre world of *1984*. The oppressors in *1984* ultimately clash with human personality. Orwell shows us how an amnesiac society cannot be created because the past lingers in the present, not as ideas but as life itself. He also shows us that when the total conditioning of an individual is achieved, it reduces him to a lifeless, passive creature. The destruction of the will does not lead to an inner persuasion, does not create fervent crusaders.

Domination, however, does not terrorize; nor does it persuade on rational grounds. It erects a structure that obliterates alternative styles of life and lures the mind by what it offers. The goal of domination is to actualize the predicament of Plato's cave whose inhabitants know nothing but the world of appearance which becomes their one and only reality. Domination amounts to a continuous political act, of manipulation of appearance into social reality, destroying all nuances and intimations of reality itself. It is the inversion of the real and the fabricated. The continuous success of domination warrants a systematic interplay between external structure and internal, psychological conditioning and acceptance of the external structure. Neither the external nor the internal alone constitutes the condition of domination. Their reciprocal interaction and mutual verification become indispensable. The individual is not hypnotized, mystified, and thus transformed into an automaton for ever. Rather than being a mere instance in existence which changes it permanently, domination is a systemic, structural process in constant motion.

Domination is not habituation which can be mechanically repeated. Nor is it overpowering others. The dominated are not defeated in the contest for power. The novelty of the concept rests precisely in its psychopolitical connotation, which indicates the oblivious acceptance of the disproportionate accumulation of power and consequent exercise of control in society. Domination is not rooted in the presence of power as such but in the monopolization of power in a context which obscures this fact as well as its purpose. The powerless do not feel their impotence.

Domination historically is preceded by other forms of oppression. The falsification of reality is gradual. The erasure of the real and possible is prepared by the forceful intervention of power in human life in the service of personal interest and advantage. The most primitive form of tyranny paves the way for domination by first effecting submission and then erecting a social organization to consolidate and perpetuate the inequity established by force.[21] It is as if the memory of a non-tyrannical experience must be forcefully weakened or removed before an interpretation falsifying the world can be advanced.

The use of force disturbs and alters both the balance of reality and its perception, and it obliterates the origins of the new social reality. Forced inequality becomes an actuality into which subsequent generations are born. It is at this historic juncture that psycho-existential configurations tend to repress the ontological, which in its natural purity is no longer anywhere to be found. The critique of actual social structure can be articulated but can be visualized only in the mental world; the empirical reality refutes ideas about other alternative structures. Domination makes its inroads when the history of oppression serves as evidence of the need for oppression – which soon ceases being perceived as oppression.

Domination is the story of social inequality and the acceptance by its victims of a falsified social context in which it must be interpreted. This inequality hides the actual relation between social organization and a certain mode of the division of labour. The social division of labour is not established on rational criteria; human bondage is rooted in the disproportionate allocation of toil and benefit. Perhaps the most lasting negative mental effect of oppression is our near inability to discuss seriously the division of labour without either some retreat into utopia or the acceptance of its inevitable anomaly. Domination shrouds the fact of anomaly and mocks utopia as immature fantasy.

Domination undergoes transformations and reaches its climax in the contemporary advanced industrial society. The reification of the system is so complete that de-humanization is invisible, unrecognizable. Reality becomes one-dimensional. Greater and more intense immersion in a system which denies visualization of alternatives, offering instead only variations of the same theme, becomes the prevailing logic and rule. Monotony prevails.

To speak of domination we need not constantly think of conspiratorial political schemes or monolithic power élites. Deception leads to self-deception, both well entrenched in a cultural, sociopolitical, economic structure cemented by the psychological distortion of what constitutes meaningful existence.

The dominators control and consciously falsify but do not achieve for themselves a level of humanity. They come to believe that the very meaning of existence is derived from the exercise of domination. Though they know the false world they sell, they know not any genuine reality.[22] Domination as a form of social falsehood politically executed encapsulates both masters and slaves in a complex artificiality. The success of the masters demands the striving for success by the dominated, and such striving only verifies the value of the success of the dominators. Because domination, as Marcuse so aptly expressed it, amounts to surplus-repression, excess repression above and beyond what either nature or reason demand, it must always be exposed by comparison to a genuine human possibility rather than to a worse condition of domination or human misery. Theoretically, there is no need to settle for the lesser evil instead of seeking and demanding what is possible. The comparative scale is, and must always be, between freedom and its denial.

If one were to draw a parallel from prison systems surely it would be agreed that some prisons are less inhumane than others, but all nonetheless are prisons; none transcends the boundary of freedom. The problem with domination is that by its very nature it tends to deny the damage it does by altering the mode of its oppressive quality; it destroys the traditional categories of common sense and experience. It is a paradox in that the worse domination gets the less it is experienced as oppression. From its archaic, primitive origins, domination arches into the modern age as the pseudo-happiness of acquisition and consumption.

If in the past domination increased the already severe demands of scarcity, which were imposed upon a technologically immature civilization, by preventing a cooperative, rational, equitable division of labour and allocation of resources, under conditions of a mature technological society domination becomes a more pernicious scourge on humanity. For now what is denied is the implementation of all inherent potentialities – material, technological, and ontological. At stake now is the emergence of free society and not just the equitable distribution of scarcity in an already meager existence. Marcuse's relentless critique of advanced industrial societies rests precisely on this point.

Domination does not imply that the intellectual abilities of the human mind are destroyed. It does stress the psychological foundations of human consciousness. Domination does not disappear through an act of cognition. The instinctual-sensual constitution of the individual must be restored, must be placed in a liberating non-repressive context before awareness can be born and acted upon.

As far as domination is concerned, the nexus between mind and body is psychic energy or structure. In this sense domination encompasses a more complex relation than that of infrastructure and superstructure, for now the whole is indeed more than its parts. Psychology, a category which cannot be reduced fully either to body or mind, refracts and amplifies the interaction of the infra and superstructures, creating a condition not reducible to any single aspect of either. As such, then, the notion of domination is an expansive transformation of Marx's concept of alienation.[23]

Marx's concept of alienation refers to the active negation of free, creative human activity, itself central to ontology. Human emancipation presupposes and coincides with the recovery of this authentic human activity. Hidden in alienation, the human essence lies ready to unfold, constricted, negated, but not eradicated. It is from this negation of ontological creativity, through its inversion, that alienation is set in motion and engulfs the world. Its totality can be reduced to an activity. Adjacent to, but distinct from, alienated activity lies the alienation of the capitalist, who in Marx's terms is the agent of that inhuman force over humanity, capital itself.[24]

It is precisely because of this predicament that the worker is the only one who is still engaged actively with the world, whose existence is the distortion and perversion of the ontological activity, and who can thus achieve the awareness of his oppressive condition and seek the liberation of human activity. In Marx's view, the proletariat mirrors negatively what free activity should be. The capitalist, far removed from alienated activity, cannot sense the meaning of and need for free creative activity. His alienation is passive, activity-less. Marx's insistence on the emancipatory qualities of the proletariat is, on philosophical grounds, rooted in the fact that the worker in his alienated activity comes closer than any one else to conceptualizing and feeling the concrete meaning of what is denied to him and renounced by the capitalist. The actively damaged life becomes the gate to the full awareness of the universality of damaged life and the desire and willingness to reclaim the fully human active life. The moment of recognition is found in the depths of the activity that dishonours the dignity of free, human creative activity – alienated labour. Here Marx, in class formulation, captures the individualistic metaphor of Master-Slave expounded by Hegel. The actor, the doer, is the liberator.

What Marx did not wish to entertain is the possibility that the active, concrete predicament might be the least conducive to recovering genuine, free activity. Being thrust actively into alienation might be denying the distance necessary for reflection and recognition. The vision of the positive activity need not be captured by those fully immersed in its active negation. But for Marx the assertion that doing and awareness are so intimately related rests on his obsessive hostility towards the abstract, his fascination with the concrete and actual. The neat, consistent logic of Marx's argument reveals his ontological dialectic as primary over his sociology and political economy. The infrastructure is the physical, concrete, and real, the direct metabolism of Nature. It is there and only there that the mutilation-restoration can and does occur according to Marx. There the radical comprehension of humanity, its universal suffering and emancipation, is reflected in the particular which is transcended. To hypostatize any other nexus or space is to fly against the very structure of life and world. But the fact that a particular condition mirrors the universal historical predicament of negated, damaged life does not necessarily imply that those who actually live it will recognize it as such. There might be an abysmal distance between a lived experience and the appropriation of its meaning. Concentration camps, torture chambers, houses of prostitution speak with eloquence beyond the necessary understanding of their inhabitants. Suffering and dehumanization are not best expressed by victims. Philosophers and poets speak with passion and elegance without having experienced the very situations they condemn. Pain is followed by silence. The victims become witnesses, non-comprehending accusers in defence of humanity. It is not Odysseus who comprehends the meaning of his journey but Homer. Marx must have felt the inner tension between the concrete inertness of proletarian consciousness and the vicariousness of the dynamic, imaginative interpretation of his own. But the truth always speaks by proxy, in parables and metaphors. Marx wanted the actual victims to become the story tellers.

The point that concerns us here, however, is that alienation has its genesis in a specific activity which according to Marx constitutes the most vital nerve of ontology and society. Domination is an all-pervasive condition which cannot be traced back to any single activity.[25] The world and the images which sustain it *are* the constituent parts of domination. The distorted, falsified world *is* the context of domination and no mere byproduct of it. While alienation stresses the economic context of social organization, domination emphasizes the psychological-cultural features of social life which embrace the totality and cement its structural patterns. Domination does not intensify the condition of alienation, it creates a distinct condition.

It is in this sense that the systemic, dialectical aspects of alienation, in the Marxian sense of the phenomenon, appear rudimentary and insufficient in explaining domination. What we do not need is merely a more detailed, methodical examination and understanding of the economic structure which supposedly would enlighten us as to the capitalistic mechanisms which delay the culmination of the internal contradictions. All such efforts are futile because they are based upon the implicit assumption of the inevitable collapse of capitalism and the dawn of an emancipated future. Thus, it takes only a touch of imagination to discover the episodes that diverted the dialectical movement. Once the arrival of the Messiah is taken for granted, his present absence can always be accounted for.

Domination, in the sense of total control through an all-pervasive system, need not deny the day of apocalypse, but most certainly does change its meaning and mode of arrival. Domination as deception and falsification requires conscious control. The masters act consciously, willingly, as power holders[26] who know that they must procure obedience, docility, and active passivity and remain invisible as well. The masters are not agents. It is not denied that in dominating they dehumanize themselves. I only wish to disclaim the suggestion that the dominators and the dominated are imprisoned in their dehumanizing postures by systemic forces, by some negative, pernicious cunning of unreason or malice. The system exists and is verified, but it has been brought into existence by its masters. It is the manipulation of the instruments of domination by actual individuals or groups of individuals which denies and mocks a fully dialectical approach or perspective on domination and, consequently, liberation.

Precisely because domination is the result of human effort, it never gains full systemic autonomy. It requires continuous political reinforcement. The psychological basis of domination legitimates the social reality so that the success of the élite becomes the gravitational centre of social aspirations. Their luxuries signify success, status, and prestige. They must be emulated, sought after with passion and zeal. The whole of one's energy must be invested in the achievement of a station in life that bestows upon it the grace of the system, its material blessings, its supposed satisfactions. And those with less fortune, those whose standard of living falls short of the glories of dominated society, must accept the discrepancy between their condition and that of the successful not only as just but as the natural consequence of their natural differences. They must admire the successful and not resent them. The logic and meaning of the human condition must be that of the social world as created by domination. The system articulates the goals, establishes the criteria. Alternatives must be reduced to the ridiculous, to failure to achieve, to defeat. Reason must be silenced by unreason pretending to be reason, freedom must be exorcised by the idiocy of unfreedom and the hollowness of leisure time; travel, once a genuine educational and existential experience, becomes tourism.

The masters of dominated society pursue the extinction of other world views from the minds of their subjects. They extract not resignation, fear, and defeatism, but an active, zealous embrace of their embellished system of values and needs so that critical thought would be impossible. Domination, unlike the Inquisition, does not fight or punish heresy; it destroys its possibility, nullifies its effectiveness. The masters become administrators of social benefits. No commands are issued, only rational, self-evident, seductive participation is offered.

Domination in advanced industrial societies no longer needs to extract obedience on austere, puritanical grounds of renunciation. It now provides access, mobility, tangibility of progressive advancement. Domination confines violence to the background, stressing the multifarious world of objects, services, where the web of falsehood is firmly woven around all aspects of life.

The images of one-dimensionality, false happiness, eclipse of reason, Fanon's masks, R.D. Laing's happy scenarios, expose poignantly the discrepancy between reality and the dominated human psyche, revealing the shrouded mind, the regulated body and its energy, the atrophized self-determined individual, the lies that sustain the frightening avoidance of truth.

These and similar metaphors suggest the completion of what Orwell thought impossible. But metaphors can be misleading if taken literally. They are ideal-types, vivid signals of on-going tendencies, of a propensity but not a finalized crystallization.[27] Their hegemonic definitional character alerts us about the spreading disease and does not proclaim the devastation of an epidemic.

The metaphors of domination, when taken literally, have a numbing finality. No fury is expressed, no target is visible. It is an irony that the more vividly one criticizes domination the less political it appears; the less immediate, the more alien it becomes. Other forms of oppression concretize and personalize the enemy. Domination denies a visible figure; it offers only a systemic universe.

The metaphors articulate the erosion of the most fundamental elements of life and human personality. They accurately convey the prevailing aura and texture of the dominant culture, mode of thought, and behaviour, which reflect a social structure and perpetuate it.

The reality of the dominated has the semblance of the natural. It never becomes natural. The mask hides the face but it does not become the face.

The actual, the real, is not fully obliterated. Denial of the discrepancy between reality and social reality, between ontology and history, between culture and existence, is continuous and intense, devious and dexterous, but not fully successful. The actual lingers on. Its total denial, its concrete defeat, is pathology, individual insanity. Sociopolitical delusions remain anchored to an objective but dimmed reality. Denial does not achieve abolition. Reality has its nemesis.

Though the mask does not become the face, the wearing of the mask is not perceived. The suspension between the actual and its active denial, the dim and muted context in which humanity breathes creates a current of anxiety and tension. This current is not necessarily a source of hope, a chance for recovery of an illuminated, reason-guided reality. The system of domination that generates the psychological anxiety unintentionally and unavoidably propels the individual deeper into the system. On the verge of despair, without awareness, like addicted gamblers, all return to try their luck again, for they know no other game, no other fortune lurks in their hearts. But the tension and anxiety remain and even grow. The happiness of the kingdom of the darkness is false, its sleep troubled, because its subjects are not fully convinced of their earthly paradise. It is not that they are happy and ought not to be. They are anxious, bored, exhausted; not truly happy. Their energy lacks the tranquility of confidence, the zest of joy. Their righteousness disturbs them; their security does not comfort them. Their emptiness inarticulate, they remain fragments of wasted lives.

The inner, secret psychological dislocation of self and world does not lead to a dialogue, to reflection. It only testifies to the inability of domination to come full circle and complete its metaphor; it testifies to the unreflective, invisibly damaged lives, scarred without battle, without heroics, without anamnesis.

The deep, silent anxiety of the dominated becomes diversified in intensity and scope as they seek relief. Within the boundaries of dominated life the quest for a meaningful experience – from mysticism to complete, hysterical servility to the system – manifests what cannot always be politicized. Domination breeds an internal disharmony and fragmentation full of anxiety, the pacification of which can be sought in an infinite variety of irrational, frustrated modes of thought and action. Anxiety does not seek refuge in the light of reason. The mutilated congregate in the darkness. They are marginal creatures, neither fully drowned in a lie nor seeing the simple truth of the solid land. Tamed, yet untransformed, they are capable of volcanic eruptions but not of visions of a 'politically other' world. Frustrated, they frequently pursue the oppression of others. Social mass movements achieve the mobilization of this psychological dislocation.

The bored rich lust after novelty; the poor seek wealth. Their shallow existence calls for excitement, demands new gods who might grant them meaning. In the meantime they all buy what they do not need. Rich and poor lack wisdom; their routinized, habitual life, with its premeditated, bureaucratized spontaneity – spasms of unreflective inadequacy – drives them away from the critical visions which dissect their impoverished humanity, and yet it satiates them not. For they are afflicted by domination, what they cannot name and – when it is named for them – cannot understand. And life goes on.

And the social structure of politics is mechanically advocated by some, vehemently refuted by others. Neither in alliance with a dialectical miracle worker nor in resignation does the world change or is understood.

Domination, the highest stage of dehumanization, is a sinister act against humanity. Only by insisting on examining political experience from its perspective, its foundation and modalities, can one be irreverent enough to commit the ultimate sacrilege of exposing the emperor as the thief of humanity. The emperor as tyrant does not unveil this other, deeper version of human history.

NOTES

1 It is an infernal predicament which negates humanity without allowing awareness of this fact. Its damaged lives cannot cry out their pain. With simplicity and brilliance Franz Kafka captures the notion of unawareness, but of an impending event, in the opening passages of *The Castle*. 'The Castle hill was hidden, veiled in mist and darkness, nor was there even a glimmer of light to show that a castle was there. On the wooden bridge leading from the main road to the village, K. stood for a long time gazing into the illusory emptiness above him.' The Castle will exhaust and consume K. in the future. The illusory dimension does not render domination less hellish, it only transforms its condition to a loss without overt suffering.
2 *The Prince and the Discourses* (New York 1950), 56, 32
3 Ibid., 64, 44, 22, 139
4 The term is not Machiavelli's but Jean-Parul Sartre's. Similar themes are to be found in Merleau-Ponty and Albert Camus, though each treats the dilemma differently.
5 Machiavelli, *The Prince*, 44. 'The chief foundations of all states ... are good laws and good arms. And as there cannot be good laws where there are not good arms ... '
6 Success is not the imperative for Machiavelli. Many of his heroes failed and not all blessed with success are necessarily admired by him. How and why success and failure come about determine a man's greatness. See Alkis Kontos, 'Success and Knowledge in Machiavelli,' in *The Political Calculus: Essays on Machiavelli's Philosophy*, ed. Anthony Parel (Toronto 1972). With regard to Machiavelli's famous dictum that he loved his city more than his soul, see Leo Stauss, *Thoughts on Machiavelli* (Illinois 1958), which establishes that neither Florence nor Italy constituted Machiavelli's true fatherland. For a political interpretation of the statement asserting a passion for politics divorced from crude or vulgar opportunism or utilitarianism see Hannah Arendt, *On Revolution* (New York 1963), 290.
7 *Leviathan*, ed. with introduction by C.B. Macpherson, (Harmondworth 1968), part II, chapter 17, 227
8 Ibid., part I, chapter 11, 166
9 Idem.
10 Politics as power struggle is affirmed by an ideologically diverse number of scholars: Max Weber, Harold Lasswell, David Easton, Bertrand de Jouvenel in *The Pure Theory of Politics* (New Haven 1963), 30. In international politics, the classic advocate of power politics remains Hans J. Morgenthau, *Politics Among Nations* (New York 1968), and, of course, Karl von Clausewitz, *War, Politics and Power*, ed. and trans. Edward M. Collins (Chicago 1962).
11 Aristotle, 'Politics,' in *The Basic Works of Aristotle*, ed. Richard McKeon (New York 1941), Book 1, chapter 2, 1129-30
12 C.B. Macpherson, *The Political Theory of Possessive Individualism: Hobbes to Locke* (Oxford 1962)
13 We should always remember that Socrates was, at least, allowed to defend himself. Death without defence, or, even worse, without allowing Plato to immortalize the philosophic life could be a much more severe fate imposed on philosophers.
14 Karl A. Wittfogel, *Oriental Despotism: A Comparative Study of Total Power* (New Haven 1957), 27, 47
15 Max Weber's seminal work on comparative religious dogmas attacks and refutes any narrow deterministic view of economic life as the basis of such dogmas, but it does not deny the role of economic activity or social structure.
16 Vittorio Alfieri, *Of Tyranny*, trans. Julius A. Molinaro and Beatrice Corrigan (Toronto 1961), 11; Alfred Cobban, *Dictatorship: Its History and Theory* (London 1939), 26; Kenneth H. Waters, *Herodotos on Tyrants and Despots: A Study in Objectivity* (Wiesbaden 1971), 6-7; *P.N. Ure, The Origin of Tyranny* (Cambridge 1922), 2, 11, 25, 51, 70, 85 (this is primarily an economic interpretation of the rise of tyranny in classical Greece); A. Andrewes, *The Greek Tyrants* (London 1956), 12, 34ff., 152. On the philosophical

aspects of tyranny, ancient and modern, see the great debate between Strauss and Kojève in Leo Strauss, *On Tyranny* (Ithaca 1968); see also George Grant's thoughtful commentary 'Tyranny and Wisdom,' in his *Technology and Empire: Perspectives on North America* (Toronto 1969).

17 On this see Eric Voegelin's review of *The Origins of Totalitarianism* and Arendt's response in *The Review of Politics*, (January 1953), 68-85

18 Hannah Arendt, *The Human Condition* (Chicago 1958), chapter 2

19 Domination as power over others, as overpowering others, constitutes a totally different category.

20 Orwell writes, 'Their embrace had been a battle, the climax a victory. It was a blow struck against the Party. It was a political act,' 104. But he also states, 'Tragedy, he perceived, belonged to the ancient time when there was still privacy, love, and friendship, and when the members of a family stood by one another without needing to know the reason,' 27. 'Today there were fear, hatred, and pain, but no dignity of emotion, no deep or complex sorrows,' 28 (Penguin edition).

21 Herbert Marcuse, *Eros and Civilization* (New York 1962), 55-6, suggests the origin of domination in the desire of the dominator to avoid toil, and hence increase pleasure. In a context of scarcity impatience towards equalization of the burden of survival is conceivable. In other words, the perennial question of why did some choose to dominate is answerable and comprehensible in a given sociohistorical context and does not indicate an ontological propensity towards domination.

22 Karl Marx, *Economic and Philosophic Manuscripts of 1844* (Moscow 1961), 83, 126. Also see C. Wright Mills, *The Power Elite* (New York 1956) on the phenomenon of celebrity veneration.

23 Marcuse comes close to this usage but he is not consistent. At times domination equals alienation. Surplus repression-domination is called 'surplus alienation.' See Herbert Marcuse, 'A Revolution in Values,' in *Political Ideologies*, ed. James A. Gould and Willis H. Truitt (New York 1973), 333. On the history of the concept of alienation, see Nathan Rotenstreich, *Basic Problems of Marx's Philosophy* (Indianapolis 1965), chapter 7, 'Concept of Alienation and its Metamorphoses.'

24 Intimated in *Economic and Philosophic Manuscripts*, 37, 126, and stated explicitly in *Capital* (Moscow 1962), vol. 3, 798 ' ... the capitalist is merely capital personified and functions in the process of production solely as the agent of capital ... '; also 259 and elsewhere.

25 Alienation for Marx originates in the loss of one's product: *Economic and Philosophic Manuscripts*, 69. The activity of producing, without this loss is positive. This position renders the arrival of alienation something of a mystery, unless it is reduced to an ontological flaw. Not how, but why a previously non-alienated world begins to exploit is not treated satisfactorily by Marx. Domination tends to suggest the burdensome nature of work as necessity. It is the originally negative character of labour that an inequitable division of labour intensifies. Avoidance of work is explainable on psychological grounds and is not the result of an inherent exploitative propensity in human nature.

26 The work of Marcuse, C. Wright Mills, *Power Elite*, and Ralph Miliband, *The State in Capitalist Society* (London 1969), is pertinent here.

27 Herbert Marcuse, *One-Dimensional Man* (Boston 1968), regarding the underprivileged outsiders of the system. *An Essay on Liberation* (Boston 1969), regarding the young who are not coopted. Frantz Fanon, *The Wretched of the Earth*, trans. Constance Farrington (New York 1963), regarding the colonized peoples' night dreams and dances, chapter 1, 'Concerning Violence.' In all three instance, perfect, total internalization is not achieved.

Contributors

BEN AGGER is completing a doctoral dissertation in the department of political economy, University of Toronto.

ELIZABETH BRADY teaches and writes in London, Ontario.

DAVID COOK teaches in the department of political economy and is Assistant to the Vice-President and Provost, University of Toronto.

ALKIS KONTOS teaches in the department of political economy and at Erindale College, University of Toronto.

MONIKA LANGER teaches in the department of philosophy, Yale University.

CHRISTIAN LENHARDT teaches in the department of political science, York University.

C.B. MACPHERSON is University Professor and teaches in the department of political economy, University of Toronto.

R.O. MATTHEWS teaches in the department of political economy, University of Toronto.

KEITH McCALLUM was working for his doctorate at the University of Toronto until 1974; he is now studying in England.

R.T. NAYLOR teaches in the department of economics, McGill University.

ATO SEKYI-OTU teaches in the division of social science, York University.

O. WEININGER teaches in the Ontario Institute for Studies in Education, University of Toronto.